NATHANIEL HAWTHORNE was born on July 4, 1804, in Salem, Massachusetts, the son and grandson of proud New England seafarers. He lived in genteel poverty with his widowed mother and two young sisters in a house filled with Puritan ideals and family pride in a prosperous past. His boyhood was, in most respects, pleasant and normal. In 1825 he was graduated from Bowdoin College, Brunswick, Maine, and he returned to Salem determined to become a writer of short stories. For the next twelve years he was plagued with unhappiness and self-doubts as he struggled to master his craft. He finally secured some small measure of success with the publication of his *Twice-Told Tales* (1837). His marriage to Sophia Peabody in 1842 was a happy one. *The Scarlet Letter* (1850), which brought him immediate recognition, was followed by *The House of the Seven Gables* (1851). After serving four years as the American Consul in Liverpool, England, he traveled in Italy; he returned home to Massachusetts in 1860. Depressed, weary of writing, and failing in health, he died on May 19, 1864, at Plymouth, New Hampshire.

NATHANIEL HAWTHORNE

THE

SCARLET

LETTER

With a Foreword by
LEO MARX

Revised and Updated Bibliography

A SIGNET CLASSIC

NEW AMERICAN LIBRARY

NEW YORK AND SCARBOROUGH. ONTARIO

NATHANIEL HAWTHORNE

THE

SCARLET

A

LETTER

FOREWORD © 1959 BY NAL PENGUIN INC.
BIBLIOGRAPHY COPYRIGHT © 1980 BY NAL PENGUIN INC,

Ⓒ

SIGNET CLASSIC TRADEMARK REG. U.S. PAT. OFF. AND FOREIGN COUNTRIES
REGISTERED TRADEMARK—MARCA REGISTRADA
HECHO EN CHICAGO, U.S.A.

SIGNET, SIGNET CLASSIC, MENTOR, ONYX, PLUME, MERIDIAN AND
NAL BOOKS are published *in the United States* by
NAL PENGUIN INC.,
1633 Broadway, New York, New York 10019,
in Canada by The New American Library of Canada Limited,
81 Mack Avenue, Scarborough, Ontario M1L 1M8

36   37   38   39   40   41   42   43   44

PRINTED IN THE UNITED STATES OF AMERICA

Contents

FOREWORD

I N JUNE, 1849, Nathaniel Hawthorne lost the job in the Salem Custom House that he had held for three years. He was forty-five years old, and although he had gained some reputation as an author of short tales, he had never earned enough by writing to support his family. Clearly his career was at a turning point. Then a few weeks later his mother died. In the aftermath he became ill. When he recovered late in the summer he began to write The Scarlet Letter, and he wrote steadily, with a speed and purpose he had never known before. He turned his suffering into imaginative energy. Perhaps that accounts for the sense of powerful emotions barely held in check that permeates the "hell-fired story," as he called it. In any event, on February 3, 1850, he read the final pages to his wife. "It broke her heart," he wrote to a friend, "and sent her to bed with a grievous headache, which I look upon as a triumphant success."

Today all the world acknowledges Hawthorne's triumph. Among the classics of American fiction The Scarlet Letter is remarkable in several ways. It is the most economical, the most thoroughly composed and unified of our great novels. But of course these qualities cannot be accounted for by the shocking events of the previous summer. The truth is that Hawthorne had been preparing himself to write this book for twenty years. In the brooding, painstaking creation of his tales he had put in order his feelings about the New England past. He had sifted and resifted the themes and images that he uses in The Scarlet Letter. As early as 1837, for example, he had mentioned a woman condemned by

Puritan justice to wear a scarlet "A." * His long and devoted preparation is what best explains the sureness of touch, the clarity, force and precision of the work he began in 1849. It is also a key to the style. As many readers have observed, the tight structure and figurative language of the book make it seem more like lyric poetry than most novels. Entering the world of The Scarlet Letter is like walking into a large, many-sided hall of mirrors. It is a bright yet shadowy place where we see every fact in an unending succession of relations to every other fact.

Consider, for example, the landscape and the way it affects every aspect of the story. From the beginning, even before Hawthorne directs our attention to the wilderness that surrounds Boston, he makes its presence felt. We feel it in the grim mood of the crowd waiting at the prison door. To be sure, some of the grimness can be explained in other ways. These people are led by militant Puritans, men of faith who are passionately committed to an experiment in utopian Christian politics. In seventeenth-century Boston the laws are rigorously enforced. The stark authority of the regime is indicated by the prison, scaffold and pillory that dominate the opening scene. And yet there is something besides religious zeal in the atmosphere. On reflection we realize that it has to do with the community's location in space—with geography. Here is a tiny outpost of English society cut off from civilization by the ocean on one side and a vast, unexplored reach of wild nature on the other. What this may portend is quietly suggested by the appearance of a savage at the edge of the crowd. In The Scarlet Letter landscape is no mere backdrop; it is inseparable from policy and action and meaning.

In fact the setting bears directly on the story of Hester Prynne. The forest, plausibly enough, is the place where Hester and Arthur most freely acknowledge their bond. In the woods they momentarily escape the strict Puritan code. Under the circumstances, what more likely spot

* "Endicott and the Red Cross," the story which contains this germ of the novel, is reprinted on pp. 247–254 of the present edition. Besides the key image, the tale embodies many of Hawthorne's general attitudes toward the Puritans.

can we imagine for a meeting of secret lovers? The forest, then, is identified with love. But it is characteristic of Hawthorne's art that he can turn this fact, at first glance so obvious, so prosaic, into a stunning metaphor. Indeed he turns the whole landscape into a metaphor. We soon find, for example, that the forest is called a "moral wilderness." What makes this idea so compelling is that Hawthorne has prepared us for it by first showing us the plain fact. It is literally true that in this story the forest is a place where people elude the rules of the community. Hawthorne does not say to the reader, as it were, "let the forest stand for x." The forest means what the forest is: a place where no laws obtain, in short, a moral wilderness. Now if we also happen to know that Hawthorne is working in a distinguished tradition, that Dante, for instance, used the same metaphor, so much the better. The main point is, however, that Hawthorne so constructs the terrain of The Scarlet Letter that the town is a sphere of rigidly enforced law, and the forest of tempting license, and that between the two extremes there is no ground where Hester and Dimmesdale can take their stand.

But the contrast between the town and the forest is only one expression of the root conflict. At the outset Hawthorne introduces an elaborate set of parallel contrasts. He sets off the prison, "black flower of civilized society," with a wild rosebush. In opposition to the authoritarian politics of the iron Puritans, he invokes the name of Anne Hutchinson, the rebellious woman who was banished for heresy during the early years of the colony. (He again links her name with Hester's in Chapter 13.) Each side of the tableau has its appropriate color—black or red; each has a key word—"iron" or "wild." As we read on, these images recur with ever expanding significance. Arthur wears black and Hester red. In his role as pastor as well as by temperament, Arthur is committed to the iron side, with all that that implies about man's weakness and his inescapable need for restraint, order and institutional control. (Iron, after all, is man-made, cold to the touch, hard, strong, yet subject to rust.) But Hester sees life differently. She values the impulsive, passional and spontaneous. (Roses grow wild; they are delicate, soft, fragrant, thorny; they bloom only for a brief moment.) At bottom the difference comes to this: Hester trusts the heart.

Now of course Hawthorne deliberately enlists us all on Hester's side. Who can resist the dark beauty standing alone with her babe like "the image of Divine Maternity"? Who can say a good word for her self-righteous accusers, or for the craven father of her child? Hawthorne calls forth our warmest impulses—our sympathy for the lonely, our solidarity with the persecuted, our anarchic urge toward fulfillment now; and then, when our gentlest selves have been exposed, he forces us to recognize their fallibility. Having weighted the argument so heavily on the sentimental side, it is no easy task to restore the balance. Whether Hawthorne succeeds is for each reader to judge. But the test is our feeling about what happens to Hester in the end. Can we accept her defeat? If we accept her fate as true (in Hawthorne's phrase) to the laws of the human heart, then he has won his triumph over a seductive but inherently sentimental view of life. Neither Hester nor Dimmesdale has the answer. Without the other each is incomplete. Pearl cannot become fully human until she has a father as well as a mother. Or, to put it in more abstract terms, Hawthorne finally would have us see that as a principle the wild rose is no more adequate than iron.

The action of The Scarlet Letter has the effect of breaking down the terrible dualism with which it begins. For Hawthorne there is a double victory in this process. First, he squares himself with his Puritan ancestors. What he most dislikes about them is the inhuman dogmatism exemplified by the sign Hester is forced to wear: "A" = adulteress. As if a human being could be contained in so mechanical an allegory! The moment Hester steps out of prison she begins to demonstrate the preposterousness of the idea. Her needlework already has invested the simple sign with another significance. It is a thing of beauty. Before long it will come to stand for many things, just as all the images take on complicated meanings.

But in 1850 there was no trick to winning a victory over the Puritans. For Hawthorne's contemporaries were, in his opinion, all too willing to dismiss Calvinism, with its deep suspicion of human motives, and go to the opposite extreme. In their unbounded capacity for self-approval they would wholeheartedly endorse Hester's position. "What we did," she tells Dimmesdale in the forest, "had a consecration of its own." This might easily be the voice of nineteenth-century America with its unlimited confidence in man, nature and itself. To have her way Hester is perfectly willing to disregard all that men have inherited from the past—religion, tradition, law, and society. She believes in the new beginning. Right here Hawthorne takes the measure of his own age. For all her heroic self-reliance, or rather because of it, Hester destroys the object of her love.

It is not necessary to say a great deal about Chillingworth, who represents a third point of view. Hawthorne does not ask us to give him much sympathy. He stands for the detached scientific intelligence, an ideal that he betrays in his obsession with revenge. This cold-blooded man is a stock character, a villain out of the Faust myth who anticipates the heartless psychiatrist of current lore. If his presence does not offend our common sense it is because we realize that Hawthorne does not try for life-likeness in any of his characters. *The Scarlet Letter* is not a realistic novel. Even little Pearl, who sometimes seems more like a clockwork doll than a child, finally makes sense in psychological terms. Hawthorne is not attempting to create a mirror image of actuality. *The Scarlet Letter* is a romance, a highly stylized symbolic fable, and only in its moral significance is it firmly linked with the world we inhabit.

Unlike novels in the realistic tradition, *The Scarlet Letter* has a moral. It is curious that so few readers discover it. At the end of Chapter 1 Hawthorne tells us to look for it. He plucks a rose and presents it to us as if, he says, to symbolize a moral blossom to be found in the story. In the final chapter he fulfills his promise. Reflecting on the implications of the tale, he spells out the lesson in the simplest language. Perhaps that is the difficulty. The language is so simple, the author so outspoken, and the meaning so plain that we scarcely recognize the moral—much less its profundity.

One final word. When Hawthorne finished *The Scarlet*

Letter he realized that it was too long to include in a volume of tales as he had planned. But it was not quite long enough to stand alone. Hence the introductory chapter, "The Custom House." This elegant essay, a charming specimen of its kind, does help some readers cross the bridge into Hawthorne's fictional world. But it is not an integral part of the story, and the impatient reader may begin immediately with the novel and save the other for his leisure.

LEO MARX
Amherst College
Amherst, Mass.

PREFACE

TO THE SECOND EDITION OF *The Scarlet Letter*

MUCH to the author's surprise, and (if he may say so without additional offence) considerably to his amusement, he finds that his sketch of official life, introductory to *The Scarlet Letter*, has created an unprecedented excitement in the respectable community immediately around him. It could hardly have been more violent, indeed, had he burned down the Custom House, and quenched its last smoking ember in the blood of a certain venerable personage, against whom he is supposed to cherish a peculiar malevolence. As the public disapprobation would weigh very heavily on him, were he conscious of deserving it, the author begs leave to say that he has carefully read over the introductory pages with a purpose to alter or expunge whatever might be found amiss, and to make the best reparation in his power for the atrocities of which he has been adjudged guilty. But it appears to him, that the only remarkable features of the sketch are its frank and genuine good humor, and the general accuracy with which he has conveyed his sincere impressions of the characters therein described. As to enmity, or ill feeling of any kind, personal or political, he utterly disclaims such motives. The sketch might, perhaps, have been wholly omitted, without loss to the public or detriment to the book; but, having undertaken to write it, he conceives that it could not have been done in a better or a kindlier spirit, nor,

so far as his abilities availed, with a livelier effect of
truth.

The author is constrained, therefore, to republish
his introductory sketch without the change of a word.

Salem,
March 30, 1850

NOTE: Originally, as he explains in his footnote (p. 52), Hawthorne
had intended to publish several other tales and sketches along with
the main narrative, which he felt to be too short to stand alone.
But the first edition included only "The Custom House." Certain
political figures in Salem protested that Hawthorne was making an
unfair attack on them. Hence this preface. Most editors have
followed Hawthorne's lead in treating "The Custom House" as
an introduction to the romance itself.

—L. M.

The Custom House

INTRODUCTORY TO *THE SCARLET LETTER*

IT IS A LITTLE REMARKABLE that—though disinclined to talk overmuch of myself and my affairs at the fireside, and to my personal friends—an autobiographical impulse should twice in my life have taken possession of me, in addressing the public. The first time was three or four years since, when I favored the reader —inexcusably, and for no earthly reason that either the indulgent reader or the intrusive author could imagine —with a description of my way of life in the deep quietude of an Old Manse. And now—because, beyond my deserts, I was happy enough to find a listener or two on the former occasion—I again seize the public by the button, and talk of my three years' experience in a Custom House. The example of the famous "P.P., Clerk of this Parish," was never more faithfully followed. The truth seems to be, however, that, when he casts his leaves forth upon the wind, the author addresses, not the many who will fling aside his volume, or never take it up, but the few who will understand him, better than most of his schoolmates or lifemates. Some authors, indeed, do far more than this, and indulge themselves in such confidential depths of revelation as could fittingly be addressed, only and exclusively, to the one heart and mind of perfect sympathy; as if the printed book, thrown at large on the wide world, were certain to find out the divided segment of the writer's own nature, and complete his circle of existence by bringing him into communion with it. It is scarcely decorous, however, to speak all, even where we speak impersonally. But, as thoughts are frozen and utterance benumbed unless the speaker stand in some true relation with his audience, it may be pardonable to imagine that a friend, a kind and apprehensive, though not the closest friend, is listening to our talk; and then, a native reserve being thawed by this genial consciousness, we may prate of the circumstances that lie around us, and even of ourself, but still keep the inmost Me behind its veil. To this extent, and within these limits, an author, methinks, may be autobiographical, without violating either the reader's rights or his own.

It will be seen, likewise, that this Custom House sketch has a certain propriety, of a kind always recognized in literature, as explaining how a large portion of the following pages came into my possession, and as offering proofs of the authenticity of a narrative therein contained. This, in fact—a desire to put myself in my true position as editor, or very little more, of the most prolix among the tales that make up my volume—this, and no other, is my true reason for assuming a personal relation with the public. In accomplishing the main purpose, it has appeared allowable, by a few extra touches, to give a faint representation of a mode of life not heretofore described, together with some of the characters that move in it, among whom the author happened to make one.

In my native town of Salem, at the head of what, half a century ago, in the days of old King Derby, was a bustling wharf—but which is now burdened with decayed wooden warehouses, and exhibits few or no symptoms of commercial life; except, perhaps, a bark or brig, halfway down its melancholy length, discharging hides; or, nearer at hand, a Nova Scotia schooner, pitching out her cargo of fire-wood—at the head, I say, of this dilapidated wharf, which the tide often overflows, and along which, at the base and in the rear of the row of buildings, the track of many languid years is seen in a border of unthrifty grass—here, with a view from its front windows adown this not very enlivening prospect, and thence across the harbor, stands a spacious edifice of brick. From the loftiest point of its roof, during precisely three and a half hours of each forenoon, floats or droops, in breeze or calm, the banner of the republic; but with the thirteen stripes turned vertically, instead of horizontally, and thus indicating that a civil, and not a military post of Uncle Sam's government, is here established. Its front is ornamented with a portico of half a dozen wooden pillars supporting a balcony, beneath which a flight of wide granite steps descends towards the street. Over the entrance hovers an enormous specimen of the American eagle, with outspread wings, a shield before her breast, and, if I recollect aright, a bunch of intermingled thunderbolts and barbed arrows in each claw. With the customary infirmity of temper that characterizes this unhappy fowl, she appears, by the fierceness of her beak and eye, and the general truculency of her attitude, to threaten mischief to the inoffensive community; and especially to warn all citizens, careful of their safety, against intruding on the premises which she overshadows with her wings. Nevertheless, vixenly as she looks, many people are seeking, at this very moment, to shelter themselves under the wing of the federal eagle; imagining, I presume, that her bosom has all the softness and snugness of an eiderdown pillow. But she has no great tenderness, even in her best of moods, and, sooner or later—oftener soon than late—is apt to fling off her nestlings, with a scratch of her claw, a dab of her beak, or a rankling wound from her barbed arrows.

The pavement round about the above-described edifice —which we may as well name at once as the Custom House of the port—has grass enough growing in its chinks to show that it has not, of late days, been worn by any multitudinous resort of business. In some months of the year, however, there often chances a forenoon when affairs move onward with a livelier tread. Such occasions might remind the elderly citizen of that period before the last war with England, when Salem was a port by itself; not scorned, as she is now, by her own merchants and ship-owners, who permit her wharves to crumble to ruin, while their ventures go to swell, needlessly and imperceptibly, the mighty flood of commerce at New York or Boston. On some such morning, when three or four vessels happen to have arrived at once—usually from Africa or South America—or to be on the verge of their departure thitherward, there is a sound of frequent feet, passing briskly up and down the granite steps. Here, before his own wife has greeted him, you may greet the sea-flushed shipmaster, just in port, with his vessel's papers under his arm, in a tarnished tin box. Here, too, comes his owner, cheerful or sombre, gracious or in the sulks, accordingly as his scheme of the now accomplished voyage has been realized in merchandise that will readily be turned to gold, or has buried him under a bulk of incommodities such as nobody will care to rid him of. Here, likewise—the germ of the wrinkle-browed, grizzly-bearded, careworn merchant—we have the smart young clerk, who gets the taste of traffic as a wolf cub does of blood, and already sends adventures in his master's ships, when he had better be sailing mimic boats upon a mill-pond. Another figure in the scene is the outward-bound sailor, in quest of a protection; or the recently arrived one, pale and feeble, seeking a passport to the hospital. Nor must we forget the captains of the rusty little schooners that bring firewood from the British provinces; a rough-looking set of tarpaulins, without the alertness of the Yankee aspect, but contributing an item of no slight importance to our decaying trade.

Cluster all these individuals together, as they sometimes were, with other miscellaneous ones to diversify the group, and, for the time being, it made the Custom House a stirring scene. More frequently, however, on ascending the steps, you would discern—in the entry, if it were summer time, or in their appropriate rooms, if wintry or inclement weather—a row of venerable figures, sitting in old-fashioned chairs, which were tipped on their hind legs back against the wall. Oftentimes they were asleep, but occasionally might be heard talking together, in voices between speech and a snore, and with that lack of energy that distinguishes the occupants of alms-houses, and all other human beings who depend for subsistence on charity, on monopolized labor, or anything else but their own independent exertions. These old gentlemen—seated, like Matthew, at the receipt of custom, but not very liable to be summoned thence, like him, for apostolic errands—were Custom House officers.

Furthermore, on the left hand as you enter the front

door, is a certain room or office about fifteen feet square and of a lofty height, with two of its arched windows commanding a view of the aforesaid dilapidated wharf, and the third looking across a narrow lane, and along a portion of Derby Street. All three give glimpses of the shops of grocers, block-makers, slop-sellers, and ship-chandlers; around the doors of which are generally to be seen, laughing and gossiping, clusters of old salts, and such other wharf-rats as haunt the Wapping of a seaport. The room itself is cobwebbed and dingy with old paint; its floor is strewn with gray sand in a fashion that has elsewhere fallen into long disuse; and it is easy to conclude, from the general slovenliness of the place, that this is a sanctuary into which womankind, with her tools of magic, the broom and mop, has very infrequent access. In the way of furniture, there is a stove with a voluminous funnel; an old pine desk with a three-legged stool beside it; two or three wooden-bottom chairs, exceedingly decrepit and infirm; and—not to forget the library—on some shelves, a score or two of volumes of the Acts of Congress, and a bulky Digest of the Revenue Laws. A tin pipe ascends through the ceiling, and forms a medium of vocal communication with other parts of the edifice. And here, some six months ago—pacing from corner to corner, or lounging on the long-legged stool, with his elbow on the desk, and his eyes wandering up and down the columns of the morning newspaper—you might have recognized, honored reader, the same individual who welcomed you into this cheery little study, where the sunshine glimmered so pleasantly through the willow branches, on the western side of the Old Manse. But now, should you go thither to seek him, you would inquire in vain for the Locofoco Surveyor. The besom of reform has swept him out of office; and a worthier successor wears his dignity, and pockets his emoluments.

This old town of Salem—my native place, though I have dwelt much away from it, both in boyhood and maturer years—possesses, or did possess, a hold on my affections, the force of which I have never realized during my seasons of actual residence here. Indeed, so far as its physical aspect is concerned, with its flat, unvaried surface, covered chiefly with wooden houses, few or none of which pretend to architectural beauty—its irregularity, which is neither picturesque nor quaint, but only tame— its long and lazy street, lounging wearisomely through the whole extent of the peninsula, with Gallows Hill and New Guinea at one end, and a view of the alms-house at the other—such being the features of my native town, it would be quite as reasonable to form a sentimental attachment to a disarranged checkerboard. And yet, though invariably happiest elsewhere, there is within me a feeling for old Salem, which, in lack of a better phrase, I must be content to call affection. The sentiment is probably assignable to the deep and aged roots which my family has struck into the soil. It is now nearly two centuries and a quarter since the original Briton, the earliest emigrant of my name, made his appearance in the wild and forest-bordered settlement, which has since become a city. And here his descendants have been born and died, and have mingled their earthy substance with the soil; until no small portion of it must necessarily be akin to the mortal frame wherewith, for a little while, I walk the streets. In part, therefore, the attachment which I speak of is the mere sensuous sympathy of dust for dust. Few of my countrymen can know what it is; nor, as frequent transplantation is perhaps better for the stock, need they consider it desirable to know.

But the sentiment has likewise its moral quality. The figure of that first ancestor, invested by family tradition with a dim and dusky grandeur, was present to my boyish imagination as far back as I can remember. It still haunts me, and induces a sort of home-feeling with the past, which I scarcely claim in reference to the present phase of the town. I seem to have a stronger claim to a residence here on account of this grave, bearded, sable-cloaked and steeple-crowned progenitor—who came so early, with his Bible and his sword, and trode the unworn street with such a stately port, and made so large a figure, as a man of war and peace—a stronger claim than for myself, whose name is seldom heard and my face hardly known. He was a soldier, legislator, judge; he was a ruler in the Church; he had all the Puritanic traits, both good and evil. He was likewise a better persecutor; as witness the Quakers, who have remembered him in their histories, and relate an incident of his hard severity toward a woman of their sect, which will last longer, it is to be feared, than any record of his better deeds, although these were many. His son, too, inherited the persecuting spirit, and made himself so conspicuous in the martyrdom of the witches, that their blood may fairly be said to have left a stain upon him. So deep a stain, indeed, that his old dry bones, in the Charter Street burial ground, must still retain it, if they have not crumbled utterly to dust! I know not whether these ancestors of mine bethought themselves to repent, and ask pardon of heaven for their cruelties; or whether they are now groaning under the heavy consequences of them, in another state of being. At all events, I, the present writer, as their representative, hereby take shame upon myself for their sakes, and pray that any curse incurred by them—as I have heard, and as the dreary and unprosperous condition of the race, for many a long year back, would argue to exist—may be now and henceforth removed.

Doubtless, however, either of these stern and black-browed Puritans would have thought it quite a sufficient retribution for his sins, that, after so long a lapse of years, the old trunk of the family tree, with so much venerable moss upon it, should have borne, as its topmost bough, an idler like myself. No aim that I have ever cherished would they recognize as laudable; no success of mine—if my life, beyond its domestic scope, had ever been brightened by success—would they deem otherwise than worthless, if not positively disgraceful. "What is he?" murmurs one gray shadow of my forefathers to the other. "A writer of storybooks! What kind of a business in life—what mode of glorifying God, or being serviceable to mankind in his day and generation—may that be? Why, the degenerate fellow might as well have been a fiddler!" Such are the compliments bandied between my great-grandsires and myself, across the gulf of time! And yet, let them scorn me as they will, strong traits of their nature have intertwined themselves with mine.

Planted deep in the town's earliest infancy and childhood by these two earnest and energetic men, the race has ever since subsisted here; always, too, in respectability; never, so far as I have known, disgraced by a single unworthy member! but seldom or never, on the other hand, after the first two generations, performing any memorable deed, or so much as putting forward a claim to public notice. Gradually, they have sunk almost out of sight; as old houses, here and there about the streets, get covered halfway to the eaves by the accumulation of new soil. From father to son, for above a hundred years, they followed the sea; a gray-headed shipmaster, in each generation, retiring from the quarter-deck to the homestead, while a boy of fourteen took the hereditary place before the mast, confronting the salt spray and the gale, which had blustered against his sire and grandsire. The boy, also, in due time, passed from the forecastle to the cabin, spent a tempestuous manhood, and returned from his world wanderings, to grow old, and die, and mingle his dust with the natal earth. This long connection of a family with one spot, as its place of birth and burial, creates a kindred between the human being and the locality, quite independent of any charm in the scenery or moral circumstances that surround him. It is not love, but instinct. The new inhabitant—who came himself from a foreign land, or whose father or grandfather came—has little claim to be called a Salemite; he has no conception of the oysterlike tenacity with which an old settler, over whom his third century is creeping, clings to the spot where his successive generations have been imbedded. It is no matter that the place is joyless for him; that he is weary of the old wooden houses, the mud and dust, the dead level of site and sentiment, the chill east wind, and the chillest of social atmospheres—all these, and whatever faults besides he may see or imagine, are nothing to the purpose. The spell survives, and just as powerfully as if the natal spot were an earthly paradise. So has it been in my case. I felt it almost as a destiny to make Salem my home; so that the mould of features and cast of character which had all along been familiar here—ever, as one representative of the race lay down in his grave, another assuming, as it were, his sentry-march along the main street—might still in my little day be seen and recognized in the old town. Nevertheless, this very sentiment is an evidence that the connection, which has become an unhealthy one, should at last be severed. Human nature will not flourish, any more than a potato, if it be planted and replanted for too long a series of generations in the same worn-out soil. My children have had other birthplaces, and, so far as their fortunes may be within my control, shall strike their roots into unaccustomed earth.

On emerging from the Old Manse, it was chiefly this strange, indolent, unjoyous attachment for my native town, that brought me to fill a place in Uncle Sam's brick edifice, when I might as well, or better, have gone somewhere else. My doom was on me. It was not the first time, nor the second, that I had gone away—as it seemed, permanently—but yet returned, like the bad halfpenny; or as if Salem were for me the inevitable centre of the universe. So, one fine morning, I ascended the flight of granite steps, with the President's commission in my pocket, and was introduced to the corps of gentlemen who were to aid me in my weighty responsibility, as chief executive officer of the Custom House.

I doubt greatly—or, rather, I do not doubt at all—whether any public functionary of the United States, either in the civil or military line, has ever had such a patriarchal body of veterans under his orders as myself. The whereabouts of the Oldest Inhabitant was at once settled when I looked at them. For upwards of twenty years before this epoch, the independent position of the Collector had kept the Salem Custom House out of the whirlpool of political vicissitude, which makes the tenure of office generally so fragile. A soldier—New England's most distinguished soldier—he stood firmly on the pedestal of his gallant services; and, himself secure in the wise liberality of the successive administrations through which he had held office, he had been the safety of his subordinates in many an hour of danger and heartquake. General Miller was radically conservative; a man over whose kindly nature habit had no slight influence; attaching himself strongly to familiar faces, and with difficulty moved to change, even when change might have brought unquestionable improvement. Thus, on taking charge of my department, I found few but aged men. They were ancient sea captains, for the most part, who, after being tossed on every sea, and standing up sturdily against life's tempestuous blast, had finally drifted into this quiet nook,

where, with little to disturb them, except the periodical
terrors of a Presidential election, they one and all acquired
a new lease of existence. Though by no means less liable
than their fellow-men to age and infirmity, they had evidently some talisman or other that kept death at bay.
Two or three of their number, as I was assured, being
gouty and rheumatic, or perhaps bedridden, never
dreamed of making their appearance at the Custom
House during a large part of the year; but, after a torpid
winter, would creep out into the warm sunshine of May
or June, go lazily about what they termed duty, and, at
their own leisure and convenience, betake themselves to
bed again. I must plead guilty to the charge of abbreviat-
ing the official breath of more than one of these venerable
servants of the republic. They were allowed, on my
representation, to rest from their arduous labors, and soon
afterwards—as if their sole principle of life had been
zeal for their country's service, as I verily believe it was—
withdrew to a better world. It is a pious consolation to
me, that, through my interference, a sufficient space was
allowed them for repentance of the evil and corrupt practices into which, as a matter of course, every Custom
House officer must be supposed to fall. Neither the front
nor the back entrance of the Custom House opens on the
road to Paradise.

The greater part of my officers were Whigs. It was well
for their venerable brotherhood that the new Surveyor
was not a politician, and though a faithful Democrat in
principle, neither received nor held his office with any
reference to political services. Had it been otherwise—
had an active politician been put into this influential post,
to assume the easy task of making head against a Whig
Collector, whose infirmities withheld him from the personal administration of his office—hardly a man of the
old corps would have drawn the breath of official life
within a month after the exterminating angel had come
up the Custom House steps. According to the received
code in such matters, it would have been nothing short
of duty, in a politician, to bring every one of those white
heads under the axe of the guillotine. It was plain enough
to discern, that the old fellows dreaded some such dis-
courtesy at my hands. It pained, and at the same time

amused me, to behold the terrors that attended my advent; to see a furrowed cheek, weather-beaten by half a century of storm, turn ashy pale at the glance of so harmless an individual as myself; to detect, as one or another addressed me, the tremor of a voice, which, in long-past days, had been wont to bellow through a speaking-trumpet, hoarsely enough to frighten Boreas himself to silence. They knew, these excellent old persons, that, by all established rule—and, as regarded some of them, weighed by their own lack of efficiency for business—they ought to have given place to younger men, more orthodox in politics, and altogether fitter than themselves to serve our common Uncle. I knew it too, but could never quite find in my heart to act upon the knowledge. Much and deservedly to my own discredit, therefore, and considerably to the detriment of my official conscience, they continued, during my incumbency, to creep about the wharves, and loiter up and down the Custom House steps. They spent a good deal of time, also, asleep in their accustomed corners, with their chairs tilted back against the wall; awaking, however, once or twice in a forenoon, to bore one another with the several thousandth repetition of old sea stories, and mouldy jokes, that had grown to be passwords and countersigns among them.

The discovery was soon made, I imagine, that the new Surveyor had no great harm in him. So, with lightsome hearts, and the happy consciousness of being usefully employed—in their own behalf, at least, if not for our beloved country—these good old gentlemen went through the various formalities of office. Sagaciously, under their spectacles, did they peep into the holds of vessels! Mighty was their fuss about little matters, and marvellous, sometimes, the obtuseness that allowed greater ones to slip between their fingers! Whenever such a mischance occurred—when a wagonload of valuable merchandise had been smuggled ashore, at noonday, perhaps, and directly beneath their unsuspicious noses—nothing could exceed the vigilance and alacrity with which they proceeded to lock, and double-lock, and secure with tape and sealing-wax, all the avenues of the delinquent vessel. Instead of a reprimand for their previous negligence, the case seemed rather to require an eulogium on their praiseworthy caution, after the mischief had happened; a grateful recognition of the promptitude of their zeal, the moment that there was no longer any remedy.

Unless people are more than commonly disagreeable, it is my foolish habit to contract a kindness for them. The better part of my companion's character, if it have a better part, is that which usually comes uppermost in my regard, and forms the type whereby I recognize the man. As most of these old Custom House officers had good traits, and as my position in reference to them, being paternal and protective, was favorable to the growth of friendly sentiments, I soon grew to like them all. It was pleasant, in the summer forenoons—when the fervent heat, that almost liquefied the rest of the human family, merely communicated a genial warmth to their half-torpid systems—it was pleasant to hear them chatting in the back entry, a row of them all tipped against the wall, as usual; while the frozen witticisms of past generations were thawed out, and came bubbling with laughter from their lips. Externally, the jollity of aged men has much in common with the mirth of children; the intellect, any more than a deep sense of humor, has little to do with the matter; it is, with both, a gleam that plays upon the surface, and imparts a sunny and cheery aspect alike to the green branch, and gray, mouldering trunk. In one case, however, it is real sunshine; in the other, it more resembles the phosphorescent glow of decaying wood.

It would be sad injustice, the reader must understand, to represent all my excellent old friends as in their dotage. In the first place, my coadjutors were not invariably old; there were men among them in their strength and prime, of marked ability and energy, and altogether superior to the sluggish and dependent mode of life on which their evil stars had cast them. Then, moreover, the white locks of age were sometimes found to be the thatch of an intellectual tenement in good repair. But, as respects the majority of my corps of veterans, there will be no wrong done if I characterize them generally as a set of wearisome old souls, who had gathered nothing worth preservation from their varied experience of life. They seemed to have flung away all the golden grain of practical wisdom, which they had enjoyed so many opportunities of harvesting, and most carefully to have stored their memories with the husks. They spoke with far more interest and unction of their morning's breakfast, or yesterday's, today's, or tomorrow's dinner than of the shipwreck of forty or fifty years ago, and all the world's wonders which they had witnessed with their youthful eyes.

The father of the Custom House—the patriarch, not only of this little squad of officials, but, I am bold to say, of the respectable body of tide-waiters all over the United States—was a certain permanent Inspector. He might truly be termed a legitimate son of the revenue system, dyed in the wool, or, rather, born in the purple; since his sire, a Revolutionary colonel, and formerly collector of the port, had created an office for him, and appointed him to fill it, at a period of the early ages which few living men can now remember. This Inspector, when I first knew him, was a man of fourscore years, or thereabouts, and certainly one of the most wonderful specimens of winter-green that you would be likely to discover in a lifetime's search. With his florid cheek, his compact figure, smartly arrayed in a bright-buttoned blue coat, his brisk and vigorous step and his hale and hearty aspect, altogether he seemed—not young, indeed—but a kind of new contrivance of Mother Nature in the shape of man, whom age and infirmity had no business to touch. His voice and laugh, which perpetually reëchoed through the Custom House, had nothing of the tremulous quaver and cackle of an old man's utterance; they came strutting out of his lungs like the crow of a cock or the blast of a clarion. Looking at him merely as an animal—and there was very little else to look at—he was a most satisfactory object, from the thorough healthfulness and wholesomeness of his system, and his capacity, at that extreme age, to enjoy all, or nearly all, the delights which he had ever aimed at, or conceived of. The careless security of his life in the Custom House, on a regular income, and with but slight and infrequent

apprehensions of removal, had no doubt contributed to
make time pass lightly over him. The original and more
potent causes, however, lay in the rare perfection of his
animal nature, the moderate proportion of intellect,
and the very trifling admixture of moral and spiritual
ingredients; these latter qualities, indeed, being in barely
enough measure to keep the old gentleman from walking on all fours. He possessed no power of thought, no
depth of feeling, no troublesome sensibilities; nothing,
in short, but a few commonplace instincts, which, aided
by the cheerful temper that grew inevitably out of his
physical well-being, did duty very respectably, and to
general acceptance, in lieu of a heart. He had been
the husband of three wives, all long since dead; the
father of twenty children, most of whom, at every age
of childhood or maturity, had likewise returned to dust.
Here, one would suppose, might have been sorrow
enough to imbue the sunniest disposition, through and
through, with a sable tinge. Not so with our old Inspector! One brief sigh sufficed to carry off the entire
burden of these dismal reminiscences. The next moment,
he was as ready for sport as any unbreeched infant; far
readier than the Collector's junior clerk, who, at nine-
teen years, was much the elder and graver man of the
two.

I used to watch and study this patriarchal personage
with, I think, livelier curiosity, than any other form of
humanity there presented to my notice. He was, in
truth, a rare phenomenon; so perfect, in one point of
view; so shallow, so delusive, so impalpable, such an
absolute nonentity, in every other. My conclusion was
that he had no soul, no heart, no mind; nothing, as I
have already said, but instincts; and yet, withal, so
cunningly had the few materials of his character been
put together, that there was no painful perception of
deficiency, but, on my part, an entire contentment with
what I found in him. It might be difficult—and it was
so—to conceive how he should exist hereafter, so earthy
and sensuous did he seem; but surely his existence here,
admitting that it was to terminate with his last breath,
had been not unkindly given; with no higher moral
responsibilities than the beasts of the field, but with a

larger scope of enjoyment than theirs, and with all their blessed immunity from the dreariness and duskiness of age.

One point, in which he had vastly the advantage over his four-footed brethren, was his ability to recollect the good dinners which it had made no small portion of the happiness of his life to eat. His gourmandism was a highly agreeable trait; and to hear him talk of roast meat was as appetizing as a pickle or an oyster. As he possessed no higher attribute, and neither sacrificed nor vitiated any spiritual endowment by devoting all his energies and ingenuities to subserve the delight and profit of his maw, it always pleased and satisfied me to hear him expatiate on fish, poultry, and butcher's meat, and the most eligible methods of preparing them for the table. His reminiscences of good cheer, however ancient the date of the actual banquet, seemed to bring the savor of pig or turkey under one's very nostrils. There were flavors on his palate, that had lingered there not less than sixty or seventy years, and were still apparently as fresh as that of the mutton chop which he had just devoured for his breakfast. I have heard him smack his lips over dinners, every guest at which, except himself, had long been food for worms. It was marvellous to observe how the ghosts of bygone meals were continually rising up before him; not in anger or retribution, but as if grateful for his former appreciation, and seeking to repudiate an endless series of enjoyment, at once shadowy and sensual. A tenderloin of beef, a hind-quarter of veal, a sparerib of pork, a particular chicken, or a remarkably praiseworthy turkey, which had perhaps adorned his board in the days of the elder Adams, would be remembered; while all the subsequent experience of our race, and all the events that brightened or darkened his individual career, had gone over him with as little permanent effect as the passing breeze. The chief tragic event of the old man's life, so far as I could judge, was his mishap with a certain goose, which lived and died some twenty or forty years ago; a goose of most promising figure, but which, at table, proved so inveterately tough that the carving knife would make no impression on its carcass, and it could only be divided with an axe and handsaw.

But it is time to quit this sketch; on which, however, I should be glad to dwell at considerably more length, because, of all men whom I have ever known, this individual was fittest to be a Custom House officer. Most persons, owing to causes which I may not have space to hint at, suffer moral detriment from this peculiar mode of life. The old Inspector was incapable of it; and, were he to continue in office to the end of time, would be as good as he was then, and sit down to dinner with just as good an appetite.

There is one likeness, without which my gallery of Custom House portraits would be strangely incomplete, but which my comparatively few opportunities for observation enable me to sketch only in the merest outline. It is that of the Collector, our gallant old General, who, after his brilliant military service, subsequently to which he had ruled over a wild Western territory, had come hither, twenty years before, to spend the decline of his varied and honorable life. The brave soldier had already numbered, nearly or quite, his threescore years and ten, and was pursuing the remainder of his earthly march, burdened with infirmities which even the martial music of his own spirit-stirring recollections could do little towards lightening. The step was palsied now, that had been foremost in the charge. It was only with the assistance of a servant, and by leaning his hand heavily on the iron balustrade, that he could slowly and painfully ascend the Custom House steps, and, with a toilsome progress across the floor, attain his customary chair beside the fireplace. There he used to sit, gazing with a somewhat dim serenity of aspect at the figures that came and went; amid the rustle of papers, the administering of oaths, the discussion of business, and the casual talk of the office; all which sounds and circumstances seemed but indistinctly to impress his senses, and hardly to make their way into his inner sphere of contemplation. His countenance, in this repose, was mild and kindly. If his notice was sought, an expression of courtesy and interest gleamed out upon his features; proving that there was light within him, and that it was only the outward medium of the intellectual lamp that obstructed the rays in their passage. The closer you penetrated to the substance of his mind, the sounder it appeared. When no longer called upon to speak, or listen, either of which operations cost him an evident effort, his face would briefly subside into its former not uncheerful quietude. It was not painful to behold this look; for, though dim, it had not the imbecility of decaying age. The framework of his nature, originally strong and massive, was not yet crumbled into ruin.

To observe and define his character, however, under such disadvantages, was as difficult a task as to trace out and build up anew, in imagination, an old fortress like Ticonderoga, from a view of its gray and broken ruins. Here and there, perchance, the walls may remain almost complete; but elsewhere may be only a shapeless mound, cumbrous with its very strength, and overgrown, through long years of peace and neglect, with grass and alien weeds.

Nevertheless, looking at the old warrior with affection—for, slight as was the communication between us, my feeling towards him, like that of all bipeds and quadrupeds who knew him, might not improperly be termed so—I could discern the main points of his portrait. It was marked with the noble and heroic qualities which showed it to be not by a mere accident, but of good right, that he had won a distinguished name. His spirit could never, I conceive, have been characterized by an uneasy activity; it must, at any period of his life, have required an impulse to set him in motion; but, once stirred up, with obstacles to overcome, and an adequate object to be attained, it was not in the man to give out or fail. The heat that had formerly pervaded his nature, and which was not yet extinct, was never of the kind that flashes and flickers in a blaze; but, rather, a deep, red glow, as of iron in a furnace. Weight, solidity, firmness; this was the expression of his repose, even in such decay as had crept untimely over him, at the period of which I speak. But I could imagine, even then, that, under some excitement which should go deeply into his consciousness—roused by a trumpet peal loud enough to awaken all of his energies that were not dead, but only slumbering—he was yet capable of flinging off his infirmities like a sick man's gown, dropping the staff of age to seize a battle sword, and starting up once more a warrior. And, in so intense a moment, his demeanor would have still been calm. Such an exhibition, however, was but to be pictured in fancy; not to be anticipated, nor desired. What I saw in him—as evidently as the indestructible ramparts of Old Ticonderoga, already cited as the most appropriate simile—were the features of stubborn and ponderous endurance, which might well have amounted to obstinacy in his earlier days; of integrity, that, like most of his other endowments, lay in a somewhat heavy mass, and was just as unmalleable and unmanageable as a ton of iron ore; and of benevolence, which, fiercely as he led the bayonets on at Chippewa or Fort Erie, I take to be of quite as genuine a stamp as what actuates any or all of the polemical philanthropists of the age. He had slain men with his own hand, for aught I know—certainly, they had fallen, like blades of grass at the sweep of the scythe, before the charge to which his spirit imparted its triumphant energy—but, be that as it might, there was never in his heart so much cruelty as would have brushed the down off a butterfly's wing. I have not known the man to whose innate kindliness I would more confidently make an appeal.

Many characteristics—and those, too, which contribute not the least forcibly to impart resemblance in a sketch —must have vanished, or been obscured, before I met the General. All merely graceful attributes are usually the most evanescent; nor does Nature adorn the human ruin with blossoms of new beauty, that have their roots and proper nutriment only in the chinks and crevices of decay, as she sows wall-flowers over the ruined fortress of Ticonderoga. Still, even in respect of grace and beauty, there were points well worth noting. A ray of humor, now and then, would make its way through the veil of dim obstruction, and glimmer pleasantly upon our faces. A trait of native elegance, seldom seen in the masculine character after childhood or early youth, was shown in the General's fondness for the sight and fragrance of flowers. An old soldier might be supposed to prize only the bloody laurel on his brow; but here was one, who seemed to have a young girl's appreciation of the floral tribe.

There, beside the fireplace, the brave old General used to sit; while the Surveyor—though seldom, when it could be avoided, taking upon himself the difficult task of engaging him in conversation—was fond of standing at a distance, and watching his quiet and almost slumberous countenance. He seemed away from us, although we saw him but a few yards off; remote, though we passed close beside his chair; unattainable, though we might have stretched forth our hands and touched his own. It might be that he lived a more real life within his thoughts than amid the unappropriate environment of the Collector's office. The evolutions of the parade; the tumult of the battle; the flourish of old, heroic music, heard thirty years before—such scenes and sounds, perhaps, were all alive before his intellectual sense. Meanwhile, the merchants and shipmasters, the spruce clerks and uncouth sailors, entered and departed; the bustle of this commercial and Custom House life kept up its little murmur round about him; and neither with the men nor their affairs did the General appear to sustain the most distant relation. He was as much out of place as an old sword—now rusty, but which had flashed once in the battle's front, and showed still a bright gleam along its blade—would have been, among the inkstands, paper folders, and mahogany rulers on the Deputy Collector's desk.

There was one thing that much aided me in renewing and re-creating the stalwart soldier of the Niagara frontier—the man of true and simple energy. It was the recollection of those memorable words of his—"I'll try, Sir!"—spoken on the very verge of a desperate and heroic enterprise, and breathing the soul and spirit of New England hardihood, comprehending all perils, and encountering all. If, in our country, valor were rewarded by heraldic honor, this phrase—which it seems so easy to speak, but which only he, with such a task of danger and glory before him, has ever spoken—would be the best and fittest of all mottoes for the General's shield of arms.

It contributes greatly towards a man's moral and intellectual health, to be brought into habits of companionship with individuals unlike himself, who care little for his pursuits, and whose sphere and abilities he must go out of himself to appreciate. The accidents of my life have often afforded me this advantage, but never with more fulness and variety than during my continuance in office. There was one man, especially, the observation of whose character gave me a new idea of talent. His gifts were emphatically those of a man of business; prompt, acute, clear-minded; with an eye that saw through all perplexities, and a faculty of arrangement that made them vanish, as by the waving of an enchanter's wand. Bred up from boyhood in the Custom House, it was his proper field of activity; and the many intricacies of business, so harassing to the interloper, presented themselves before him with the regularity of a perfectly comprehended system. In my contemplation, he stood as the ideal of his class. He was, indeed, the Custom House in himself, or, at all events, the mainspring that kept its variously revolving wheels in motion; for, in an institution like this, where its officers are appointed to subserve their own profit and convenience and seldom with a leading reference to their fitness for the duty to be performed, they must perforce seek elsewhere the dexterity which is not in them. Thus, by an inevitable necessity, as a magnet attracts steel filings, so did our man of business draw to himself the difficulties which everybody met with. With an easy condescension, and kind forbearance towards our stupidity—which, to his order of mind, must have seemed little short of crime—would he forthwith, by the merest touch of his finger, make the incomprehensible as clear as daylight. The merchants valued him not less than we, his esoteric friends. His integrity was perfect; it was a law of nature with him, rather than a choice or a principle; nor can it be otherwise than the main condition of an intellect so remarkably clear and accurate as his, to be honest and regular in the administration of affairs. A stain on his conscience, as to anything that came within the range of his vocation, would trouble such a man very much in the same way, though to a far greater degree, than an error in the balance of an account, or an ink-blot on the fair page of a book of record. Here, in a word—and it is a rare instance in my life—I had met with a person thoroughly adapted to the situation which he held.

Such were some of the people with whom I now found myself connected. I took it in good part, at the hands of Providence, that I was thrown into a position so little akin to my past habits, and set myself seriously to gather from it whatever profit was to be had. After my fellowship of toil and impracticable schemes with the dreamy brethren of Brook Farm; after living for three years within the subtile influence of an intellect like Emerson's; after those wild, free days on the Assabeth, indulging fantastic speculations beside our fire of fallen boughs with Ellery Channing; after talking with Thoreau about pine trees and Indian relics in his hermitage at Walden; after growing fastidious by sympathy with the classic refinement of Hillard's culture; after becoming imbued with poetic sentiment at Longfellow's hearthstone—it was time, at length, that I should exercise other faculties of my nature, and nourish myself with food for which I had hitherto had little appetite. Even the old Inspector was desirable, as a change of diet, to a man who had known Alcott. I looked upon it as an evidence, in some measure, of a system naturally well balanced, and lacking no essential part of a thorough organization, that, with such associates to remember, I could mingle at once with men of altogether different qualities and never murmur at the change.

Literature, its exertions and objects, were now of little moment in my regard. I cared not, at this period, for books; they were apart from me. Nature—except it were human nature—the nature that is developed in earth and sky, was, in one sense, hidden from me; and all the imaginative delight, wherewith it had been spiritualized, passed away out of my mind. A gift, a faculty, if it had not departed, was suspended and inanimate within me. There would have been something sad, unutterably dreary, in all this, had I not been conscious that it lay at my own option to recall what-

ever was valuable in the past. It might be true, indeed,
that this was a life which could not, with impunity, be
lived too long, else it might make me permanently
other than I had been, without transforming me into
any shape which it would be worth my while to take.
But I never considered it as other than a transitory life.
There was always a prophetic instinct, a low whisper
in my ear, that within no long period, and whenever a
new change of custom should be essential to my good,
a change would come.

Meanwhile, there I was, a Surveyor of the Revenue,
and, so far as I have been able to understand, as good
a Surveyor as need be. A man of thought, fancy, and
sensibility (had he ten times the Surveyor's proportion
of those qualities) may, at any time, be a man of affairs,
if he will only choose to give himself the trouble. My
fellow-officers, and the merchants and sea captains with
whom my official duties brought me into any manner of
connection, viewed me in no other light, and probably
knew me in no other character. None of them, I presume, had ever read a page of my inditing, or would
have cared a fig the more for me, if they had read them
all; nor would it have mended the matter, in the least,
had those same unprofitable pages been written with a
pen like that of Burns or of Chaucer, each of whom
was a Custom House officer in his day, as well as I. It
is a good lesson—though it may often be a hard one—
for a man who has dreamed of literary fame, and of
making for himself a rank among the world's dignitar-
ies by such means, to step aside out of the narrow circle
in which his claims are recognized, and to find how
utterly devoid of significance, beyond that circle, is all
that he achieves and all he aims at. I know not that I
especially needed the lesson, either in the way of warning or rebuke; but, at any rate, I learned it thoroughly;
nor, it gives me pleasure to reflect, did the truth, as it
came home to my perception, ever cost me a pang, or
require to be thrown off in a sigh. In the way of literary
talk, it is true, the Naval Officer—an excellent fellow,
who came into office with me and went out only a little
later—would often engage me in a discussion about one
or the other of his favorite topics, Napoleon or Shake-

speare. The Collector's junior clerk, too—a young gentle-man who, it was whispered, occasionally covered a sheet of Uncle Sam's letter paper with what (at the distance of a few yards) looked very much like poetry—used now and then to speak to me of books, as matters with which I might possibly be conversant. This was my all of lettered intercourse; and it was quite sufficient for my necessities.

No longer seeking nor caring that my name should be blazoned abroad on title pages, I smiled to think that it had now another kind of vogue. The Custom House marker imprinted it with a stencil and black paint, on pepper-bags, and baskets of anatto, and cigar boxes, and bales of all kinds of dutiable merchandise, in testimony that these commodities had paid the impost, and gone regularly through the office. Borne on such queer vehicle of fame, a knowledge of my existence, so far as a name conveys it, was carried where it had never been before, and, I hope, will never go again.

But the past was not dead. Once in a great while, the thoughts, that had seemed so vital and so active, yet had been put to rest so quietly, revived again. One of the most remarkable occasions, when the habit of by-gone days awoke in me, was that which brings it within the law of literary propriety to offer the public the sketch which I am now writing.

In the second story of the Custom House, there is a large room, in which the brick-work and naked rafters have never been covered with panelling and plaster. The edifice—originally projected on a scale adapted to the old commercial enterprise of the port, and with an idea of subsequent prosperity destined never to be realized —contains far more space than its occupants know what to do with. This airy hall, therefore, over the Collector's apartments, remains unfinished to this day, and, in spite of the aged cobwebs that festoon its dusky beams, appears still to await the labor of the carpenter and mason. At one end of the room, in a recess, were a number of barrels, piled one upon another, contain-ing bundles of official documents. Large quantities of similar rubbish lay lumbering the floor. It was sorrow-ful to think how many days, and weeks, and months, and years of toil, had been wasted on these musty papers, which were now only an encumbrance on earth, and were hidden away in this forgotten corner, never more to be glanced at by human eyes. But, then, what reams of other manuscripts—filled not with the dulness of official formalities, but with the thought of inventive brains and the rich effusion of deep hearts—had gone equally to oblivion; and that, moreover, without serving a purpose in their day, as these heaped-up papers had, and—saddest of all—without purchasing for their writers the comfortable livelihood which the clerks of the Custom House had gained by these worthless scratchings of the pen! Yet not altogether worthless, perhaps, as materials of local history. Here, no doubt, statistics of the former commerce of Salem might be discovered, and memorials of her princely merchants— old King Derby, old Billy Gray, old Simon Forrester, and many another magnate in his day, whose powdered head, however, was scarcely in the tomb before his mountain-pile of wealth began to dwindle. The founders of the greater part of the families which now compose the aristocracy of Salem might here be traced, from the petty and obscure beginnings of their traffic, at periods generally much posterior to the Revolution, upward to what their children look upon as long-established rank.

Prior to the Revolution, there is a dearth of records; the earlier documents and archives of the Custom House having, probably, been carried off to Halifax when all the King's officials accompanied the British army in its flight from Boston. It has often been a matter of regret with me; for, going back, perhaps, to the days of the Protectorate, those papers must have contained many references to forgotten or remembered men, and to antique customs, which would have affected me with the same pleasure as when I used to pick up Indian arrowheads in the field near the Old Manse.

But, one idle and rainy day, it was my fortune to make a discovery of some little interest. Poking and burrowing into the heaped-up rubbish in the corner, unfolding one and another document, and reading the names of vessels that had long ago foundered at sea or rotted at the wharves, and those of merchants, never heard of now on 'Change, nor very readily decipherable on their mossy tombstones; glancing at such matters with the saddened, weary, half-reluctant interest which we bestow on the corpse of dead activity—and exerting my fancy, sluggish with little use, to raise up from these dry bones an image of the old town's brighter aspect, when India was a new region, and only Salem knew the way thither—I chanced to lay my hand on a small package, carefully done up in a piece of ancient yellow parchment. This envelope had the air of an official record of some period long past, when clerks engrossed their stiff and formal chirography on more substantial materials than at present. There was something about it that quickened an instinctive curiosity, and made me undo the faded red tape that tied up the package with the sense that a treasure would here be brought to light. Unbending the rigid folds of the parchment cover, I found it to be a commission, under the hand and seal of Governor Shirley, in favor of one Jonathan Pue, as Surveyor of his Majesty's Customs for the port of Salem, in the Province of Massachusetts Bay. I remembered to have read (probably in Felt's Annals) a notice of the decease of Mr. Surveyor Pue about fourscore years ago; and likewise, in a newspaper of recent times, an account of the digging up of his remains in the little graveyard of St. Peter's Church during the renewal of that edifice. Nothing, if I rightly call to mind, was left of my respected predecessor, save an imperfect skeleton, and some fragments of apparel, and a wig of majestic frizzle; which, unlike the head that it once adorned, was in very satisfactory preservation. But, on examining the papers which the parchment commission served to envelop, I found more traces of Mr. Pue's mental part, and the internal operations of his head, than the frizzled wig had contained of the venerable skull itself.

They were documents, in short, not official, but of a private nature, or at least written in his private capacity, and apparently with his own hand. I could account for their being included in the heap of Custom House lumber only by the fact that Mr. Pue's death had happened suddenly; and that these papers, which he probably kept in his official desk, had never come to the knowledge of his heirs, or were supposed to relate to the business of the revenue. On the transfer of the archives to Halifax, this package, proving to be of no public concern, was left behind, and had remained ever since unopened.

The ancient Surveyor—being little molested, I suppose, at that early day, with business pertaining to his office—seems to have devoted some of his many leisure hours to researches as a local antiquarian, and other inquisitions of a similar nature. These supplied material for petty activity to a mind that would otherwise have been eaten up with rust. A portion of his facts, by the by, did me good service in the preparation of the article entitled "Main Street," included in the present volume.* The remainder may perhaps be applied to purposes equally valuable, hereafter; or not impossibly may be worked up, so far as they go, into a regular history of Salem, should my veneration for the natal soil ever impel me to so pious a task. Meanwhile, they shall be at the command of any gentleman, inclined, and competent, to take the unprofitable labor off my hands. As a final disposition, I contemplate depositing them with the Essex Historical Society.

But the object that most drew my attention in the mysterious package was a certain affair of fine red cloth, much worn and faded. There were traces about it of gold embroidery, which, however, was greatly frayed and defaced; so that none, or very little, of the glitter was left. It had been wrought, as was easy to perceive, with wonderful skill of needlework; and the stitch (as I am assured by ladies conversant with such mysteries) gives evidence of a now forgotten art, not to be recovered even by the process of picking out the threads. This rag of scarlet cloth—for time, and wear, and a sacrilegious moth, had reduced it to little other than a rag—on careful examination, assumed the shape of a letter. It was the capital letter "A." By an accurate measurement, each limb proved to be precisely three

* See note p. 52.

inches and a quarter in length. It had been intended, there could be no doubt, as an ornamental article of dress; but how it was to be worn, or what rank, honor, and dignity, in by-past times, were signified by it, was a riddle which (so evanescent are the fashions of the world in these particulars) I saw little hope of solving. And yet it strangely interested me. My eyes fastened themselves upon the old scarlet letter, and would not be turned aside. Certainly, there was some deep meaning in it, most worthy of interpretation, and which, as it were, streamed forth from the mystic symbol, subtly communicating itself to my sensibilities, but evading the analysis of my mind.

While thus perplexed—and cogitating, among other hypotheses, whether the letter might not have been one of those decorations which the white men used to contrive, in order to take the eyes of Indians—I happened to place it on my breast. It seemed to me—the reader may smile, but must not doubt my word—it seemed to me then that I experienced a sensation not altogether physical, yet almost so, as of burning heat; and as if the letter were not of red cloth, but red-hot iron. I shuddered, and involuntarily let it fall upon the floor.

In the absorbing contemplation of the scarlet letter, I had hitherto neglected to examine a small roll of dingy paper, around which it had been twisted. This I now opened and had the satisfaction to find, recorded by the old Surveyor's pen, a reasonably complete explanation of the whole affair. There were several foolscap sheets, containing many particulars respecting the life and conversation of one Hester Prynne, who appeared to have been rather a noteworthy personage in the view of our ancestors. She had flourished during the period between the early days of Massachusetts and the close of the seventeenth century. Aged persons, alive in the time of Mr. Surveyor Pue, and from whose oral testimony he had made up his narrative, remembered her in their youth as a very old, but not decrepit woman, of a stately and solemn aspect. It had been her habit from an almost immemorial date to go about the country as a kind of voluntary nurse, and doing whatever

miscellaneous good she might; taking upon herself, likewise, to give advice in all matters, especially those of
the heart; by which means, as a person of such propensi-
ties inevitably must, she gained from many people the
reverence due to an angel, but, I should imagine, was
looked upon by others as an intruder and a nuisance.
Prying further into the manuscript, I found the record
of other doings and sufferings of this singular woman,
for most of which the reader is referred to the story
entitled *The Scarlet Letter;* and it should be borne
carefully in mind, that the main facts of that story are
authorized and authenticated by the document of Mr.
Surveyor Pue. The original papers, together with the
scarlet letter itself—a most curious relic—are still in my
possession, and shall be freely exhibited to whomsoever,
induced by the great interest of the narrative, may desire
a sight of them. I must not be understood as affirming
that, in the dressing up of the tale, and imagining the
motives and modes of passion that influenced the
characters who figure in it, I have invariably confined
myself within the limits of the old Surveyor's half a
dozen sheets of foolscap. On the contrary, I have
allowed myself, as to such points, nearly or altogether
as much license as if the facts had been entirely of my
own invention. What I contend for is the authenticity
of the outline.

This incident recalled my mind, in some degree, to
its old track. There seemed to be here the groundwork
of a tale. It impressed me as if the ancient Surveyor,
in his garb of a hundred years gone by, and wearing his
immortal wig—which was buried with him, but did not
perish in the grave—had met me in the deserted chamber of the Custom House. In his port was the dignity
of one who had borne his Majesty's commission, and
who was therefore illuminated by a ray of the splendor
that shone so dazzlingly about the throne. How unlike,
alas! the hangdog look of a republican official, who, as
the servant of the people, feels himself less than the
least, and below the lowest, of his masters. With his
own ghostly hand, the obscurely seen but majestic figure
had imparted to me the scarlet symbol, and the little
roll of explanatory manuscript. With his own ghostly

voice, he had exhorted me, on the sacred consideration of my filial duty and reverence towards him—who might reasonably regard himself as my official ancestor—to bring his mouldy and moth-eaten lucubrations before the public. "Do this," said the ghost of Mr. Surveyor Pue, emphatically nodding the head that looked so imposing within its memorable wig, "do this and the profit shall be all your own! You will shortly need it; for it is not in your days as it was in mine, when a man's office was a life-lease, and oftentimes an heirloom. But, I charge you, in this matter of old Mistress Prynne, give to your predecessor's memory the credit which will be rightfully its due!" And I said to the ghost of Mr. Surveyor Pue, "I will!"

On Hester Prynne's story, therefore, I bestowed much thought. It was the subject of my meditations for many an hour while pacing to and fro across my room; or traversing, with a hundredfold repetition, the long extent from the front door of the Custom House to the side entrance, and back again. Great were the weariness and annoyance of the old Inspector and the Weighers and Gaugers, whose slumbers were disturbed by the unmercifully lengthened tramp of my passing and returning footsteps. Remembering their own former habits, they used to say that the Surveyor was walking the quarter-deck. They probably fancied that my sole object —and, indeed, the sole object for which a sane man could ever put himself into voluntary motion—was to get an appetite for dinner. And to say the truth, an appetite, sharpened by the east wind that generally blew along the passage, was the only valuable result of so much indefatigable exercise. So little adapted is the atmosphere of a Custom House to the delicate harvest of fancy and sensibility, that, had I remained there through ten Presidencies yet to come, I doubt whether the tale of The Scarlet Letter would ever have been brought before the public eye. My imagination was a tarnished mirror. It would not reflect, or only with miserable dimness, the figures with which I did my best to people it. The characters of the narrative would not be warmed and rendered malleable by any heat that I could kindle at my intellectual forge. They would take

neither the glow of passion nor the tenderness of sentiment, but retained all the rigidity of dead corpses, and
stared me in the face with a fixed and ghastly grin of
contemptuous defiance. "What have you to do with us?"
that expression seemed to say. "The little power you
might once have possessed over the tribe of unrealities
is gone! You have bartered it for a pittance of the
public gold. Go, then, and earn your wages!" In short,
the almost torpid creatures of my own fancy twitted
me with imbecility, and not without fair occasion.

It was not merely during the three hours and a half
which Uncle Sam claimed as his share of my daily life
this wretched numbness held possession of me. It went
with me on my seashore walks and rambles into the
country, whenever—which was seldom and reluctantly
—I bestirred myself to seek that invigorating charm of
Nature, which used to give me such freshness and activity of thought the moment that I stepped across
the threshold of the Old Manse. The same torpor, as
regarded the capacity for intellectual effort, accompanied me home, and weighed upon me in the chamber
which I most absurdly termed my study. Nor did it
quit me, when, late at night, I sat in the deserted parlor,
lighted only by the glimmering coal fire and the moon,
striving to picture forth imaginary scenes, which, the
next day, might flow out on the brightening page in
many-hued description.

If the imaginative faculty refused to act at such an
hour, it might well be deemed a hopeless case. Moonlight, in a familiar room, falling so white upon the car-
pet, and showing all its figures so distinctly—making
every object so minutely visible, yet so unlike a morning or noontide visibility—is a medium the most suitable for a romance writer to get acquainted with his
illusive guests. There is the little domestic scenery of
the well-known apartment; the chairs, with each its
separate individuality; the centre-table, sustaining a work-
basket, a volume or two, and an extinguished lamp;
the sofa; the bookcase: the picture on the wall—all these
details, so completely seen, are so spiritualized by the
unusual light, that they seem to lose their actual substance, and become things of intellect. Nothing is too

small or too trifling to undergo this change, and acquire dignity thereby. A child's shoe; the doll, seated in her little wicker carriage; the hobby-horse—whatever, in a word, has been used or played with during the day is now invested with a quality of strangeness and remoteness, though still almost as vividly present as by daylight. Thus, therefore, the floor of our familiar room has become a neutral territory, somewhere between the real world and fairyland, where the Actual and the Imaginary may meet, and each imbue itself with the nature of the other. Ghosts might enter here without affrighting us. It would be too much in keeping with the scene to excite surprise, were we to look about us and discover a form, beloved, but gone hence, now sitting quietly in a streak of this magic moonshine, with an aspect that would make us doubt whether it had returned from afar, or had never once stirred from our fireside.

The somewhat dim coal fire has an essential influence in producing the effect which I would describe. It throws its unobtrusive tinge throughout the room, with a faint ruddiness upon the walls and ceiling and a reflected gleam from the polish of the furniture. This warmer light mingles itself with the cold spirituality of the moonbeams, and communicates, as it were, a heart and sensibilities of human tenderness to the forms which fancy summons up. It converts them from snow-images into men and women. Glancing at the looking glass, we behold—deep within its haunted verge—the smouldering glow of the half-extinguished anthracite, the white moonbeams on the floor, and a repetition of all the gleam and shadow of the picture, with one remove further from the actual, and nearer to the imaginative. Then, at such an hour, and with this scene before him, if a man sitting all alone cannot dream strange things and make them look like truth, he need never try to write romances.

But, for myself, during the whole of my Custom House experience, moonlight and sunshine and the glow of firelight were just alike in my regard; and neither of them was of one whit more avail than the twinkle of a tallow candle. An entire class of susceptibilities, and a gift connected with them—of no great richness or value, but the best I had—was gone from me.

It is my belief, however, that, had I attempted a different order of composition, my faculties would not have been found so pointless and inefficacious. I might, for instance, have contented myself with writing out the narratives of a veteran shipmaster, one of the Inspectors, whom I should be most ungrateful not to mention, since scarcely a day passed that he did not stir me to laughter and admiration by his marvellous gifts as a story-teller. Could I have preserved the picturesque force of his style and the humorous coloring which nature taught him how to throw over his descriptions, the result, I honestly believe, would have been something new in literature. Or I might readily have found a more serious task. It was a folly, with the materiality of this daily life pressing so intrusively upon me, to attempt to fling myself back into another age; or to insist on creating the semblance of a world out of airy matter, when, at every moment, the impalpable beauty of my soap-bubble was broken by the rude contact of some actual circumstance. The wiser effort would have been to diffuse thought and imagination through the opaque substance of today, and thus to make it a bright transparency; to spiritualize the burden that began to weigh so heavily; to seek, resolutely, the true and indestructible value that lay hidden in the petty and wearisome incidents and ordinary characters with which I was now conversant. The fault was mine. The page of life that was spread out before me seemed dull and commonplace, only because I had not fathomed its deeper import. A better book than I shall ever write was there; leaf after leaf presenting itself to me, just as it was written out by the reality of the flitting hour, and vanishing as fast as written, only because my brain wanted the insight and my hand the cunning to transcribe it. At some future day, it may be, I shall remember a few scattered fragments and broken paragraphs, and write them down, and find the letters turn to gold upon the page.

These perceptions have come too late. At the instant, I was only conscious that what would have been a pleasure once was now a hopeless toil. There was no occasion to make much moan about this state of affairs. I had ceased to be a writer of tolerably poor tales and essays, and had become a tolerably good Surveyor of the Customs. That was all. But, nevertheless, it is anything but agreeable to be haunted by a suspicion that one's intellect is dwindling away, or exhaling, without your consciousness, like ether out of a phial, so that, at every glance, you find a smaller and less volatile residuum. Of the fact, there could be no doubt; and, examining myself and others, I was led to conclusions, in reference to the effect of public office on the character, not very favorable to the mode of life in question. In some other form, perhaps, I may hereafter develop these effects. Suffice it here to say that a Custom House officer of long continuance can hardly be a very praiseworthy or respectable personage, for many reasons; one of them, the tenure by which he holds his situation, and another, the very nature of his business, which—though, I trust, an honest one—is of such a sort that he does not share in the united effort of mankind.

An effect—which I believe to be observable, more or less, in every individual who has occupied the position—is, that, while he leans on the mighty arm of the Republic, his own proper strength departs from him. He loses, in an extent proportioned to the weakness or force of his original nature, the capability of self-support. If he possess an unusual share of native energy, or the enervating magic of place do not operate too long upon him, his forfeited powers may be redeemable. The ejected officer—fortunate in the unkindly shove that sends him forth betimes to struggle amid a struggling world—may return to himself and become all that he has ever been. But this seldom happens. He usually keeps his ground just long enough for his own ruin, and is then thrust out, with sinews all unstrung, to totter along the difficult footpath of life as he best may. Conscious of his own infirmity—that his tempered steel and elasticity are lost—he forever afterwards looks wistfully about him in quest of support external to himself. His pervading and continual hope—a hallucination, which

in the face of all discouragement, and making light o
impossibilities, haunts him while he lives, and, I fancy
like the convulsive throes of the cholera, torments hin
for a brief space after death—is, that finally, and in nc
long time, by some happy coincidence of circumstances
he shall be restored to office. This faith, more than any
thing else, steals the pith and availability out of whateve
enterprise he may dream of undertaking. Why shoulc
he toil and moil, and be at so much trouble to pick him
self up out of the mud, when, in a little while hence
the strong arm of his Uncle will raise and support him?
Why should he work for his living here, or go to dig
gold in California, when he is so soon to be made happy,
at monthly intervals, with a little pile of glittering coin
out of his Uncle's pocket? It is sadly curious to observe
how slight a taste of office suffices to infect a poor fellow
with this singular disease. Uncle Sam's gold—meaning
no disrespect to the worthy old gentleman—has, in this
respect, a quality of enchantment like that of the Devil's
wages. Whoever touches it should look well to himself,
or he may find the bargain to go hard against him,
involving, if not his soul, yet many of its better attributes;
its sturdy force, its courage and constancy, its truth, its
self-reliance, and all that gives the emphasis to manly
character.

Here was a fine prospect in the distance! Not that
the Surveyor brought the lesson home to himself, or
admitted that he could be so utterly undone, either by
continuance in office, or ejectment. Yet my reflections
were not the most comfortable. I began to grow melancholy and restless; continually prying into my mind, to
discover which of its poor properties were gone and
what degree of detriment had already accrued to the
remainder. I endeavored to calculate how much longer
I could stay in the Custom House, and yet go forth a
man. To confess the truth, it was my greatest apprehension—as it would never be a measure of policy to turn
out so quiet an individual as myself, and it being hardly
in the nature of a public officer to resign—it was my chief
trouble, therefore, that I was likely to grow gray and
decrepit in the Surveyorship, and become much such
another animal as the old Inspector. Might it not, in

the tedious lapse of official life that lay before me, finally be with me as it was with this venerable friend—to make the dinner hour the nucleus of the day, and to spend the rest of it as an old dog spends it, asleep in the sunshine or in the shade? A dreary look-forward this, for a man who felt it to be the best definition of happiness to live throughout the whole range of his faculties and sensibilities! But, all this while, I was giving myself very unnecessary alarm. Providence had meditated better things for me than I could possibly imagine for myself.

A remarkable event of the third year of my Surveyorship—to adopt the tone of "P. P."—was the election of General Taylor to the Presidency. It is essential, in order to a complete estimate of the advantages of official life, to view the incumbent at the in-coming of a hostile administration. His position is then one of the most singularly irksome, and, in every contingency, disagreeable, that a wretched mortal can possibly occupy; with seldom an alternative of good, on either hand, although what presents itself to him as the worst event may very probably be the best. But it is a strange experience, to a man of pride and sensibility, to know that his interests are within the control of individuals who neither love nor understand him, and by whom, since one or the other must needs happen, he would rather be injured than obliged. Strange, too, for one who has kept his calmness throughout the contest, to observe the bloodthirstiness that is developed in the hour of triumph, and to be conscious that he is himself among its objects! There are few uglier traits of human nature than this tendency —which I now witnessed in men no worse than their neighbors—to grow cruel, merely because they possessed the power of inflicting harm. If the guillotine, as applied to office holders, were a literal fact instead of one of the most apt of metaphors, it is my sincere belief that the active members of the victorious party were sufficiently excited to have chopped off all our heads, and have thanked Heaven for the opportunity! It appears to me—who have been a calm and curious observer, as well in victory as defeat—that this fierce and bitter spirit of malice and revenge has never distinguished the many triumphs of my own party as it now did that of the Whigs. The Democrats take the offices, as a general rule, because they need them, and because the practice of many years has made it the law of political warfare, which, unless a different system be proclaimed, it were weakness and cowardice to murmur at. But the long habit of victory has made them generous. They know how to spare, when they see occasion; and when they strike, the axe may be sharp, indeed, but its edge is seldom poisoned with ill will; nor is it their custom ignominiously to kick the head which they have just struck off.

In short, unpleasant as was my predicament at best, I saw much reason to congratulate myself that I was on the losing side, rather than the triumphant one. If, heretofore, I had been none of the warmest of partisans, I began now, at this season of peril and adversity, to be pretty acutely sensible with which party my predilections lay; nor was it without something like regret and shame, that, according to a reasonable calculation of chances, I saw my own prospect of retaining office to be better than those of my Democratic brethren. But who can see an inch into futurity, beyond his nose? My own head was the first that fell!

The moment when a man's head drops off is seldom or never, I am inclined to think, precisely the most agreeable of his life. Nevertheless, like the greater part of our misfortunes, even so serious a contingency brings its remedy and consolation with it, if the sufferer will but make the best, rather than the worst, of the accident which has befallen him. In my particular case, the consolatory topics were close at hand, and, indeed, had suggested themselves to my meditations a considerable time before it was requisite to use them. In view of my previous weariness of office and vague thoughts of resignation, my fortune somewhat resembled that of a person who should entertain an idea of committing suicide, and, altogether beyond his hopes, meet with the good hap to be murdered. In the Custom House, as before in the Old Manse, I had spent three years; a term long enough to rest a weary brain; long enough to break off old intellectual habits, and make room for new ones; long enough, and too long, to have lived in an unnatural state, doing what was really of no advantage nor delight to any human being, and withholding myself from toil that would, at least, have stilled an unquiet impulse in me. Then, moreover, as regarded his unceremonious ejectment, the late Surveyor was not altogether ill-pleased to be recognized by the Whigs as an enemy; since his inactivity in political affairs—his tendency to roam, at will, in that broad and quiet field where all mankind may meet, rather than confine himself to those narrow paths where brethren of the same household must diverge from one another— had sometimes made it questionable with his brother Democrats whether he was a friend. Now, after he had won the crown of martyrdom (though with no longer a head to wear it on), the point might be looked upon as settled. Finally, little heroic as he was, it seemed more decorous to be overthrown in the downfall of the party with which he had been content to stand, than to remain a forlorn survivor, when so many worthier men were falling; and, at last, after subsisting for four years on the mercy of a hostile administration, to be compelled then to define his position anew, and claim the yet more humiliating mercy of a friendly one.

Meanwhile the press had taken up my affair, and kept me, for a week or two, careering through the public prints, in my decapitated state, like Irving's Headless Horseman; ghastly and grim, and longing to be buried, as a politically dead man ought. So much for my figurative self. The real human being, all this time, with his head safely on his shoulders, had brought himself to the comfortable conclusion that everything was for the best; and, making an investment in ink, paper, and steel pens, had opened his long-disused writing desk, and was again a literary man.

Now it was, that the lucubrations of my ancient predecessor, Mr. Surveyor Pue, came into play. Rusty through long idleness, some little space was requisite before my intellectual machinery could be brought to work upon the tale, with an effect in any degree satisfactory. Even yet, though my thoughts were ultimately much absorbed in the task, it wears, to my eye, a stern

and sombre aspect; too much ungladdened by genial
sunshine; too little relieved by the tender and familiar
influences which soften almost every scene of nature
and real life, and, undoubtedly, should soften every
picture of them. This uncaptivating effect is perhaps due
to the period of hardly accomplished revolution, and
still seething turmoil, in which the story shaped itself.
It is no indication, however, of a lack of cheerfulness in
the writer's mind; for he was happier while straying
through the gloom of these sunless fantasies than at any
time since he had quitted the Old Manse. Some of the
briefer articles, which contribute to make up the volume,
have likewise been written since my involuntary withdrawal from the toils and honors of public life, and the
remainder are gleaned from annuals and magazines, of
such antique date that they have gone round the circle,
and come back to novelty again.* Keeping up the metaphor of the political guillotine, the whole may be
considered as the *Posthumous Papers of a Decapitated
Surveyor;* and the sketch which I am now bringing to
a close, if too autobiographical for a modest person to
publish in his lifetime, will readily be excused in a gentleman who writes from beyond the grave. Peace be with
all the world! My blessing on my friends! My forgiveness
to my enemies! For I am in the realm of quiet!

The life of the Custom House lies like a dream behind me. The old Inspector—who, by the by, I regret
to say, was overthrown and killed by a horse, some time
ago; else he would certainly have lived forever—he, and
all those other venerable personages who sat with him
at the receipt of custom, are but shadows in my view;
white-headed and wrinkled images which my fancy used
to sport with and has now flung aside forever. The
merchants—Pingree, Phillips, Shepard, Upton, Kimball,
Bertram, Hunt—these, and many other names, which
had such a classic familiarity for my ear six months ago
—these men of traffic, who seemed to occupy so important
a position in the world—how little time has it required
to disconnect me from them all, not merely in act, but

---

* At the time of writing this article, the author intended to
publish, along with *The Scarlet Letter,* several shorter tales and
sketches. These it has been thought advisable to defer.

recollection! It is with an effort that I recall the figures and appellations of these few. Soon, likewise, my old native town will loom upon me through the haze of memory, a mist brooding over and around it; as if it were no portion of the real earth, but an overgrown village in cloudland, with only imaginary inhabitants to people its wooden houses, and walk its homely lanes, and the unpicturesque prolixity of its main street. Henceforth, it ceases to be a reality of my life. I am a citizen of somewhere else. My good townspeople will not much regret me; for—though it has been as dear an object as any, in my literary efforts, to be of some importance in their eyes, and to win myself a pleasant memory in this abode and burial place of so many of my forefathers—there has never been, for me, the genial atmosphere which a literary man requires in order to ripen the best harvest of his mind. I shall do better amongst other faces; and these familiar ones, it need hardly be said, will do just as well without me.

It may be, however—O, transporting and triumphant thought!—that the great-grandchildren of the present race may sometimes think kindly of the scribbler of by-gone days, when the antiquary of days to come, among the sites memorable in the town's history, shall point out the locality of the town pump!

1

THE PRISON DOOR

A THRONG OF BEARDED MEN, in sad-colored garments and gray, steeple-crowned hats, intermixed with women, some wearing hoods, and others
bareheaded, was assembled in front of a wooden edifice,
the door of which was heavily timbered with oak and
studded with iron spikes.

The founders of a new colony, whatever Utopia of
human virtue and happiness they might originally project,
have invariably recognized it among their earliest practical necessities to allot a portion of the virgin soil as
a cemetery, and another portion as the site of a prison.
In accordance with this rule, it may safely be assumed
that the forefathers of Boston had built the first prison
house somewhere in the vicinity of Cornhill almost as
seasonably as they marked out the first burial ground,
on Isaac Johnson's lot and round about his grave, which
subsequently became the nucleus of all the congregated
sepulchres in the old churchyard of King's Chapel.
Certain it is that, some fifteen or twenty years after the
settlement of the town, the wooden jail was already
marked with weather-stains and other indications of age
which gave a yet darker aspect to its beetle-browed and
gloomy front. The rust on the ponderous iron-work of
its oaken door looked more antique than anything else in
the New World. Like all that pertains to crime, it
seemed never to have known a youthful era. Before this

ugly edifice, and between it and the wheel-track of the street, was a grass plot, much overgrown with burdock, pigweed, apple peru, and such unsightly vegetation, which evidently found something congenial in the soil that had so early borne the black flower of civilized society, a prison. But on one side of the portal, and rooted almost at the threshold, was a wild rosebush, covered, in this month of June, with its delicate gems, which might be imagined to offer their fragrance and fragile beauty to the prisoner as he went in, and to the condemned criminal as he came forth to his doom, in token that the deep heart of Nature could pity and be kind to him.

This rosebush, by a strange chance, has been kept alive in history; but whether it had merely survived out of the stern old wilderness, so long after the fall of the gigantic pines and oaks that originally overshadowed it —or whether, as there is fair authority for believing, it had sprung up under the footsteps of the sainted Ann Hutchinson, as she entered the prison door—we shall not take upon us to determine. Finding it so directly on the threshold of our narrative, which is now about to issue from that inauspicious portal, we could hardly do otherwise than pluck one of its flowers, and present it to the reader. It may serve, let us hope, to symbolize some sweet moral blossom that may be found along the track, or relieve the darkening close of a tale of human frailty and sorrow.

2

THE MARKET PLACE

THE GRASS PLOT BEFORE THE JAIL, in Prison Lane, on a certain summer morning not less than two centuries ago, was occupied by a pretty large number of the inhabitants of Boston, all with their eyes intently fastened on the iron-clamped oaken door. Amongst any other population, or at a later period in the history of New England, the grim rigidity that petrified the bearded physiognomies of these good people would have augured some awful business in hand. It could have betokened nothing short of the anticipated execution of some noted culprit, on whom the sentence of a legal tribunal had but confirmed the verdict of public sentiment. But in that early severity of the Puritan character, an inference of this kind could not so indubitably be drawn. It might be that a sluggish bond-servant, or an undutiful child, whom his parents had given over to the civil authority, was to be corrected at the whipping-post. It might be that an Antinomian, a Quaker, or other heterodox religionist, was to be scourged out of the town, or an idle and vagrant Indian, whom the white man's firewater had made riotous about the streets, was to be driven with stripes into the shadow of the forest. It might be, too, that a witch, like old Mistress Hibbins, the bitter-tempered widow of the magistrate, was to die upon the gallows. In either case, there was very much the same solemnity of demeanor on the part of the spectators; as befitted a people amongst whom religion and law

were almost identical, and in whose character both were
so thoroughly interfused, that the mildest and the sever-
est acts of public discipline were alike made venerable
and awful. Meagre, indeed, and cold, was the sympathy
that a transgressor might look for from such bystanders
at the scaffold. On the other hand, a penalty which in
our days would infer a degree of mocking infamy and
ridicule might then be invested with almost as stern
a dignity as the punishment of death itself.

It was a circumstance to be noted, on the summer
morning when our story begins its course, that the
women, of whom there were several in the crowd, appeared to take a peculiar interest in whatever penal
infliction might be expected to ensue. The age had
not so much refinement that any sense of impropriety
restrained the wearers of petticoat and farthingale from
stepping forth into the public ways and wedging their
not unsubstantial persons, if occasion were, into the
throng nearest to the scaffold at an execution. Morally,
as well as materially, there was a coarser fibre in those
wives and maidens of old English birth and breeding
than in their fair descendants, separated from them
by a series of six or seven generations; for, throughout
that chain of ancestry, every successive mother has
transmitted to her child a fainter bloom, a more delicate
and briefer beauty, and a slighter physical frame, if not
a character of less force and solidity, than her own. The
women who were now standing about the prison door
stood within less than half a century of the period when
the manlike Elizabeth had been the not altogether un-
suitable representative of the sex. They were her country-
women; and the beef and ale of their native land, with
a moral diet not a whit more refined, entered largely into
their composition. The bright morning sun, therefore,
shone on broad shoulders and well-developed busts and
on round and ruddy cheeks that had ripened in the far-
off island, and had hardly yet grown paler or thinner in
the atmosphere of New England. There was, moreover,
a boldness and rotundity of speech among these matrons,
as most of them seemed to be, that would startle us at
the present day, whether in respect to its purport or its
volume of tone.

"Goodwives," said a hard-featured dame of fifty, "I'll tell ye a piece of my mind. It would be greatly for the public behoof, if we women, being of mature age and church members in good repute, should have the handling of such malefactresses as this Hester Prynne. What think ye, gossips? If the hussy stood up for judgment before us five, that are now here in a knot together, would she come off with such a sentence as the worshipful magistrates have awarded? Marry, I trow not!"

"People say," said another, "that the Reverend Master Dimmesdale, her godly pastor, takes it very grievously to heart that such a scandal should have come upon his congregation."

"The magistrates are God-fearing gentlemen, but merciful overmuch—that is a truth," added a third autumnal matron. "At the very least, they should have put the brand of a hot iron on Hester Prynne's forehead. Madam Hester would have winced at that, I warrant me. But she—the naughty baggage—little will she care what they put upon the bodice of her gown! Why, look you, she may cover it with a brooch, or suchlike heathenish adornment, and so walk the streets as brave as ever!"

"Ah, but," interposed, more softly, a young wife, holding a child by the hand, "let her cover the mark as she will, the pang of it will be always in her heart."

"What do we talk of marks and brands, whether on the bodice of her gown, or the flesh of her forehead?" cried another female, the ugliest as well as the most pitiless of these self-constituted judges. "This woman has brought shame upon us all, and ought to die. Is there not law for it? Truly there is, both in the Scripture and the statute-book. Then let the magistrates, who have made it of no effect, thank themselves if their own wives and daughters go astray!"

"Mercy on us, goodwife," exclaimed a man in the crowd, "is there no virtue in woman, save what springs from a wholesome fear of the gallows? That is the hardest word yet! Hush, now, gossips! for the lock is turning in the prison door, and here comes Mistress Prynne herself."

The door of the jail being flung open from within, there appeared, in the first place, like a black shadow

emerging into the sunshine, the grim and grisly presence
of the town beadle, with a sword by his side and his
staff of office in his hand. This personage prefigured and
represented in his aspect the whole dismal severity of
the Puritanic code of law, which it was his business to
administer in its final and closest application to the of-
fender. Stretching forth the official staff in his left hand,
he laid his right upon the shoulder of a young woman,
whom he thus drew forward; until, on the threshold of
the prison door, she repelled him, by an action marked
with natural dignity and force of character, and stepped
into the open air, as if by her own free will. She bore in
her arms a child, a baby of some three months old,
who winked and turned aside its little face from the
too vivid light of day; because its existence, heretofore,
had brought it acquainted only with the gray twilight
of a dungeon, or other darksome apartment of the prison.

When the young woman—the mother of this child
—stood fully revealed before the crowd, it seemed to be
her first impulse to clasp the infant closely to her bosom;
not so much by an impulse of motherly affection, as that
she might thereby conceal a certain token, which was
wrought or fastened into her dress. In a moment, however, wisely judging that one token of her shame would
but poorly serve to hide another, she took the baby on
her arm, and, with a burning blush, and yet a haughty
smile, and a glance that would not be abashed, looked
around at her townspeople and neighbors. On the breast
of her gown, in fine red cloth surrounded with an elaborate embroidery and fantastic flourishes of gold thread,
appeared the letter "A." It was so artistically done, and
with so much fertility and gorgeous luxuriance of fancy,
that it had all the effect of a last and fitting decoration
to the apparel which she wore; and which was of a
splendor in accordance with the taste of the age, but
greatly beyond what was allowed by the sumptuary regulations of the colony.

The young woman was tall, with a figure of perfect
elegance on a large scale. She had dark and abundant
hair, so glossy that it threw off the sunshine with a
gleam, and a face which, besides being beautiful from
regularity of feature and richness of complexion, had

the impressiveness belonging to a marked brow and deep black eyes. She was ladylike, too, after the manner of the feminine gentility of those days; characterized by a certain state and dignity, rather than by the delicate, evanescent, and indescribable grace, which is now recognized as its indication. And never had Hester Prynne appeared more ladylike, in the antique interpretation of the term, than as she issued from the prison. Those who had before known her and had expected to behold her dimmed and obscured by a disastrous cloud, were astonished, and even startled, to perceive how her beauty shone out and made a halo of the misfortune and ignominy in which she was enveloped. It may be true that, to a sensitive observer, there was something exquisitely painful in it. Her attire, which, indeed, she had wrought for the occasion, in prison, and had modelled much after her own fancy, seemed to express the attitude of her spirit, the desperate recklessness of her mood, by its wild and picturesque peculiarity. But the point which drew all eyes and, as it were, transfigured the wearer—so that both men and women, who had been familiarly acquainted with Hester Prynne, were now impressed as if they beheld her for the first time—was that *Scarlet Letter*, so fantastically embroidered and illuminated upon her bosom. It had the effect of a spell, taking her out of the ordinary relations with humanity and enclosing her in a sphere by herself.

"She hath good skill at her needle, that's certain," remarked one of her female spectators; "but did ever a woman, before this brazen hussy, contrive such a way of showing it! Why, gossips, what is it but to laugh in the faces of our godly magistrates, and make a pride out of what they, worthy gentlemen, meant for a punishment?"

"It were well," muttered the most iron-visaged of the old dames, "if we stripped Madam Hester's rich gown off her dainty shoulders; and as for the red letter, which she hath stitched so curiously, I'll bestow a rag of mine own rheumatic flannel, to make a fitter one!"

"O, peace, neighbors, peace!" whispered their youngest companion; "do not let her hear you! Not a stitch in that embroidered letter, but she has felt it in her heart."

The grim beadle now made a gesture with his staff.

"Make way, good people, make way, in the King's name!" cried he. "Open a passage; and, I promise ye, Mistress Prynne shall be set where man, woman and child may have a fair sight of her brave apparel, from this time till an hour past meridian. A blessing on the righteous Colony of the Massachusetts, where iniquity is dragged out into the sunshine! Come along, Madam Hester, and show your scarlet letter in the market place!"

A lane was forthwith opened through the crowd of spectators. Preceded by the beadle, and attended by an irregular procession of stern-browed men and unkindly visaged women, Hester Prynne set forth towards the place appointed for her punishment. A crowd of eager and curious schoolboys, understanding little of the matter in hand except that it gave them a half-holiday, ran before her progress, turning their heads continually to stare into her face, and at the winking baby in her arms, and at the ignominious letter on her breast. It was no great distance, in those days, from the prison door to the market place. Measured by the prisoner's experience, however, it might be reckoned a journey of some length; for, haughty as her demeanor was, she perchance underwent an agony from every footstep of those that thronged to see her, as if her heart had been flung into the street for them all to spurn and trample upon. In our nature, however, there is a provision, alike marvellous and merciful, that the sufferer should never know the intensity of what he endures by its present torture, but chiefly by the pang that rankles after it. With almost a serene deportment, therefore, Hester Prynne passed through this portion of her ordeal, and came to a sort of scaffold, at the western extremity of the market place. It stood nearly beneath the eaves of Boston's earliest church, and appeared to be a fixture there.

In fact, this scaffold constituted a portion of a penal machine, which now, for two or three generations past, has been merely historical and traditionary among us, but was held, in the old time, to be as effectual an agent n the promotion of good citizenship as ever was the guillotine among the terrorists of France. It was, in short, the platform of the pillory; and above it rose the framework of that instrument of discipline, so fashioned as to confine the human head in its tight grasp, and thus hold it up to the public gaze. The very ideal of ignominy was embodied and made manifest in this contrivance of wood and iron. There can be no outrage, methinks, against our common nature—whatever be the delinquencies of the individual—no outrage more flagrant than to forbid the culprit to hide his face for shame; as it was the essence of this punishment to do. In Hester Prynne's instance, however, as not unfrequently in other cases, her sentence bore, that she should stand a certain time upon the platform but without undergoing that gripe about the neck and confinement of the head, the proneness to which was the most devilish characteristic of this ugly engine. Knowing well her part, she ascended a flight of wooden steps, and was thus displayed to the surrounding multitude, at about the height of a man's shoulders above the street.

Had there been a Papist among the crowd of Puritans, he might have seen in this beautiful woman, so picturesque in her attire and mien, and with the infant at her bosom, an object to remind him of the image of Divine Maternity, which so many illustrious painters have vied with one another to represent; something which should remind him, indeed, but only by contrast, of that sacred image of sinless motherhood, whose infant was to redeem the world. Here, there was the taint of deepest sin in the most sacred quality of human life, working such effect that the world was only the darker for this woman's beauty, and the more lost for the infant that she had borne.

The scene was not without a mixture of awe, such as must always invest the spectacle of guilt and shame in a fellow-creature, before society shall have grown corrupt enough to smile, instead of shuddering, at it. The witnesses of Hester Prynne's disgrace had not yet passed beyond their simplicity. They were stern enough to look upon her death, had that been the sentence, without a murmur at its severity, but had none of the heartlessness of another social state, which would find only a theme for jest in an exhibition like the present. Even had there been a disposition to turn the matter into ridicule, it must have been repressed and over-powered by the solemn presence of men no less dignified than the Governor and several of his counsellors, a judge, a general, and the ministers of the town; all of whom sat or stood in a balcony of the meeting house, looking down upon the platform. When such personages could constitute a part of the spectacle without risking the majesty or reverence of rank and office, it was safely to be inferred that the infliction of a legal sentence would have an earnest and effectual meaning. Accordingly, the crowd was sombre and grave. The unhappy culprit sustained herself as best a woman might, under the heavy weight of a thousand unrelenting eyes, all fastened upon her and concentred at her bosom. It was almost intol-erable to be borne. Of an impulsive and passionate nature, she had fortified herself to encounter the stings and venomous stabs of public contumely, wreaking itself in every variety of insult; but there was a quality so much more terrible in the solemn mood of the popular mind, that she longed rather to behold all those rigid countenances contorted with scornful merriment, and herself the object. Had a roar of laughter burst from the multitude—each man, each woman, each little shrill-voiced child, contributing their individual parts—Hester Prynne might have repaid them all with a bitter and disdainful smile. But under the leaden infliction which it was her doom to endure, she felt, at moments, as if she must needs shriek out with the full power of her lungs and cast herself from the scaffold down upon the ground, or else go mad at once.

Yet there were intervals when the whole scene, in which she was the most conspicuous object, seemed to vanish from her eyes, or, at least, glimmered indistinctly before them, like a mass of imperfectly shaped and spectral images. Her mind, and especially her memory, was preternaturally active, and kept bringing up other scenes than this roughly hewn street of a little town on the edge of the Western wilderness; other faces than were lowering upon her from beneath the brims of those steeple-crowned hats. Reminiscences, the most trifling and immaterial, passages of infancy and school-days, sports, childish quarrels, and the little domestic traits of her maiden years, came swarming back upon her, intermingled with recollections of whatever was gravest in her subsequent life; one picture precisely as vivid as another; as if all were of similar importance, or all alike a play. Possibly it was an instinctive device of her spirit to relieve itself, by the exhibition of these phantasmagoric forms, from the cruel weight and hard-ness of the reality.

Be that as it might, the scaffold of the pillory was a point of view that revealed to Hester Prynne the entire track along which she had been treading since her happy infancy. Standing on that miserable eminence, she saw again her native village, in Old England, and her paternal home; a decayed house of gray stone, with a poverty-stricken aspect, but retaining a half-obliterated shield of arms over the portal, in token of antique gentility. She saw her father's face, with its bald brow and reverend white beard that flowed over the old-fashioned Elizabethan ruff; her mother's, too, with the look of heedful and anxious love which it always wore in her remembrance, and which, even since her death, had so often laid the impediment of a gentle remon-strance in her daughter's pathway. She saw her own face, glowing with girlish beauty, and illuminating all the interior of the dusky mirror in which she had been wont to gaze at it. There she beheld another countenance, of a man well stricken in years, a pale, thin, scholar-like visage, with eyes dim and bleared by the lamplight that had served them to pore over many ponderous books. Yet those same bleared optics had a strange, penetrating power, when it was their owner's purpose to read the human soul. This figure of the study and the cloister, as Hester Prynne's womanly fancy failed not to recall, was slightly deformed, with the left shoulder a trifle higher than the right. Next rose before her, in memory's picture gallery, the intricate and narrow thoroughfares, the tall, gray houses, the huge cathedrals, and the public edifices, ancient in date and quaint in architecture, of a Continental city, where a new life had awaited her, still in connection with the misshapen scholar; a new life, but feeding itself on time-worn materials, like a tuft of green moss on a crumbling wall. Lastly, in lieu of these shifting scenes, came back the rude market place of the Puritan settlement, with all the townspeople assembled and levelling their stern regards at Hester Prynne—yes, at herself—who stood on the scaffold of the pillory, an infant on her arm, and the letter "A" in scarlet, fantastically embroidered with gold thread, upon her bosom!

Could it be true? She clutched the child so fiercely to her breast that it sent forth a cry; she turned her eyes downward at the scarlet letter, and even touched it with her finger, to assure herself that the infant and the shame were real. Yes!—these were her realities—all else had vanished!

3

THE RECOGNITION

FROM THIS INTENSE CONSCIOUSNESS of being the object of severe and universal observation, the wearer of the scarlet letter was at length relieved, by discerning on the outskirts of the crowd a figure which irresistibly took possession of her thoughts. An Indian in his native garb was standing there; but the red men were not so infrequent visitors of the English settlements, that one of them would have attracted any notice from Hester Prynne at such a time; much less would he have excluded all other objects and ideas from her mind. By the Indian's side, and evidently sustaining a companionship with him, stood a white man, clad in a strange disarray of civilized and savage costume.

He was small in stature, with a furrowed visage which, as yet, could hardly be termed aged. There was a remarkable intelligence in his features, as of a person who had so cultivated his mental part that it could not fail to mould the physical to itself, and become manifest by unmistakable tokens. Although, by a seemingly careless arrangement of his heterogeneous garb, he had endeavored to conceal or abate the peculiarity, it was sufficiently evident to Hester Prynne that one of this man's shoulders rose higher than the other. Again, at the first instant of perceiving that thin visage and the slight deformity of the figure, she pressed her infant to her bosom with so convulsive a force that the poor babe uttered another cry of pain. But the mother did not seem to hear it.

At his arrival in the market place, and some time before she saw him, the stranger had bent his eyes on Hester Prynne. It was carelessly, at first, like a man chiefly accustomed to look inward, and to whom external matters are of little value and import unless they bear relation to something within his mind. Very soon, however, his look became keen and penetrative. A writhing horror twisted itself across his features, like a snake gliding swiftly over them, and making one little pause, with all its wreathed intervolutions in open sight. His face darkened with some powerful emotion, which, nevertheless, he so instantaneously controlled by an effort of his will, that, save at a single moment, its expression might have passed for calmness. After a brief space, the convulsion grew almost imperceptible, and finally subsided into the depths of his nature. When he found the eyes of Hester Prynne fastened on his own, and saw that she appeared to recognize him, he slowly and calmly raised his finger, made a gesture with it in the air, and laid it on his lips.

Then, touching the shoulder of a townsman who stood next to him, he addressed him in a formal and courteous manner.

"I pray you, good Sir," said he, "who is this woman? —and wherefore is she here set up to public shame?"

"You must needs be a stranger in this region, friend,"

answered the townsman, looking curiously at the questioner and his savage companion, "else you would surely have heard of Mistress Hester Prynne, and her evil doings. She hath raised a great scandal, I promise you, in godly Master Dimmesdale's church."

"You say truly," replied the other. "I am a stranger, and have been a wanderer, sorely against my will. I have met with grievous mishaps by sea and land, and have been long held in bonds among the heathen folk, to the southward; and am now brought hither by this Indian, to be redeemed out of my captivity. Will it please you, therefore, to tell me of Hester Prynne's— have I her name rightly?—of this woman's offences, and what has brought her to yonder scaffold?"

"Truly, friend; and methinks it must gladden your heart, after your troubles and sojourn in the wilderness," said the townsman, "to find yourself, at length, in a land where iniquity is searched out, and punished in the sight of rulers and people; as here in our godly New England. Yonder woman, Sir, you must know, was the wife of a certain learned man, English by birth, but who had long dwelt in Amsterdam, whence, some good time agone, he was minded to cross over and cast in his lot with us of the Massachusetts. To this purpose, he sent his wife before him, remaining himself to look after some necessary affairs. Marry, good Sir, in some two years, or less, that the woman has been a dweller here in Boston, no tidings have come of this learned gentleman, Master Prynne; and his young wife, look you, being left to her own misguidance—"

"Ah!—aha!—I conceive you," said the stranger, with a bitter smile. "So learned a man as you speak of should have learned this too in his books. And who, by your favor, Sir, may be the father of yonder babe—it is some three or four months old, I should judge—which Mistress Prynne is holding in her arms?"

"Of a truth, friend, that matter remaineth a riddle; and the Daniel who shall expound it is yet a-wanting," answered the townsman. "Madam Hester absolutely refuseth to speak, and the magistrates have laid their heads together in vain. Peradventure the guilty one stands looking on at this sad spectacle, unknown of man, and forgetting that God sees him."

"The learned man," observed the stranger, with another smile, "should come himself, to look into the mystery."

"It behooves him well, if he be still in life," responded the townsman. "Now, good Sir, our Massachusetts magistracy, bethinking themselves that this woman is youthful and fair, and doubtless was strongly tempted to her fall—and that, moreover, as is most likely, her husband may be at the bottom of the sea—they have not been bold to put in force the extremity of our righteous law against her. The penalty thereof is death. But in their great mercy and tenderness of heart, they have doomed Mistress Prynne to stand only a space of three hours on the platform of the pillory, and then and thereafter, for the remainder of her natural life, to wear a mark of shame upon her bosom."

"A wise sentence!" remarked the stranger, gravely bowing his head. "Thus she will be a living sermon against sin, until the ignominious letter be engraved upon her tombstone. It irks me, nevertheless, that the partner of her iniquity should not, at least, stand on the scaffold by her side. But he will be known!—he will be known!—he will be known!"

He bowed courteously to the communicative townsman, and, whispering a few words to his Indian attendant, they both made their way through the crowd.

While this passed, Hester Prynne had been standing on her pedestal, still with a fixed gaze towards the stranger; so fixed a gaze, that, at moments of intense absorption, all other objects in the visible world seemed to vanish, leaving only him and her. Such an interview, perhaps, would have been more terrible than even to meet him as she now did, with the hot, midday sun burning down upon her face and lighting up its shame; with the scarlet token of infamy on her breast; with the sin-born infant in her arms; with a whole people, drawn forth as to a festival, staring at the features that should have been seen only in the quiet gleam of the fireside, in the happy shadow of a home, or beneath a matronly veil, at church. Dreadful as it was, she was conscious

of a shelter in the presence of these thousand witnesses.
It was better to stand thus, with so many betwixt him
and her, than to greet him, face to face, they two alone.
She fled for refuge, as it were, to the public exposure,
and dreaded the moment when its protection should be
withdrawn from her. Involved in these thoughts, she
scarcely heard a voice behind her, until it had repeated
her name more than once, in a loud and solemn tone,
audible to the whole multitude.

"Hearken unto me, Hester Prynne!" said the voice.

It has already been noticed that directly over the
platform on which Hester Prynne stood was a kind of
balcony, or open gallery, appended to the meeting house.
It was the place whence proclamations were wont to be
made, amidst an assemblage of the magistracy, with all
the ceremonial that attended such public observances in
those days. Here, to witness the scene which we are
describing, sat Governor Bellingham himself, with four
sergeants about his chair, bearing halberds, as a guard of
honor. He wore a dark feather in his hat, a border of
embroidery on his cloak, and a black velvet tunic beneath;
a gentleman advanced in years, with a hard experience
written in his wrinkles. He was not ill fitted to be the
head and representative of a community which owed
its origin and progress and its present state of development, not to the impulses of youth, but to the stern and
tempered energies of manhood and the sombre sagacity
of age; accomplishing so much, precisely because it
imagined and hoped so little. The other eminent characters by whom the chief ruler was surrounded were
distinguished by a dignity of mien belonging to a period
when the forms of authority were felt to possess the
sacredness of Divine institutions. They were, doubtless,
good men, just, and sage. But, out of the whole human
family, it would not have been easy to select the same
number of wise and virtuous persons who should be
less capable of sitting in judgment on an erring woman's
heart, and disentangling its mesh of good and evil, than
the sages of rigid aspect towards whom Hester Prynne
now turned her face. She seemed conscious, indeed,
that whatever sympathy she might expect lay in the
larger and warmer heart of the multitude; for, as she

lifted her eyes towards the balcony, the unhappy woman grew pale and trembled.

The voice which had called her attention was that of the reverend and famous John Wilson, the eldest clergyman of Boston, a great scholar like most of his contemporaries in the profession, and withal a man of kind and genial spirit. This last attribute, however, had been less carefully developed than his intellectual gifts, and was, in truth, rather a matter of shame than self-congratulation with him. There he stood, with a border of grizzled locks beneath his skullcap, while his gray eyes, accustomed to the shaded light of his study, were winking, like those of Hester's infant, in the unadulterated sunshine. He looked like the darkly engraved portraits which we see prefixed to old volumes of sermons; and had no more right than one of those portraits would have, to step forth, as he now did, and meddle with a question of human guilt, passion and anguish.

"Hester Prynne," said the clergyman, "I have striven with my young brother here, under whose preaching of the word you have been privileged to sit"—here Mr. Wilson laid his hand on the shoulder of a pale young man beside him—"I have sought, I say, to persuade this godly youth that he should deal with you, here in the face of Heaven, and before these wise and upright rulers, and in hearing of all the people as touching the vileness and blackness of your sin. Knowing your natural temper better than I, he could the better judge what arguments to use, whether of tenderness or terror, such as might prevail over your hardness and obstinacy; insomuch that you should no longer hide the name of him who tempted you to this grievous fall. But he opposes to me (with a young man's oversoftness, albeit wise beyond his years) that it were wronging the very nature of woman to force her to lay open her heart's secrets in such broad daylight, and in presence of so great a multitude. Truly, as I sought to convince him, the shame lay in the commission of the sin, and not in the showing of it forth. What say you to it, once again, Brother Dimmesdale? Must it be thou, or I, that shall deal with this poor sinner's soul?"

There was a murmur among the dignified and reverend

occupants of the balcony; and Governor Bellingham gave expression to its purport, speaking in an authoritative voice, although tempered with respect towards the youthful clergyman whom he addressed.

"Good Master Dimmesdale," said he, "the responsibility of this woman's soul lies greatly with you. It behooves you, therefore, to exhort her to repentance and to confession, as a proof and consequence thereof."

The directness of this appeal drew the eyes of the whole crowd upon the Reverend Mr. Dimmesdale; a young clergyman who had come from one of the great English universities, bringing all the learning of the age into our wild forestland. His eloquence and religious fervor had already given the earnest of high eminence in his profession. He was a person of very striking aspect, with a white, lofty, and impending brow, large, brown, melancholy eyes, and a mouth which, unless when he forcibly compressed it, was apt to be tremulous, expressing both nervous sensibility and a vast power of self-restraint. Notwithstanding his high native gifts and scholarlike attainments, there was an air about this young minister—an apprehensive, a startled, a half-frightened look—as of a being who felt himself quite astray and at a loss in the pathway of human existence, and could only be at ease in some seclusion of his own. Therefore, so far as his duties would permit, he trod in the shadowy bypaths, and thus kept himself simple and childlike, coming forth, when occasion was, with a freshness, and fragrance, and dewy purity of thought, which, as many people said, affected them like the speech of an angel.

Such was the young man whom the Reverend Mr. Wilson and the Governor had introduced so openly to the public notice, bidding him speak, in the hearing of all men, to that mystery of a woman's soul, so sacred even in its pollution. The trying nature of his position drove the blood from his cheek, and made his lips tremulous.

"Speak to the woman, my brother," said Mr. Wilson. "It is of moment to her soul, and therefore, as the worshipful Governor says, momentous to thine own, in whose charge hers is. Exhort her to confess the truth!"

The Reverend Mr. Dimmesdale bent his head, in silent prayer, as it seemed, and then came forward.

"Hester Prynne," said he, leaning over the balcony, and looking down steadfastly into her eyes, "thou hearest what this good man says, and seest the accountability under which I labor. If thou feelest it to be for thy soul's peace, and that thy earthly punishment will thereby be made more effectual to salvation, I charge thee to speak out the name of thy fellow-sinner and fellow-sufferer! Be not silent from any mistaken pity and tenderness for him; for, believe me, Hester, though he were to step down from a high place, and stand there beside thee on thy pedestal of shame, yet better were it so, than to hide a guilty heart through life. What can thy silence do for him, except it tempt him—yea, compel him, as it were—to add hypocrisy to sin? Heaven hath granted thee an open ignominy, that thereby thou mayest work out an open triumph over the evil within thee, and the sorrow without. Take heed how thou deniest to him —who, perchance, hath not the courage to grasp it for himself—the bitter, but wholesome, cup that is now presented to thy lips!"

The young pastor's voice was tremulously sweet, rich, deep, and broken. The feeling that it so evidently manifested, rather than the direct purport of the words, caused it to vibrate within all hearts, and brought the listeners into one accord of sympathy. Even the poor baby at Hester's bosom was affected by the same influence, for it directed its hitherto vacant gaze towards Mr. Dimmesdale, and held up its little arms, with a half pleased, half plaintive murmur. So powerful seemed the minister's appeal, that the people could not believe but that Hester Prynne would speak out the guilty name; or else that the guilty one himself, in whatever high or lowly place he stood, would be drawn forth by an inward and inevitable necessity, and compelled to ascend the scaffold.

Hester shook her head.

"Woman, transgress not beyond the limits of Heaven's mercy!" cried the Reverend Mr. Wilson, more harshly than before. "That little babe hath been gifted with a voice to second and confirm the counsel which thou

hast heard. Speak out the name! That, and thy repentance, may avail to take the scarlet letter off thy breast."

"Never!" replied Hester Prynne, looking, not at Mr.
Wilson, but into the deep and troubled eyes of the
younger clergyman. "It is too deeply branded. Ye
cannot take it off. And would that I might endure his
agony, as well as mine!"

"Speak, woman!" said another voice, coldly and sternly,
proceeding from the crowd about the scaffold. "Speak;
and give your child a father!"

"I will not speak!" answered Hester, turning pale as
death, but responding to this voice, which she too surely
recognized. "And my child must seek a heavenly Father;
she shall never know an earthly one!"

"She will not speak!" murmured Mr. Dimmesdale,
who, leaning over the balcony, with his hand upon his
heart, had awaited the result of his appeal. He now drew
back, with a long respiration. "Wondrous strength and
generosity of a woman's heart! She will not speak!"

Discerning the impracticable state of the poor culprit's
mind, the elder clergyman, who had carefully prepared
himself for the occasion, addressed to the multitude a
discourse on sin, in all its branches, but with continual
reference to the ignominious letter. So forcibly did he
dwell upon this symbol, for the hour or more during
which his periods were rolling over the people's heads,
that it assumed new terrors in their imagination, and
seemed to derive its scarlet hue from the flames of the
infernal pit. Hester Prynne, meanwhile, kept her place
upon the pedestal of shame, with glazed eyes, and an
air of weary indifference. She had borne, that morning,
all that nature could endure; and as her temperament
was not of the order that escapes from too intense suffering by a swoon, her spirit could only shelter itself
beneath a stony crust of insensibility, while the faculties
of animal life remained entire. In this state, the voice
of the preacher thundered remorselessly, but unavailingly,
upon her ears. The infant, during the latter portion of
her ordeal, pierced the air with its wailings and screams;
she strove to hush it, mechanically, but seemed scarcely
to sympathize with its trouble. With the same hard
demeanor, she was led back to prison, and vanished

from the public gaze within its iron-clamped portal. It was whispered, by those who peered after her, that the scarlet letter threw a lurid gleam along the dark passageway of the interior.

4

THE INTERVIEW

AFTER HER RETURN TO THE PRISON, Hester Prynne was found to be in a state of nervous excitement that demanded constant watchfulness, lest she should perpetrate violence on herself, or do some halffrenzied mischief to the poor babe. As night approached, it proving impossible to quell her insubordination by rebuke or threats of punishment, Master Brackett, the jailer, thought fit to introduce a physician. He described him as a man of skill in all Christian modes of physical science, and likewise familiar with whatever the savage people could teach, in respect to medicinal herbs and roots that grew in the forest. To say the truth, there was much need of professional assistance, not merely for Hester herself, but still more urgently for the child, who, drawing its sustenance from the maternal bosom, seemed to have drunk in with it all the turmoil, the anguish and despair, which pervaded the mother's system. It now writhed in convulsions of pain, and was a forcible type, in its little frame, of the moral agony which Hester Prynne had borne throughout the day.

Closely following the jailer into the dismal apartment appeared that individual of singular aspect, whose presence in the crowd had been of such deep interest to the wearer of the scarlet letter. He was lodged in the prison, not as suspected of any offence, but as the most convenient and suitable mode of disposing of him until the magistrates should have conferred with the Indian sagamores respecting his ransom. His name was announced as Roger Chillingworth. The jailer, after ushering him into the room, remained a moment, marvelling at the comparative quiet that followed his entrance; for Hester Prynne had immediately become as still as death, although the child continued to moan.

"Prithee, friend, leave me alone with my patient," said the practitioner. "Trust me, good jailer, you shall briefly have peace in your house; and, I promise you, Mistress Prynne shall hereafter be more amenable to just authority than you may have found her heretofore."

"Nay, if your worship can accomplish that," answered Master Brackett, "I shall own you for a man of skill indeed! Verily, the woman hath been like a possessed one; and there lacks little, that I should take in hand to drive Satan out of her with stripes."

The stranger had entered the room with the characteristic quietude of the profession to which he announced himself as belonging. Nor did his demeanor change when the withdrawal of the prison-keeper left him face to face with the woman, whose absorbed notice of him in the crowd had intimated so close a relation between himself and her. His first care was given to the child, whose cries, indeed, as she lay writhing on the trundle bed, made it of peremptory necessity to postpone all other business to the task of soothing her. He examined the infant carefully, and then proceeded to unclasp a leathern case, which he took from beneath his dress. It appeared to contain certain medical preparations, one of which he mingled with a cup of water.

"My old studies in alchemy," observed he, "and my sojourn, for above a year past, among a people well versed in the kindly properties of simples, have made a better physician of me than many that claim the medical degree. Here, woman! The child is yours—she is none of mine—neither will she recognize my voice or aspect as a father's. Administer this draught, therefore, with thine own hand."

Hester repelled the offered medicine, at the same time gazing with strongly marked apprehension into his face.

"Wouldst thou avenge thyself on the innocent babe?" whispered she.

"Foolish woman!" responded the physician, half coldly, half soothingly. "What should ail me, to harm this misbegotten and miserable babe? The medicine is potent for good; and were it my child—yea, mine own, as well as thine!—I could do no better for it."

As she still hesitated, being, in fact, in no reasonable state of mind, he took the infant in his arms, and himself administered the draught. It soon proved its efficacy, and redeemed the leech's pledge. The moans of the little patient subsided; its convulsive tossings gradually ceased; and, in a few moments, as is the custom of young children after relief from pain, it sank into a profound and dewy slumber. The physician, as he had a fair right to be termed, next bestowed his attention on the mother. With calm and intent scrutiny, he felt her pulse, looked into her eyes—a gaze that made her heart shrink and shudder, because so familiar, and yet so strange and cold—and, finally, satisfied with his investigation, proceeded to mingle another draught.

"I know not Lethe nor Nepenthe," remarked he, "but I have learned many new secrets in the wilderness, and here is one of them—a recipe that an Indian taught me, in requital of some lessons of my own, that were as old as Paracelsus. Drink it! It may be less soothing than a sinless conscience. That I cannot give thee. But it will calm the swell and heaving of thy passion, like oil thrown on the waves of a tempestuous sea."

He presented the cup to Hester, who received it with a slow, earnest look into his face; not precisely a look of fear, yet full of doubt and questioning, as to what his purposes might be. She looked also at her slumbering child.

"I have thought of death," said she, "have wished for it, would even have prayed for it, were it fit that such as I should pray for anything. Yet, if death be in this cup, I bid thee think again, ere thou beholdest me quaff it. See! It is even now at my lips."

"Drink, then," replied he, still with the same cold composure. "Dost thou know me so little, Hester Prynne? Are my purposes wont to be so shallow? Even if I imagine a scheme of vengeance, what could I do better for my object than to let thee live—than to give thee medicines against all harm and peril of life—so that this burning shame may still blaze upon thy bosom?" As he spoke, he laid his long forefinger on the scarlet letter, which forthwith seemed to scorch into Hester's breast, as if it had been red-hot. He noticed her involuntary gesture, and smiled. "Live, therefore, and bear about thy doom with thee, in the eyes of men and women—in the eyes of him whom thou didst call thy husband—in the eyes of yonder child! And, that thou mayest live, take off this draught."

Without further expostulation or delay, Hester Prynne drained the cup, and, at the motion of the man of skill, seated herself on the bed where the child was sleeping; while he drew the only chair which the room afforded, and took his own seat beside her. She could not but tremble at these preparations; for she felt that —having now done all that humanity, or principle, or, if so it were, a refined cruelty, impelled him to do, for the relief of physical suffering—he was next to treat with her as the man whom she had most deeply and irreparably injured.

"Hester," said he, "I ask not wherefore, nor how, thou hast fallen into the pit, or say, rather, thou hast ascended to the pedestal of infamy on which I found thee. The reason is not far to seek. It was my folly, and thy weakness. I—a man of thought, the bookworm of great libraries—a man already in decay, having given my best years to feed the hungry dream of knowledge —what had I to do with youth and beauty like thine own! Misshapen from my birth-hour, how could I delude myself with the idea that intellectual gifts might veil physical deformity in a young girl's fantasy! Men call me wise. If sages were ever wise in their own behoof, I might have foreseen all this. I might have known that, as I came out of the vast and dismal forest and entered this settlement of Christian men, the very first object to meet my eyes would be thyself, Hester Prynne, standing up, a statue of ignominy, before the people. Nay, from the moment when we came down the old church steps together, a married pair, I might have beheld the bale-fire of that scarlet letter blazing at the end of our path!"

"Thou knowest," said Hester—for, depressed as she was, she could not endure this last quiet stab at the token of her shame—"thou knowest that I was frank with thee. I felt no love, nor feigned any."

"True," replied he. "It was my folly! I have said it. But, up to that epoch of my life, I had lived in vain. The world had been so cheerless! My heart was a habitation large enough for many guests, but lonely and chill, and without a household fire. I longed to kindle one! It seemed not so wild a dream—old as I was, and sombre as I was, and misshapen as I was—that the simple bliss, which is scattered far and wide for all mankind to gather up, might yet be mine. And so, Hester, I drew thee into my heart, into its innermost chamber, and sought to warm thee by the warmth which thy presence made there!"

"I have greatly wronged thee," murmured Hester.

"We have wronged each other," answered he. "Mine was the first wrong, when I betrayed thy budding youth into a false and unnatural relation with my decay. Therefore, as a man who has not thought and philosophized in vain, I seek no vengeance, plot no evils against thee. Between thee and me, the scale hangs fairly balanced. But, Hester, the man lives who has wronged us both! Who is he?"

"Ask me not!" replied Hester Prynne, looking firmly into his face. "That thou shalt never know!"

"Never, sayest thou?" rejoined he, with a smile of dark and self-relying intelligence. "Never know him! Believe me, Hester, there are few things—whether in the outward world, or, to a certain depth, in the invisible sphere of thought—few things hidden from the man who devotes himself earnestly and unreservedly to the solution of a mystery. Thou mayest cover up thy secret from the prying multitude. Thou mayest conceal it,

too, from the ministers and magistrates, even as thou
didst this day, when they sought to wrench the name
out of thy heart and give thee a partner on thy pedestal.
But, as for me, I come to the inquest with other senses
than they possess. I shall seek this man as I have sought
truth in books, as I have sought gold in alchemy. There
is a sympathy that will make me conscious of him. I
shall see him tremble. I shall feel myself shudder, suddenly and unawares. Sooner or later, he must needs be
mine!"

The eyes of the wrinkled scholar glowed so intensely
upon her that Hester Prynne clasped her hands over
her heart, dreading lest he should read the secret there
at once.

"Thou wilt not reveal his name? Not the less he is
mine," resumed he, with a look of confidence, as if
destiny were at one with him. "He bears no letter of
infamy wrought into his garment, as thou dost; but
I shall read it on his heart. Yet fear not for him! Think
not that I shall interfere with Heaven's own method
of retribution, or, to my own loss, betray him to the
gripe of human law. Neither do thou imagine that I
shall contrive aught against his life; no, nor against his
fame, if, as I judge, he be a man of fair repute. Let him
live! Let him hide himself in outward honor, if he may!
Not the less he shall be mine!"

"Thy acts are like mercy," said Hester, bewildered
and appalled. "But thy words interpret thee as a terror!"

"One thing, thou that wast my wife, I would enjoin
upon thee," continued the scholar. "Thou hast kept the
secret of thy paramour. Keep, likewise, mine! There
are none in this land that know me. Breathe not, to any
human soul, that thou didst ever call me husband! Here,
on this wild outskirt of the earth, I shall pitch my tent;
for, elsewhere a wanderer, and isolated from human
interests, I find here a woman, a man, a child, amongst
whom and myself there exist the closest ligaments. No
matter whether of love or hate; no matter whether of
right or wrong! Thou and thine, Hester Prynne, belong
to me. My home is where thou art, and where he is.
But betray me not!"

"Wherefore dost thou desire it?" inquired Hester,

shrinking, she hardly knew why, from this secret bond. "Why not announce thyself openly, and cast me off at once?"

"It may be," he replied, "because I will not encounter the dishonor that besmirches the husband of a faithless woman. It may be for other reasons. Enough, it is my purpose to live and die unknown. Let, therefore, thy husband be to the world as one already dead, and of whom no tidings shall ever come. Recognize me not, by word, by sign, by look! Breathe not the secret, above all, to the man thou wottest of. Shouldst thou fail me in this, beware! His fame, his position, his life, will be in my hands. Beware!"

"I will keep thy secret, as I have his," said Hester.

"Swear it!" rejoined he.

And she took the oath.

"And now, Mistress Prynne," said old Roger Chillingworth, as he was hereafter to be named, "I leave thee alone; alone with thy infant, and the scarlet letter! How is it, Hester? Doth thy sentence bind thee to wear the token in thy sleep? Art thou not afraid of nightmares and hideous dreams?"

"Why dost thou smile so at me?" inquired Hester, troubled at the expression of his eyes. "Art thou like the Black Man that haunts the forest round about us? Hast thou enticed me into a bond that will prove the ruin of my soul?"

"Not thy soul," he answered, with another smile. "No, not thine!"

5

HESTER AT HER NEEDLE

HESTER PRYNNE'S TERM OF CONFINEMENT was now at an end. Her prison door was thrown open and she came forth into the sunshine, which, falling on all alike, seemed, to her sick and morbid heart, as if meant for no other purpose than to reveal the scarlet letter on her breast. Perhaps there was a more real torture in her first unattended footsteps from the threshold of the prison than even in the procession and spectacle that have been described, where she was made the common infamy at which all mankind was summoned to point its finger. Then, she was supported by an unnatural tension of the nerves and by all the combative energy of her character, which enabled her to convert the scene into a kind of lurid triumph. It was, moreover, a separate and insulated event, to occur but once in her lifetime, and to meet which, therefore, reckless of economy, she might call up the vital strength that would have sufficed for many quiet years. The very law that condemned her—a giant of stern features, but with vigor to support, as well as to annihilate, in his iron arm —had held her up through the terrible ordeal of her ignominy. But now, with this unattended walk from her prison door began the daily custom; and she must either sustain and carry it forward by the ordinary resources of her nature, or sink beneath it. She could no longer borrow from the future to help her through the present grief. Tomorrow would bring its own trial with it; so would the next day, and so would the next; each its own trial, and yet the very same that was now so unutterably grievous to be borne. The days of the far-off future would toil onward; still with the same burden for her to take up and bear along with her, but never to fling down; for the accumulating days and added years would pile up their misery upon the heap of shame. Throughout them all, giving up her individuality, she would become the general symbol at which the preacher and moralist might point, and in which they might vivify and embody their images of woman's frailty and sinful passion. Thus the young and pure would be taught to look at her, with the scarlet letter flaming on her breast—at her, the child of honorable parents, at her, the mother of a babe, that would hereafter be a woman, at her, who had once been innocent—as the figure, the body, the reality of sin. And over her grave, the infamy that she must carry thither would be her only monument.

It may seem marvellous, that, with the world before her—kept by no restrictive clause of her condemnation within the limits of the Puritan settlement, so remote and so obscure, free to return to her birthplace, or to any other European land, and there hide her character and identity under a new exterior, as completely as if emerging into another state of being, and having also the passes of the dark, inscrutable forest open to her, where the wildness of her nature might assimilate itself with a people whose customs and life were alien from the law that had condemned her—it may seem marvellous, that this woman should still call that place her home, where, and where only, she must needs be the type of shame. But there is a fatality, a feeling so irresistible and inevitable that it has the force of doom, which almost invariably compels human beings to linger around and haunt, ghostlike, the spot where some great and marked event has given the color to their lifetime; and still the more irresistibly, the darker the tinge that saddens it. Her sin, her ignominy, were the roots which she had struck into the soil. It was as if a new birth, with stronger assimilations than the first, had converted the forestland, still so uncongenial to every other pilgrim and wanderer, into Hester Prynne's wild and dreary but lifelong home. All other scenes of earth —even that village of rural England, where happy infancy and stainless maidenhood seemed yet to be in her mother's keeping, like garments put off long ago —were foreign to her, in comparison. The chain that bound her here was of iron links, and galling to her inmost soul, but could never be broken.

It might be, too—doubtless it was so, although she hid the secret from herself, and grew pale whenever it struggled out of her heart, like a serpent from its hole —it might be that another feeling kept her within the scene and pathway that had been so fatal. There dwelt, there trod the feet of one with whom she deemed herself connected in a union, that, unrecognized on earth, would bring them together before the bar of final judgment, and make that their marriage altar, for a joint futurity of endless retribution. Over and over again, the tempter of souls had thrust this idea upon Hester's contemplation, and laughed at the passionate and desperate joy with which she seized, and then strove to cast it from her. She barely looked the idea in the face, and hastened to bar it in its dungeon. What she compelled herself to believe—what, finally, she reasoned upon as her motive for continuing a resident of New England— was half a truth, and half a self-delusion. Here, she said to herself, had been the scene of her guilt, and here should be the scene of her earthly punishment; and so, perchance, the torture of her daily shame would at length purge her soul and work out another purity than that which she had lost; more saintlike, because the result of martyrdom.

Hester Prynne, therefore, did not flee. On the outskirts of town, within the verge of the peninsula, but not in close vicinity to any other habitation, there was a small thatched cottage. It had been built by an earlier settler, and abandoned because the soil about it was too sterile for cultivation, while its comparative remoteness put it out of the sphere of that social activity which already marked the habits of the emigrants. It stood on the shore, looking across a basin of the sea at the forest-covered hills toward the west. A clump of scrubby trees, such as alone grew on the peninsula, did not so much conceal the cottage from view, as seem to denote that there was some object which would fain have been, or at least ought to be, concealed. In this little, lonesome dwelling, with some slender means that she possessed, and by the license of the magistrates, who still kept an inquisitorial watch over her, Hester established herself, with her infant child. A mystic shadow of suspicion immediately attached itself to the spot. Children, too young to comprehend wherefore this woman should be shut out from the sphere of human charities, would creep nigh enough to behold her plying her needle at the cottage window, or standing in the doorway, or laboring in her little garden, or coming forth along the pathway that led townward; and, discerning the scarlet letter on her breast, would scamper off with a strange, contagious fear.

Lonely as was Hester's situation, and without a friend on earth who dared to show himself, she, however, incurred even no risk of want. She possessed an art that sufficed, even in a land that afforded comparatively little scope for its exercise, to supply food for her thriving infant and herself. It was the art—then, as now, almost the only one within a woman's grasp—of needlework. She bore on her breast, in the curiously embroidered letter, a specimen of her delicate and imaginative skill of which the dames of a court might gladly have availed themselves, to add the richer and more spiritual adornment of human ingenuity to their fabrics of silk and gold. Here, indeed, in the sable simplicity that generally characterized the Puritanic modes of dress, there might be an infrequent call for the finer productions of her handiwork. Yet the taste of the age, demanding whatever was elaborate in compositions of this kind, did not fail to extend its influence over our stern progenitors, who had cast behind them so many fashions which it might seem harder to dispense with. Public ceremonies, such as ordinations, the installation of magistrates, and all that could give majesty to the forms in which a new government manifested itself to the people, were, as a matter of policy, marked by a stately and well-conducted ceremonial and a sombre,

but yet a studied magnificence. Deep ruffs, painfully
wrought bands and gorgeously embroidered gloves
were all deemed necessary to the official state of men
assuming the reins of power; and were readily allowed
to individuals dignified by rank or wealth, even while
sumptuary laws forbade these and similar extravagances
to the plebeian order. In the array of funerals, too—
whether for the apparel of the dead body, or to typify,
by manifold emblematic devices of sable cloth and
snowy lawn, the sorrow of the survivors—there was a
frequent and characteristic demand for such labor as
Hester Prynne could supply. Baby linen—for babies
then wore robes of state—afforded still another possibility of toil and emolument.

By degrees, nor very slowly, her handiwork became
what would now be termed the fashion. Whether from
commiseration for a woman of so miserable a destiny;
or from the morbid curiosity that gives a fictitious value
even to common or worthless things; or by whatever
other intangible circumstance was then, as now, sufficient to bestow on some persons what others might
seek in vain; or because Hester really filled a gap which
must otherwise have remained vacant; it is certain that
she had ready and fairly requited employment for as
many hours as she saw fit to occupy with her needle.
Vanity, it may be, chose to mortify itself by putting
on, for ceremonials of pomp and state, the garments
that had been wrought by her sinful hands. Her needlework was seen on the ruff of the Governor; military men
wore it on their scarfs, and the minister on his band; it
decked the baby's little cap; it was shut up, to be mil-
dewed and moulder away, in the coffins of the dead.
But it is not recorded that, in a single instance, her
skill was called in aid to embroider the white veil which
was to cover the pure blushes of a bride. The exception
indicated the ever relentless vigor with which society
frowned upon her sin.

Hester sought not to acquire anything beyond a subsistence, of the plainest and most ascetic description,
for herself, and a simple abundance for her child. Her
own dress was of the coarsest materials and the most
sombre hue; with only that one ornament—the scarlet

letter—which it was her doom to wear. The child's attire, on the other hand, was distinguished by a fanci-
ful, or, we might rather say, a fantastic ingenuity, which
served, indeed, to heighten the airy charm that early
began to develop itself in the little girl, but which appeared to have also a deeper meaning. We may speak
further of it hereafter. Except for that small expenditure
in the decoration of her infant, Hester bestowed all her
superfluous means in charity, on wretches less miserable
than herself, and who not unfrequently insulted the
hand that fed them. Much of the time which she might
readily have applied to the better efforts of her art, she
employed in making coarse garments for the poor. It is
probable that there was an idea of penance in this mode
of occupation, and that she offered up a real sacrifice
of enjoyment in devoting so many hours to such rude
handiwork. She had in her nature a rich, voluptuous,
Oriental characteristic—a taste for the gorgeously beautiful, which, save in the exquisite productions of her
needle, found nothing else in all the possibilities of her
life to exercise itself upon. Women derive a pleasure,
incomprehensible to the other sex, from the delicate
toil of the needle. To Hester Prynne it might have been
a mode of expressing, and therefore soothing, the passion of her life. Like all other joys, she rejected it as
a sin. This morbid meddling of conscience with an immaterial matter betokened, it is to be feared, no genuine
and steadfast penitence, but something doubtful, something that might be deeply wrong, beneath.

In this manner, Hester Prynne came to have a part to
perform in the world. With her native energy of character and rare capacity, it could not entirely cast her
off, although it had set a mark upon her more intolerable to a woman's heart than that which branded the
brow of Cain. In all her intercourse with society, however, there was nothing that made her feel as if she
belonged to it. Every gesture, every word, and even the
silence of those with whom she came in contact, implied, and often expressed, that she was banished, and
as much alone as if she inhabited another sphere, or
communicated with the common nature by other
organs and senses than the rest of human kind. She

stood apart from moral interests, yet close beside them,
like a ghost that revisits the familiar fireside and can no
longer make itself seen or felt, no more smile with the
household joy, nor mourn with the kindred sorrow; or,
should it succeed in manifesting its forbidden sympathy,
awakening only terror and horrible repugnance. These
emotions, in fact, and its bitterest scorn besides, seemed
to be the sole portion that she retained in the universal
heart. It was not an age of delicacy; and her position,
although she understood it well and was in little danger
of forgetting it, was often brought before her vivid
self-perception, like a new anguish, by the rudest touch
upon the tenderest spot. The poor, as we have already
said, whom she sought out to be the objects of her
bounty, often reviled the hand that was stretched
forth to succor them. Dames of elevated rank, likewise,
whose doors she entered in the way of her occupation,
were accustomed to distil drops of bitterness into her
heart, sometimes through that alchemy of quiet malice,
by which women can concoct a subtile poison from
ordinary trifles, and sometimes, also, by a coarser expression, that fell upon the sufferer's defenceless breast
like a rough blow upon an ulcerated wound. Hester had
schooled herself long and well; she never responded to
these attacks, save by a flush of crimson that rose irrepressibly over the pale cheek, and again subsided
into the depths of her bosom. She was patient—a martyr,
indeed—but she forebore to pray for her enemies, lest,
in spite of her forgiving aspirations, the words of the
blessing should stubbornly twist themselves into a curse.

Continually, and in a thousand other ways, did she
feel the innumerable throbs of anguish that had been
so cunningly contrived for her by the undying, the ever-
active sentence of the Puritan tribunal. Clergymen
paused in the street to address words of exhortation that
brought a crowd, with its mingled grin and frown,
around the poor, sinful woman. If she entered a church,
trusting to share the Sabbath smile of the Universal
Father, it was often her mishap to find herself the text
of the discourse. She grew to have a dread of children;
for they had imbibed from their parents a vague idea
of something horrible in this dreary woman, gliding

silently through the town, with never any companion but one only child. Therefore, first allowing her to pass, they pursued her at a distance with shrill cries, and the utterance of a word that had no distinct purport to their own minds, but was none the less terrible to her, as proceeding from lips that babbled it unconsciously. It seemed to argue so wide a diffusion of her shame that all nature knew of it; it could have caused her no deeper pang had the leaves of the trees whispered the dark story among themselves, had the summer breeze murmured about it—had the wintry blast shrieked it aloud! Another peculiar torture was felt in the gaze of a new eye. When strangers looked curiously at the scarlet letter—and none ever failed to do so—they branded it afresh into Hester's soul; so that, oftentimes, she could scarcely refrain, yet always did refrain, from covering the symbol with her hand. But then, again, an accustomed eye had likewise its own anguish to inflict. Its cool stare of familiarity was intolerable. From first to last, in short, Hester Prynne had always this dreadful agony in feeling a human eye upon the token; the spot never grew callous; it seemed, on the contrary, to grow more sensitive with daily torture.

But sometimes, once in many days, or perchance in many months, she felt an eye—a human eye—upon the ignominious brand, that seemed to give a momentary relief, as if half of her agony were shared. The next instant, back it all rushed again, with still a deeper throb of pain; for, in that brief interval, she had sinned anew. Had Hester sinned alone?

Her imagination was somehow affected, and, had she been of a softer moral and intellectual fibre, would have been still more so, by the strange and solitary anguish of her life. Walking to and fro with those lonely footsteps in the little world with which she was outwardly connected, it now and then appeared to Hester—if altogether fancy, it was nevertheless too potent to be resisted—she felt or fancied, then, that the scarlet letter had endowed her with a new sense. She shuddered to believe, yet could not help believing, that it gave her a sympathetic knowledge of the hidden sin in other hearts. She was terror-stricken by the revelations that were thus made. What were they? Could they be other than the insidious whispers of the bad angel, who would fain have persuaded the struggling woman, as yet only half his victim, that the outward guise of purity was but a lie, and that, if truth were everywhere to be shown, a scarlet letter would blaze forth on many a bosom besides Hester Prynne's? Or, must she receive those intimations—so obscure, yet so distinct—as truth? In all her miserable experience, there was nothing else so awful and so loathsome as this sense. It perplexed as well as shocked her by the irreverent inopportuneness of the occasions that brought it into vivid action. Sometimes the red infamy upon her breast would give a sympathetic throb, as she passed near a venerable minister or magistrate, the model of piety and justice, to whom that age of antique reverence looked up as to a mortal man in fellowship with angels. "What evil thing is at hand?" would Hester say to herself. Lifting her reluctant eyes, there would be nothing human within the scope of view, save the form of this earthly saint! Again, a mystic sisterhood would contumaciously assert itself as she met the sanctified frown of some matron, who, according to the rumor of all tongues, had kept cold snow within her bosom throughout life. That unsunned snow in the matron's bosom, and the burning shame on Hester Prynne's—what had the two in common? Or, once more, the electric thrill would give her warning— "Behold, Hester, here is a companion!"—and, looking up, she would detect the eyes of a young maiden glancing at the scarlet letter, shyly and aside, and quickly averted, with a faint, chill crimson in her cheeks as if her purity were somewhat sullied by that momentary glance. O Fiend, whose talisman was that fatal symbol, wouldst thou leave nothing, whether in youth or age, for this poor sinner to revere?—such loss of faith is ever one of the saddest results of sin. Be it accepted as a proof that all was not corrupt in this poor victim of her own frailty, and man's hard law, that Hester Prynne yet struggled to believe that no fellow-mortal was guilty like herself.

The vulgar, who, in those dreary old times, were always contributing a grotesque horror to what inter-

ested their imaginations, had a story about the scarlet
letter which we might readily work up into a terrific
legend. They averred that the symbol was not mere
scarlet cloth tinged in an earthly dyepot, but was red-
hot with infernal fire, and could be seen glowing all
alight whenever Hester Prynne walked abroad in the
nighttime. And we must needs say it seared Hester's
bosom so deeply, that perhaps there was more truth in
the rumor than our modern incredulity may be inclined to admit.

6

PEARL

WE HAVE AS YET HARDLY SPOKEN of the infant;
that little creature, whose innocent life had
sprung, by the inscrutable decree of Providence, a lovely
and immortal flower, out of the rank luxuriance of a guilty
passion. How strange it seemed to the sad woman as she
watched the growth, and the beauty that became every
day more brilliant, and the intelligence that threw its
quivering sunshine over the tiny features of this child!
Her Pearl!—For so had Hester called her; not as a
name expressive of her aspect, which had nothing of the
calm, white, unimpassioned lustre that would be indicated by the comparison. But she named the infant
"Pearl," as being of great price—purchased with all
she had—her mother's only treasure! How strange,
indeed! Man had marked this woman's sin by a scarlet
letter, which had such potent and disastrous efficacy that
no human sympathy could reach her, save it were sin-

ful like herself. God, as a direct consequence of the
sin which man thus punished, had given her a lovely
child, whose place was on that same dishonored bosom,
to connect her parent forever with the race and descent
of mortals, and to be finally a blessed soul in heaven!
Yet these thoughts affected Hester Prynne less with
hope than apprehension. She knew that her deed had
been evil; she could have no faith, therefore, that its
result would be for good. Day after day, she looked fearfully into the child's expanding nature; ever dreading
to detect some dark and wild peculiarity, that should
correspond with the guiltiness to which she owed her
being.

Certainly, there was no physical defect. By its perfect shape, its vigor, and its natural dexterity in the
use of all its untried limbs, the infant was worthy to
have been brought forth in Eden; worthy to have been
left there, to be the plaything of the angels, after the
world's first parents were driven out. The child had
a native grace which does not invariably coexist with
faultless beauty; its attire, however simple, always impressed the beholder as if it were the very garb that
precisely became it best. But little Pearl was not clad
in rustic weeds. Her mother, with a morbid purpose
that may be better understood hereafter, had bought
the richest tissues that could be procured, and allowed
her imaginative faculty its full play in the arrangement
and decoration of the dresses which the child wore
before the public eye. So magnificent was the small
figure when thus arrayed, and such was the splendor
of Pearl's own proper beauty, shining through the
gorgeous robes which might have extinguished a paler
loveliness, that there was an absolute circle of radiance
around her on the darksome cottage floor. And yet a
russet gown, torn and soiled with the child's rude play,
made a picture of her just as perfect. Pearl's aspect was
imbued with a spell of infinite variety; in this one child
there were many children, comprehending the full scope
between the wild-flower prettiness of a peasant baby, and
the pomp, in little, of an infant princess. Throughout all,
however, there was a trait of passion, a certain depth of
hue, which she never lost; and if, in any of her changes,

she had grown fainter or paler, she would have ceased to
be herself—it would have been no longer Pearl!

This outward mutability indicated, and did not more
than fairly express, the various properties of her inner
life. Her nature appeared to possess depth, too, as well
as variety; but—or else Hester's fears deceived her—it
lacked reference and adaptation to the world into which
she was born. The child could not be made amenable
to rules. In giving her existence, a great law had been
broken, and the result was a being whose elements were
perhaps beautiful and brilliant, but all in disorder; or
with an order peculiar to themselves, amidst which the
point of variety and arrangement was difficult or impossible to be discovered. Hester could only account
for the child's character—and even then most vaguely
and imperfectly—by recalling what she herself had been,
during that momentous period while Pearl was im-
bibing her soul from the spiritual world, and her bodily
frame from its material of earth. The mother's impas-
sioned state had been the medium through which were
transmitted to the unborn infant the rays of its moral
life; and, however white and clear originally, they had
taken the deep stains of crimson and gold, the fiery
lustre, the black shadow, and the untempered light, of
the intervening substance. Above all, the warfare of
Hester's spirit, at that epoch, was perpetuated in
Pearl. She could recognize her wild, desperate, de-
fiant mood, the flightiness of her temper, and even
some of the very cloud-shapes of gloom and despondency that had brooded in her heart. They were now
illuminated by the morning radiance of a young child's
disposition, but, later in the day of earthly existence,
might be prolific of the storm and whirlwind.

The discipline of the family, in those days, was of
a far more rigid kind than now. The frown, the harsh
rebuke, the frequent application of the rod, enjoined
by Scriptural authority, were used, not merely in the
way of punishment for actual offences, but as a wholesome regimen for the growth and promotion of all childish virtues. Hester Prynne, nevertheless, the lonely
mother of this one child, ran little risk of erring on
the side of undue severity. Mindful, however, of her
own errors and misfortunes, she early sought to im-

pose a tender but strict control over the infant immortality that was committed to her charge. But the task was beyond her skill. After testing both smiles and frowns, and proving that neither mode of treatment possessed any calculable influence, Hester was ultimately compelled to stand aside, and permit the child to be swayed by her own impulses. Physical compulsion or restraint was effectual, of course, while it lasted. As to any other kind of discipline, whether addressed to her mind or heart, little Pearl might or might not be within its reach, in accordance with the caprice that ruled the moment. Her mother, while Pearl was yet an infant, grew acquainted with a certain peculiar look that warned her when it would be labor thrown away to insist, persuade, or plead. It was a look so intelligent, yet inexplicable, so perverse, sometimes so malicious, but generally accompanied by a wild flow of spirits, that Hester could not help questioning, at such moments, whether Pearl was a human child. She seemed rather an airy sprite, which, after playing its fantastic sports for a little while upon the cottage floor, would flit away with a mocking smile. Whenever that look appeared in her wild, bright, deeply black eyes, it invested her with a strange remoteness and intangibility; it was as if she were hovering in the air and might vanish, like a glimmering light that comes we know not whence and goes we know not whither. Beholding it, Hester was constrained to rush towards the child to pursue the little elf in the flight which she invariably began, to snatch her to her bosom, with a close pressure and earnest kisses—not so much from overflowing love, as to assure herself that Pearl was flesh and blood, and not utterly delusive. But Pearl's laugh, when she was caught, though full of merriment and music, made her mother more doubtful than before.

Heart-smitten at this bewildering and baffling spell that so often came between herself and her sole treasure, whom she had bought so dear and who was all her world, Hester sometimes burst into passionate tears. Then, perhaps—for there was no foreseeing how it might affect her—Pearl would frown, and clench her little fist, and harden her small features into a stern, unsympathizing look of discontent. Not seldom, she would laugh anew, and louder than before, like a thing incapable and unintelligent of human sorrow. Or—but this more rarely happened—she would be convulsed with a rage of grief, and sob out her love for her mother in broken words, and seem intent on proving that she had a heart, by breaking it. Yet Hester was hardly safe in confiding herself to that gusty tenderness; it passed as suddenly as it came. Brooding over all these matters, the mother felt like one who has evoked a spirit, but, by some irregularity in the process of conjuration, has failed to win the master-word that should control this new and incomprehensible intelligence. Her only real comfort was when the child lay in the placidity of sleep. Then she was sure of her, and tasted hours of quiet, sad, delicious happiness; until—perhaps with that perverse expression glimmering from beneath her opening lids—little Pearl awoke!

How soon—with what strange rapidity, indeed!—did Pearl arrive at an age that was capable of social intercourse, beyond the mother's ever-ready smile and nonsense words! And then what a happiness would it have been, could Hester Prynne have heard her clear, birdlike voice mingling with the uproar of other childish voices, and have distinguished and unravelled her own darling's tones, amid all the entangled outcry of a group of sportive children! But this could never be. Pearl was a born outcast of the infantile world. An imp of evil, emblem and product of sin, she had no right among christened infants. Nothing was more remarkable than the instinct, as it seemed, with which the child comprehended her loneliness; the destiny that had drawn an inviolable circle round about her; the whole peculiarity, in short, of her position in respect to other children. Never, since her release from prison, had Hester met the public gaze without her. In all her walks about the town, Pearl, too, was there; first as the babe in arms, and afterwards as the little girl, small companion of her mother, holding a forefinger with her whole grasp, and tripping along at the rate of three or four footsteps to one of Hester's. She saw the children of the settlement, on the grassy margin of the street, or

at the domestic thresholds, disporting themselves in such
grim fashions as the Puritanic nurture would permit;
playing at going to church, perchance; or at scourging
Quakers; or taking scalps in a sham-fight with the Indians;
or scaring one another with freaks of imitative witchcraft.
Pearl saw, and gazed intently; but never sought to make
acquaintance. If spoken to, she would not speak again. If
the children gathered about her, as they sometimes did,
Pearl would grow positively terrible in her puny wrath,
snatching up stones to fling at them, with shrill, inco-
herent exclamations that made her mother tremble because they had so much the sound of a witch's anathemas
in some unknown tongue.

The truth was that the little Puritans, being of the
most intolerant brood that ever lived, had got a vague
idea of something outlandish, unearthly, or at variance
with ordinary fashions, in the mother of the child; and
therefore scorned them in their hearts, and not unfrequently reviled them with their tongues. Pearl felt the
sentiment, and requited it with the bitterest hatred that
can be supposed to rankle in a childish bosom. These out-
breaks of a fierce temper had a kind of value, and even
comfort, for her mother, because there was at least an
intelligible earnestness in the mood, instead of the fitful
caprice that so often thwarted her in the child's manifesta-
tions. It appalled her, nevertheless, to discern here, again,
a shadowy reflection of the evil that had existed in herself. All this enmity and passion had Pearl inherited, by
inalienable right, out of Hester's heart. Mother and
daughter stood together in the same circle of seclusion
from human society; and in the nature of the child
seemed to be perpetuated those unquiet elements that
had distracted Hester Prynne before Pearl's birth, but
had since begun to be soothed away by the softening influences of maternity.

At home, within and around her mother's cottage,
Pearl wanted not a wide and various circle of acquaintance. The spell of life went forth from her ever creative
spirit and communicated itself to a thousand objects, as
a torch kindles a flame wherever it may be applied. The
unlikeliest materials—a stick, a bunch of rags, a flower—
were the puppets of Pearl's witchcraft, and, without un-

dergoing any outward change, became spiritually adapted
to whatever drama occupied the stage of her inner world.
Her one baby-voice served a multitude of imaginary personages, old and young, to talk withal. The pine trees,
aged, black and solemn, and flinging groans and other
melancholy utterances on the breeze, needed little transformation to figure as Puritan elders; the ugliest weeds
of the garden were their children, whom Pearl smote
down and uprooted, most unmercifully. It was wonderful, the vast variety of forms into which she threw her
intellect, with no continuity, indeed, but darting up and
dancing, always in a state of preternatural activity, soon
sinking down as if exhausted by so rapid and feverish a
tide of life, and succeeded by other shapes of a similar
wild energy. It was like nothing so much as the phantasmagoric play of the northern lights. In the mere exercise
of the fancy, however, and the sportiveness of a growing
mind, there might be little more than was observable in
other children of bright faculties; except as Pearl, in the
dearth of human playmates, was thrown more upon the
visionary throng which she created. The singularity lay
in the hostile feelings with which the child regarded all
these offspring of her own heart and mind. She never
created a friend, but seemed always to be sowing broad-
cast the dragon's teeth, whence sprung a harvest of
armed enemies against whom she rushed to battle. It was
inexpressibly sad—then what depth of sorrow to a mother,
who felt in her own heart the cause!—to observe, in one
so young, this constant recognition of an adverse world,
and so fierce a training of the energies that were to make
good her cause in the contest that must ensue.

Gazing at Pearl, Hester Prynne often dropped her work
upon her knees, and cried out with an agony which she
would fain have hidden, but which made utterance for
itself, betwixt speech and a groan, "O Father in Heaven—
if Thou art still my Father—what is this being which I
have brought into the world!" And Pearl, overhearing
the ejaculation, or aware through some more subtle chan-
nel of those throbs of anguish, would turn her vivid and
beautiful little face upon her mother, smile with sprite-
like intelligence, and resume her play.

One peculiarity of the child's deportment remains yet

to be told. The very first thing which she had noticed in her life, was—what?—not the mother's smile, responding to it, as other babies do, by that faint, embryo smile of the little mouth, remembered so doubtfully afterwards, and with such fond discussion whether it were indeed a smile. By no means! But that first object of which Pearl seemed to become aware was—shall we say it?—the scarlet letter on Hester's bosom! One day, as her mother stooped over the cradle, the infant's eyes had been caught by the glimmering of the gold embroidery about the letter; and, putting up her little hand, she grasped at it, smiling, not doubtfully, but with a decided gleam, that gave her face the look of a much older child. Then, gasping for breath, did Hester Prynne clutch the fatal token, instinctively endeavoring to tear it away; so infinite was the torture inflicted by the intelligent touch of Pearl's baby hand. Again, as if her mother's agonized gesture were meant only to make sport for her, did little Pearl look into her eyes, and smile! From that epoch, except when the child was asleep, Hester had never felt a moment's safety; not a moment's calm enjoyment of her. Weeks, it is true, would sometimes elapse, during which Pearl's gaze might never once be fixed upon the scarlet letter; but then, again, it would come at unawares, like the stroke of sudden death, and always with that peculiar smile and odd expression of the eyes.

Once this freakish, elvish cast came into the child's eyes while Hester was looking at her own image in them, as mothers are fond of doing; and, suddenly—for women in solitude, and with troubled hearts, are pestered with unaccountable delusions—she fancied that she beheld, not her own miniature portrait, but another face, in the small black mirror of Pearl's eye. It was a face, fiendlike, full of smiling malice, yet bearing the semblance of features that she had known full well, though seldom with a smile, and never with malice in them. It was as if an evil spirit possessed the child, and had just then peeped forth in mockery. Many a time afterwards had Hester been tortured, though less vividly, by the same illusion.

In the afternoon of a certain summer's day, after Pearl grew big enough to run about, she amused herself with gathering handfuls of wild-flowers and flinging them, one

by one, at her mother's bosom, dancing up and down
like a little elf whenever she hit the scarlet letter. Hester's first motion had been to cover her bosom with her
clasped hands. But, whether from pride or resignation or
a feeling that her penance might best be wrought out by
this unutterable pain, she resisted the impulse, and sat
erect, pale as death, looking sadly into little Pearl's wild
eyes. Still came the battery of flowers, almost invariably
hitting the mark, and covering the mother's breast with
hurts for which she could find no balm in this world, nor
knew how to seek it in another. At last, her shot being
all expended, the child stood still and gazed at Hester
with that little, laughing image of a fiend peeping out—
or, whether it peeped or no, her mother so imagined it—
from the unsearchable abyss of her black eyes.

"Child, what art thou?" cried the mother.

"O, I am your little Pearl!" answered the child.

But, while she said it, Pearl laughed, and began to
dance up and down, with the humorsome gesticulation of
a little imp whose next freak might be to fly up the
chimney.

"Art thou my child, in very truth?" asked Hester.

Nor did she put the question altogether idly, but, for
the moment, with a portion of genuine earnestness; for
such was Pearl's wonderful intelligence that her mother
half doubted whether she were not acquainted with the
secret spell of her existence, and might not now reveal
herself.

"Yes; I am little Pearl!" repeated the child, continuing
her antics.

"Thou art not my child! Thou art no Pearl of mine!"
said the mother, half playfully; for it was often the case
that a sportive impulse came over her, in the midst of
her deepest suffering. "Tell me, then, what thou art, and
who sent thee hither?"

"Tell me, Mother!" said the child seriously, coming
up to Hester, and pressing herself close to her knees. "Do
thou tell me!"

"Thy Heavenly Father sent thee!" answered Hester
Prynne.

But she said it with a hesitation that did not escape the
acuteness of the child. Whether moved only by her ordi-

nary freakishness, or because an evil spirit prompted her, she put up her small forefinger, and touched the scarlet letter.

"He did not send me!" cried she, positively. "I have no Heavenly Father!"

"Hush, Pearl, hush! Thou must not talk so!" answered the mother, suppressing a groan. "He sent us all into this world. He sent even me, thy mother. Then, much more, thee! Or, if not, thou strange and elfish child, whence didst thou come?"

"Tell me! Tell me!" repeated Pearl, no longer seriously, but laughing, and capering about the floor. "It is thou that must tell me!"

But Hester could not resolve the query, being herself in a dismal labyrinth of doubt. She remembered—betwixt a smile and a shudder—the talk of the neighboring townspeople, who, seeking vainly elsewhere for the child's paternity, and observing some of her odd attributes, had given out that poor little Pearl was a demon offspring; such as, ever since old Catholic times, had occasionally been seen on earth, through the agency of their mother's sin, and to promote some foul and wicked purpose. Luther, according to the scandal of his monkish enemies, was a brat of that hellish breed; nor was Pearl the only child to whom this inauspicious origin was assigned, among the New England Puritans.

7

THE GOVERNOR'S HALL

HESTER PRYNNE went one day to the mansion of Governor Bellingham with a pair of gloves, which she had fringed and embroidered to his order, and which were to be worn on some great occasion of state; for, though the chances of a popular election had caused this former ruler to descend a step or two from the highest rank, he still held an honorable and influential place among the colonial magistracy.

Another and far more important reason than the delivery of a pair of embroidered gloves impelled Hester, at this time, to seek an interview with a personage of so much power and activity in the affairs of the settlement. It had reached her ears that there was a design on the part of some of the leading inhabitants, cherishing the more rigid order of principles in religion and government, to deprive her of her child. On the supposition that Pearl, as already hinted, was of demon origin, these good people not unreasonably argued that a Christian interest in the mother's soul required them to remove such a stumbling block from her path. If the child, on the other hand, were really capable of moral and religious growth and possessed the elements of ultimate salvation, then, surely, it would enjoy all the fairer prospect of these advantages by being transferred to wiser and better guardianship than Hester Prynne's. Among those who promoted the design, Governor Bellingham was said to be one of the most busy. It may appear singular, and, indeed, not a little ludicrous,

that an affair of this kind, which in later days would have
been referred to no higher jurisdiction than that of the
selectmen of the town, should then have been a question
publicly discussed, and on which statesmen of eminence
took sides. At that epoch of pristine simplicity, however,
matters of even slighter public interest, and of far less
intrinsic weight, than the welfare of Hester and her child
were strangely mixed up with the deliberations of legislators and acts of state. The period was hardly, if at all,
earlier than that of our story, when a dispute concerning
the right of property in a pig not only caused a fierce and
bitter contest in the legislative body of the colony, but
resulted in an important modification of the framework
itself of the legislature.

Full of concern, therefore—but so conscious of her own
right that it seemed scarcely an unequal match between
the public, on the one side, and a lonely woman, backed
by the sympathies of nature, on the other—Hester Prynne
set forth from her solitary cottage. Little Pearl, of course,
was her companion. She was now of an age to run lightly
along by her mother's side, and, constantly in motion
from morn till sunset, could have accomplished a much
longer journey than that before her. Often, nevertheless,
more from caprice than necessity, she demanded to be
taken up in arms; but was soon as imperious to be set
down again, and frisked onward before Hester on the
grassy pathway, with many a harmless trip and tumble.
We have spoken of Pearl's rich and luxuriant beauty; a
beauty that shone with deep and vivid tints; a bright
complexion, eyes possessing intensity both of depth and
glow, and hair already of a deep, glossy brown, and which,
in after years, would be nearly akin to black. There was
fire in her and throughout her; she seemed the unpre-
meditated offshoot of a passionate moment. Her mother,
in contriving the child's garb, had allowed the gorgeous
tendencies of her imagination their full play; arraying her
in a crimson velvet tunic of a peculiar cut, abundantly
embroidered with fantasies and flourishes of gold thread.
So much strength of coloring, which must have given a
wan and pallid aspect to cheeks of a fainter bloom, was
admirably adapted to Pearl's beauty and made her the

very brightest little jet of flame that ever danced upon
the earth.

But it was a remarkable attribute of this garb, and, indeed, of the child's whole appearance, that it irresistibly
and inevitably reminded the beholder of the token which
Hester Prynne was doomed to wear upon her bosom. It
was the scarlet letter in another form; the scarlet letter
endowed with life! The mother herself—as if the red ignominy were so deeply scorched into her brain that all
her conceptions assumed its form—had carefully wrought
out the similitude; lavishing many hours of morbid ingenuity to create an analogy between the object of her
affection and the emblem of her guilt and torture. But,
in truth, Pearl was the one as well as the other; and only
in consequence of that identity had Hester contrived so
perfectly to represent the scarlet letter in her appearance.

As the two wayfarers came within the precincts of the
town, the children of the Puritans looked up from their
play—or what passed for play with those sombre little
urchins—and spoke gravely one to another:

"Behold, verily, there is the woman of the scarlet
letter, and, of a truth, moreover, there is the likeness of
the scarlet letter running along by her side! Come,
therefore, and let us fling mud at them!"

But Pearl, who was a dauntless child, after frowning,
stamping her foot, and shaking her little hand with a
variety of threatening gestures, suddenly made a rush
at the knot of her enemies, and put them all to flight.
She resembled, in her fierce pursuit of them, an infant
pestilence—the scarlet fever, or some such half-fledged
angel of judgment—whose mission was to punish the
sins of the rising generation. She screamed and shouted,
too, with a terrific volume of sound which, doubtless,
caused the hearts of the fugitives to quake within them.
The victory accomplished, Pearl returned quietly to
her mother, and looked up, smiling, into her face.

Without further adventure, they reached the dwelling of Governor Bellingham. This was a large wooden
house, built in a fashion of which there are specimens
still extant in the streets of our elder towns; now moss-
grown, crumbling to decay, and melancholy at heart
with the many sorrowful or joyful occurrences, remem-

bered or forgotten, that have happened and passed
away within their dusky chambers. Then, however,
there was the freshness of the passing year on its exterior, and the cheerfulness, gleaming forth from the
sunny windows, of a human habitation into which death
had never entered. It had, indeed, a very cheery aspect;
the walls being overspread with a kind of stucco, in
which fragments of broken glass were plentifully intermixed; so that, when the sunshine fell aslant-wise over
the front of the edifice, it glittered and sparkled as if
diamonds had been flung against it by the double
handful. The brilliancy might have befitted Aladdin's
palace rather than the mansion of a grave old Puritan
ruler. It was further decorated with strange and seemingly cabalistic figures and diagrams, suitable to the
quaint taste of the age, which had been drawn in the
stucco when newly laid on, and had now grown hard
and durable, for the admiration of after times.

Pearl, looking at this bright wonder of a house, began
to caper and dance, and imperatively required that the
whole breadth of sunshine should be stripped off its
front, and given her to play with.

"No, my little Pearl!" said her mother. "Thou must
gather thine own sunshine. I have none to give thee!"

They approached the door, which was of an arched
form, and flanked on each side by a narrow tower or
projection of the edifice, in both of which were lattice
windows, with wooden shutters to close over them at
need. Lifting the iron hammer that hung at the portal,
Hester Prynne gave a summons, which was answered
by one of the Governor's bond-servants; a free-born
Englishman, but now a seven years' slave. During that
term he was to be the property of his master, and as
much a commodity of bargain and sale as an ox, or a
joint-stool. The serf wore the blue coat, which was the
customary garb of serving-men at that period, and long
before, in the old hereditary halls of England.

"Is the worshipful Governor Bellingham within?"
inquired Hester.

"Yea, forsooth," replied the bond-servant, staring with
wide-open eyes at the scarlet letter, which, being a
newcomer in the country, he had never before seen.

"Yea, his honorable worship is within. But he hath a godly minister or two with him, and likewise a leech. Ye may not see his worship now."

"Nevertheless, I will enter," answered Hester Prynne; and the bond-servant, perhaps judging from the decision of her air and the glittering symbols in her bosom that she was a great lady in the land, offered no opposition.

So the mother and little Pearl were admitted into the hall of entrance. With many variations suggested by the nature of his building-materials, diversity of climate, and a different mode of social life, Governor Bellingham had planned his new habitation after the residences of gentlemen of fair estate in his native land. Here, then, was a wide and reasonably lofty hall, extending through the whole depth of the house and forming a medium of general communication, more or less directly, with all the other apartments. At one extremity, this spacious room was lighted by the windows of the two towers, which formed a small recess on either side of the portal. At the other end, though partly muffled by a curtain, it was more powerfully illuminated by one of those embowed hall windows which we read of in old books, and which was provided with a deep and cushioned seat. Here, on the cushion, lay a folio tome, probably of the Chronicles of England or other such substantial literature; even as, in our own days, we scatter gilded volumes on the centre-table, to be turned over by the casual guest. The furniture of the hall consisted of some ponderous chairs, the backs of which were elaborately carved with wreaths of oaken flowers; and likewise a table in the same taste; the whole being of the Elizabethan age, or perhaps earlier, and heirlooms, transferred hither from the Governor's paternal home. On the table—in token that the sentiment of old English hospitality had not been left behind—stood a large pewter tankard, at the bottom of which, had Hester or Pearl peeped into it, they might have seen the frothy remnant of a recent draught of ale.

On the wall hung a row of portraits, representing the forefathers of the Bellingham lineage, some with armor on their breasts, and others with stately ruffs and robes of peace. All were characterized by the sternness and severity which old portraits so invariably put on; as if they were the ghosts, rather than the pictures, of departed worthies, and were gazing with harsh and intolerant criticism at the pursuits and enjoyments of living men.

At about the centre of the oaken panels that lined the hall was suspended a suit of mail, not, like the pictures, an ancestral relic, but of the most modern date; for it had been manufactured by a skilful armorer in London the same year in which Governor Bellingham came over to New England. There was a steel headpiece, a cuirass, a gorget, and greaves, with a pair of gauntlets and a sword hanging beneath; all, and especially the helmet and breastplate, so highly burnished as to glow with white radiance and scatter an illumination everywhere about upon the floor. This bright panoply was not meant for mere idle show, but had been worn by the Governor on many a solemn muster and training field, and had glittered, moreover, at the head of a regiment in the Pequod war. For, though bred a lawyer and accustomed to speak of Bacon, Coke, Noye, and Finch as his professional associates, the exigences of this new country had transformed Governor Bellingham into a soldier, as well as a statesman and ruler.

Little Pearl—who was as greatly pleased with the gleaming armor as she had been with the glittering frontispiece of the house—spent some time looking into the polished mirror of the breastplate.

"Mother," cried she, "I see you here. Look! Look!"

Hester looked, by way of humoring the child; and she saw that, owing to the peculiar effect of this convex mirror, the scarlet letter was represented in exaggerated and gigantic proportions, so as to be greatly the most prominent feature of her appearance. In truth, she seemed absolutely hidden behind it. Pearl pointed upward, also, at a similar picture in the headpiece, smiling at her mother, with the elfish intelligence that was so familiar an expression on her small physiognomy. That look of naughty merriment was likewise reflected in the mirror, with so much breadth and intensity of effect, that it made Hester Prynne feel as if it could not be the image of her own child, but of an imp who was seeking to mould itself into Pearl's shape.

"Come along, Pearl," said she, drawing her away. "Come and look into this fair garden. It may be we shall see flowers there; more beautiful ones than we find in the woods."

Pearl, accordingly, ran to the bow window at the further end of the hall and looked along the vista of a garden walk, carpeted with closely shaven grass and bordered with some rude and immature attempt at shrubbery. But the proprietor appeared already to have relinquished as hopeless the effort to perpetuate on this side of the Atlantic, in a hard soil and amid the close struggle for subsistence, the native English taste for ornamental gardening. Cabbages grew in plain sight; and a pumpkin vine, rooted at some distance, had run across the intervening space and deposited one of its gigantic products directly beneath the hall window; as if to warn the Governor that this great lump of vegetable gold was as rich an ornament as New England earth would offer him. There were a few rosebushes, however, and a number of apple trees, probably the descendants of those planted by the Reverend Mr. Blackstone, the first settler of the peninsula, that half-mythological personage, who rides through our early annals seated on the back of a bull.

Pearl, seeing the rosebushes, began to cry for a red rose, and would not be pacified.

"Hush, child, hush!" said her mother, earnestly. "Do not cry, dear little Pearl! I hear voices in the garden. The Governor is coming, and gentlemen along with him!"

In fact, adown the vista of the garden avenue a number of persons were seen approaching towards the house. Pearl, in utter scorn of her mother's attempt to quiet her, gave an eldritch scream and then became silent; not from any notion of obedience, but because the quick and mobile curiosity of her disposition was excited by the appearance of these new personages.

8

THE ELF-CHILD AND THE MINISTER

GOVERNOR BELLINGHAM, IN A LOOSE GOWN and easy cap—such as elderly gentlemen loved to endue themselves with, in their domestic privacy—walked foremost, and appeared to be showing off his estate and expatiating on his projected improvements. The wide circumference of an elaborate ruff beneath his gray beard, in the antiquated fashion of King James' reign, caused his head to look not a little like that of John the Baptist in a charger. The impression made by his aspect, so rigid and severe, and frostbitten with more than autumnal age, was hardly in keeping with the appliances of worldly enjoyment wherewith he had evidently done his utmost to surround himself. But it is an error to suppose that our grave forefathers—though accustomed to speak and think of human existence as a state merely of trial and warfare, and though unfeignedly prepared to sacrifice goods and life at the behest of duty—made it a matter of conscience to reject such means of comfort, or even luxury, as lay fairly within their grasp. This creed was never taught, for instance, by the venerable pastor, John Wilson, whose beard, white as a snowdrift, was seen over Governor Bellingham's shoulder; while its wearer suggested that pears and peaches might yet be naturalized in the New England climate, and that purple grapes might possibly be compelled to flourish against the sunny garden wall. The old clergyman, nurtured at the rich bosom of the English Church, had a long-established and legitimate taste for all good and comfortable things; and however stern he might show himself in the pulpit or in his public reproof of such transgressions as that of Hester Prynne, still, the genial benevolence of his private life had won him warmer affection than was accorded to any of his professional contemporaries.

Behind the Governor and Mr. Wilson came two other guests; one, the Reverend Arthur Dimmesdale, whom the reader may remember, as having taken a brief and reluctant part in the scene of Hester Prynne's disgrace; and, in close companionship with him, old Roger Chillingworth, a person of great skill in physic, who, for two or three years past, had been settled in the town. It was understood that this learned man was the physician as well as friend of the young minister, whose health had severely suffered, of late, by his too unreserved self-sacrifice to the labors and duties of the pastoral relation.

The Governor, in advance of his visitors, ascended one or two steps, and, throwing open the leaves of the great hall window, found himself close to little Pearl. The shadow of the curtain fell on Hester Prynne, and partially concealed her.

"What have we here?" said Governor Bellingham, looking with surprise at the scarlet little figure before him. "I profess, I have never seen the like, since my days of vanity, in old King James' time, when I was wont to esteem it a high favor to be admitted to a court mask! There used to be a swarm of these small apparitions, in holiday time; and we called them children of the Lord of Misrule. But how gat such a guest into my hall?"

"Ay, indeed!" cried good old Mr. Wilson. "What little bird of scarlet plumage may this be? Methinks I have seen just such figures when the sun has been shining through a richly painted window and tracing out the golden and crimson images across the floor. But that was in the old land. Prithee, young one, who art thou, and what has ailed thy mother to bedizen thee in this strange fashion? Art thou a Christian child—ha? Dost know thy catechism? Or art thou one of those naughty elfs or fairies whom we thought to have left behind us, with other relics of Papistry, in merry old England?"

"I am Mother's child," answered the scarlet vision, "and my name is Pearl!"

"Pearl?—Ruby, rather!—or Coral!—or Red Rose, at the very least, judging from thy hue!" responded the old minister, putting forth his hand in a vain attempt to pat little Pearl on the cheek. "But where is this mother of thine? Ah! I see," he added; and, turning to Governor Bellingham, whispered, "This is the selfsame child of whom we have held speech together; and behold here the unhappy woman, Hester Prynne, her mother!"

"Sayest thou so?" cried the Governor. "Nay, we might have judged that such a child's mother must needs be a scarlet woman, and a worthy type of her of Babylon! But she comes at a good time; and we will look into this matter forthwith."

Governor Bellingham stepped through the window into the hall, followed by his three guests.

"Hester Prynne," said he, fixing his naturally stern regard on the wearer of the scarlet letter, "there hath been much question concerning thee, of late. The point hath been weightily discussed, whether we, that are of authority and influence, do well discharge our consciences by trusting an immortal soul, such as there is in yonder child, to the guidance of one who hath stumbled and fallen amid the pitfalls of this world. Speak thou, the child's own mother! Were it not, thinkest thou, for thy little one's temporal and eternal welfare, that she be taken out of thy charge, and clad soberly, and disciplined strictly, and instructed in the truths of heaven and earth? What canst thou do for the child, in this kind?"

"I can teach my little Pearl what I have learned from this!" answered Hester Prynne, laying her finger on the red token.

"Woman, it is thy badge of shame!" replied the stern magistrate. "It is because of the stain which that letter indicates, that we would transfer thy child to other hands."

"Nevertheless," said the mother calmly, though growing more pale, "this badge hath taught me—it daily teaches me—it is teaching me at this moment—lessons whereof my child may be the wiser and better, albeit they can profit nothing to myself."

"We will judge warily," said Bellingham, "and look well what we are about to do. Good Master Wilson, I pray you, examine this Pearl—since that is her name—and see whether she hath had such Christian nurture as befits a child of her age."

The old minister seated himself in an armchair, and made an effort to draw Pearl betwixt his knees. But the child, unaccustomed to the touch or familiarity of any but her mother, escaped through the open window, and stood on the upper step, looking like a wild tropical bird of rich plumage ready to take flight into the upper air. Mr. Wilson, not a little astonished at this outbreak —for he was a grandfatherly sort of personage, and usually a vast favorite with children—essayed, however, to proceed with the examination.

"Pearl," said he, with great solemnity, "thou must take heed to instruction, that so, in due season, thou mayest wear in thy bosom the pearl of great price. Canst thou tell me, my child, who made thee?"

Now Pearl knew well enough who made her; for Hester Prynne, the daughter of a pious home, very soon after her talk with the child about her Heavenly Father, had begun to inform her of those truths which the human spirit, at whatever stage of immaturity, imbibes with such eager interest. Pearl, therefore, so large were the attainments of her three years' lifetime, could have borne a fair examination in the New England Primer, or the first column of the Westminster Catechism, although unacquainted with the outward form of either of those celebrated works. But that perversity, which all children have more or less of, and of which little Pearl had a tenfold portion, now, at the most inopportune moment, took thorough possession of her and closed her lips, or impelled her to speak words amiss. After putting her fingers in her mouth, with many ungracious refusals to answer good Mr. Wilson's question, the child finally announced that she had not been made at all, but had been plucked by her mother off the bush of wild roses that grew by the prison door.

This fantasy was probably suggested by the near

proximity of the Governor's red roses, as Pearl stood
outside of the window; together with her recollection
of the prison rosebush, which she had passed in coming hither.

Old Roger Chillingworth, with a smile on his face,
whispered something in the young clergyman's ear. Hester Prynne looked at the man of skill, and even then,
with her fate hanging in the balance, was startled to
perceive what a change had come over his features—
how much uglier they were—how his dark complexion
seemed to have grown duskier, and his figure more misshapen—since the days when she had familiarly known
him. She met his eyes for an instant, but was immediately constrained to give all her attention to the scene
now going forward.

"This is awful!" cried the Governor, slowly recover-
ing from the astonishment into which Pearl's response
had thrown him. "Here is a child of three years old,
and she cannot tell who made her! Without question,
she is equally in the dark as to her soul, its present
depravity, and future destiny! Methinks, gentlemen, we
need inquire no further."

Hester caught hold of Pearl, and drew her forcibly
into her arms, confronting the old Puritan magistrate
with almost a fierce expression. Alone in the world, cast
off by it, and with this sole treasure to keep her heart
alive, she felt that she possessed indefeasible rights
against the world, and was ready to defend them to the
death.

"God gave me the child!" cried she. "He gave her
in requital of all things else, which ye had taken from
me. She is my happiness!—she is my torture, none the
less! Pearl keeps me here in life! Pearl punishes me too!
See ye not, she is the scarlet letter, only capable of
being loved, and so endowed with a millionfold the
power of retribution for my sin? Ye shall not take her!
I will die first!"

"My poor woman," said the not unkind old minister,
"the child shall be well cared for!—far better than thou
canst do it."

"God gave her into my keeping," repeated Hester
Prynne, raising her voice almost to a shriek. "I will

not give her up!"—And here, by a sudden impulse, she turned to the young clergyman, Mr. Dimmesdale, at whom, up to this moment, she had seemed hardly so much as once to direct her eyes. "Speak thou for me!" cried she. "Thou wast my pastor, and hadst charge of my soul, and knowest me better than these men can. I will not lose the child! Speak for me! Thou knowest —for thou hast sympathies which these men lack—thou knowest what is in my heart, and what are a mother's rights, and how much the stronger they are when that mother has but her child and the scarlet letter! Look thou to it! I will not lose the child! Look to it!"

At this wild and singular appeal, which indicated that Hester Prynne's situation had provoked her to little less than madness, the young minister at once came forward, pale, and holding his hand over his heart, as was his custom whenever his peculiarly nervous temperament was thrown into agitation. He looked now more careworn and emaciated than as we described him at the scene of Hester's public ignominy; and whether it were his failing health, or whatever the cause might be, his large dark eyes had a world of pain in their troubled and melancholy depth.

"There is truth in what she says," began the minister, with a voice sweet, tremulous, but powerful, insomuch that the hall reëchoed, and the hollow armor rang with it—"truth in what Hester says, and in the feeling which inspires her! God gave her the child, and gave her, too, an instinctive knowledge of its nature and requirements—both seemingly so peculiar—which no other mortal being can possess. And, moreover, is there not a quality of awful sacredness in the relation between this mother and this child?"

"Ay!—how is that, good Master Dimmesdale?" interrupted the Governor. "Make that plain, I pray you!"

"It must be even so," resumed the minister. "For, if we deem it otherwise, do we not thereby say that the Heavenly Father, the Creator of all flesh, hath lightly recognized a deed of sin and made of no account the distinction between unhallowed lust and holy love? This child of its father's guilt and its mother's shame hath come from the hand of God, to work in many ways upon her heart, who pleads so earnestly, and with such bitterness of spirit, the right to keep her. It was meant for a blessing; for the one blessing of her life! It was meant, doubtless, as the mother herself hath told us, for a retribution too; a torture to be felt at many an unthought-of moment; a pang, a sting, an ever-recurring agony, in the midst of a troubled joy! Hath she not expressed this thought in the garb of the poor child, so forcibly reminding us of that red symbol which sears her bosom?"

"Well said, again!" cried good Mr. Wilson. "I feared the woman had no better thought than to make a mountebank of her child!"

"O, not so!—not so!" continued Mr. Dimmesdale. "She recognizes, believe me, the solemn miracle which God hath wrought, in the existence of that child. And may she feel, too—what, methinks, is the very truth—that this boon was meant, above all things else, to keep the mother's soul alive, and to preserve her from blacker depths of sin into which Satan might else have sought to plunge her! Therefore it is good for this poor, sinful woman that she hath an infant immortality, a being capable of eternal joy or sorrow, confided to her care—to be trained up by her to righteousness—to remind her, at every moment, of her fall—but yet to teach her, as it were by the Creator's sacred pledge, that, if she bring the child to heaven, the child also will bring its parent thither! Herein is the sinful mother happier than the sinful father. For Hester Prynne's sake, then, and no less for the poor child's sake, let us leave them as Providence hath seen fit to place them!"

"You speak, my friend, with a strange earnestness," said old Roger Chillingworth, smiling at him.

"And there is a weighty import in what my young brother hath spoken," added the Reverend Mr. Wilson. "What say you, worshipful Master Bellingham? Hath he not pleaded well for the poor woman?"

"Indeed hath he," answered the magistrate, "and hath adduced such arguments that we will even leave the matter as it now stands, so long, at least, as there shall be no further scandal in the woman. Care must be had, nevertheless, to put the child to due and stated examination in the catechism, at thy hands or Master Dimmesdale's. Moreover, at a proper season, the tithing-men must take heed that she go both to school and to meeting."

The young minister, on ceasing to speak, had withdrawn a few steps from the group and stood with his face partially concealed in the heavy folds of the window curtain, while the shadow of his figure, which the sunlight cast upon the floor, was tremulous with the vehemence of his appeal. Pearl, that wild and flighty little elf, stole softly towards him, and taking his hand in the grasp of both of her own, laid her cheek against it; a caress so tender, and withal so unobtrusive, that her mother, who was looking on, asked herself, "Is that my Pearl?" Yet she knew that there was love in the child's heart, although it mostly revealed itself in passion, and hardly twice in her lifetime had been softened by such gentleness as now. The minister—for, save the long-sought regards of woman, nothing is sweeter than these marks of childish preference, accorded spontaneously by a spiritual instinct, and therefore seeming to imply in us something truly worthy to be loved—the minister looked round, laid his hand on the child's head, hesitated an instant, and then kissed her brow. Little Pearl's unwonted mood of sentiment lasted no longer; she laughed, and went capering down the hall, so airily, that old Mr. Wilson raised a question whether even her tiptoes touched the floor.

"The little baggage hath witchcraft in her, I profess," said he to Mr. Dimmesdale. "She needs no old woman's broomstick to fly withal!"

"A strange child!" remarked old Roger Chillingworth. "It is easy to see the mother's part in her. Would it be beyond a philosopher's research, think ye, gentlemen, to analyze that child's nature, and, from its make and mould, to give a shrewd guess at the father?"

"Nay; it would be sinful, in such a question, to follow the clew of profane philosophy," said Mr. Wilson. "Better to fast and pray upon it; and still better, it may be, to leave the mystery as we find it, unless Providence reveal it of its own accord. Thereby, every good Christian man hath a title to show a father's kindness to-wards the poor, deserted babe."

The affair being so satisfactorily concluded, Hester Prynne, with Pearl, departed from the house. As they descended the steps, it is averred that the lattice of a chamber window was thrown open, and forth into the sunny day was thrust the face of Mistress Hibbins, Governor Bellingham's bitter-tempered sister, and the same who, a few years later, was executed as a witch.

"Hist, hist!" said she, while her ill-omened physiognomy seemed to cast a shadow over the cheerful newness of the house. "Wilt thou go with us tonight? There will be a merry company in the forest; and I well-nigh promised the Black Man that comely Hester Prynne should make one."

"Make my excuse to him, so please you!" answered Hester, with a triumphant smile. "I must tarry at home, and keep watch over my little Pearl. Had they taken her from me, I would willingly have gone with thee into the forest, and signed my name in the Black Man's book too, and that with mine own blood!"

"We shall have thee there anon!" said the witch-lady, frowning, as she drew back her head.

But here—if we suppose this interview betwixt Mistress Hibbins and Hester Prynne to be authentic, and not a parable—was already an illustration of the young minister's argument against sundering the relation of a fallen mother to the offspring of her frailty. Even thus early had the child saved her from Satan's snare.

9

THE LEECH

UNDER THE APPELLATION of Roger Chillingworth, the reader will remember, was hidden another name, which its former wearer had resolved should never more be spoken. It has been related, how, in the crowd that witnessed Hester Prynne's ignominious exposure, stood a man, elderly, travel-worn, who, just emerging from the perilous wilderness, beheld the woman, in whom he hoped to find embodied the warmth and cheerfulness of home, set up as a type of sin before the people. Her matronly fame was trodden under all men's feet. Infamy was babbling around her in the public market place. For her kindred, should the tidings ever reach them, and for the companions of her unspotted life, there remained nothing but the contagion of her dishonor, which would not fail to be distributed in strict accordance and proportion with the intimacy and sacredness of their previous relationship. Then why—since the choice was with himself—should the individual, whose connection with the fallen woman had been the most intimate and sacred of them all, come forward to vindicate his claim to an inheritance so little desirable? He resolved not to be pilloried beside her on her pedestal of shame. Unknown to all but Hester Prynne, and possessing the lock and key of her silence, he chose to withdraw his name from the roll of mankind, and, as regarded his former ties and interests, to vanish out of life as completely as if he indeed

lay at the bottom of the ocean, whither rumor had
long ago consigned him. This purpose once effected,
new interests would immediately spring up, and likewise a new purpose; dark, it is true, if not guilty, but
of force enough to engage the full strength of his
faculties.

In pursuance of this resolve, he took up his residence
in the Puritan town as Roger Chillingworth, without
other introduction than the learning and intelligence
of which he possessed more than a common measure.
As his studies at a previous period of his life had made
him extensively acquainted with the medical science of
the day, it was as a physician that he presented himself,
and as such was cordially received. Skilful men of the
medical and chirurgical profession were of rare occur-
rence in the colony. They seldom, it would appear,
partook of the religious zeal that brought other emigrants across the Atlantic. In their researches into the
human frame, it may be that the higher and more
subtile faculties of such men were materialized, and
that they lost the spiritual view of existence amid the
intricacies of that wondrous mechanism, which seemed
to involve art enough to comprise all of life within
itself. At all events, the health of the good town of
Boston, so far as medicine had aught to do with it, had
hitherto lain in the guardianship of an aged deacon and
apothecary, whose piety and godly deportment were
stronger testimonials in his favor than any that he could
have produced in the shape of a diploma. The only
surgeon was one who combined the occasional exercise
of that noble art with the daily and habitual flourish of
a razor. To such a professional body Roger Chillingworth was a brilliant acquisition. He soon manifested
his familiarity with the ponderous and imposing machinery of antique physic, in which every remedy contained a multitude of far-fetched and heterogeneous
ingredients as elaborately compounded as if the pro-
posed result had been the Elixir of Life. In his Indian
captivity, moreover, he had gained much knowledge
of the properties of native herbs and roots; nor did he
conceal from his patients, that these simple medicines,
Nature's boon to the untutored savage, had quite as

large a share of his own confidence as the European pharmacopœia, which so many learned doctors had spent centuries in elaborating.

This learned stranger was exemplary, as regarded, at least, the outward forms of a religious life, and, early after his arrival, had chosen for his spiritual guide the Reverend Mr. Dimmesdale. The young divine, whose scholar-like renown still lived in Oxford, was considered by his more fervent admirers as little less than a heavenly-ordained apostle, destined, should he live and labor for the ordinary term of life, to do as great deeds for the now feeble New England Church, as the early Fathers had achieved for the infancy of the Christian faith. About this period, however, the health of Mr. Dimmesdale had evidently begun to fail. By those best acquainted with his habits, the paleness of the young minister's cheek was accounted for by his too earnest devotion to study, his scrupulous fulfilment of parochial duty, and, more than all, by the fasts and vigils of which he made a frequent practice, in order to keep the grossness of this earthly state from clogging and obscuring his spiritual lamp. Some declared, that, if Mr. Dimmesdale were really going to die, it was cause enough that the world was not worthy to be any longer trodden by his feet. He himself, on the other hand, with characteristic humility, avowed his belief that if Providence should see fit to remove him, it would be because of his own unworthiness to perform its humblest mission here on earth. With all this difference of opinion as to the cause of his decline, there could be no question of the fact. His form grew emaciated; his voice, though still rich and sweet, had a certain melancholy prophecy of decay in it; he was often observed, on any slight alarm or other sudden accident, to put his hand over his heart, with first a flush and then a paleness, indicative of pain.

Such was the young clergyman's condition, and so imminent the prospect that his dawning light would be extinguished, all untimely, when Roger Chillingworth made his advent to the town. His first entry on the scene, few people could tell whence, dropping down, as it were, out of the sky, or starting from the nether earth, had an aspect of mystery which was easily heightened to the miraculous. He was now known to be a man of skill; it was observed that he gathered herbs, and the blossoms of wild-flowers, and dug up roots, and plucked off twigs from the forest trees, like one acquainted with hidden virtues in what was valueless to common eyes. He was heard to speak of Sir Kenelm Digby, and other famous men—whose scientific attainments were esteemed hardly less than supernatural—as having been his correspondents or associates. Why, with such rank in the learned world, had he come hither? What could he, whose sphere was in great cities, be seeking in the wilderness? In answer to this query, a rumor gained ground—and, however absurd, was entertained by some very sensible people—that Heaven had wrought an absolute miracle by transporting an eminent Doctor of Physic from a German university bodily through the air and setting him down at the door of Mr. Dimmesdale's study! Individuals of wiser faith, indeed, who knew that Heaven promotes its purposes without aiming at the stage effect of what is called miraculous interposition, were inclined to see a providential hand in Roger Chillingworth's so opportune arrival.

This idea was countenanced by the strong interest which the physician ever manifested in the young clergyman; he attached himself to him as a parishioner, and sought to win a friendly regard and confidence from his naturally reserved sensibility. He expressed great alarm at his pastor's state of health, but was anxious to attempt the cure, and, if early undertaken, seemed not despondent of a favorable result. The elders, the deacons, the motherly dames, and the young and fair maidens of Mr. Dimmesdale's flock were alike importunate that he should make trial of the physician's frankly offered skill. Mr. Dimmesdale gently repelled their entreaties.

"I need no medicine," said he.

But how could the young minister say so, when, with every successive Sabbath, his cheek was paler and thinner, and his voice more tremulous than before—when it had now become a constant habit, rather than a casual gesture, to press his hand over his heart? Was he weary of his labors? Did he wish to die? These questions were solemnly propounded to Mr. Dimmesdale by the elder ministers of Boston and the deacons of his church, who, to use their own phrase, "dealt with him" on the sin of rejecting the aid which Providence so manifestly held out. He listened in silence, and finally promised to confer with the physician.

"Were it God's will," said the Reverend Mr. Dimmesdale, when, in fulfilment of this pledge, he requested old Roger Chillingworth's professional advice, "I could be well content that my labors, and my sorrows, and my sins, and my pains, should shortly end with me, and what is earthly of them be buried in my grave, and the spiritual go with me to my eternal state, rather than that you should put your skill to the proof in my behalf."

"Ah," replied Roger Chillingworth, with that quietness which, whether imposed or natural, marked all his deportment, "it is thus that a young clergyman is apt to speak. Youthful men, not having taken a deep root, give up their hold of life so easily! And saintly men, who walk with God on earth, would fain be away, to walk with him on the golden pavements of the New Jerusalem."

"Nay," rejoined the young minister, putting his hand to his heart, with a flush of pain flitting over his brow, "were I worthier to walk there, I could be better content to toil here."

"Good men ever interpret themselves too meanly," said the physician.

In this manner, the mysterious old Roger Chillingworth became the medical adviser of the Reverend Mr. Dimmesdale. As not only the disease interested the physician, but he was strongly moved to look into the character and qualities of the patient, these two men, so different in age, came gradually to spend much time together. For the sake of the minister's health, and to enable the leech to gather plants with healing balm in them, they took long walks on the seashore or in the forest; mingling various talk with the plash and murmur of the waves, and the solemn wind anthem among the treetops. Often, likewise, one was the guest of the other in his place of study and retirement. There was a fascination for the minister in the company of the man of science, in whom he recognized an intellectual cultivation of no moderate depth or scope, together with a range and freedom of ideas that he would have vainly looked for among

the members of his own profession. In truth, he was
startled, if not shocked, to find this attribute in the physician. Mr. Dimmesdale was a true priest, a true religionist, with the reverential sentiment largely developed, and
an order of mind that impelled itself powerfully along
the track of a creed and wore its passage continually
deeper with the lapse of time. In no state of society
would he have been what is called a man of liberal views;
it would always be essential to his peace to feel the pressure of a faith upon him, supporting, while it confined
him within its iron framework. Not the less, however,
though with a tremulous enjoyment, did he feel the occasional relief of looking at the universe through the
medium of another kind of intellect than those with
which he habitually held converse. It was as if a window
were thrown open, admitting a freer atmosphere into the
close and stifled study where his life was wasting itself
away, amid lamplight, or obstructed day-beams, and the
musty fragrance, be it sensual or moral, that exhales from
books. But the air was too fresh and chill to be long
breathed with comfort. So the minister, and the physician
with him, withdrew again within the limits of what their
church defined as orthodox.

Thus Roger Chillingworth scrutinized his patient carefully, both as he saw him in his ordinary life, keeping an
accustomed pathway in the range of thoughts familiar to
him, and as he appeared when thrown amidst other moral
scenery, the novelty of which might call out something
new to the surface of his character. He deemed it essential, it would seem, to know the man before attempting
to do him good. Wherever there is a heart and an intellect, the diseases of the physical frame are tinged with the
peculiarities of these. In Arthur Dimmesdale, thought
and imagination were so active, and sensibility so intense,
that the bodily infirmity would be likely to have its
groundwork there. So Roger Chillingworth—the man of
skill, the kind and friendly physician—strove to go deep
into his patient's bosom, delving among his principles,
prying into his recollections, and probing everything with
a cautious touch, like a treasure-seeker in a dark cavern.
Few secrets can escape an investigator who has opportunity and license to undertake such a quest and skill to

follow it up. A man burdened with a secret should especially avoid the intimacy of his physician. If the latter possess native sagacity, and a nameless something more—let us call it intuition; if he show no intrusive egotism, nor disagreeably prominent characteristics of his own; if he have the power, which must be born with him, to bring his mind into such affinity with his patient's that this last shall unawares have spoken what he imagines himself only to have thought; if such revelations be received without tumult, and acknowledged not so often by an uttered sympathy as by silence, an inarticulate breath, and here and there a word, to indicate that all is understood; if to these qualifications of a confidant be joined the advantages afforded by his recognized character as a physician—then, at some inevitable moment will the soul of the sufferer be dissolved, and flow forth in a dark but transparent stream, bringing all its mysteries into the daylight.

Roger Chillingworth possessed all, or most, of the attributes above enumerated. Nevertheless, time went on; a kind of intimacy, as we have said, grew up between these two cultivated minds, which had as wide a field as the whole sphere of human thought and study to meet upon; they discussed every topic of ethics and religion, of public affairs, and private character; they talked much, on both sides, of matters that seemed personal to themselves; and yet no secret, such as the physician fancied must exist there, ever stole out of the minister's consciousness into his companion's ear. The latter had his suspicions, indeed, that even the nature of Mr. Dimmesdale's bodily disease had never fairly been revealed to him. It was a strange reserve!

After a time, at a hint from Roger Chillingworth, the friends of Mr. Dimmesdale effected an arrangement by which the two were lodged in the same house; so that every ebb and flow of the minister's life-tide might pass under the eye of his anxious and attached physician. There was much joy throughout the town when this greatly desirable object was attained. It was held to be the best possible measure for the young clergyman's welfare; unless, indeed, as often urged by such as felt authorized to do so, he had selected some one of the many blooming damsels, spiritually devoted to him, to become his devoted wife. This latter step, however, there was no present prospect that Arthur Dimmesdale would be prevailed upon to take; he rejected all suggestions of the kind, as if priestly celibacy were one of his articles of church discipline. Doomed by his own choice, therefore, as Mr. Dimmesdale so evidently was, to eat his unsavory morsel always at another's board and endure the lifelong chill which must be his lot who seeks to warm himself only at another's fireplace, it truly seemed that this sagacious, experienced, benevolent old physician, with his concord of paternal and reverential love for the young pastor, was the very man, of all mankind, to be constantly within reach of his voice.

The new abode of the two friends was with a pious widow, of good social rank, who dwelt in a house covering pretty nearly the site on which the venerable structure of King's Chapel has since been built. It had the graveyard, originally Isaac Johnson's home-field, on one side, and so was well adapted to call up serious reflections, suited to their respective employments, in both minister and man of physic. The motherly care of the good widow assigned to Mr. Dimmesdale a front apartment with a sunny exposure, and heavy window curtains to create a noontide shadow when desirable. The walls were hung round with tapestry, said to be from the Gobelin looms, and, at all events, representing the Scriptural story of David and Bathsheba, and Nathan the Prophet, in colors still unfaded, but which made the fair woman of the scene almost as grimly picturesque as the woe-denouncing seer. Here, the pale clergyman piled up his library, rich with parchment-bound folios of the Fathers and the lore of Rabbis and monkish erudition, of which the Protestant divines, even while they vilified and decried that class of writers, were yet constrained often to avail themselves. On the other side of the house, old Roger Chillingworth arranged his study and laboratory; not such as a modern man of science would reckon even tolerably complete, but provided with a distilling apparatus and the means of compounding drugs and chemicals, which the practised alchemist knew well how to turn to purpose. With such commodiousness of situation, these two learned persons sat themselves down, each in his own domain, yet familiarly passing from one apartment to the other, and bestowing a mutual and not incurious inspection into one another's business.

And the Reverend Arthur Dimmesdale's best discerning friends, as we have intimated, very reasonably imagined that the hand of Providence had done all this for the purpose—besought in so many public, and domestic, and secret prayers—of restoring the young minister to health. But—it must now be said—another portion of the community had latterly begun to take its own view of the relation betwixt Mr. Dimmesdale and the mysterious old physician. When an uninstructed multitude attempts to see with its eyes, it is exceedingly apt to be deceived. When, however, it forms its judgment, as it usually does, on the intuitions of its great and warm heart, the conclusions thus attained are often so profound and so unerring, as to possess the character of truths supernaturally revealed. The people, in the case of which we speak, could justify its prejudice against Roger Chillingworth by no fact or argument worthy of serious refutation. There was an aged handicraftsman, it is true, who had been a citizen of London at the period of Sir Thomas Overbury's murder, now some thirty years agone; he testified to having seen the physician, under some other name which the narrator of the story had now forgotten, in company with Doctor Forman, the famous old conjurer, who was implicated in the affair of Overbury. Two or three individuals hinted that the man of skill, during his Indian captivity, had enlarged his medical attainments by joining in the incantations of the savage priests, who were universally acknowledged to be powerful enchanters, often performing seemingly miraculous cures by their skill in the black art. A large number—and many of these were persons of such sober sense and practical observation that their opinions would have been valuable in other matters—affirmed that Roger Chillingworth's aspect had undergone a remarkable change while he had dwelt in town, and especially since his abode with Mr.

Dimmesdale. At first, his expression had been calm, meditative, scholar-like. Now, there was something ugly and evil in his face which they had not previously noticed, and which grew still the more obvious to sight, the oftener they looked upon him. According to the vulgar idea, the fire in his laboratory had been brought from the lower regions, and was fed with infernal fuel; and so, as might be expected, his visage was getting sooty with the smoke.

To sum up the matter, it grew to be a widely diffused opinion that the Reverend Arthur Dimmesdale, like many other personages of especial sanctity, in all ages of the Christian world, was haunted either by Satan himself, or Satan's emissary, in the guise of old Roger Chillingworth. This diabolical agent had the Divine permission, for a season, to burrow into the clergyman's intimacy and plot against his soul. No sensible man, it was confessed, could doubt on which side the victory would turn. The people looked, with an unshaken hope, to see the minister come forth out of the conflict, transfigured with the glory which he would unquestionably win. Meanwhile, nevertheless, it was sad to think of the perchance mortal agony through which he must struggle towards his triumph.

Alas! to judge from the gloom and terror in the depths of the poor minister's eyes, the battle was a sore one, and the victory anything but secure.

10

THE LEECH AND HIS PATIENT

OLD ROGER CHILLINGWORTH, throughout life, had been calm in temperament, kindly, though not of warm affections, but ever, and in all his relations with the world, a pure and upright man. He had begun an investigation, as he imagined, with the severe and equal integrity of a judge, desirous only of truth, even as if the question involved no more than the air-drawn lines and figures of a geometrical problem, instead of human passions and wrongs inflicted on himself. But, as he proceeded, a terrible fascination, a kind of fierce, though still calm, necessity seized the old man within its gripe and never set him free again, until he had done all its bidding. He now dug into the poor clergyman's heart like a miner searching for gold; or, rather, like a sexton delving into a grave, possibly in quest of a jewel that had been buried on the dead man's bosom, but likely to find nothing save mortality and corruption. Alas for his own soul, if these were what he sought!

Sometimes, a light glimmered out of the physician's eyes, burning blue and ominous, like the reflection of a furnace, or, let us say, like one of those gleams of ghastly fire that darted from Bunyan's awful doorway in the hillside and quivered on the pilgrim's face. The soil where this dark miner was working had perchance shown indications that encouraged him.

"This man," said he, at one such moment, to himself,

"pure as they deem him—all spiritual as he seems—hath inherited a strong animal nature from his father or mother. Let us dig a little further in the direction of this vein!"

Then, after long search into the minister's dim interior, and turning over many precious materials in the shape of high aspirations for the welfare of his race, warm love of souls, pure sentiments, natural piety, strengthened by thought and study, and illuminated by revelation—all of which invaluable gold was perhaps no better than rubbish to the seeker—he would turn back, discouraged, and begin his quest towards another point. He groped along as stealthily, with as cautious a tread, and as wary an outlook, as a thief entering a chamber where a man lies only half asleep—or, it may be, broad awake—with purpose to steal the very treasure which this man guards as the apple of his eye. In spite of his premeditated carefulness, the floor would now and then creak; his garments would rustle; the shadow of his presence, in a forbidden proximity, would be thrown across his victim. In other words, Mr. Dimmesdale, whose sensibility of nerve often produced the effect of spiritual intuition, would become vaguely aware that something inimical to his peace had thrust itself into relation with him. But old Roger Chillingworth, too, had perceptions that were almost intuitive; and when the minister threw his startled eyes towards him, there the physician sat; his kind, watchful, sympathizing, but never intrusive friend.

Yet Mr. Dimmesdale would perhaps have seen this individual's character more perfectly if a certain morbidness, to which sick hearts are liable, had not rendered him suspicious of all mankind. Trusting no man as his friend, he could not recognize his enemy when the latter actually appeared. He therefore still kept up a familiar intercourse with him, daily receiving the old physician in his study, or visiting the laboratory, and, for recreation's sake, watching the processes by which weeds were converted into drugs of potency.

One day, leaning his forehead on his hand and his elbow on the sill of the open window that looked towards the graveyard, he talked with Roger Chillingworth while the old man was examining a bundle of unsightly plants.

"Where," asked he, with a look askance at them—for it was the clergyman's peculiarity that he seldom, nowadays, looked straightforth at any object, whether human or inanimate—"where, my kind doctor, did you gather those herbs, with such a dark, flabby leaf?"

"Even in the graveyard here at hand," answered the physician, continuing his employment. "They are new to me. I found them growing on a grave which bore no tombstone, nor other memorial of the dead man, save these ugly weeds that have taken upon themselves to keep him in remembrance. They grew out of his heart, and typify, it may be, some hideous secret that was buried with him, and which he had done better to confess during his lifetime."

"Perchance," said Mr. Dimmesdale, "he earnestly desired it, but could not."

"And wherefore?" rejoined the physician. "Wherefore not; since all the powers of nature call so earnestly for the confession of sin, that these black weeds have sprung up out of a buried heart to make manifest an unspoken crime?"

"That, good Sir, is but a fantasy of yours," replied the minister. "There can be, if I forebode aright, no power, short of the Divine mercy, to disclose, whether by uttered words, or by type or emblem, the secrets that may be buried with a human heart. The heart, making itself guilty of such secrets, must perforce hold them, until the day when all hidden things shall be revealed. Nor have I so read or interpreted Holy Writ as to understand that the disclosure of human thoughts and deeds, then to be made, is intended as a part of the retribution. That, surely, were a shallow view of it. No; these revelations, unless I greatly err, are meant merely to promote the intellectual satisfaction of all intelligent beings, who will stand waiting, on that day, to see the dark problem of this life made plain. A knowledge of men's hearts will be needful to the completest solution of that problem. And I conceive, moreover, that the hearts holding such miserable secrets as you speak of will yield them up, at that last day, not with reluctance, but with a joy unutterable."

"Then why not reveal them here?" asked Roger Chillingworth, glancing quietly aside at the minister. "Why should not the guilty ones sooner avail themselves of this unutterable solace?"

"They mostly do," said the clergyman, griping hard at his breast, as if afflicted with an importunate throb of pain. "Many, many a poor soul hath given its confidence to me, not only on the deathbed, but while strong in life, and fair in reputation. And ever, after such an outpouring, O, what a relief have I witnessed in those sinful brethren! even as in one who at last draws free air, after long stifling with his own polluted breath. How can it be otherwise? Why should a wretched man, guilty, we will say, of murder, prefer to keep the dead corpse buried in his own heart, rather than fling it forth at once, and let the universe take care of it!"

"Yet some men bury their secrets thus," observed the calm physician.

"True; there are such men," answered Mr. Dimmesdale. "But, not to suggest more obvious reasons, it may be that they are kept silent by the very constitution of their nature. Or—can we not suppose it?—guilty as they may be, retaining, nevertheless, a zeal for God's glory and man's welfare, they shrink from displaying themselves black and filthy in the view of men; because, thenceforward, no good can be achieved by them; no evil of the past be redeemed by better service. So, to their own unutterable torment, they go about among their fellow-creatures looking pure as new-fallen snow; while their hearts are all speckled and spotted with iniquity of which they cannot rid themselves."

"These men deceive themselves," said Roger Chillingworth, with somewhat more emphasis than usual, and making a slight gesture with his forefinger. "They fear to take up the shame that rightfully belongs to them. Their love for man, their zeal for God's service—these holy impulses may or may not coexist in their hearts with the evil inmates to which their guilt has unbarred the door, and which must needs propagate a hellish breed within them. But, if they seek to glorify God, let them not lift heavenward their unclean hands! If they would serve their fellowmen, let them do it by making manifest the power and reality of conscience, in constraining them to penitential self-abasement! Wouldst thou have me to believe, O wise and pious friend, that a false show can be better—can be more for God's glory, or man's welfare—than God's own truth? Trust me, such men deceive themselves!"

"It may be so," said the young clergyman, indifferently, as waiving a discussion that he considered irrelevant or unreasonable. He had a ready faculty, indeed, of escaping from any topic that agitated his too sensitive and nervous temperament.—"But, now, I would ask of my well-skilled physician whether, in good sooth, he deems me to have profited by his kindly care of this weak frame of mine?"

Before Roger Chillingworth could answer, they heard the clear, wild laughter of a young child's voice proceeding from the adjacent burial ground. Looking instinctively from the open window—for it was summertime—the minister beheld Hester Prynne and little Pearl passing along the footpath that traversed the enclosure. Pearl looked as beautiful as the day, but was in one of those moods of perverse merriment which, whenever they occurred, seemed to remove her entirely out of the sphere of sympathy or human contact. She now skipped irreverently from one grave to another; until, coming to the broad, flat, armorial tombstone of a departed worthy—perhaps of Isaac Johnson himself—she began to dance upon it. In reply to her mother's command and entreaty that she would behave more decorously, little Pearl paused to gather the prickly burrs from a tall burdock which grew beside the tomb. Taking a handful of these, she arranged them along the lines of the scarlet letter that decorated the maternal bosom, to which the burrs, as their nature was, tenaciously adhered. Hester did not pluck them off.

Roger Chillingworth had by this time approached the window, and smiled grimly down.

"There is no law, nor reverence for authority, no regard for human ordinances or opinions, right or wrong, mixed up with that child's composition," remarked he, as much to himself as to his companion. "I saw her, the other day, bespatter the Governor himself with water, at the cattle trough in Spring Lane. What, in Heaven's name, is she? Is the imp altogether evil? Hath she affections? Hath she any discoverable principle of being?"

"None—save the freedom of a broken law," answered Mr. Dimmesdale, in a quiet way, as if he had been discussing the point within himself. "Whether capable of good, I know not."

The child probably overheard their voices; for, looking up to the window with a bright but naughty smile of mirth and intelligence, she threw one of the prickly burrs at the Reverend Mr. Dimmesdale. The sensitive clergyman shrunk with nervous dread from the light missile. Detecting his emotion, Pearl clapped her little hands in the most extravagant ecstasy. Hester Prynne, likewise, had involuntarily looked up; and all these four persons, old and young, regarded one another in silence, till the child laughed aloud, and shouted, "Come away, Mother! Come away, or yonder old Black Man will catch you! He hath got hold of the minister already. Come away, Mother, or he will catch you! But he cannot catch little Pearl!"

So she drew her mother away, skipping, dancing, and frisking fantastically among the hillocks of the dead people, like a creature that had nothing in common with a bygone and buried generation, nor owned herself akin to it. It was as if she had been made afresh out of new elements, and must perforce be permitted to live her own life, and be a law unto herself without her eccentricities being reckoned to her for a crime.

"There goes a woman," resumed Roger Chillingworth, after a pause, "who, be her demerits what they may, hath none of that mystery of hidden sinfulness which you deem so grievous to be borne. Is Hester Prynne the less miserable, think you, for that scarlet letter on her breast?"

"I do verily believe it," answer the clergyman. "Nevertheless, I cannot answer for her. There was a look of pain in her face which I would gladly have been spared the sight of. But still, methinks, it must needs be better for the sufferer to be free to show his pain, as this poor woman Hester is, than to cover it all up in his heart."

There was another pause; and the physician began anew to examine and arrange the plants which he had gathered.

"You inquired of me, a little time agone," said he, at length, "my judgment as touching your health."

"I did," answered the clergyman, "and would gladly

learn it. Speak frankly, I pray you, be it for life or death."

"Freely, then, and plainly," said the physician, still busy with his plants, but keeping a wary eye on Mr. Dimmesdale, "the disorder is a strange one; not so much in itself, nor as outwardly manifested—in so far, at least, as the symptoms have been laid open to my observation. Looking daily at you, my good Sir, and watching the tokens of your aspect now for months gone by, I should deem you a man sore sick, it may be, yet not so sick but that an instructed and watchful physician might well hope to cure you. But—I know not what to say—the disease is what I seem to know, yet know it not."

"You speak in riddles, learned Sir," said the pale minister, glancing aside out of the window.

"Then, to speak more plainly," continued the physician, "and I crave pardon, Sir—should it seem to require pardon—for this needful plainness of my speech. Let me ask—as your friend, as one having charge, under Providence, of your life and physical well-being—hath all the operation of this disorder been fairly laid open and recounted to me?"

"How can you question it?" asked the minister. "Surely, it were child's play to call in a physician and then hide the sore!"

"You would tell me, then, that I know all?" said Roger Chillingworth deliberately and fixing an eye, bright with intense and concentrated intelligence, on the minister's face. "Be it so! But again! He to whom only the outward and physical evil is laid open, knoweth, oftentimes, but half the evil which he is called upon to cure. A bodily disease, which we look upon as whole and entire within itself, may, after all, be but a symptom of some ailment in the spiritual part. Your pardon, once again, good Sir, if my speech give the shadow of offence. You, Sir, of all men whom I have known, are he whose body is the closest conjoined, and imbued, and identified, so to speak, with the spirit whereof it is the instrument."

"Then I need ask no further," said the clergyman, somewhat hastily rising from his chair. "You deal not, I take it, in medicine for the soul!"

"Thus, a sickness," continued Roger Chillingworth, going on, in an unaltered tone, without heeding the interruption—but standing up and confronting the emaciated and white-cheeked minister with his low, dark and misshapen figure—"a sickness, a sore place, if we may so call it, in your spirit, hath immediately its appropriate manifestation in your bodily frame. Would you, therefore, that your physician heal the bodily evil? How may this be, unless you first lay open to him the wound or trouble in your soul?"

"No—not to thee!—not to an earthly physician!" cried Mr. Dimmesdale passionately and turning his eyes, full and bright, and with a kind of fierceness, on old Roger Chillingworth. "Not to thee! But, if it be the soul's disease, then do I commit myself to the one Physician of the soul! He, if it stand with his good pleasure, can cure; or he can kill! Let him do with me as, in his justice and wisdom, he shall see good. But who art thou, that meddlest in this matter?—that darest thrust himself between the sufferer and his God?"

With a frantic gesture, he rushed out of the room.

"It is as well to have made this step," said Roger Chillingworth to himself, looking after the minister with a grave smile. "There is nothing lost. We shall be friends again anon. But see, now, how passion takes hold upon this man, and hurrieth him out of himself! As with one passion, so with another! He hath done a wild thing ere now, this pious Master Dimmesdale, in the hot passion of his heart!"

It proved not difficult to re-establish the intimacy of the two companions, on the same footing and in the same degree as heretofore. The young clergyman, after a few hours of privacy, was sensible that the disorder of his nerves had hurried him into an unseemly outbreak of temper which there had been nothing in the physician's words to excuse or palliate. He marvelled, indeed, at the violence with which he had thrust back the kind old man, when merely proffering the advice which it was his duty to bestow, and which the minister himself had expressly sought. With these remorseful feelings, he lost no time in making the amplest apologies, and besought his friend still to continue the care, which, if not successful in restoring him to health, had, in all probability, been the means of prolonging his feeble existence to that hour. Roger Chillingworth readily assented, and went on with his medical supervision of the minister, doing his best for him, in all good faith, but always quitting the patient's apartment at the close of a professional interview with a mysterious and puzzled smile upon his lips. This expression was invisible in Mr. Dimmesdale's presence, but grew strongly evident as the physician crossed the threshold.

"A rare case!" he muttered. "I must needs look deeper into it. A strange sympathy betwixt soul and body! Were it only for the art's sake, I must search this matter to the bottom!"

It came to pass, not long after the scene above recorded, that the Reverend Mr. Dimmesdale, at noonday, and entirely unawares, fell into a deep, deep slumber, sitting in his chair, with a large black-letter volume open before him on the table. It must have been a work of vast ability in the somniferous school of literature. The profound depth of the minister's repose was the more remarkable, inasmuch as he was one of those persons whose sleep, ordinarily, is as light, as fitful, and as easily scared away, as a small bird hopping on a twig. To such an unwonted remoteness, however, had his spirit now withdrawn into itself, that he stirred not in his chair, when old Roger Chillingworth, without any extraordinary precaution, came into the room. The physician advanced directly in front of his patient, laid his hand upon his bosom, and thrust aside the vestment, that, hitherto, had always covered it even from the professional eye.

Then, indeed, Mr. Dimmesdale shuddered, and slightly stirred.

After a brief pause, the physician turned away.

But, with what a wild look of wonder, joy, and horror! With what a ghastly rapture, as it were, too mighty to be expressed only by the eye and features, and therefore bursting forth through the whole ugliness of his figure, and making itself even riotously manifest by the extravagant gestures with which he threw up his arms towards the ceiling, and stamped his foot upon the floor! Had a man seen old Roger Chillingworth, at that moment

of his ecstasy, he would have had no need to ask how
Satan comports himself when a precious human soul
is lost to heaven and won into his kingdom.

But what distinguished the physician's ecstasy from
Satan's was the trait of wonder in it!

11

THE INTERIOR OF A HEART

AFTER THE INCIDENT last described, the intercourse
between the clergyman and the physician,
though externally the same, was really of another character than it had previously been. The intellect of Roger
Chillingworth had now a sufficiently plain path before
it. It was not, indeed, precisely that which he had laid
out for himself to tread. Calm, gentle, passionless as
he appeared, there was yet, we fear, a quiet depth of
malice, hitherto latent, but active now, in this unfortunate old man, which led him to imagine a more
intimate revenge than any mortal had ever wreaked upon
an enemy. To make himself the one trusted friend to
whom should be confided all the fear, the remorse, the
agony, the ineffectual repentance, the backward rush
of sinful thoughts, expelled in vain! All that guilty
sorrow, hidden from the world, whose great heart would
have pitied and forgiven, to be revealed to him, the
Pitiless, to him, the Unforgiving! All that dark treasure
to be lavished on the very man to whom nothing else
could so adequately pay the debt of vengeance!

The clergyman's shy and sensitive reserve had balked
this scheme. Roger Chillingworth, however, was inclined
to be hardly, if at all, less satisfied with the aspect of

affairs which Providence—using the avenger and his victim for its own purposes, and, perchance, pardoning, where it seemed most to punish—had substituted for his black devices. A revelation, he could almost say, had been granted to him. It mattered little, for his object, whether celestial, or from what other region. By its aid, in all the subsequent relations betwixt him and Mr. Dimmesdale, not merely the external presence, but the very inmost soul of the latter seemed to be brought out before his eyes, so that he could see and comprehend its every movement. He became, thenceforth, not a spectator only, but a chief actor in the poor minister's interior world. He could play upon him as he chose. Would he arouse him with a throb of agony? The victim was forever on the rack; it needed only to know the spring that controlled the engine—and the physician knew it well! Would he startle him with sudden fear? As at the waving of a magician's wand, uprose a grisly phantom—uprose a thousand phantoms—in many shapes, of death, or more awful shame, all flocking round about the clergyman, and pointing with their fingers at his breast!

All this was accomplished with a subtlety so perfect, that the minister, though he had constantly a dim perception of some evil influence watching over him, could never gain a knowledge of its actual nature. True, he looked doubtfully, fearfully—even, at times, with horror and the bitterness of hatred—at the deformed figure of the old physician. His gestures, his gait, his grizzled beard, his slightest and most indifferent acts, the very fashion of his garments, were odious in the clergyman's sight; a token implicitly to be relied on of a deeper antipathy in the breast of the latter than he was willing to acknowledge to himself. For, as it was impossible to assign a reason for such distrust and abhorrence, so Mr. Dimmesdale, conscious that the poison of one morbid spot was infecting his heart's entire substance, attributed all his presentiments to no other cause. He took himself to task for his bad sympathies in reference to Roger Chillingworth, disregarded the lesson that he should have drawn from them, and did his best to root them out. Unable to accomplish this, he nevertheless, as a matter of principle, continued his habits of social familiarity with the old man, and thus

gave him constant opportunities for perfecting the purpose to which—poor, forlorn creature that he was, and
more wretched than his victim—the avenger had devoted
himself.

While thus suffering under bodily disease, and gnawed
and tortured by some black trouble of the soul, and
given over to the machinations of his deadliest enemy,
the Reverend Mr. Dimmesdale had achieved a brilliant
popularity in his sacred office. He won it, indeed, in
great part, by his sorrows. His intellectual gifts, his moral
perceptions, his power of experiencing and communicating emotion, were kept in a state of preternatural
activity by the prick and anguish of his daily life. His
fame, though still on its upward slope, already overshadowed the soberer reputations of his fellow-clergy-
men, eminent as several of them were. There were
scholars among them who had spent more years in
acquiring abstruse lore connected with the divine profession than Mr. Dimmesdale had lived;* and who might
well, therefore, be more profoundly versed in such solid
and valuable attainments than their youthful brother.
There were men, too, of a sturdier texture of mind than
his, and endowed with a far greater share of shrewd, hard,
iron, or granite understanding; which, duly mingled
with a fair proportion of doctrinal ingredient, constitutes
a highly respectable, efficacious, and unamiable variety
of the clerical species. There were others, again, true
saintly fathers, whose faculties had been elaborated by
weary toil among their books, and by patient thought,
and etherealized, moreover, by spiritual communications
with the better world, into which their purity of life
had almost introduced these holy personages with their
garments of mortality still clinging to them. All that
they lacked was the gift that descended upon the chosen
disciples at Pentecost, in tongues of flame; symbolizing,
it would seem, not the power of speech in foreign and
unknown languages, but that of addressing the whole
human brotherhood in the heart's native language.
These fathers, otherwise so apostolic, lacked Heaven's
last and rarest attestation of their office, the Tongue
of Flame. They would have vainly sought—had they
ever dreamed of seeking—to express the highest truths

through the humblest medium of familiar words and images. Their voices came down, afar and indistinctly, from the upper heights where they habitually dwelt.

Not improbably, it was to this latter class of men that Mr. Dimmesdale, by many of his traits of character, naturally belonged. To the high mountain peaks of faith and sanctity he would have climbed, had not the tendency been thwarted by the burden, whatever it might be, of crime or anguish, beneath which it was his doom to totter. It kept him down, on a level with the lowest; him, the man of ethereal attributes, whose voice the angels might else have listened to and answered! But this very burden it was that gave him sympathies so intimate with the sinful brotherhood of mankind; so that his heart vibrated in unison with theirs, and received their pain into itself, and sent its own throb of pain through a thousand other hearts, in gushes of sad, persuasive eloquence. Oftenest persuasive, but sometimes terrible! The people knew not the power that moved them thus. They deemed the young clergyman a miracle of holiness. They fancied him the mouthpiece of Heaven's messages of wisdom and rebuke and love. In their eyes, the very ground on which he trod was sanctified. The virgins of his church grew pale around him, victims of a passion so imbued with religious sentiment that they imagined it to be all religion, and brought it openly, in their white bosoms, as their most acceptable sacrifice before the altar. The aged members of his flock, beholding Mr. Dimmesdale's frame so feeble while they were themselves so rugged in their infirmity, believed that he would go heavenward before them, and enjoined it upon their children that their old bones should be buried close to their young pastor's holy grave. And, all this time, perchance, when poor Mr. Dimmesdale was thinking of his grave, he questioned with himself whether the grass would ever grow on it, because an accursed thing must there be buried!

It is inconceivable, the agony with which this public veneration tortured him! It was his genuine impulse to adore the truth, and to reckon all things shadowlike, and utterly devoid of weight or value, that had not its divine essence as the life within their life. Then, what

was he?—a substance?—or the dimmest of all shadows?
He longed to speak out from his own pulpit at the full
height of his voice, and tell the people what he was.
"I, whom you behold in these black garments of the
priesthood—I, who ascend the sacred desk, and turn
my pale face heavenward, taking upon myself to hold
communion, in your behalf, with the Most High Omnis-
cience—I, in whose daily life you discern the sanctity
of Enoch—I, whose footsteps, as you suppose, leave a
gleam along my earthly track, whereby the pilgrims that
shall come after me may be guided to the regions of
the blest—I, who have laid the hand of baptism upon
your children—I, who have breathed the parting prayer
over your dying friends, to whom the Amen sounded
faintly from a world which they had quitted—I, your
pastor, whom you so reverence and trust, am utterly
a pollution and a lie!"

More than once, Mr. Dimmesdale had gone into the
pulpit, with a purpose never to come down its steps
until he should have spoken words like the above. More
than once, he had cleared his throat and drawn in the
long, deep, and tremulous breath, which, when sent
forth again, would come burdened with the black secret
of his soul. More than once—nay, more than a hundred
times—he had actually spoken! Spoken! But how? He
had told his hearers that he was altogether vile, a viler
companion of the vilest, the worst of sinners, an abomi-
nation, a thing of unimaginable iniquity; and that the
only wonder was that they did not see his wretched
body shrivelled up before their eyes by the burning
wrath of the Almighty! Could there be plainer speech
than this? Would not the people start up in their
seats by a simultaneous impulse, and tear him down
out of the pulpit which he defiled? Not so, indeed!
They heard it all, and did but reverence him the more.
They little guessed what deadly purport lurked in those
self-condemning words. "The godly youth!" said they
among themselves. "The saint on earth! Alas, if he discern such sinfulness in his own white soul, what horrid
spectacle would he behold in thine or mine!" The
minister well knew—subtile, but remorseful hypocrite
that he was!—the light in which his vague confession

would be viewed. He had striven to put a cheat upon himself by making the avowal of a guilty conscience, but had gained only one other sin, and a self-acknowledged shame, without the momentary relief of being self-deceived. He had spoken the very truth, and transformed it into the veriest falsehood. And yet, by the constitution of his nature, he loved the truth and loathed the lie, as few men ever did. Therefore, above all things else, he loathed his miserable self!

His inward trouble drove him to practices more in accordance with the old, corrupted faith of Rome than with the better light of the church in which he had been born and bred. In Mr. Dimmesdale's secret closet, under lock and key, there was a bloody scourge. Oftentimes, this Protestant and Puritan divine had plied it on his own shoulders, laughing bitterly at himself the while, and smiting so much the more pitilessly because of that bitter laugh. It was his custom, too, as it has been that of many other pious Puritans, to fast—not, however, like them, in order to purify the body and render it the fitter medium of celestial illumination, but rigorously, and until his knees trembled beneath him, as an act of penance. He kept vigils, likewise, night after night, sometimes in utter darkness; sometimes with a glimmering lamp; and sometimes, viewing his own face in a looking glass, by the most powerful light which he could throw upon it. He thus typified the constant introspection wherewith he tortured, but could not purify, himself. In these lengthened vigils, his brain often reeled and visions seemed to flit before him; perhaps seen doubtfully, and by a faint light of their own, in the remote dimness of the chamber, or more vividly, and close beside him, within the looking glass. Now it was a herd of diabolic shapes that grinned and mocked at the pale minister, and beckoned him away with them; now a group of shining angels, who flew upward heavily, as sorrow-laden, but grew more ethereal as they rose. Now came the dead friends of his youth, and his white-bearded father, with a saintlike frown, and his mother, turning her face away as she passed by. Ghost of a mother—thinnest fantasy of a mother—methinks she might yet have thrown a pitying glance towards her son! And now, through the chamber which these spectral thoughts had made so ghastly, glided Hester Prynne, leading along little Pearl in her scarlet garb, and pointing her forefinger, first at the scarlet letter on her bosom, and then at the clergyman's own breast.

None of these visions ever quite deluded him. At any moment, by an effort of his will, he could discern substances through their misty lack of substance, and convince himself that they were not solid in their nature, like yonder table of carved oak, or that big, square, leathern-bound and brazen-clasped volume of divinity. But, for all that, they were, in one sense, the truest and most substantial things which the poor minister now dealt with. It is the unspeakable misery of a life so false as his, that it steals the pith and substance out of whatever realities there are around us, and which were meant by Heaven to be the spirit's joy and nutriment. To the untrue man, the whole universe is false— it is impalpable—it shrinks to nothing within his grasp. And he himself, in so far as he shows himself in a false light, becomes a shadow, or, indeed, ceases to exist. The only truth that continued to give Mr. Dimmesdale a real existence on this earth was the anguish in his inmost soul, and the undissembled expression of it in his aspect. Had he once found power to smile, and wear a face of gayety, there would have been no such man!

On one of those ugly nights, which we have faintly hinted at but forborne to picture forth, the minister started from his chair. A new thought had struck him. There might be a moment's peace in it. Attiring himself with as much care as if it had been for public worship, and precisely in the same manner, he stole softly down the staircase, undid the door, and issued forth.

12

THE MINISTER'S VIGIL

Walking in the shadow of a dream, as it were, and perhaps actually under the influence of a species of somnambulism, Mr. Dimmesdale reached the spot where, now so long since, Hester Prynne had lived through her first hours of public ignominy. The same platform or scaffold, black and weather-stained with the storm or sunshine of seven long years, and foot-worn, too, with the tread of many culprits who had since ascended it, remained standing beneath the balcony of the meeting house. The minister went up the steps.

It was an obscure night of early May. An unvaried pall of cloud muffled the whole expanse of sky from zenith to horizon. If the same multitude which had stood as eyewitnesses while Hester Prynne sustained her punishment could now have been summoned forth, they would have discerned no face above the platform, nor hardly the outline of a human shape, in the dark gray of the midnight. But the town was all asleep. There was no peril of discovery. The minister might stand there, if it so pleased him, until morning should redden in the east, without other risk than that the dank and chill night air would creep into his frame and stiffen his joints with rheumatism and clog his throat with catarrh and cough, thereby defrauding the expectant audience of tomorrow's prayer and sermon. No eye could see him, save that ever-wakeful one which

had seen him in his closet wielding the bloody scourge.
Why, then, had he come hither? Was it but the mockery
of penitence? A mockery, indeed, but in which his
soul trifled with itself! A mockery at which angels blushed
and wept, while fiends rejoiced with jeering laughter!
He had been driven hither by the impulse of that
Remorse which dogged him everywhere, and whose own
sister and closely linked companion was that Cowardice
which invariably drew him back with her tremulous gripe,
just when the other impulse had hurried him to the
verge of a disclosure. Poor, miserable man! what right
had infirmity like his to burden itself with crime? Crime
is for the iron-nerved, who have their choice either to
endure it, or, if it press too hard, to exert their fierce
and savage strength for a good purpose, and fling it off
at once! This feeble and most sensitive of spirits could
do neither, yet continually did one thing or another,
which intertwined, in the same inextricable knot, the
agony of heaven-defying guilt and vain repentance.

And thus, while standing on the scaffold, in this
vain show of expiation, Mr. Dimmesdale was overcome
with a great horror of mind, as if the universe were
gazing at a scarlet token on his naked breast, right
over his heart. On that spot, in very truth, there was,
and there had long been, the gnawing and poisonous
tooth of bodily pain. Without any effort of his will
or power to restrain himself, he shrieked aloud; an
outcry that went pealing through the night, and was
beaten back from one house to another, and reverberated
from the hills in the background as if a company of
devils, detecting so much misery and terror in it, had
made a plaything of the sound, and were bandying
it to and fro.

"It is done!" muttered the minister, covering his face
with his hands. "The whole town will awake, and hurry
forth, and find me here!"

But it was not so. The shriek had perhaps sounded
with a far greater power to his own startled ears than
it actually possessed. The town did not awake; or, if
it did, the drowsy slumberers mistook the cry either
for something frightful in a dream, or for the noise of
witches, whose voices, at that period, were often heard

to pass over the settlements or lonely cottages, as they rode with Satan through the air. The clergyman, therefore, hearing no symptoms of disturbance, uncovered his eyes and looked about him. At one of the chamber windows of Governor Bellingham's mansion, which stood at some distance on the line of another street, he beheld the appearance of the old magistrate himself, with a lamp in his hand, a white nightcap on his head, and a long white gown enveloping his figure. He looked like a ghost, evoked unseasonably from the grave. The cry had evidently startled him. At another window of the same house, moreover, appeared old Mistress Hibbins, the Governor's sister, also with a lamp, which, even thus far off, revealed the expression of her sour and discontented face. She thrust forth her head from the lattice, and looked anxiously upward. Beyond the shadow of a doubt, this venerable witch-lady had heard Mr. Dimmesdale's outcry, and interpreted it, with its multitudinous echoes and reverberations, as the clamor of the fiends and night-hags, with whom she was well known to make excursions into the forest.

Detecting the gleam of Governor Bellingham's lamp, the old lady quickly extinguished her own, and vanished. Possibly, she went up among the clouds. The minister saw nothing further of her motions. The magistrate, after a wary observation of the darkness—into which, nevertheless, he could see but little further than he might into a millstone—retired from the window.

The minister grew comparatively calm. His eyes, however, were soon greeted by a little, glimmering light, which, at first a long way off, was approaching up the street. It threw a gleam of recognition on here a post, and there a garden fence, and here a latticed window-pane, and there a pump with its full trough of water, and here, again, an arched door of oak, with an iron knocker, and a rough log for the doorstep. The Reverend Mr. Dimmesdale noted all these minute particulars, even while firmly convinced that the doom of his existence was stealing onward in the footsteps which he now heard; and that the gleam of the lantern would fall upon him, in a few moments more, and reveal his long-hidden secret. As the light drew nearer, he beheld, within its illuminated circle, his brother clergyman—or, to speak more accurately, his professional father, as well as highly valued friend—the Reverend Mr. Wilson; who, as Mr. Dimmesdale now conjectured, had been praying at the bedside of some dying man. And so he had. The good old minister came freshly from the death chamber of Governor Winthrop, who had passed from earth to heaven within that very hour. And now, surrounded, like the saintlike personages of olden times, with a radiant halo that glorified him amid this gloomy night of sin—as if the departed Governor had left him an inheritance of his glory, or as if he had caught upon himself the distant shine of the celestial city while looking thitherward to see the triumphant pilgrim pass within its gates—now, in short, good Father Wilson was moving homeward, aiding his footsteps with a lighted lantern! The glimmer of this luminary suggested the above conceits to Mr. Dimmesdale, who smiled—nay, almost laughed at them—and then wondered if he were going mad.

As the Reverend Mr. Wilson passed beside the scaffold, closely muffling his Geneva cloak about him with one arm and holding the lantern before his breast with the other, the minister could hardly restrain himself from speaking.

"A good evening to you, venerable Father Wilson! Come up hither, I pray you, and pass a pleasant hour with me!"

Good heavens! Had Mr. Dimmesdale actually spoken? For one instant, he believed that these words had passed his lips. But they were uttered only within his imagination. The venerable Father Wilson continued to step slowly onward, looking carefully at the muddy pathway before his feet, and never once turning his head towards the guilty platform. When the light of the glimmering lantern had faded quite away, the minister discovered, by the faintness which came over him, that the last few moments had been a crisis of terrible anxiety, although his mind had made an involuntary effort to relieve itself by a kind of lurid playfulness.

Shortly afterwards, the like grisly sense of the humorous again stole in among the solemn phantoms of his thought. He felt his limbs growing stiff with the unaccustomed chilliness of the night, and doubted whether he should be able to descend the steps of the scaffold. Morning would break, and find him there. The neighborhood would begin to rouse itself. The earliest riser, coming forth in the dim twilight, would perceive a vaguely defined figure aloft on the place of shame; and, half crazed betwixt alarm and curiosity, would go, knocking from door to door, summoning all the people to behold the ghost—as he needs must think it— of some defunct transgressor. A dusky tumult would flap its wings from one house to another. Then—the morning light still waxing stronger—old patriarchs would rise up in great haste, each in his flannel gown, and matronly dames, without pausing to put off their night-gear. The whole tribe of decorous personages, who had never heretofore been seen with a single hair of their heads awry, would start into public view with the disorder of a nightmare in their aspects. Old Governor Bellingham would come grimly forth with his King James' ruff fastened askew; and Mistress Hibbins, with some twigs of the forest clinging to her skirts, and looking sourer than ever, as having hardly got a wink of sleep after her night ride; and good Father Wilson, too, after spending half the night at a deathbed and liking ill to be disturbed, thus early, out of his dreams about the glorified saints. Hither, likewise, would come the elders and deacons of Mr. Dimmesdale's church, and the young virgins who so idolized their minister, and had made a shrine for him in their white bosoms; which now, by the by, in their hurry and confusion, they would scantly have given themselves time to cover with their kerchiefs. All people, in a word, would come stumbling over their thresholds, and turning up their amazed and horror-stricken visages around the scaffold. Whom would they discern there, with the red eastern light upon his brow? Whom, but the Reverend Arthur Dimmesdale, half frozen to death, overwhelmed with shame, and standing where Hester Prynne had stood!

Carried away by the grotesque horror of this picture, the minister, unawares, and to his own infinite alarm, burst into a great peal of laughter. It was immediately

responded to by a light, airy, childish laugh, in which
with a thrill of the heart—but he knew not whether of
exquisite pain, or pleasure as acute—he recognized the
tones of little Pearl.

"Pearl! Little Pearl!" cried he, after a moment's pause;
then, suppressing his voice, "Hester! Hester Prynne!
Are you there?"

"Yes; it is Hester Prynne!" she replied, in a tone of
surprise; and the minister heard her footsteps approaching from the sidewalk, along which she had been passing.
"It is I, and my little Pearl."

"Whence come you, Hester?" asked the minister.
"What sent you hither?"

"I have been watching at a deathbed," answered Hester
Prynne—"at Governor Winthrop's deathbed, and have
taken his measure for a robe, and am now going homeward to my dwelling."

"Come up hither, Hester, thou and little Pearl," said
the Reverend Mr. Dimmesdale. "Ye have both been
here before, but I was not with you. Come up hither
once again, and we will stand all three together!"

She silently ascended the steps, and stood on the
platform, holding little Pearl by the hand. The minister
felt for the child's other hand, and took it. The moment
that he did so, there came what seemed a tumultuous
rush of new life, other life than his own, pouring like
a torrent into his heart and hurrying through all his
veins, as if the mother and the child were communicating their vital warmth to his half-torpid system. The
three formed an electric chain.

"Minister!" whispered little Pearl.

"What wouldst thou say, child?" asked Mr. Dimmesdale.

"Wilt thou stand here with Mother and me, tomorrow
noontide?" inquired Pearl.

"Nay; not so, my little Pearl," answered the minister;
for, with the new energy of the moment, all the dread
of public exposure that had so long been the anguish
of his life had returned upon him; and he was already
trembling at the conjunction in which—with a strange
joy, nevertheless—he now found himself. "Not so, my

child. I shall, indeed, stand with thy mother and thee one other day, but not tomorrow."

Pearl laughed, and attempted to pull away her hand. But the minister held it fast.

"A moment longer, my child!" said he.

"But wilt thou promise," asked Pearl, "to take my hand, and Mother's hand, tomorrow noontide?"

"Not then, Pearl," said the minister, "but another time."

"And what other time?" persisted the child.

"At the great judgment day," whispered the minister —and, strangely enough, the sense that he was a professional teacher of the truth impelled him to answer the child so. "Then, and there, before the judgment seat, thy mother, and thou, and I, must stand together. But the daylight of this world shall not see our meeting!"

Pearl laughed again.

But, before Mr. Dimmesdale had done speaking, a light gleamed far and wide over all the muffled sky. It was doubtless caused by one of those meteors which the night-watcher may so often observe burning out to waste in the vacant regions of the atmosphere. So powerful was its radiance, that it thoroughly illuminated the dense medium of cloud betwixt the sky and earth. The great vault brightened, like the dome of an immense lamp. It showed the familiar scene of the street, with the distinctness of midday, but also with the awfulness that is always imparted to familiar objects by an unaccustomed light. The wooden houses, with their jutting stories and quaint gable peaks; the doorsteps and thresholds, with the early grass springing up about them; the garden plots, black with freshly turned earth; the wheeltrack, little worn, and, even in the market place, margined with green on either side—all were visible, but with a singularity of aspect that seemed to give another moral interpretation to the things of this world than they had ever borne before. And there stood the minister, with his hand over his heart; and Hester Prynne, with the embroidered letter glimmering on her bosom; and little Pearl, herself a symbol, and the connecting link between those two. They stood in the noon of that strange and solemn splendor as if it were the light that is to reveal all secrets and the daybreak that shall unite all who belong to one another.

There was witchcraft in little Pearl's eyes, and her face, as she glanced upward at the minister, wore that naughty smile which made its expression frequently so elvish. She withdrew her hand from Mr. Dimmesdale's and pointed across the street. But he clasped both his hands over his breast, and cast his eyes towards the zenith.

Nothing was more common in those days than to interpret all meteoric appearances, and other natural phenomena that occurred with less regularity than the rise and set of sun and moon, as so many revelations from a supernatural source. Thus, a blazing spear, a sword of flame, a bow, or a sheaf of arrows, seen in the midnight sky, prefigured Indian warfare. Pestilence was known to have been foreboded by a shower of crimson light. We doubt whether any marked event, for good or evil, ever befell New England, from its settlement down to Revolutionary times, of which the inhabitants had not been previously warned by some spectacle of this nature. Not seldom, it had been seen by multitudes. Oftener, however, its credibility rested on the faith of some lonely eyewitness, who beheld the wonder through the colored, magnifying, and distorting medium of his imagination, and shaped it more distinctly in his afterthought. It was, indeed, a majestic idea that the destiny of nations should be revealed, in these awful hieroglyphics, on the cope of heaven. A scroll so wide might not be deemed too expansive for Providence to write a people's doom upon. The belief was a favorite one with our forefathers, as betokening that their infant commonwealth was under a celestial guardianship of peculiar intimacy and strictness. But what shall we say when an individual discovers a revelation, addressed to himself alone, on the same vast sheet of record! In such a case, it could only be the symptom of a highly disordered mental state, when a man, rendered morbidly self-contemplative by long, intense, and secret pain, had extended his egotism over the whole expanse of nature, until the firmament itself should appear no more than a fitting page for his soul's history and fate!

We impute it, therefore, solely to the disease in his own eye and heart, that the minister, looking upward to the zenith, beheld there the appearance of an immense letter—the letter "A"—marked out in lines of dull red light. Not but the meteor may have shown itself at that point, burning duskily through a veil of cloud; but with no such shape as his guilty imagination gave it; or, at least, with so little definiteness, that another's guilt might have seen another symbol in it.

There was a singular circumstance that characterized Mr. Dimmesdale's psychological state at this moment. All the time that he gazed upward to the zenith, he was, nevertheless, perfectly aware that little Pearl was pointing her finger towards old Roger Chillingworth, who stood at no great distance from the scaffold. The minister appeared to see him with the same glance that discerned the miraculous letter. To his features, as to all other objects, the meteoric light imparted a new expression; or it might well be that the physician was not careful then, as at all other times, to hide the malevolence with which he looked upon his victim. Certainly, if the meteor kindled up the sky and disclosed the earth with an awfulness that admonished Hester Prynne and the clergyman of the day of judgment, then might Roger Chillingworth have passed with them for the archfiend, standing there with a smile and scowl, to claim his own. So vivid was the expression, or so intense the minister's perception of it, that it seemed still to remain painted on the darkness after the meteor had vanished, with an effect as if the street and all things else were at once annihilated.

"Who is that man, Hester?" gasped Mr. Dimmesdale, overcome with terror. "I shiver at him! Dost thou know the man? I hate him, Hester!"

She remembered her oath, and was silent.

"I tell thee, my soul shivers at him!" muttered the minister again. "Who is he? Who is he? Canst thou do nothing for me? I have a nameless horror of the man!"

"Minister," said little Pearl, "I can tell thee who he is!"

"Quickly, then, child!" said the minister, bending

his ear close to her lips. "Quickly!—and as low as thou canst whisper."

Pearl mumbled something into his ear that sounded, indeed, like human language, but was only such gibberish as children may be heard amusing themselves with by the hour together. At all events, if it involved any secret information in regard to old Roger Chillingworth, it was in a tongue unknown to the erudite clergyman, and did but increase the bewilderment of his mind. The elvish child then laughed aloud.

"Dost thou mock me now?" said the minister.

"Thou wast not bold!—thou wast not true!" answered the child. "Thou wouldst not promise to take my hand, and Mother's hand, tomorrow noontide!"

"Worthy Sir," answered the physician, who had now advanced to the foot of the platform. "Pious Master Dimmesdale! can this be you? Well, well, indeed! We men of study, whose heads are in our books, have need to be straitly looked after! We dream in our waking moments, and walk in our sleep. Come, good Sir, and my dear friend, I pray you, let me lead you home!"

"How knewest thou that I was here?" asked the minister, fearfully.

"Verily, and in good faith," answered Roger Chillingworth, "I knew nothing of the matter. I had spent the better part of the night at the bedside of the worshipful Governor Winthrop, doing what my poor skill might to give him ease. He going home to a better world, I, likewise, was on my way homeward, when this strange light shone out. Come with me, I beseech you, Reverend Sir; else you will be poorly able to do Sabbath duty tomorrow. Aha! see now, how they trouble the brain—these books!—these books! You should study less, good Sir, and take a little pastime; or these night-whimseys will grow upon you."

"I will go home with you," said Mr. Dimmesdale.

With a chill despondency, like one awaking all nerveless from an ugly dream, he yielded himself to the physician, and was led away.

The next day, however, being the Sabbath, he preached a discourse which was held to be the richest and most powerful, and the most replete with heavenly influences, that had ever proceeded from his lips. Souls, it is said, more souls than one, were brought to the truth by the efficacy of that sermon, and vowed within themselves to cherish a holy gratitude towards Mr. Dimmesdale throughout the long hereafter. But, as he came down the pulpit steps, the gray-bearded sexton met him, holding up a black glove, which the minister recognized as his own.

"It was found," said the sexton, "this morning, on the scaffold where evil-doers are set up to public shame. Satan dropped it there, I take it, intending a scurrilous jest against your reverence. But, indeed, he was blind and foolish, as he ever and always is. A pure hand needs no glove to cover it!"

"Thank you, my good friend," said the minister, gravely, but startled at heart; for, so confused was his remembrance, that he had almost brought himself to look at the events of the past night as visionary. "Yes, it seems to be my glove, indeed!"

"And, since Satan saw fit to steal it, your reverence must needs handle him without gloves, henceforward," remarked the old sexton, grimly smiling. "But did your reverence hear of the portent that was seen last night?—a great red letter in the sky—the letter 'A' which we interpret to stand for 'Angel.' For, as our good Governor Winthrop was made an angel this past night, it was doubtless held fit that there should be some notice thereof!"

"No," answered the minister, "I had not heard of it."

13

ANOTHER VIEW OF HESTER

IN HER LATE SINGULAR INTERVIEW with Mr.
Dimmesdale, Hester Prynne was shocked at
the condition to which she found the clergyman reduced.
His nerve seemed absolutely destroyed. His moral force
was abased into more than childish weakness. It grovelled
helpless on the ground, even while his intellectual faculties retained their pristine strength, or had perhaps
acquired a morbid energy, which disease only could have
given them. With her knowledge of a train of circumstances hidden from all others, she could readily infer
that, besides the legitimate action of his own conscience,
a terrible machinery had been brought to bear, and was
still operating, on Mr. Dimmesdale's well-being and
repose. Knowing what this poor, fallen man had once
been, her whole soul was moved by the shuddering terror
with which he had appealed to her—the outcast woman
—for support against his instinctively discovered enemy.
She decided, moreover, that he had a right to her utmost
aid. Little accustomed, in her long seclusion from society,
to measure her ideas of right and wrong by any standard
external to herself, Hester saw—or seemed to see—that
there lay a responsibility upon her in reference to the
clergyman which she owed to no other, nor to the whole
world besides. The links that united her to the rest of
human kind—links of flowers, or silk, or gold, or whatever
the material—had all been broken. Here was the iron link
of mutual crime, which neither he nor she could break.

Like all other ties, it brought along with it its obligations.

Hester Prynne did not now occupy precisely the same position in which we beheld her during the earlier periods of her ignominy. Years had come and gone. Pearl was now seven years old. Her mother, with the scarlet letter on her breast, glittering in its fantastic embroidery, had long been a familiar object to the townspeople. As is apt to be the case when a person stands out in any prominence before the community, and, at the same time, interferes neither with public nor individual interests and convenience, a species of general regard had ultimately grown up in reference to Hester Prynne. It is to the credit of human nature, that, except where its selfishness is brought into play, it loves more readily than it hates. Hatred, by a gradual and quiet process, will even be transformed to love, unless the change be impeded by a continually new irritation of the original feeling of hostility. In this matter of Hester Prynne, there was neither irritation nor irksomeness. She never battled with the public, but submitted uncomplainingly to its worst usage; she made no claim upon it in requital for what she suffered; she did not weigh upon its sympathies. Then, also, the blameless purity of her life during all these years in which she had been set apart to infamy was reckoned largely in her favor. With nothing now to lose in the sight of mankind, and with no hope, and seemingly no wish, of gaining anything, it could only be a genuine regard for virtue that had brought back the poor wanderer to its paths.

It was perceived, too, that while Hester never put forward even the humblest title to share in the world's privileges—further than to breathe the common air, and earn daily bread for little Pearl and herself by the faithful labor of her hands—she was quick to acknowledge her sisterhood with the race of man, whenever benefits were to be conferred. None so ready as she to give of her little substance to every demand of poverty; even though the bitter-hearted pauper threw back a gibe in requital of the food brought regularly to his door, or the garments wrought for him by the fingers that could have embroidered a monarch's robe. None so self-devoted as Hester, when pestilence stalked through the town. In all seasons of calamity, indeed, whether general or of individuals, the outcast of society at once found her place. She came, not as a guest, but as a rightful inmate, into the household that was darkened by trouble, as if its gloomy twilight were a medium in which she was entitled to hold intercourse with her fellow-creatures. There glimmered the embroidered letter, with comfort in its unearthly ray. Elsewhere the token of sin, it was the taper of the sick-chamber. It had even thrown its gleam, in the sufferer's hard extremity, across the verge of time. It had shown him where to set his foot, while the light of earth was fast becoming dim, and ere the light of futurity could reach him. In such emergencies, Hester's nature showed itself warm and rich; a wellspring of human tenderness, unfailing to every real demand, and inexhaustible by the largest. Her breast, with its badge of shame, was but the softer pillow for the head that needed one. She was self-ordained a Sister of Mercy; or, we may rather say, the world's heavy hand had so ordained her, when neither the world nor she looked forward to this result. The letter was the symbol of her calling. Such helpfulness was found in her—so much power to do and power to sympathize—that many people refused to interpret the scarlet "A" by its original signification. They said that it meant "Able"; so strong was Hester Prynne, with a woman's strength.

It was only the darkened house that could contain her. When sunshine came again, she was not there. Her shadow had faded across the threshold. The helpful inmate had departed, without one backward glance to gather up the meed of gratitude, if any were in the hearts of those whom she had served so zealously. Meeting them in the street, she never raised her head to receive their greeting. If they were resolute to accost her, she laid her finger on the scarlet letter, and passed on. This might be pride, but was so like humility, that it produced all the softening influence of the latter quality on the public mind. The public is despotic in its temper; it is capable of denying common justice when too strenuously demanded as a right; but quite as frequently it awards more than justice when the appeal is made, as despots love to have it made, entirely to its generosity. Interpreting

Hester Prynne's deportment as an appeal of this nature, society was inclined to show its former victim a more benign countenance than she cared to be favored with, or, perchance, than she deserved.

The rulers, and the wise and learned men of the community, were longer in acknowledging the influence of Hester's good qualities than the people. The prejudices which they shared in common with the latter were fortified in themselves by an iron framework of reasoning, that made it a far tougher labor to expel them. Day by day, nevertheless, their sour and rigid wrinkles were relaxing into something which, in the due course of years, might grow to be an expression of almost benevolence. Thus it was with the men of rank, on whom their eminent position imposed the guardianship of the public morals. Individuals in private life, meanwhile, had quite forgiven Hester Prynne for her frailty; nay, more, they had begun to look upon the scarlet letter as the token, not of that one sin, for which she had borne so long and dreary a penance, but of her many good deeds since. "Do you see that woman with the embroidered badge?" they would say to strangers. "It is our Hester—the town's own Hester—who is so kind to the poor, so helpful to the sick, so comforting to the afflicted!" Then, it is true, the propensity of human nature to tell the very worst of itself, when embodied in the person of another, would constrain them to whisper the black scandal of bygone years. It was none the less a fact, however, that, in the eyes of the very men who spoke thus, the scarlet letter had the effect of the cross on a nun's bosom. It imparted to the wearer a kind of sacredness which enabled her to walk securely amid all peril. Had she fallen among thieves, it would have kept her safe. It was reported, and believed by many, that an Indian had drawn his arrow against the badge, and that the missile struck it, but fell harmless to the ground.

The effect of the symbol—or, rather, of the position in respect to society that was indicated by it—on the mind of Hester Prynne herself was powerful and peculiar. All the light and graceful foliage of her character had been withered up by this red-hot brand, and had long ago fallen away, leaving a bare and harsh outline which

might have been repulsive, had she possessed friends
or companions to be repelled by it. Even the attractive-
ness of her person had undergone a similar change. It
might be partly owing to the studied austerity of her
dress, and partly to the lack of demonstration in her
manners. It was a sad transformation, too, that her rich
and luxuriant hair had either been cut off, or was so
completely hidden by a cap, that not a shining lock of
it ever once gushed into the sunshine. It was due in part
to all these causes, but still more to something else,
that there seemed to be no longer anything in Hester's
face for Love to dwell upon; nothing in Hester's form,
though majestic and statue-like, that Passion would ever
dream of clasping in its embrace; nothing in Hester's
bosom to make it ever again the pillow of Affection.
Some attribute had departed from her, the permanence
of which had been essential to keep her a woman. Such
is frequently the fate, and such the stern development,
of the feminine character and person, when the woman
has encountered, and lived through, an experience of
peculiar severity. If she be all tenderness, she will die.
If she survive, the tenderness will either be crushed out
of her, or—and the outward semblance is the same—
crushed so deeply into her heart that it can never show
itself more. The latter is perhaps the truest theory. She
who has once been woman, and ceased to be so, might
at any moment become a woman again, if there were
only the magic touch to effect the transfiguration. We
shall see whether Hester Prynne were ever afterwards
so touched, and transfigured.

Much of the marble coldness of Hester's impression
was to be attributed to the circumstance that her life
had turned, in a great measure, from passion and feeling
to thought. Standing alone in the world—alone, as to
any dependence on society, and with little Pearl to be
guided and protected—alone, and hopeless of retrieving
her position, even had she not scorned to consider it desirable—she cast away the fragments of a broken chain.
The world's law was no law for her mind. It was an age
in which the human intellect, newly emancipated, had
taken a more active and a wider range than for many centuries before. Men of the sword had overthrown nobles

and kings. Men bolder than these had overthrown and re-arranged—not actually, but within the sphere of theory, which was their most real abode—the whole system of ancient prejudice, wherewith was linked much of ancient principle. Hester Prynne imbibed this spirit. She assumed a freedom of speculation, then common enough on the other side of the Atlantic, but which our fore-fathers, had they known it, would have held to be a deadlier crime than that stigmatized by the scarlet letter. In her lonesome cottage by the seashore, thoughts visited her, such as dared to enter no other dwelling in New England; shadowy guests that would have been as perilous as demons to their entertainer, could they have been seen so much as knocking at her door.

It is remarkable that persons who speculate the most boldly often conform with the most perfect quietude to the external regulations of society. The thought suffices them, without investing itself in the flesh and blood of action. So it seemed to be with Hester. Yet, had little Pearl never come to her from the spiritual world, it might have been far otherwise. Then, she might have come down to us in history, hand in hand with Ann Hutchin-son, as the foundress of a religious sect. She might, in one of her phases, have been a prophetess. She might, and not improbably would, have suffered death from the stern tribunals of the period for attempting to un-dermine the foundations of the Puritan establishment. But, in the education of her child, the mother's en-thusiasm of thought had something to wreak itself upon. Providence, in the person of this little girl, had assigned to Hester's charge the germ and blossom of womanhood, to be cherished and developed amid a host of difficulties. Everything was against her. The world was hostile. The child's own nature had something wrong in it which continually betokened that she had been born amiss—the effluence of her mother's lawless passion—and often impelled Hester to ask, in bitterness of heart, whether it were for ill or good that the poor little creature had been born at all.

Indeed, the same dark question often rose into her mind with reference to the whole race of womanhood. Was existence worth accepting, even to the happiest

among them? As concerned her own individual existence,
she had long ago decided in the negative, and dismissed
the point as settled. A tendency to speculation, though
it may keep woman quiet, as it does man, yet makes
her sad. She discerns, it may be, such a hopeless task
before her. As a first step, the whole system of society
is to be torn down and built up anew. Then, the very
nature of the opposite sex, or its long hereditary habit
which has become like nature, is to be essentially modified before woman can be allowed to assume what seems
a fair and suitable position. Finally, all other difficulties
being obviated, woman cannot take advantage of these
preliminary reforms until she herself shall have undergone a still mightier change; in which, perhaps, the
ethereal essence, wherein she has her truest life, will be
found to have evaporated. A woman never overcomes
these problems by any exercise of thought. They are not
to be solved, or only in one way. If her heart chance to
come uppermost, they vanish. Thus, Hester Prynne,
whose heart had lost its regular and healthy throb,
wandered without a clew in the dark labyrinth of mind;
now turned aside by an insurmountable precipice; now
starting back from a deep chasm. There was wild and
ghastly scenery all around her, and a home and comfort
nowhere. At times, a fearful doubt strove to possess her
soul, whether it were not better to send Pearl at once
to heaven, and go herself to such futurity as Eternal
Justice should provide.

The scarlet letter had not done its office.

Now, however, her interview with the Reverend Mr.
Dimmesdale on the night of his vigil had given her a
new theme of reflection, and held up to her an object
that appeared worthy of any exertion and sacrifice for
its attainment. She had witnessed the intense misery
beneath which the minister struggled, or, to speak more
accurately, had ceased to struggle. She saw that he stood
on the verge of lunacy, if he had not already stepped
across it. It was impossible to doubt, that, whatever painful efficacy there might be in the secret sting of remorse,
a deadlier venom had been infused into it by the hand
that proffered relief. A secret enemy had been continually
by his side, under the semblance of a friend and helper,

and had availed himself of the opportunities thus afforded for tampering with the delicate springs of Mr. Dimmesdale's nature. Hester could not but ask herself whether there had not originally been a defect of truth, courage and loyalty on her own part in allowing the minister to be thrown into a position where so much evil was to be foreboded, and nothing auspicious to be hoped. Her only justification lay in the fact that she had been able to discern no method of rescuing him from the blacker ruin than had overwhelmed herself, except by acquiescing in Roger Chillingworth's scheme of disguise. Under that impulse, she had made her choice, and had chosen, as it now appeared, the more wretched alternative of the two. She determined to redeem her error, so far as it might yet be possible. Strengthened by years of hard and solemn trial, she felt herself no longer so inadequate to cope with Roger Chillingworth as on that night, abased by sin, and half maddened by the ignomity that was still new, when they had talked together in the prison chamber. She had climbed her way, since then, to a higher point. The old man, on the other hand, had brought himself nearer to her level, or perhaps below it, by the revenge which he had stooped for.

In fine, Hester Prynne resolved to meet her former husband, and do what might be in her power for the rescue of the victim on whom he had so evidently set his gripe. The occasion was not long to seek. One afternoon, walking with Pearl in a retired part of the peninsula, she beheld the old physician, with a basket on one arm and a staff in the other hand, stooping along the ground, in quest of roots and herbs to concoct his medicines withal.

14

HESTER AND THE PHYSICIAN

Hester bade little Pearl run down to the margin of the water and play with the shells and tangled seaweed, until she should have talked awhile with yonder gatherer of herbs. So the child flew away like a bird, and, making bare her small white feet, went pattering along the moist margin of the sea. Here and there she came to a full stop, and peeped curiously into a pool, left by the retiring tide as a mirror for Pearl to see her face in. Forth peeped at her, out of the pool, with dark, glistening curls around her head and an elf-smile in her eyes, the image of a little maid, whom Pearl, having no other playmate, invited to take her hand and run a race with her. But the visionary little maid, on her part, beckoned likewise, as if to say—"This is a better place! Come thou into the pool!" And Pearl, stepping in, mid-leg deep, beheld her own white feet at the bottom, while, out of a still lower depth, came the gleam of a kind of fragmentary smile, floating to and fro in the agitated water.

Meanwhile, her mother had accosted the physician.

"I would speak a word with you," said she, "a word that concerns us much."

"Aha! and is it Mistress Hester that has a word for old Roger Chillingworth?" answered he, raising himself from his stooping posture. "With all my heart! Why, Mistress, I hear good tidings of you, on all hands! No longer ago than yester-eve, a magistrate, a wise and godly man, was discoursing of your affairs, Mistress Hester, and whispered me that there had been question concerning you in the council. It was debated whether or no, with safety to the common weal, yonder scarlet letter might be taken off your bosom. On my life, Hester, I made my entreaty to the worshipful magistrate that it might be done forthwith!"

"It lies not in the pleasure of the magistrates to take off this badge," calmly replied Hester. "Were I worthy to be quit of it, it would fall away of its own nature, or be transformed into something that should speak a different purport."

"Nay, then, wear it, if it suit you better," rejoined he. "A woman must needs follow her own fancy, touching the adornment of her person. The letter is gayly embroidered, and shows right bravely on your bosom!"

All this while, Hester had been looking steadily at the old man, and was shocked, as well as wonder-smitten, to discern what a change had been wrought upon him within the past seven years. It was not so much that he had grown older; for though the traces of advancing life were visible, he bore his age well and seemed to retain a wiry vigor and alertness. But the former aspect of an intellectual and studious man, calm and quiet, which was what she best remembered in him, had altogether vanished and been succeeded by an eager, searching, almost fierce, yet carefully guarded look. It seemed to be his wish and purpose to mask this expression with a smile; but the latter played him false, and flickered over his visage so derisively, that the spectator could see his blackness all the better for it. Ever and anon, too, there came a glare of red light out of his eyes; as if the old man's soul were on fire, and kept on smouldering duskily within his breast, until, by some casual puff of passion, it was blown into a momentary flame. This he repressed, as speedily as possible, and strove to look as if nothing of the kind had happened.

In a word, old Roger Chillingworth was a striking evidence of man's faculty of transforming himself into a devil, if he will only, for a reasonable space of time, undertake a devil's office. This unhappy person had effected such a transformation by devoting himself, for seven years, to the constant analysis of a heart full of torture, and deriving his enjoyment thence, and adding fuel to those fiery tortures which he analyzed and gloated over.

The scarlet letter burned on Hester Prynne's bosom. Here was another ruin, the responsibility of which came partly home to her.

"What see you in my face," asked the physician, "that you look at it so earnestly?"

"Something that would make me weep, if there were any tears bitter enough for it," answered she. "But let it pass! It is of yonder miserable man that I would speak."

"And what of him?" cried Roger Chillingworth, eagerly, as if he loved the topic, and were glad of an opportunity to discuss it with the only person of whom he could make a confidant. "Not to hide the truth, Mistress Hester, my thoughts happen just now to be busy with the gentleman. So speak freely; and I will make answer."

"When we last spake together," said Hester, "now seven years ago, it was your pleasure to extort a promise of secrecy, as touching the former relation betwixt yourself and me. As the life and good fame of yonder man were in your hands, there seemed no choice to me save to be silent, in accordance with your behest. Yet it was not without heavy misgivings that I thus bound myself; for, having cast off all duty towards other human beings, there remained a duty towards him; and something whispered me that I was betraying it in pledging myself to keep your counsel. Since that day, no man is so near to him as you. You tread behind his every footstep. You are beside him, sleeping and waking. You search his thoughts. You burrow and rankle in his heart! Your clutch is on his life, and you cause him to die daily a living death; and still he knows you not. In permitting this, I have surely acted a false part by the only man to whom the power was left me to be true!"

"What choice had you?" asked Roger Chillingworth. "My finger, pointed at this man, would have hurled him from his pulpit into a dungeon—thence, peradventure, to the gallows!"

"It had been better so!" said Hester Prynne.

"What evil have I done the man?" asked Roger Chillingworth again. "I tell thee, Hester Prynne, the richest fee that ever physician earned from monarch could not have bought such care as I have wasted on this miserable priest! But for my aid, his life would have burned away in torments within the first two years after the perpetration of his crime and thine. For, Hester, his spirit lacked the strength that could have borne up, as thine has, beneath a burden like thy scarlet letter. O, I could reveal a goodly secret! But enough! What art can do, I have exhausted on him. That he now breathes, and creeps about on earth, is owing all to me!"

"Better he had died at once!" said Hester Prynne.

"Yea, woman, thou sayest truly!" cried old Roger Chillingworth, letting the lurid fire of his heart blaze out before her eyes. "Better had he died at once! Never did mortal suffer what this man has suffered. And all, all, in the sight of his worst enemy! He has been conscious of me. He has felt an influence dwelling always upon him like a curse. He knew, by some spiritual sense— for the Creator never made another being so sensitive as this—he knew that no friendly hand was pulling at his heart-strings, and that an eye was looking curiously into him, which sought only evil, and found it. But he knew not that the eye and hand were mine! With the superstition common to his brotherhood, he fancied himself given over to a fiend, to be tortured with frightful dreams, and desperate thoughts, the sting of remorse, and despair of pardon, as a foretaste of what awaits him beyond the grave. But it was the constant shadow of my presence!—the closest propinquity of the man whom he had most vilely wronged!—and who had grown to exist only by this perpetual poison of the direst revenge! Yea, indeed!—he did not err!—there was a fiend at his elbow! A mortal man, with once a human heart, has become a fiend for his especial torment!"

The unfortunate physician, while uttering these words, lifted his hands with a look of horror, as if he had beheld some frightful shape, which he could not recognize, usurping the place of his own image in a glass. It was one of those moments—which sometimes occur only at the interval of years—when a man's moral aspect is faithfully revealed to his mind's eye. Not improbably, he had never before viewed himself as he did now.

"Hast thou not tortured him enough?" said Hester, noticing the old man's look. "Has he not paid thee all?"

"No!—no!—He has but increased the debt!" answered the physician; and as he proceeded, his manner lost its fiercer characteristics and subsided into gloom. "Dost thou remember me, Hester, as I was nine years agone? Even then, I was in the autumn of my days, nor was it the early autumn. But all my life had been made up of earnest, studious, thoughtful, quiet years, bestowed faithfully for the increase of mine own knowledge, and faithfully, too, though this latter object was but casual to the other—faithfully for the advancement of human welfare. No life had been more peaceful and innocent than mine; few lives so rich with benefits conferred. Dost thou remember me? Was I not, though you might deem me cold, nevertheless a man thoughtful for others, craving little for himself—kind, true, just, and of constant if not warm affections? Was I not all this?"

"All this, and more," said Hester.

"And what am I now?" demanded he, looking into her face, and permitting the whole evil within him to be written on his features. "I have already told thee what I am! A fiend! Who made me so?"

"It was myself!" cried Hester, shuddering. "It was I, not less than he. Why hast thou not avenged thyself on me?"

"I have left thee to the scarlet letter," replied Roger Chillingworth. "If that have not avenged me, I can do no more!"

He laid his finger on it, with a smile.

"It has avenged thee!" answered Hester Prynne.

"I judged no less," said the physician. "And now, what wouldst thou with me touching this man?"

"I must reveal the secret," answered Hester, firmly. "He must discern thee in thy true character. What may be the result, I know not. But this long debt of confidence, due from me to him, whose bane and ruin I have been, shall at length be paid. So far as concerns the overthrow or preservation of his fair fame and his earthly state, and perchance his life, he is in thy hands. Nor do I—whom the scarlet letter has disciplined to truth, though it be the truth of red-hot iron, entering into the soul—nor do I perceive such advantages in his living any longer a life of ghastly emptiness, that I shall stoop to implore thy mercy. Do with him as thou wilt! There is no good for him—no good for me—no good for thee! There is no good for little Pearl! There is no path to guide us out of this dismal maze!"

"Woman, I could well-nigh pity thee!" said Roger Chillingworth, unable to restrain a thrill of admiration too; for there was a quality almost majestic in the despair which she expressed. "Thou hadst great elements. Peradventure, hadst thou met earlier with a better love than mine, this evil had not been. I pity thee, for the good that has been wasted in thy nature!"

"And I thee," answered Hester Prynne, "for the hatred that has transformed a wise and just man to a fiend! Wilt thou yet purge it out of thee, and be once more human? If not for his sake, then doubly for thine own! Forgive, and leave his further retribution to the Power that claims it! I said, but now, that there could be no good event for him, or thee, or me, who are here wandering together in this gloomy maze of evil, and stumbling at every step over the guilt wherewith we have strewn our path. It is not so! There might be good for thee, and thee alone, since thou hast been deeply wronged, and hast it at thy will to pardon. Wilt thou give up that only privilege? Wilt thou reject that priceless benefit?"

"Peace, Hester, peace!" replied the old man, with gloomy sternness. "It is not granted me to pardon. I have no such power as thou tellest me of. My old faith, long forgotten, comes back to me, and explains all that we do, and all we suffer. By thy first step awry, thou didst plant the germ of evil; but since that moment, it has all been a dark necessity. Ye that have wronged me are not sinful, save in a kind of typical illusion; neither am I fiendlike, who have snatched a fiend's office from his hands. It is our fate. Let the black flower blossom as it may. Now go thy ways, and deal as thou wilt with yonder man."

He waved his hand, and betook himself again to his employment of gathering herbs.

15

HESTER AND PEARL

So ROGER CHILLINGWORTH—a deformed old figure, with a face that haunted men's memories longer than they liked—took leave of Hester Prynne, and went stooping away along the earth. He gathered here and there an herb, or grubbed up a root, and put it into the basket on his arm. His gray beard almost touched the ground, as he crept onward. Hester gazed after him a little while, looking with a half-fantastic curiosity to see whether the tender grass of early spring would not be blighted beneath him and show the wavering track of his footsteps, sere and brown, across its cheerful verdure. She wondered what sort of herbs they were, which the old man was so sedulous to gather. Would not the earth, quickened to an evil purpose by the sympathy of his eye, greet him with poisonous shrubs, of species hitherto unknown, that would start up under his fingers? Or might it suffice him, that every wholesome growth should be converted into something deleterious and malignant at his touch? Did the sun, which shone so brigl.tly everywhere else, really fall upon him? Or was there, as it rather seemed, a circle of ominous shadow moving along with his deformity, whichever way he turned himself? And whither was he now going? Would he not suddenly sink into the earth, leaving a barren and blasted spot, where, in due course of time, would be seen deadly nightshade, dogwood, henbane, and whatever else of vegetable wickedness the climate could produce, all flourishing with hideous luxuriance? Or would he spread bat's wings and flee away, looking so much the uglier, the higher he rose towards heaven?

"Be it sin or no," said Hester Prynne, bitterly, as she still gazed after him, "I hate the man!"

She upbraided herself for the sentiment, but could not overcome or lessen it. Attempting to do so, she thought of those long-past days in a distant land, when he used to emerge at eventide from the seclusion of his study and sit down in the firelight of their home, and in the light of her nuptial smile. He needed to bask himself in that smile, he said, in order that the chill of so many lonely hours among his books might be taken off the scholar's heart. Such scenes had once appeared not otherwise than happy, but now, as viewed through the dismal medium of her subsequent life, they classed themselves among her ugliest remembrances. She marvelled how such scenes could have been! She marvelled how she could ever have been wrought upon to marry him! She deemed it her crime most to be repented of, that she had ever endured, and reciprocated, the luke-warm grasp of his hand, and had suffered the smile of her lips and eyes to mingle and melt into his own. And it seemed a fouler offence committed by Roger Chillingworth than any which had since been done him, that, in the time when her heart knew no better, he had persuaded her to fancy herself happy by his side.

"Yes, I hate him!" repeated Hester, more bitterly than before. "He betrayed me! He has done me worse wrong than I did him!"

Let men tremble to win the hand of woman, unless they win along with it the utmost passion of her heart! Else it may be their miserable fortune, as it was Roger Chillingworth's, when some mightier touch than their own may have awakened all her sensibilities, to be reproached even for the calm content, the marble image of happiness, which they will have imposed upon her as the warm reality. But Hester ought long ago to have done with this injustice. What did it betoken? Had seven long years, under the torture of the scarlet letter, inflicted so much of misery and wrought out no repentance?

The emotions of that brief space, while she stood gazing after the crooked figure of old Roger Chillingworth, threw a dark light on Hester's state of mind, revealing much that she might not otherwise have acknowledged to herself.

He being gone, she summoned back her child.

"Pearl! Little Pearl! Where are you?"

Pearl, whose activity of spirit never flagged, had been at no loss for amusement while her mother talked with the old gatherer of herbs. At first, as already told, she had flirted fancifully with her own image in a pool of water, beckoning the phantom forth, and—as it declined to venture—seeking a passage for herself into its sphere of impalpable earth and unattainable sky. Soon finding, however, that either she or the image was unreal, she turned elsewhere for better pastime. She made little boats out of birch-bark, and freighted them with snail shells, and sent out more ventures on the mighty deep than any merchant in New England; but the larger part of them foundered near the shore. She seized a live horseshoe by the tail, and made prize of several five-fingers, and laid out a jellyfish to melt in the warm sun. Then she took up the white foam that streaked the line of the advancing tide, and threw it upon the breeze, scampering after it with winged footsteps to catch the great snowflakes ere they fell. Perceiving a flock of beach birds that fed and fluttered along the shore, the naughty child picked up her apron full of pebbles, and, creeping from rock to rock after these small seafowl, displayed remarkable dexterity in pelting them. One little gray bird with a white breast, Pearl was almost sure, had been hit by a pebble, and fluttered away with a broken wing. But then the elf-child sighed, and gave up her sport; because it grieved her to have done harm to a little being that was as wild as the sea breeze, or as wild as Pearl herself.

Her final employment was to gather seaweed of various

kinds and make herself a scarf, or mantle, and a head-dress, and thus assume the aspect of a little mermaid. She inherited her mother's gift for devising drapery and costume. As the last touch to her mermaid's garb, Pearl took some eelgrass, and imitated, as best she could, on her own bosom, the decoration with which she was so familiar on her mother's. A letter—the letter "A"—but freshly green, instead of scarlet! The child bent her chin upon her breast, and contemplated this device with strange interest; even as if the one only thing for which she had been sent into the world was to make out its hidden import.

"I wonder if Mother will ask me what it means?" thought Pearl.

Just then she heard her mother's voice, and flitting along as lightly as one of the little sea birds, appeared before Hester Prynne, dancing, laughing, and pointing her finger to the ornament upon her bosom.

"My little Pearl!" said Hester, after a moment's silence, "the green letter, and on thy childish bosom, has no purport. But dost thou know, my child, what this letter means which thy mother is doomed to wear?"

"Yes, Mother," said the child. "It is the great letter 'A.' Thou hast taught me in the hornbook."

Hester looked steadily into her little face; but, though there was that singular expression which she had so often remarked in her black eyes, she could not satisfy herself whether Pearl really attached any meaning to the symbol. She felt a morbid desire to ascertain the point.

"Dost thou know, child, wherefore thy mother wears this letter?"

"Truly do I!" answered Pearl, looking brightly into her mother's face. "It is for the same reason that the minister keeps his hand over his heart!"

"And what reason is that?" asked Hester, half smiling at the absurd incongruity of the child's observation; but, on second thoughts, turning pale. "What has the letter to do with any heart, save mine?"

"Nay, Mother, I have told all I know," said Pearl more seriously than she was wont to speak. "Ask yonder old man whom thou hast been talking with! It may be he can tell. But in good earnest now, Mother dear, what does this scarlet letter mean?—and why dost thou wear it on thy bosom?—and why does the minister keep his hand over his heart?"

She took her mother's hand in both her own, and gazed into her eyes with an earnestness that was seldom seen in her wild and capricious character. The thought occurred to Hester that the child might really be seeking to approach her with childlike confidence, and doing what she could, and as intelligently as she knew how, to establish a meeting point of sympathy. It showed Pearl in an unwonted aspect. Heretofore, the mother, while loving her child with the intensity of a sole affection, had schooled herself to hope for little other return than the waywardness of an April breeze, which spends its time in airy sport, and has its gusts of inexplicable passion, and is petulant in its best of moods, and chills oftener than caresses you, when you take it to your bosom; in requital of which misdemeanors, it will sometimes, of its own vague purpose, kiss your cheek with a kind of doubtful tenderness, and play gently with your hair, and then be gone about its other idle business, leaving a dreamy pleasure at your heart. And this, moreover, was a mother's estimate of the child's disposition. Any other observer might have seen few but unamiable traits, and have given them a far darker coloring. But now the idea came strongly into Hester's mind that Pearl, with her remarkable precocity and acuteness, might already have approached the age when she could be made a friend, and intrusted with as much of a mother's sorrow as could be imparted, without irreverence either to the parent or the child. In the little chaos of Pearl's character, there might be seen emerging—and could have been, from the very first—the steadfast principles of an unflinching courage—an uncontrollable will—a sturdy pride, which might be disciplined into self-respect—and a bitter scorn of many things, which, when examined, might be found to have the taint of falsehood in them. She possessed affections, too, though hitherto acrid and disagreeable as are the richest flavors of unripe fruit. With all these sterling attributes, thought Hester, the evil which she inherited from her mother must be great indeed, if a noble woman do not grow out of this elfish child.

Pearl's inevitable tendency to hover about the enigma of the scarlet letter seemed an innate quality of her being. From the earliest epoch of her conscious life, she had entered upon this as her appointed mission. Hester had often fancied that Providence had a design of justice and retribution, in endowing the child with this marked propensity; but never, until now, had she bethought herself to ask, whether, linked with that design, there might not likewise be a purpose of mercy and beneficence. If little Pearl were entertained with faith and trust, as a spirit messenger no less than an earthly child, might it not be her errand to soothe away the sorrow that lay cold in her mother's heart, and converted it into a tomb?—and to help her to overcome the passion, once so wild, and even yet neither dead nor asleep, but only imprisoned within the same tomb-like heart?

Such were some of the thoughts that now stirred in Hester's mind, with as much vivacity of impression as if they had actually been whispered into her ear. And there was little Pearl, all this while, holding her mother's hand in both her own, and turning her face upward, while she put these searching questions, once, and again, and still a third time.

"What does the letter mean, Mother?—and why dost thou wear it?—and why does the minister keep his hand over his heart?"

"What shall I say?" thought Hester to herself. "No! If this be the price of the child's sympathy, I cannot pay it."

Then she spoke aloud.

"Silly Pearl," said she, "what questions are these? There are many things in this world that a child must not ask about. What know I of the minister's heart? And as for the scarlet letter, I wear it for the sake of its gold thread."

In all the seven bygone years, Hester Prynne had never before been false to the symbol on her bosom. It may be that it was the talisman of a stern and severe, but yet a guardian spirit, who now forsook her, as recognizing that, in spite of his strict watch over her heart, some new evil had crept into it, or some old one had never been expelled. As for little Pearl, the earnestness soon passed out of her face.

But the child did not see fit to let the matter drop. Two or three times, as her mother and she went home- ward, and as often at suppertime, and while Hester was putting her to bed, and once after she seemed to be fairly asleep, Pearl looked up, with mischief gleaming in her black eyes.

"Mother," said she, "what does the scarlet letter mean?"

And the next morning, the first indication the child gave of being awake was by popping up her head from the pillow and making that other inquiry, which she had so unaccountably connected with her investigations about the scarlet letter:

"Mother!—Mother!—Why does the minister keep his hand over his heart?"

"Hold thy tongue, naughty child!" answered her mother, with an asperity that she had never permitted to herself before. "Do not tease me; else I shall shut thee into the dark closet!"

16

A FOREST WALK

HESTER PRYNNE REMAINED CONSTANT in her re- solve to make known to Mr. Dimmesdale, at whatever risk of present pain or ulterior consequences, the true character of the man who had crept into his intimacy. For several days, however, she vainly sought an opportunity of addressing him in some of the meditative walks which she knew him to be in the habit of taking, along the shores of the peninsula, or on the wooded hills of the neighboring country. There would have been no scandal, indeed, nor peril to the holy whiteness of the clergyman's good fame, had she visited him in his own study, where many a penitent, ere now, had confessed sins of perhaps as deep a dye as the one betokened by the scarlet letter. But, partly that she dreaded the secret or undisguised interference of old Roger Chillingworth, and partly that her conscious heart imputed suspicion where none could have been felt, and partly that both the minister and she would need the whole wide world to breathe in while they talked together—for all these reasons, Hester never thought of meeting him in any narrower privacy than beneath the open sky.

At last, while attending in a sick chamber, whither the Reverend Mr. Dimmesdale had been summoned to make a prayer, she learnt that he had gone the day before to visit the Apostle Eliot, among his Indian converts. He would probably return by a certain hour in the afternoon of the morrow. Betimes, therefore, the next day, Hester took little Pearl—who was necessarily the companion of all her mother's expeditions, however inconvenient her presence—and set forth.

The road, after the two wayfarers had crossed from the peninsula to the mainland, was no other than a footpath. It straggled onward into the mystery of the primeval forest. This hemmed it in so narrowly, and stood so black and dense on either side, and disclosed such imperfect glimpses of the sky above, that, to Hester's mind, it imaged not amiss the moral wilderness in which she had so long been wandering. The day was chill and sombre. Overhead was a gay expanse of cloud, slightly stirred, however, by a breeze, so that a gleam of flickering sunshine might now and then be seen at its solitary play along the path. This flitting cheerfulness was always at the further extremity of some long vista through the forest. The sportive sunlight—feebly sportive, at best, in the predominant pensiveness of the day and scene—withdrew itself as they came nigh, and left the spots where it had danced the drearier, because they had hoped to find them bright.

"Mother," said little Pearl, "the sunshine does not love you. It runs away and hides itself, because it is afraid of something on your bosom. Now, see! There it is, playing, a good way off. Stand you here, and let me run and catch it. I am but a child. It will not flee from me; for I wear nothing on my bosom yet!"

"Nor ever will, my child, I hope," said Hester.

"And why not, Mother?" asked Pearl, stopping short,

just at the beginning of her race. "Will not it come of its own accord, when I am a woman grown?"

"Run away, child," answered her mother, "and catch the sunshine! It will soon be gone."

Pearl set forth at a great pace, and, as Hester smiled to perceive, did actually catch the sunshine, and stood laughing in the midst of it, all brightened by its splendor, and scintillating with the vivacity excited by rapid motion. The light lingered about the lonely child, as if glad of such a playmate, until her mother had drawn almost nigh enough to step into the magic circle too.

"It will go now," said Pearl, shaking her head.

"See!" answered Hester, smiling. "Now I can stretch out my hand, and grasp some of it."

As she attempted to do so, the sunshine vanished; or, to judge from the bright expression that was dancing in Pearl's features, her mother could have fancied that the child had absorbed it into herself, and would give it forth again, with a gleam about her path, as they should plunge into some gloomier shade. There was no other attribute that so much impressed her with a sense of new and untransmitted vigor in Pearl's nature, as this never-failing vivacity of spirits; she had not the disease of sadness, which almost all children, in these latter days, inherit, with the scrofula, from the troubles of their ancestors. Perhaps this too was a disease, and but the reflex of the wild energy with which Hester had fought against her sorrows, before Pearl's birth. It was certainly a doubtful charm, imparting a hard, metallic lustre to the child's character. She wanted—what some people want throughout life—a grief that should deeply touch her, and thus humanize and make her capable of sympathy. But there was time enough yet for little Pearl.

"Come, my child!" said Hester, looking about her from the spot where Pearl stood still in the sunshine. "We will sit down a little way within the wood, and rest ourselves."

"I am not aweary, Mother," replied the little girl. "But you may sit down, if you will tell me a story meanwhile."

"A story, child!" said Hester. "And about what?"

"O, a story about the Black Man," answered Pearl, taking hold of her mother's gown, and looking up, half earnestly, half mischievously, into her face. "How he haunts this forest, and carries a book with him—a big, heavy book, with iron clasps; and how this ugly Black Man offers his book and an iron pen to everybody that meets him here among the trees; and they are to write their names with their own blood. And then he sets his mark on their bosoms! Didst thou ever meet the Black Man, Mother?"

"And who told you this story, Pearl?" asked her mother, recognizing a common superstition of the period.

"It was the old dame in the chimney-corner, at the house where you watched last night," said the child. "But she fancied me asleep while she was 'alking of it. She said that a thousand and a thousand people had met him here, and had written in his book, and have his mark on them. And that ugly-tempered lady, old Mistress Hibbins, was one. And, Mother, the old dame said that this scarlet letter was the Black Man's mark on thee, and that it glows like a red flame when thou meetest him at midnight, here in the dark wood. Is it true, Mother? And dost thou go to meet him in the nighttime?"

"Didst thou ever awake, and find thy mother gone?" asked Hester.

"Not that I remember," said the child. "If thou fearest to leave me in our cottage, thou mightest take me along with thee. I would very gladly go! But, Mother, tell me now! Is there such a Black Man? And didst thou ever meet him? And is this his mark?"

"Wilt thou let me be at peace, if I once tell thee?" asked her mother.

"Yes, if thou tellest me all," answered Pearl.

"Once in my life I met the Black Man!" said her mother. "This scarlet letter is his mark!"

Thus conversing, they entered sufficiently deep into the wood to secure themselves from the observation of any casual passenger along the forest track. Here they sat down on a luxuriant heap of moss, which, at some epoch of the preceding century, had been a gigantic pine, with its root and trunk in the darksome shade, and its head aloft in the upper atmosphere. It was a little dell where they had seated themselves, with a leaf-strewn bank rising gently on either side, and a brook flowing through the midst over a bed of fallen and drowned leaves. The trees impending over it had flung down great branches from time to time, which choked up the current and compelled it to form eddies and black depths at some points, while, in its swifter and livelier passages, there appeared a channel-way of pebbles, and brown, sparkling sand. Letting the eyes follow along the course of the stream, they could catch the reflected light from its water at some short distance within the forest, but soon lost all traces of it amid the bewilderment of tree-trunks and underbrush, and here and there a huge rock covered over with gray lichens. All these giant trees and boulders of granite seemed intent on making a mystery of the course of this small brook; fearing, perhaps, that, with its never-ceasing loquacity, it should whisper tales out of the heart of the old forest whence it flowed, or mirror its revelations on the smooth surface of a pool. Continually, indeed, as it stole onward, the streamlet kept up a babble, kind, quiet, soothing, but melancholy, like the voice of a young child that was spending its infancy without playfulness, and knew not how to be merry among sad acquaintance and events of sombre hue.

"O brook! O foolish and tiresome little brook!" cried Pearl, after listening awhile to its talk. "Why art thou so sad? Pluck up a spirit, and do not be all the time sighing and murmuring!"

But the brook, in the course of its little lifetime among the forest trees, had gone through so solemn an experience that it could not help talking about it and seemed to have nothing else to say. Pearl resembled the brook, inasmuch as the current of her life gushed from a wellspring as mysterious, and had flowed through scenes shadowed as heavily with gloom. But, unlike the little stream, she danced and sparkled, and prattled airily along her course.

"What does this sad little brook say, Mother?" inquired she.

"If thou hadst a sorrow of thine own, the brook might

tell thee of it," answered her mother, "even as it is telling me of mine! But now, Pearl, I hear a footstep along the path, and the noise of one putting aside the branches. I would have thee betake thyself to play, and leave me to speak with him that comes yonder."

"Is it the Black Man?" asked Pearl.

"Wilt thou go and play, child?" repeated her mother. "But do not stray far into the wood. And take heed that thou come at my first call."

"Yes, Mother," answered Pearl. "But if it be the Black Man, wilt thou not let me stay a moment, and look at him, with his big book under his arm?"

"Go, silly child!" said her mother, impatiently. "It is no Black Man! Thou canst see him now, through the trees. It is the minister!"

"And so it is!" said the child. "And, Mother, he has his hand over his heart! Is it because, when the minister wrote his name in the book, the Black Man set his mark in that place? But why does he not wear it outside his bosom, as thou dost, Mother?"

"Go now, child, and thou shalt tease me as thou wilt another time," cried Hester Prynne. "But do not stray far. Keep where thou canst hear the babble of the brook."

The child went singing away, following up the current of the brook and striving to mingle a more lightsome cadence with its melancholy voice. But the little stream would not be comforted, and still kept telling its unintelligible secret of some very mournful mystery that had happened—or making a prophetic lamentation about something that was yet to happen—within the verge of the dismal forest. So Pearl, who had enough of shadow in her own little life, chose to break off all acquaintance with this repining brook. She set herself, therefore, to gathering violets and wood anemones, and some scarlet columbines that she found growing in the crevices of a high rock.

When her elf-child had departed, Hester Prynne made a step or two towards the track that led through the forest, but still remained under the deep shadow of the trees. She beheld the minister advancing along the path, entirely alone, and leaning on a staff which he had cut by the wayside. He looked haggard and feeble, and betrayed a nerveless despondency in his air which had never so remarkably characterized him in his walks about the settlement, nor in any other situation where he deemed himself liable to notice. Here it was woefully visible, in this intense seclusion of the forest, which of itself would have been a heavy trial to the spirits. There was a listlessness in his gait, as if he saw no reason for taking one step further, nor felt any desire to do so, but would have been glad, could he be glad of anything, to fling himself down at the root of the nearest tree, and lie there passive, forevermore. The leaves might bestrew him and the soil gradually accumulate and form a little hillock over his frame, no matter whether there were life in it or no. Death was too definite an object to be wished for, or avoided.

To Hester's eye, the Reverend Mr. Dimmesdale exhibited no symptom of positive and vivacious suffering, except that, as little Pearl had remarked, he kept his hand over his heart.

17

THE PASTOR AND HIS PARISHIONER

SLOWLY AS THE MINISTER WALKED, he had almost gone by before Hester Prynne could gather voice enough to attract his observation. At length, she succeeded.

"Arthur Dimmesdale!" she said, faintly at first; then louder, but hoarsely. "Arthur Dimmesdale!"

"Who speaks?" answered the minister.

Gathering himself quickly up, he stood more erect, like a man taken by surprise in a mood to which he was reluctant to have witnesses. Throwing his eyes anxiously in the direction of the voice, he indistinctly beheld a form under the trees, clad in garments so sombre, and so little relieved from the gray twilight into which the

clouded sky and the heavy foliage had darkened the noontide, that he knew not whether it were a woman or a
shadow. It may be that his pathway through life was
haunted thus, by a spectre that had stolen out from
among his thoughts.

He made a step nigher, and discovered the scarlet
letter.

"Hester! Hester Prynne!" said he. "Is it thou? Art
thou in life?"

"Even so!" she answered. "In such life as has been
mine these seven years past! And thou, Arthur Dimmesdale, dost thou yet live?"

It was no wonder that they thus questioned one another's actual and bodily existence, and even doubted
of their own. So strangely did they meet in the dim wood,
that it was like the first encounter, in the world beyond
the grave, of two spirits who had been intimately connected in their former life, but now stood coldly shuddering, in mutual dread, as not yet familiar with their state,
nor wonted to the companionship of disembodied beings.
Each a ghost, and awe-stricken at the other ghost! They
were awe-stricken likewise at themselves; because the
crisis flung back to them their consciousness, and revealed to each heart its history and experience, as life
never does, except at such breathless epochs. The soul
beheld its features in the mirror of the passing moment.
It was with fear, and tremulously, and, as it were, by a
slow, reluctant necessity, that Arthur Dimmesdale put
forth his hand, chill as death, and touched the chill hand
of Hester Prynne. The grasp, cold as it was, took away
what was dreariest in the interview. They now felt themselves, at least, inhabitants of the same sphere.

Without a word more spoken—neither he nor she assuming the guidance, but with an unexpressed consent
—they glided back into the shadow of the woods whence
Hester had emerged, and sat down on the heap of moss
where she and Pearl had before been sitting. When they
found voice to speak, it was at first only to utter remarks
and inquiries such as any two acquaintances might have
made, about the gloomy sky, the threatening storm, and,
next, the health of each. Thus they went onward, not
boldly, but step by step, into the themes that were brood-

ing deepest in their hearts. So long estranged by fate
and circumstances, they needed something slight and
casual to run before, and throw open the doors of intercourse, so that their real thoughts might be led across
the threshold.

After a while, the minister fixed his eyes on Hester
Prynne's.

"Hester," said he, "hast thou found peace?"

She smiled drearily, looking down upon her bosom.

"Hast thou?" she asked.

"None!—nothing but despair!" he answered. "What
else could I look for being what I am, and leading such
a life as mine? Were I an atheist—a man devoid of conscience—a wretch with coarse and brutal instincts—
I might have found peace, long ere now. Nay, I never
should have lost it! But, as matters stand with my soul,
whatever of good capacity there originally was in me,
all of God's gifts that were the choicest have become
the ministers of spiritual torment. Hester, I am most
miserable!"

"The people reverence thee," said Hester. "And surely
thou workest good among them! Doth this bring thee no
comfort?"

"More misery, Hester!—only the more misery!" answered the clergyman, with a bitter smile. "As concerns
the good which I may appear to do, I have no faith in
it. It must needs be a delusion. What can a ruined soul
like mine effect towards the redemption of other souls?
—or a polluted soul, towards their purification? And as
for the people's reverence, would that it were turned to
scorn and hatred! Canst thou deem it, Hester, a consolation, that I must stand up in my pulpit and meet
so many eyes turned upward to my face, as if the light
of heaven were beaming from it!—must see my flock
hungry for the truth, and listening to my words as if a
tongue of Pentecost were speaking!—and then look inward, and discern the black reality of what they idolize?
I have laughed, in bitterness and agony of heart, at the
contrast between what I seem and what I am! And Satan
laughs at it!"

"You wrong yourself in this," said Hester, gently. "You
have deeply and sorely repented. Your sin is left behind

you, in the days long past. Your present life is no less holy, in very truth, than it seems in people's eyes. Is there no reality in the penitence thus sealed and witnessed by good works? And wherefore should it not bring you peace?"

"No, Hester, no!" replied the clergyman. "There is no substance in it! It is cold and dead, and can do nothing for me! Of penance, I have had enough! Of penitence, there has been none! Else, I should long ago have thrown off these garments of mock holiness and have shown myself to mankind as they will see me at the judgment seat. Happy are you, Hester, that wear the scarlet letter openly upon your bosom! Mine burns in secret! Thou little knowest what a relief it is, after the torment of a seven years' cheat, to look into an eye that recognizes me for what I am! Had I one friend—or were it my worst enemy!—to whom, when sickened with the praises of all other men, I could daily betake myself and be known as the vilest of all sinners, methinks my soul might keep itself alive thereby. Even thus much of truth would save me! But, now, it is all falsehood!—all emptiness!— all death!"

Hester Prynne looked into his face, but hesitated to speak. Yet, uttering his long-restrained emotions so vehemently as he did, his words here offered her the very point of circumstances in which to interpose what she came to say. She conquered her fears, and spoke.

"Such a friend as thou hast even now wished for," said she, "with whom to weep over thy sin, thou hast in me, the partner of it!"—Again she hesitated, but brought out the words with an effort. "Thou hast long had such an enemy, and dwellest with him, under the same roof!"

The minister started to his feet gasping for breath and clutching at his heart, as if he would have torn it out of his bosom.

"Ha! What sayest thou!" cried he. "An enemy! And under mine own roof! What mean you?"

Hester Prynne was now fully sensible of the deep injury for which she was responsible to this unhappy man, in permitting him to lie for so many years, or, indeed, for a single moment, at the mercy of one whose purposes could not be other than malevolent. The very contiguity of his enemy, beneath whatever mask the latter might conceal himself, was enough to disturb the magnetic sphere of a being so sensitive as Arthur Dimmesdale. There had been a period when Hester was less alive to this consideration; or, perhaps, in the misanthropy of her own trouble, she left the minister to bear what she might picture to herself as a more tolerable doom. But of late, since the night of his vigil, all her sympathies towards him had been both softened and invigorated. She now read his heart more accurately. She doubted not that the continual presence of Roger Chillingworth—the secret poison of his malignity, infecting all the air about him, and his authorized interference, as a physician, with the minister's physical and spiritual infirmities—that these bad opportunities had been turned to a cruel purpose. By means of them, the sufferer's conscience had been kept in an irritated state, the tendency of which was, not to cure by wholesome pain, but to disorganize and corrupt his spiritual being. Its result, on earth, could hardly fail to be insanity, and hereafter, that eternal alienation from the Good and True, of which madness is perhaps the earthly type.

Such was the ruin to which she had brought the man, once—nay, why should we not speak it?—still so passionately loved! Hester felt that the sacrifice of the clergyman's good name, and death itself, as she had already told Roger Chillingworth, would have been infinitely preferable to the alternative which she had taken upon herself to choose. And now, rather than have had this grievous wrong to confess, she would gladly have lain down on the forest leaves and died there, at Arthur Dimmesdale's feet.

"O Arthur," cried she, "forgive me! In all things else, I have striven to be true! Truth was the one virtue which I might have held fast, and did hold fast, through all extremity; save when thy good—thy life—thy fame—were put in question! Then I consented to a deception. But a lie is never good, even though death threaten on the other side! Dost thou not see what I would say? That old man!—the physician!—he whom they call Roger Chillingworth!—he was my husband!"

The minister looked at her, for an instant, with all

that violence of passion, which—intermixed, in more shapes than one, with his higher, purer, softer qualities —was, in fact, the portion of him which the Devil claimed, and through which he sought to win the rest. Never was there a blacker or a fiercer frown than Hester now encountered. For the brief space that it lasted, it was a dark transfiguration. But his character had been so much enfeebled by suffering, that even its lower energies were incapable of more than a temporary struggle. He sank down on the ground, and buried his face in his hands.

"I might have known it," murmured he. "I did know it! Was not the secret told me, in the natural recoil of my heart, at the first sight of him, and as often as I have seen him since? Why did I not understand? O Hester Prynne, thou little, little knowest all the horror of this thing! And the shame!—the indelicacy!—the horrible ugliness of this exposure of a sick and guilty heart to the very eye that would gloat over it! Woman, woman, thou art accountable for this! I cannot forgive thee!"

"Thou shalt forgive me!" cried Hester, flinging herself on the fallen leaves beside him. "Let God punish! Thou shalt forgive!"

With sudden and desperate tenderness, she threw her arms around him, and pressed his head against her bosom; little caring though his cheek rested on the scarlet letter. He would have released himself, but strove in vain to do so. Hester would not set him free, lest he should look her sternly in the face. All the world had frowned on her —for seven long years had it frowned upon this lonely woman—and still she bore it all, nor ever once turned away her firm, sad eyes. Heaven, likewise, had frowned upon her, and she had not died. But the frown of this pale, weak, sinful, and sorrow-stricken man was what Hester could not bear, and live!

"Wilt thou yet forgive me?" she repeated over and over again. "Wilt thou not frown? Wilt thou forgive?"

"I do forgive you, Hester," replied the minister, at length, with a deep utterance out of an abyss of sadness, but no anger. "I freely forgive you now. May God forgive us both! We are not, Hester, the worst sinners in the world. There is one worse than even the polluted priest!

That old man's revenge has been blacker than my sin. He has violated, in cold blood, the sanctity of a human heart. Thou and I, Hester, never did so!"

"Never, never!" whispered she. "What we did had a consecration of its own. We felt it so! We said so to each other! Hast thou forgotten it?"

"Hush, Hester!" said Arthur Dimmesdale, rising from the ground. "No! I have not forgotten!"

They sat down again, side by side, and hand clasped in hand, on the mossy trunk of the fallen tree. Life had never brought them a gloomier hour; it was the point whither their pathway had so long been tending, and darkening ever as it stole along—and yet it enclosed a charm that made them linger upon it, and claim another, and another, and, after all, another moment. The forest was obscure around them, and creaked with a blast that was passing through it. The boughs were tossing heavily above their heads; while one solemn old tree groaned dolefully to another, as if telling the sad story of the pair that sat beneath, or constrained to forebode evil to come.

And yet they lingered. How dreary looked the forest track that led backward to the settlement, where Hester Prynne must take up again the burden of her ignominy, and the minister the hollow mockery of his good name! So they lingered an instant longer. No golden light had ever been so precious as the gloom of this dark forest. Here, seen only by his eyes, the scarlet letter need not burn into the bosom of the fallen woman! Here, seen only by her eyes, Arthur Dimmesdale, false to God and man, might be, for one moment, true!

He started at a thought that suddenly occurred to him.

"Hester," cried he, "here is a new horror! Roger Chillingworth knows your purpose to reveal his true character. Will he continue, then, to keep our secret? What will now be the course of his revenge?"

"There is a strange secrecy in his nature," replied Hester thoughtfully, "and it has grown upon him by the hidden practices of his revenge. I deem it not likely that he will betray the secret. He will doubtless seek other means of satiating his dark passions."

"And I!—how am I to live longer, breathing the same

air with this deadly enemy?" exclaimed Arthur Dimmesdale, shrinking within himself, and pressing his hand nervously against his heart—a gesture that had grown involuntary with him. "Think for me, Hester! Thou art strong. Resolve for me!"

"Thou must dwell no longer with this man," said Hester, slowly and firmly. "Thy heart must be no longer under his evil eye!"

"It were far worse than death!" replied the minister. "But how to avoid it? What choice remains to me? Shall I lie down again on these withered leaves, where I cast myself when thou didst tell me what he was? Must I sink down here, and die at once?"

"Alas, what a ruin has befallen thee!" said Hester, with the tears gushing into her eyes. "Wilt thou die for very weakness? There is no other cause!"

"The judgment of God is on me," answered the conscience-stricken priest. "It is too mighty for me to struggle with!"

"Heaven would show mercy," rejoined Hester, "hadst thou but the strength to take advantage of it."

"Be thou strong for me!" answered he. "Advise me what to do."

"Is the world, then, so narrow?" exclaimed Hester Prynne, fixing her deep eyes on the minister's and instinctively exercising a magnetic power over a spirit so shattered and subdued that it could hardly hold itself erect. "Doth the universe lie within the compass of yonder town, which only a little time ago was but a leaf-strewn desert, as lonely as this around us? Whither leads yonder forest track? Backwards to the settlement, thou sayest! Yes; but onward, too! Deeper it goes, and deeper, into the wilderness, less plainly to be seen at every step! until, some few miles hence, the yellow leaves will show no vestige of the white man's tread. There thou art free! So brief a journey would bring thee from a world where thou hast been most wretched, to one where thou mayest still be happy! Is there not shade enough in all this boundless forest to hide thy heart from the gaze of Roger Chillingworth?"

"Yes, Hester; but only under the fallen leaves!" replied the minister, with a sad smile.

"Then there is the broad pathway of the sea!" continued Hester. "It brought thee hither. If thou so choose, it will bear thee back again. In our native land, whether in some remote rural village or in vast London—or surely, in Germany, in France, in pleasant Italy—thou wouldst be beyond his power and knowledge! And what hast thou to do with all these iron men, and their opinions? They have kept thy better part in bondage too long already!"

"It cannot be!" answered the minister, listening as if he were called upon to realize a dream. "I am powerless to go! Wretched and sinful as I am, I have had no other thought than to drag on my earthly existence in the sphere where Providence hath placed me. Lost as my own soul is, I would still do what I may for other human souls! I dare not quit my post, though an unfaithful sentinel, whose sure reward is death and dishonor, when his dreary watch shall come to an end!"

"Thou art crushed under this seven years' weight of misery," replied Hester, fervently resolved to buoy him up with her own energy. "But thou shalt leave it all behind thee! It shall not cumber thy steps as thou treadest along the forest path; neither shalt thou freight the ship with it, if thou prefer to cross the sea. Leave this wreck and ruin here where it happened. Meddle no more with it! Begin all anew! Hast thou exhausted possibility in the failure of this one trial? Not so! The future is yet full of trial and success. There is happiness to be enjoyed! There is good to be done! Exchange this false life of thine for a true one. Be, if thy spirit summon thee to such a mission, the teacher and apostle of the red men. Or—as is more thy nature—be a scholar and a sage among the wisest and the most renowned of the cultivated world. Preach! Write! Act! Do anything, save to lie down and die! Give up this name of Arthur Dimmesdale and make thyself another, and a high one, such as thou canst wear without fear or shame. Why shouldst thou tarry so much as one other day in the torments that have gnawed into thy life!—that have made thee feeble to will and to do!—that will leave thee powerless even to repent! Up, and away!"

"O Hester!" cried Arthur Dimmesdale, in whose eyes a fitful light, kindled by her enthusiasm, flashed up and died away, "thou tellest of running a race to a man whose knees are tottering beneath him! I must die here! There is not the strength or courage left me to venture into the wide, strange, difficult world, alone!"

It was the last expression of the despondency of a broken spirit. He lacked energy to grasp the better fortune that seemed within his reach.

He repeated the word.

"Alone, Hester!"

"Thou shalt not go alone!" answered she, in a deep whisper.

Then, all was spoken!

18

A FLOOD OF SUNSHINE

A RTHUR DIMMESDALE GAZED into Hester's face with a look in which hope and joy shone out, indeed, but with fear betwixt them, and a kind of horror at her boldness, who had spoken what he vaguely hinted at, but dared not speak.

But Hester Prynne, with a mind of native courage and activity, and for so long a period not merely estranged, but outlawed, from society, had habituated herself to such latitude of speculation as was altogether foreign to the clergyman. She had wandered, without rule or guidance, in a moral wilderness; as vast, as intricate and shadowy, as the untamed forest, amid the gloom of which they were now holding a colloquy that was to decide their fate. Her intellect and heart had their home, as it were, in desert places, where she roamed as freely

as the wild Indian in his woods. For years past she had
looked from this estranged point of view at human institutions, and whatever priests or legislators had established; criticizing all with hardly more reverence than
the Indian would feel for the clerical band, the judicial
robe, the pillory, the gallows, the fireside, or the church.
The tendency of her fate and fortunes had been to set her
free. The scarlet letter was her passport into regions where
other women dared not tread. Shame, Despair, Solitude!
These had been her teachers—stern and wild ones—and
they had made her strong, but taught her much amiss.

The minister, on the other hand had never gone
through an experience calculated to lead him beyond
the scope of generally received laws, although, in a single
instance, he had so fearfully transgressed one of the
most sacred of them. But this had been a sin of passion,
not of principle, nor even purpose. Since that wretched
epoch, he had watched, with morbid zeal and minuteness,
not his acts—for those it was easy to arrange—but each
breath of emotion, and his every thought. At the head
of the social system, as the clergymen of that day stood,
he was only the more trammelled by its regulations,
its principles, and even its prejudices. As a priest, the
framework of his order inevitably hemmed him in. As
a man who had once sinned, but who kept his conscience
all alive and painfully sensitive by the fretting of an un-
healed wound, he might have been supposed safer
within the line of virtue than if he had never sinned at
all.

Thus, we seem to see that, as regarded Hester Prynne,
the whole seven years of outlaw and ignominy had been
little other than a preparation for this very hour. But
Arthur Dimmesdale! Were such a man once more to
fall, what plea could be urged in extenuation of his crime?
None; unless it avail him somewhat, that he was broken
down by long and exquisite suffering; that his mind
was darkened and confused by the very remorse which
harrowed it; that, between fleeing as an avowed criminal,
and remaining as a hypocrite, conscience might find it
hard to strike the balance; that it was human to avoid
the peril of death and infamy, and the inscrutable machinations of an enemy; that, finally, to this poor pilgrim

on his dreary and desert path, faint, sick, miserable, there appeared a glimpse of human affection and sympathy, a new life, and a true one, in exchange for the heavy doom which he was now expiating. And be the stern and sad truth spoken, that the breach which guilt has once made into the human soul is never, in this mortal state, repaired. It may be watched and guarded, so that the enemy shall not force his way again into the citadel and might even, in his subsequent assaults, select some other avenue, in preference to that where he had formerly succeeded. But there is still the ruined wall, and, near it, the stealthy tread of the foe that would win over again his unforgotten triumph.

The struggle, if there were one, need not be described. Let it suffice, that the clergyman resolved to flee, and not alone.

"If, in all these past seven years," thought he, "I could recall one instant of peace or hope, I would yet endure, for the sake of that earnest of Heaven's mercy. But now —since I am irrevocably doomed—wherefore should I not snatch the solace allowed to the condemned culprit before his execution? Or, if this be the path to a better life, as Hester would persuade me, I surely give up no fairer prospect by pursuing it! Neither can I any longer live without her companionship; so powerful is she to sustain—so tender to soothe! O Thou to whom I dare not lift mine eyes, wilt Thou yet pardon me!"

"Thou wilt go!" said Hester, calmly, as he met her glance.

The decision once made, a glow of strange enjoyment threw its flickering brightness over the trouble of his breast. It was the exhilarating effect—upon a prisoner just escaped from the dungeon of his own heart—of breathing the wild, free atmosphere of an unredeemed, unchristianized, lawless region. His spirit rose, as it were, with a bound, and attained a nearer prospect of the sky than throughout all the misery which had kept him grovelling on the earth. Of a deeply religious temperament, there was inevitably a tinge of the devotional in his mood.

"Do I feel joy again!" cried he, wondering at himself. "Methought the germ of it was dead in me! O Hester,

thou art my better angel! I seem to have flung myself
—sick, sin-stained, and sorrow-blackened—down upon
these forest leaves, and to have risen up all made anew,
and with new powers to glorify Him that hath been
merciful! This is already the better life! Why did we
not find it sooner?"

"Let us not look back," answered Hester Prynne. "The
past is gone! Wherefore should we linger upon it now?
See! With this symbol, I undo it all, and make it as it
had never been!"

So speaking, she undid the clasp that fastened the
scarlet letter, and, taking it from her bosom, threw it to
a distance among the withered leaves. The mystic token
alighted on the hither verge of the stream. With a hand's
breadth further flight it would have fallen into the water,
and have given the little brook another woe to carry
onward, besides the unintelligible tale which it still
kept murmuring about. But there lay the embroidered
letter, glittering like a lost jewel, which some ill-fated
wanderer might pick up, and thenceforth be haunted by
strange phantoms of guilt, sinkings of the heart, and unaccountable misfortune.

The stigma gone, Hester heaved a long, deep sigh, in
which the burden of shame and anguish departed from
her spirit. O exquisite relief! She had not known the
weight until she felt the freedom! By another impulse,
she took off the formal cap that confined her hair; and
down it fell upon her shoulders, dark and rich, with at
once a shadow and a light in its abundance, and imparting the charm of softness to her features. There played
around her mouth and beamed out of her eyes a radiant
and tender smile, that seemed gushing from the very
heart of womanhood. A crimson flush was glowing on
her cheek, that had been long so pale. Her sex, her youth,
and the whole richness of her beauty, came back from
what men call the irrevocable past, and clustered themselves, with her maiden hope and a happiness before unknown, within the magic circle of this hour. And, as if
the gloom of the earth and sky had been but the effluence
of these two mortal hearts, it vanished with their sorrow.
All at once, as with a sudden smile of heaven, forth
burst the sunshine, pouring a very flood into the obscure

forest, gladdening each green leaf, transmuting the yellow fallen ones to gold, and gleaming adown the gray trunks of the solemn trees. The objects that had made a shadow hitherto embodied the brightness now. The course of the little brook might be traced by its merry gleam afar into the wood's heart of mystery, which had become a mystery of joy.

Such was the sympathy of Nature—that wild, heathen Nature of the forest, never subjugated by human law, nor illumined by higher truth—with the bliss of these two spirits! Love, whether newly born, or aroused from a deathlike slumber, must always create a sunshine, filling the heart so full of radiance that it overflows upon the outward world. Had the forest still kept its gloom, it would have been bright in Hester's eyes, and bright in Arthur Dimmesdale's!

Hester looked at him with the thrill of another joy.

"Thou must know Pearl!" said she. "Our little Pearl! Thou hast seen her—yes, I know it!—but thou wilt see her now with other eyes. She is a strange child! I hardly comprehend her! But thou wilt love her dearly, as I do, and wilt advise me how to deal with her."

"Dost thou think the child will be glad to know me?" asked the minister, somewhat uneasily. "I have long shrunk from children, because they often show a distrust —a backwardness to be familiar with me. I have even been afraid of little Pearl!"

"Ah, that was sad!" answered the mother. "But she will love thee dearly, and thou her. She is not far off. I will call her! Pearl! Pearl!"

"I see the child," observed the minister. "Yonder she is, standing in a streak of sunshine, a good way off, on the other side of the brook. So thou thinkest the child will love me?"

Hester smiled, and again called to Pearl, who was visible at some distance, as the minister had described her, like a bright-apparelled vision in a sunbeam, which fell down upon her through an arch of boughs. The ray quivered to and fro, making her figure dim or distinct— now like a real child, now like a child's spirit—as the splendor went and came again. She heard her mother's voice, and approached slowly through the forest.

Pearl had not found the hour pass wearisomely while her mother sat talking with the clergyman. The great black forest—stern as it showed itself to those who brought the guilt and troubles of the world into its bosom —became the playmate of the lonely infant, as well as it knew how. Sombre as it was, it put on the kindest of its moods to welcome her. It offered her the partridge berries, the growth of the preceding autumn, but ripening only in the spring, and now red as drops of blood upon the withered leaves. These Pearl gathered, and was pleased with their wild flavor. The small denizens of the wilderness hardly took pains to move out of her path. A partridge, indeed, with a brood of ten behind her, ran forward threateningly, but soon repented of her fierceness, and clucked to her young ones not to be afraid. A pigeon, alone on a low branch, allowed Pearl to come beneath, and uttered a sound as much of greeting as alarm. A squirrel, from the lofty depths of his domestic tree, chattered either in anger or merriment—for a squirrel is such a choleric and humorous little personage, that it is hard to distinguish between his moods—so he chattered at the child, and flung down a nut upon her head. It was a last year's nut, and already gnawed by his sharp tooth. A fox, startled from his sleep by her light footstep on the leaves, looked inquisitively at Pearl, as doubting whether it were better to steal off, or renew his nap on the same spot. A wolf, it is said—but here the tale has surely lapsed into the improbable—came up, and smelt of Pearl's robe, and offered his savage head to be patted by her hand. The truth seems to be, however, that the mother-forest, and these wild things which it nourished, all recognized a kindred wildness in the human child.

And she was gentler here than in the grassy-margined streets of the settlement, or in her mother's cottage. The flowers appeared to know it; and one and another whispered as she passed, "Adorn thyself with me, thou beautiful child, adorn thyself with me!"—and, to please them, Pearl gathered the violets, and anemones, and columbines, and some twigs of the freshest green which the old trees held down before her eyes. With these she decorated her hair, and her young waist, and became a nymph-child, or an infant dryad, or whatever else was in closest sympathy with the antique wood. In such guise had Pearl adorned herself, when she heard her mother's voice, and came slowly back.

Slowly; for she saw the clergyman!

❧❧❧❧❧❧❧❧❧❧❧❧❧❧❧❧❧❧❧❧❧❧❧❧❧❧❧❧❧❧❧❧❧❧

19

THE CHILD AT THE BROOKSIDE

"THOU WILT LOVE HER DEARLY," repeated Hester Prynne, as she and the minister sat watching little Pearl. "Dost thou not think her beautiful? And see with what natural skill she has made those simple flowers adorn her! Had she gathered pearls, and diamonds, and rubies, in the wood, they could not have become her better. She is a splendid child! But I know whose brow she has!"

"Dost thou know, Hester," said Arthur Dimmesdale, with an unquiet smile, "that this dear child, tripping about always at thy side, hath caused me many an alarm? Methought—O Hester, what a thought is that, and how terrible to dread it!—that my own features were partly repeated in her face, and so strikingly that the world might see them! But she is mostly thine!"

"No, no! Not mostly!" answered the mother, with a tender smile. "A little longer, and thou needest not to be afraid to trace whose child she is. But how strangely beautiful she looks, with those wild flowers in her hair! It is as if one of the fairies, whom we left in our dear old England, had decked her out to meet us."

It was with a feeling which neither of them had ever before experienced, that they sat and watched Pearl's slow advance. In her was visible the tie that united them. She had been offered to the world, these seven years past, as the living hieroglyphic, in which was revealed the secret they so darkly sought to hide—all written in this symbol, all plainly manifest, had there been a prophet or magician skilled to read the character of flame! And Pearl was the oneness of their being. Be the foregone evil what it might, how could they doubt that their earthly lives and future destinies were conjoined, when they beheld at once the material union, and the spiritual idea, in whom they met, and were to dwell immortally together? Thoughts like these—and perhaps other thoughts, which they did not acknowledge or define—threw an awe about the child, as she came onward.

"Let her see nothing strange—no passion nor eagerness—in thy way of accosting her," whispered Hester. "Our Pearl is a fitful and fantastic little elf sometimes. Especially, she is seldom tolerant of emotion when she does not fully comprehend the why and wherefore. But the child hath strong affections! She loves me, and will love thee!"

"Thou canst not think," said the minister, glancing aside at Hester Prynne, "how my heart dreads this interview, and yearns for it! But, in truth, as I already told thee, children are not readily won to be familiar with me. They will not climb my knee, nor prattle in my ear, nor answer to my smile; but stand apart, and eye me strangely. Even little babies, when I take them in my arms, weep bitterly. Yet Pearl, twice in her little lifetime, hath been kind to me! The first time—thou knowest it well! The last was when thou ledst her with thee to the house of yonder stern old Governor."

"And thou didst plead so bravely in her behalf and mine!" answered the mother. "I remember it; and so shall little Pearl. Fear nothing! She may be strange and shy at first, but will soon learn to love thee!"

By this time Pearl had reached the margin of the brook and stood on the further side, gazing silently at Hester and the clergyman, who still sat together on the mossy tree-trunk, waiting to receive her. Just where she had paused, the brook chanced to form a pool, so smooth and quiet that it reflected a perfect image of her little figure, with all the brilliant picturesqueness of her beauty, in its adornment of flowers and wreathed foliage, but more refined and spiritualized than the reality. This image, so nearly identical with the living Pearl, seemed to communicate somewhat of its own shadowy and intangible quality to the child herself. It was strange the way in which Pearl stood, looking so steadfastly at them through the dim medium of the forest gloom; herself, meanwhile, all glorified with a ray of sunshine that was attracted thitherward as by a certain sympathy. In the brook beneath stood another child—another and the same—with likewise its ray of golden light. Hester felt herself, in some indistinct and tantalizing manner, estranged from Pearl; as if the child in her lonely ramble through the forest had strayed out of the sphere in which she and her mother dwelt together, and was now vainly seeking to return to it.

There was both truth and error in the impression; the child and mother were estranged, but through Hester's fault, not Pearl's. Since the latter rambled from her side, another inmate had been admitted within the circle of the mother's feelings, and so modified the aspect of them all, that Pearl, the returning wanderer, could not find her wonted place, and hardly knew where she was.

"I have a strange fancy," observed the sensitive minister, "that this brook is the boundary between two worlds, and that thou canst never meet thy Pearl again. Or is she an elfish spirit, who, as the legends of our childhood taught us, is forbidden to cross a running stream? Pray hasten her; for this delay has already imparted a tremor to my nerves."

"Come, dearest child!" said Hester encouragingly, and stretching out both her arms. "How slow thou art! When hast thou been so sluggish before now? Here is a friend of mine, who must be thy friend also. Thou wilt have twice as much love, henceforward, as thy mother alone could give thee! Leap across the brook and come to us. Thou canst leap like a young deer!"

Pearl, without responding in any manner to these honey-sweet expressions, remained on the other side of the brook. Now she fixed her bright, wild eyes on her mother, now on the minister, and now included them both in the same glance, as if to detect and explain to herself the relation which they bore to one another. For some unaccountable reason, as Arthur Dimmesdale felt the child's eyes upon himself, his hand—with that gesture so habitual as to have become involuntary—stole over his heart. At length, assuming a singular air of authority, Pearl stretched out her hand, with the small forefinger extended, and pointing evidently towards her mother's breast. And beneath, in the mirror of the brook, there was the flower-girdled and sunny image of little Pearl, pointing her small forefinger too.

"Thou strange child, why dost thou not come to me?" exclaimed Hester.

Pearl still pointed with her forefinger; and a frown gathered on her brow, the more impressive from the childish, the almost baby-like aspect of the features that conveyed it. As her mother still kept beckoning to her and arraying her face in a holiday suit of unaccustomed smiles, the child stamped her foot with a yet more imperious look and gesture. In the brook, again, was the fantastic beauty of the image, with its reflected frown, its pointed finger, and imperious gesture, giving emphasis to the aspect of little Pearl.

"Hasten, Pearl, or I shall be angry with thee!" cried Hester Prynne, who, however inured to such behavior on the elf-child's part at other seasons, was naturally anxious for a more seemly deportment now. "Leap across the brook, naughty child, and run hither! Else I must come to thee!"

But Pearl, not a whit startled at her mother's threats any more than mollified by her entreaties, now suddenly burst into a fit of passion, gesticulating violently, and throwing her small figure into the most extravagant contortions. She accompanied this wild outbreak with piercing shrieks, which the woods reverberated on all sides; so that, alone as she was in her childish and unreasonable wrath, it seemed as if a hidden multitude were lending her their sympathy and encouragement. Seen in the brook, once more, was the shadowy wrath of Pearl's image, crowned and girdled with flowers, but stamping its foot, wildly gesticulating, and, in the midst of all, still pointing its small forefinger at Hester's bosom!

"I see what ails the child," whispered Hester to the clergyman, and turning pale in spite of a strong effort to conceal her trouble and annoyance. "Children will not abide any, the slightest, change in the accustomed aspect of things that are daily before their eyes. Pearl misses something which she has always seen me wear!"

"I pray you," answered the minister, "if thou hast any means of pacifying the child, do it forthwith! Save it were the cankered wrath of an old witch, like Mistress Hibbins," added he, attempting to smile, "I know nothing that I would not sooner encounter than this passion in a child. In Pearl's young beauty, as in the wrinkled witch, it has a preternatural effect. Pacify her, if thou lovest me!"

Hester turned again towards Pearl with a crimson blush upon her cheek, a conscious glance aside at the clergyman, and then a heavy sigh; while, even before she had time to speak, the blush yielded to a deadly pallor.

"Pearl," said she, sadly, "look down at thy feet! There! —before thee!—on the hither side of the brook!"

The child turned her eyes to the point indicated; and there lay the scarlet letter, so close upon the margin of the stream that the gold embroidery was reflected in it.

"Bring it hither!" said Hester.

"Come thou and take it up!" answered Pearl.

"Was ever such a child!" observed Hester, aside to the minister. "Oh, I have much to tell thee about her! But, in very truth, she is right as regards this hateful token. I must bear its torture yet a little longer—only a few days longer—until we shall have left this region and look back hither as to a land which we have dreamed of. The forest cannot hide it! The mid-ocean shall take it from my hand and swallow it up forever!"

With these words, she advanced to the margin of the brook, took up the scarlet letter, and fastened it again into her bosom. Hopefully, but a moment ago, as Hester had spoken of drowning it in the deep sea, there was a sense of inevitable doom upon her, as she thus received back this deadly symbol from the hand of fate. She had flung it into infinite space!—she had drawn an hour's free breath!—and here again was the scarlet misery, glittering on the old spot! So it ever is, whether thus typified or no, that an evil deed invests itself with the character of doom. Hester next gathered up the heavy tresses of her hair, and confined them beneath her cap. As if there were a withering spell in the sad letter, her beauty, the warmth and richness of her womanhood, departed, like fading sunshine; and a gray shadow seemed to fall across her.

When the dreary change was wrought, she extended her hand to Pearl.

"Dost thou know thy mother now, child?" asked she, reproachfully, but with a subdued tone. "Wilt thou come across the brook and own thy mother, now that she has her shame upon her—now that she is sad?"

"Yes; now I will!" answered the child, bounding across the brook, and clasping Hester in her arms. "Now thou art my mother indeed! And I am thy little Pearl!"

In a mood of tenderness that was not usual with her, she drew down her mother's head, and kissed her brow and both her cheeks. But then—by a kind of necessity that always impelled this child to alloy whatever comfort she might chance to give with a throb of anguish— Pearl put up her mouth, and kissed the scarlet letter too!

"That was not kind!" said Hester. "When thou hast shown me a little love, thou mockest me!"

"Why doth the minister sit yonder?" asked Pearl.

"He waits to welcome thee," replied her mother. "Come thou, and entreat his blessing! He loves thee, my little Pearl, and loves thy mother too. Wilt thou not love him? Come! he longs to greet thee!"

"Doth he love us?" said Pearl, looking up with acute intelligence into her mother's face. "Will he go back with us, hand in hand, we three together, into the town?"

"Not now, dear child," answered Hester. "But in days to come he will walk hand in hand with us. We will have a home and fireside of our own; and thou shalt sit upon his knee; and he will teach thee many things, and love thee dearly. Thou wilt love him; wilt thou not?"

"And will he always keep his hand over his heart?" inquired Pearl.

"Foolish child, what a question is that!" exclaimed her mother. "Come and ask his blessing!"

But, whether influenced by the jealousy that seems instinctive with every petted child towards a dangerous rival, or from whatever caprice of her freakish nature, Pearl would show no favor to the clergyman. It was only by an exertion of force that her mother brought her up to him, hanging back and manifesting her reluctance by odd grimaces; of which, ever since her babyhood, she had possessed a singular variety, and could transform her mobile physiognomy into a series of different aspects, with a new mischief in them, each and all. The minister—painfully embarrassed, but hoping that a kiss might prove a talisman to admit him into the child's kindlier regards—bent forward, and impressed one on her brow. Hereupon, Pearl broke away from her mother, and, running to the brook, stooped over it and bathed her forehead, until the unwelcome kiss was quite washed off and diffused through a long lapse of the gliding water. She then remained apart, silently watching Hester and the clergyman, while they talked together, and made such arrangements as were suggested by their new position, and the purposes soon to be fulfilled.

And now this fateful interview had come to a close. The dell was to be left a solitude among its dark, old trees, which, with their multitudinous tongues, would whisper long of what had passed there, and no mortal be the wiser. And the melancholy brook would add this other tale to the mystery with which its little heart was already overburdened, and whereof it still kept up a murmuring babble, with not a whit more cheerfulness of tone than for ages heretofore.

20

THE MINISTER IN A MAZE

A S THE MINISTER DEPARTED, in advance of Hester Prynne and little Pearl, he threw a backward glance, half expecting that he should discover only some faintly traced features or outline of the mother and the child, slowly fading into the twilight of the woods. So great a vicissitude in his life could not at once be received as real. But there was Hester, clad in her gray robe, still standing beside the tree-trunk which some blast had overthrown a long antiquity ago, and which time had ever since been covering with moss, so that these two fated ones, with earth's heaviest burden on them, might there sit down together and find a single hour's rest and solace. And there was Pearl, too, lightly dancing from the margin of the brook—now that the intrusive third person was gone—and taking her old place by her mother's side. So the minister had not fallen asleep, and dreamed!

In order to free his mind from this indistinctness and duplicity of impression which vexed it with a strange disquietude, he recalled and more thoroughly defined the plans which Hester and himself had sketched for their departure. It had been determined between them that the Old World, with its crowds and cities, offered them a more eligible shelter and concealment than the wilds of New England, or all America, with its alternatives of an Indian wigwam or the few settlements of Europeans, scattered thinly along the seaboard.

Not to speak of the clergyman's health, so inadequate to sustain the hardships of a forest life, his native gifts, his culture, and his entire development would secure him a home only in the midst of civilization and refinement; the higher the state, the more delicately adapted to it the man. In furtherance of his choice, it so happened that a ship lay in the harbor; one of those questionable cruisers, frequent at that day, which, without being absolutely outlaws of the deep, yet roamed over its surface with a remarkable irresponsibility of character. This vessel had recently arrived from the Spanish Main, and within three days' time would sail for Bristol. Hester Prynne—whose vocation as a self-enlisted Sister of Charity had brought her acquainted with the captain and crew—could take upon herself to secure the passage of two individuals and a child with all the secrecy which circumstances rendered more than desirable.

The minister had inquired of Hester, with no little interest, the precise time at which the vessel might be expected to depart. It would probably be on the fourth day from the present. "That is most fortunate!" he had then said to himself. Now, why the Reverend Mr. Dimmesdale considered it so very fortunate, we hesitate to reveal. Nevertheless—to hold nothing back from the reader—it was because on the third day from the present he was to preach the Election Sermon; and, as such an occasion formed an honorable epoch in the life of a New England clergyman, he could not have chanced upon a more suitable mode and time of terminating his professional career. "At least they shall say of me," thought this exemplary man, "that I leave no public duty unperformed, nor ill performed!" Sad, indeed, that an introspection so profound and acute as this poor minister's should be so miserably deceived! We have had, and may still have, worse things to tell of him; but none, we apprehend, so pitiably weak; no evidence, at once so slight and irrefragable, of a subtle disease that had long since begun to eat into the real substance of his character. No man for any considerable period can wear one face to himself and another to the multitude, without finally getting bewildered as to which may be the true.

The excitement of Mr. Dimmesdale's feelings as he returned from his interview with Hester lent him unaccustomed physical energy, and hurried him townward at a rapid pace. The pathway among the woods seemed wilder, more uncouth with its rude natural obstacles and less trodden by the foot of man, than he remembered it on his outward journey. But he leaped across the plashy places, thrust himself through the clinging underbrush, climbed the ascent, plunged into the hollow, and overcame, in short, all the difficulties of the track with an unweariable activity that astonished him. He could not but recall how feebly, and with what frequent pauses for breath, he had toiled over the same ground only two days before. As he drew near the town, he took an impression of change from the series of familiar objects that presented themselves. It seemed not yesterday, not one, nor two, but many days, or even years ago, since he had quitted them. There, indeed, was each former trace of the street, as he remembered it, and all the peculiarities of the houses, with the due multitude of gable peaks, and a weathercock at every point where his memory suggested one. Not the less, however, came this importunately obtrusive sense of change. The same was true as regarded the acquaintances whom he met and all the well-known shapes of human life about the little town. They looked neither older nor younger now; the beards of the aged were no whiter, nor could the creeping babe of yesterday walk on his feet today; it was impossible to describe in what respect they differed from the individuals on whom he had so recently bestowed a parting glance; and yet the minister's deepest sense seemed to inform him of their mutability. A similar impression struck him most remarkably as he passed under the walls of his own church. The edifice had so very strange, and yet so familiar, an aspect, that Mr. Dimmesdale's mind vibrated between two ideas; either that he had seen it only in a dream hitherto, or that he was merely dreaming about it now.

This phenomenon, in the various shapes which it assumed, indicated no external change, but so sudden and important a change in the spectator of the familiar scene, that the intervening space of a single day had operated on his consciousness like the lapse of years. The minister's own will, and Hester's will, and the fate that grew between them, had wrought this transformation. It was the same town as heretofore; but the same minister returned not from the forest. He might have said to the friends who greeted him, "I am not the man for whom you take me! I left him yonder in the forest, withdrawn into a secret dell, by a mossy tree-trunk, and near a melancholy brook! Go, seek your minister, and see if his emaciated figure, his thin cheek, his white, heavy, pain-wrinkled brow, be not flung down there, like a cast-off garment!" His friends, no doubt, would still have insisted with him, "Thou art thyself the man!" but the error would have been their own, not his.

Before Mr. Dimmesdale reached home, his inner man gave him other evidences of a revolution in the sphere of thought and feeling. In truth, nothing short of a total change of dynasty and moral code in that interior kingdom was adequate to account for the impulses now communicated to the unfortunate and startled minister. At every step he was incited to do some strange, wild, wicked thing or other, with a sense that it would be at once involuntary and intentional; in spite of himself, yet growing out of a profounder self than that which opposed the impulse. For instance, he met one of his own deacons. The good old man addressed him with the paternal affection and patriarchal privilege, which his venerable age, his upright and holy character, and his station in the Church entitled him to use, and, conjoined with this, the deep, almost worshipping respect which the minister's professional and private claims alike demanded. Never was there a more beautiful example of how the majesty of age and wisdom may comport with the obeisance and respect enjoined upon it, as from a lower social rank and inferior order of endowment, towards a higher. Now, during a conversation of some two or three moments between the Reverend Mr. Dimmesdale and this excellent and hoary-bearded deacon, it was only by the most careful self-control that the former could refrain from uttering certain blasphemous suggestions that rose into his mind, respecting the communion supper. He absolutely trembled and turned pale as ashes, lest his tongue should wag itself, in utterance of these horrible matters, and plead his own consent for so doing without his having fairly given it. And, even with this terror in his heart, he could hardly avoid laughing, to imagine how the sanctified old patriarchal deacon would have been petrified by his minister's impiety!

Again, another incident of the same nature. Hurrying along the street, the Reverend Mr. Dimmesdale encountered the eldest female member of his church, a most pious and exemplary old dame; poor, widowed, lonely, and with a heart as full of reminiscences about her dead husband and children and her dead friends of long ago as a burial ground is full of storied gravestones. Yet all this, which would else have been such heavy sorrow, was made almost a solemn joy to her devout old soul by religious consolations and the truths of Scripture, wherewith she had fed herself continually for more than thirty years. And, since Mr. Dimmesdale had taken her in charge, the good grandam's chief earthly comfort—which, unless it had been likewise a heavenly comfort, could have been none at all—was to meet her pastor, whether casually, or of set purpose, and be refreshed with a word of warm, fragrant, heaven-breathing Gospel truth, from his beloved lips into her dulled but rapturously attentive ear. But on this occasion, up to the moment of putting his lips to the old woman's ear, Mr. Dimmesdale, as the great enemy of souls would have it, could recall no text of Scripture, nor aught else, except a brief, pithy, and, as it then appeared to him, unanswerable argument against the immortality of the human soul. The instilment thereof into her mind would probably have caused this aged sister to drop down dead at once, as by the effect of an intensely poisonous infusion. What he really did whisper, the minister could never afterwards recollect. There was, perhaps, a fortunate disorder in his utterance, which failed to impart any distinct idea to the good widow's comprehension, or which Providence interpreted after a method of its own. Assuredly, as the minister looked back, he beheld an expression of divine gratitude and ecstasy that seemed like the shine of the celestial city on her face, so wrinkled and ashy pale.

Again, a third instance. After parting from the old church member, he met the youngest sister of them all. It was a maiden newly won—and won by the Reverend Mr. Dimmesdale's own sermon, on the Sabbath after his vigil—to barter the transitory pleasures of the world for the heavenly hope that was to assume brighter substance as life grew dark around her, and which would gild the utter gloom with final glory. She was fair and pure as a lily that had bloomed in Paradise. The minister knew well that he was himself enshrined within the stainless sanctity of her heart, which hung its snowy curtains about his image, imparting to religion the warmth of love, and to love a religious purity. Satan, that afternoon, had surely led the poor young girl away from her mother's side, and thrown her into the pathway of this sorely tempted, or—shall we not rather say?—this lost and desperate man. As she drew nigh, the archfiend whispered him to condense into small compass and drop into her tender bosom a germ of evil that would be sure to blossom darkly soon, and bear black fruit betimes. Such was his sense of power over this virgin soul, trusting him as she did, that the minister felt potent to blight all the field of innocence with but one wicked look, and develop all its opposite with but a word. So—with a mightier struggle than he had yet sustained—he held his Geneva cloak before his face, and hurried onward, making no sign of recognition, and leaving the young sister to digest his rudeness as she might. She ransacked her conscience—which was full of harmless little matters, like her pocket or her workbag—and took herself to task, poor thing! for a thousand imaginary faults; and went about her household duties with swollen eyelids the next morning.

Before the minister had time to celebrate his victory over this last temptation, he was conscious of another impulse, more ludicrous and almost as horrible. It was —we blush to tell it—it was to stop short in the road, and teach some very wicked words to a knot of little Puritan children who were playing there, and had but just begun to talk. Denying himself this freak as unworthy of his cloth, he met a drunken seaman, one of the ship's crew from the Spanish Main. And, here, since he had so valiantly forborne all other wickedness, poor Mr. Dimmesdale longed, at least, to shake hands with the tarry blackguard, and recreate himself with a few improper jests, such as dissolute sailors so abound with, and a volley of good, round, solid, satisfactory, and heaven-defying oaths! It was not so much a better principle, as partly his natural good taste, and still more his buckramed habit of clerical decorum, that carried him safely through the latter crisis.

"What is it that haunts and tempts me thus?" cried the minister to himself, at length, pausing in the street, and striking his hand against his forehead. "Am I mad? or am I given over utterly to the fiend? Did I make a contract with him in the forest, and sign it with my blood? And does he now summon me to its fulfilment, by suggesting the performance of every wickedness which his most foul imagination can conceive?"

At the moment when the Reverend Mr. Dimmesdale thus communed with himself, and struck his forehead with his hand, old Mistress Hibbins, the reputed witch-lady, is said to have been passing by. She made a very grand appearance; having on a high headdress, a rich gown of velvet, and a ruff done up with the famous yellow starch, of which Ann Turner, her especial friend, had taught her the secret, before this last good lady had been hanged for Sir Thomas Overbury's murder. Whether the witch had read the minister's thoughts or no, she came to a full stop, looked shrewdly into his face, smiled craftily, and—though little given to converse with clergymen—began a conversation.

"So, reverend Sir, you have made a visit into the forest," observed the witch-lady, nodding her high headdress at him. "The next time, I pray you to allow me only a fair warning, and I shall be proud to bear you company. Without taking overmuch upon myself, my good word will go far towards gaining any strange gentleman a fair reception from yonder potentate you wot of!"

"I profess, Madam," answered the clergyman, with a grave obeisance, such as the lady's rank demanded and his own good-breeding made imperative—"I profess, on my conscience and character, that I am utterly bewildered as touching the purport of your words! I went not into the forest to seek a potentate; neither do I, at any future time, design a visit thither, with a view to gaining the favor of such personage. My one sufficient object was to greet that pious friend of mine, the Apostle Eliot, and rejoice with him over the many precious souls he hath won from heathendom!"

"Ha, ha, ha!" cackled the old witch-lady, still nodding her high headdress at the minister. "Well, well, we must needs talk thus in the daytime! You carry it off like an old hand! But at midnight, and in the forest, we shall have other talk together!"

She passed on with her aged stateliness, but often turning back her head and smiling at him, like one willing to recognize a secret intimacy of connection.

"Have I then sold myself," thought the minister, "to the fiend whom, if men say true, this yellow-starched and velveted old hag has chosen for her prince and master!"

The wretched minister! He had made a bargain very like it! Tempted by a dream of happiness, he had yielded himself with deliberate choice, as he had never done before, to what he knew was deadly sin. And the infectious poison of that sin had been thus rapidly diffused throughout his moral system. It had stupefied all blessed impulses, and awakened into vivid life the whole brotherhood of bad ones. Scorn, bitterness, unprovoked malignity, gratuitous desire of ill, ridicule of whatever was good and holy, all awoke, to tempt, even while they frightened him. And his encounter with old Mistress Hibbins, if it were a real incident, did but show his sympathy and fellowship with wicked mortals, and the world of perverted spirits.

He had by this time reached his dwelling on the edge of the burial ground, and, hastening up the stairs, took refuge in his study. The minister was glad to have reached this shelter without first betraying himself to the world by any of those strange and wicked eccentricities to which he had been continually impelled while passing through the streets. He entered the accustomed room and looked around him on its books, its windows, its fireplace, and the tapestried comfort of the walls, with the same perception of strangeness that had haunted him throughout his walk from the forest dell into the town, and thitherward. Here he had studied and written; here gone through fast and vigil, and come forth half alive; here, striven to pray; here, borne a hundred thousand agonies! There was the Bible, in its rich old Hebrew, with Moses and the Prophets speaking to him, and God's voice through all! There, on the table, with the inky pen beside it, was an unfinished sermon, with a sentence broken in the midst, where his thoughts had ceased to gush out upon the page, two days before. He knew that it was himself, the thin and white-cheeked minister, who had done and suffered these things, and written thus far into the Election Sermon! But he seemed to stand apart and eye this former self with scornful, pitying, but half-envious curiosity. That self was gone. Another man had returned out of the forest; a wiser one, with a knowledge of hidden mysteries which the simplicity of the former never could have reached. A bitter kind of knowledge that!

While occupied with these reflections, a knock came at the door of the study, and the minister said, "Come in!"—not wholly devoid of an idea that he might behold an evil spirit. And so he did! It was old Roger Chillingworth that entered. The minister stood, white and speechless, with one hand on the Hebrew Scriptures, and the other spread upon his breast.

"Welcome home, reverend Sir," said the physician. "And how found you that godly man, the Apostle Eliot? But methinks, dear Sir, you look pale; as if the travel through the wilderness had been too sore for you. Will not my aid be requisite to put you in heart and strength to preach your Election Sermon?"

"Nay, I think not so," rejoined the Reverend Mr. Dimmesdale. "My journey, and the sight of the holy Apostle yonder, and the free air which I have breathed, have done me good, after so long confinement in my study. I think to need no more of your drugs, my kind physician, good though they be, and administered by a friendly hand."

All this time, Roger Chillingworth was looking at the

minister with the grave and intent regard of a physician towards his patient. But, in spite of this outward show, the latter was almost convinced of the old man's knowledge, or, at least, his confident suspicion, with respect to his own interview with Hester Prynne. The physician knew then, that, in the minister's regard, he was no longer a trusted friend, but his bitterest enemy. So much being known, it would appear natural that a part of it should be expressed. It is singular, however, how long a time often passes before words embody things; and with what security two persons, who choose to avoid a certain subject, may approach its very verge, and retire without disturbing it. Thus, the minister felt no apprehension that Roger Chillingworth would touch, in express words, upon the real position which they sustained towards one another. Yet did the physician, in his dark way, creep frightfully near the secret.

"Were it not better," said he, "that you use my poor skill tonight? Verily, dear Sir, we must take pains to make you strong and vigorous for this occasion of the Election discourse. The people look for great things from you, apprehending that another year may come about, and find their pastor gone."

"Yea, to another world," replied the minister, with pious resignation. "Heaven grant it be a better one; for, in good sooth, I hardly think to tarry with my flock through the flitting seasons of another year! But, touching your medicine, kind Sir, in my present frame of body, I need it not."

"I joy to hear it," answered the physician. "It may be that my remedies, so long administered in vain, begin now to take due effect. Happy man were I, and well deserving of New England's gratitude, could I achieve this cure!"

"I thank you from my heart, most watchful friend," said the Reverend Mr. Dimmesdale, with a solemn smile. "I thank you, and can but requite your good deeds with my prayers."

"A good man's prayers are golden recompense!" rejoined old Roger Chillingworth, as he took his leave. "Yea, they are the current gold coin of the New Jerusalem, with the King's own mint-mark on them!"

Left alone, the minister summoned a servant of the house and requested food, which, being set before him, he ate with ravenous appetite. Then, flinging the already written pages of the Election Sermon into the fire, he forthwith began another, which he wrote with such an impulsive flow of thought and emotion, that he fancied himself inspired; and only wondered that Heaven should see fit to transmit the grand and solemn music of its oracles through so foul an organ-pipe as he. However, leaving that mystery to solve itself or go unsolved forever, he drove his task onward, with earnest haste and ecstasy. Thus the night fled away, as if it were a winged steed and he careering on it; morning came and peeped, blushing, through the curtains; and at last sunrise threw a golden beam into the study, and laid it right across the minister's bedazzled eyes. There he was, with the pen still between his fingers, and a vast, immeasurable tract of written space behind him!

21

THE NEW ENGLAND HOLIDAY

BETIMES IN THE MORNING of the day on which the new Governor was to receive his office at the hands of the people, Hester Prynne and little Pearl came into the market place. It was already thronged with the craftsmen and other plebeian inhabitants of the town, in considerable numbers; among whom, likewise, were many rough figures, whose attire of deerskins marked them as belonging to some of the forest settlements which surrounded the little metropolis of the colony.

On this public holiday, as on all other occasions, for seven years past, Hester was clad in a garment of coarse gray cloth. Not more by its hue than by some indescribable peculiarity in its fashion, it had the effect of making her fade personally out of sight and outline; while, again, the scarlet letter brought her back from this twilight indistinctness and revealed her under the moral aspect of its own illumination. Her face, so long familiar to the townspeople, showed the marble quietude which they were accustomed to behold there. It was like a mask; or, rather, like the frozen calmness of a dead woman's features, owing this dreary resemblance to the fact that Hester was actually dead, in respect to any claim of sympathy, and had departed out of the world with which she still seemed to mingle.

It might be, on this one day, that there was an expression unseen before, nor, indeed, vivid enough to be detected now; unless some preternaturally gifted observer should have first read the heart, and have afterwards sought a corresponding development in the countenance and mien. Such a spiritual seer might have conceived that, after sustaining the gaze of the multitude through seven miserable years as a necessity, a penance, and something which it was a stern religion to endure, she now, for one last time more, encountered it freely and voluntarily, in order to convert what had so long been agony into a kind of triumph. "Look your last on the scarlet letter and its wearer!"—the people's victim and lifelong bond-slave, as they fancied her, might say to them. "Yet a little while, and she will be beyond your reach! A few hours longer, and the deep, mysterious ocean will quench and hide forever the symbol which ye have caused to burn upon her bosom!" Nor were it an inconsistency too improbable to be assigned to human nature, should we suppose a feeling of regret in Hester's mind, at the moment when she was about to win her freedom from the pain which had been thus deeply incorporated with her being. Might there not be an irresistible desire to quaff a last, long, breathless draught of the cup of wormwood and aloes, with which nearly all her years of womanhood had been perpetually flavored? The wine of life, henceforth to be presented to her lips, must be indeed rich, delicious, and exhilarating, in its chased and golden beaker; or else leave an inevitable and weary languor, after the lees of bitterness wherewith she had been drugged, as with a cordial of intensest potency.

Pearl was decked out with airy gayety. It would have been impossible to guess that this bright and sunny apparition owed its existence to the shape of gloomy gray; or that a fancy, at once so gorgeous and so delicate as must have been requisite to contrive the child's apparel, was the same that had achieved a task perhaps more difficult, in imparting so distinct a peculiarity to Hester's simple robe. The dress, so proper was it to little Pearl, seemed an effluence, or inevitable development and outward manifestation of her character, no more to be separated from her than the many-hued brilliancy from a butterfly's wing or the painted glory from the leaf of a bright flower. As with these, so with the child; her garb was all of one idea with her nature. On this eventful day, moreover, there was a certain singular inquietude and excitement in her mood, resembling nothing so much as the shimmer of a diamond, that sparkles and flashes with the varied throbbings of the breast on which it is displayed. Children have always a sympathy in the agitations of those connected with them; always, especially, a sense of any trouble or impending revolution, of whatever kind, in domestic circumstances; and therefore Pearl, who was the gem on her mother's unquiet bosom, betrayed, by the very dance of her spirits, the emotions which none could detect in the marble passiveness of Hester's brow.

This effervescence made her flit with a birdlike movement, rather than walk by her mother's side. She broke continually into shouts of a wild, inarticulate, and sometimes piercing music. When they reached the market place, she became still more restless on perceiving the stir and bustle that enlivened the spot; for it was usually more like the broad and lonesome green before a village meeting house than the centre of a town's business.

"Why, what is this, Mother?" cried she. "Wherefore have all the people left their work today? Is it a play-day for the whole world? See, there is the blacksmith! He has washed his sooty face and put on his Sabbath-day clothes and looks as if he would gladly be merry, if any kind body would only teach him how! And there is Master Brackett, the old jailer, nodding and smiling at me. Why does he do so, Mother?"

"He remembers thee a little babe, my child," answered Hester.

"He should not nod and smile at me, for all that—the black, grim, ugly-eyed old man!" said Pearl. "He may nod at thee, if he will; for thou art clad in gray, and wearest the scarlet letter. But see, Mother, how many faces of strange people, and Indians among them, and sailors! What have they all come to do, here in the market place?"

"They wait to see the procession pass," said Hester. "For the Governor and the magistrates are to go by, and the ministers, and all the great people and good people, with the music and the soldiers marching before them."

"And will the minister be there?" asked Pearl. "And will he hold out both his hands to me, as when thou ledst me to him from the brookside?"

"He will be there, child," answered her mother. "But he will not greet thee today; nor must thou greet him."

"What a strange, sad man is he!" said the child, as if speaking partly to herself. "In the dark nighttime he calls us to him, and holds thy hand and mine, as when we stood with him on the scaffold yonder! And in the deep forest, where only the old trees can hear and the strip of sky see it, he talks with thee, sitting on a heap of moss! And he kisses my forehead, too, so that the little brook would hardly wash it off! But here, in the sunny day, and among all the people, he knows us not; nor must we know him! A strange, sad man is he, with his hand always over his heart!"

"Be quiet, Pearl! Thou understandest not these things," said her mother. "Think not now of the minister, but look about thee, and see how cheery is everybody's face today. The children have come from their schools, and the grown people from their workshops and their fields, on purpose to be happy. For today a new man is beginning to rule over them; and so—as has been the custom of mankind ever since a nation was first gathered—they make merry and rejoice; as if a good and golden year were at length to pass over the poor old world!"

It was as Hester said, in regard to the unwonted jollity that brightened the faces of the people. Into this festal season of the year—as it already was, and continued to be during the greater part of two centuries—the Puritans compressed whatever mirth and public joy they deemed allowable to human infirmity, thereby so far dispelling the customary cloud, that, for the space of a single holiday, they appeared scarcely more grave than most other communities at a period of general affliction.

But we perhaps exaggerate the gray or sable tinge which undoubtedly characterized the mood and manners of the age. The persons now in the market place of Boston had not been born to an inheritance of Puritanic gloom. They were native Englishmen whose fathers had lived in the sunny richness of the Elizabethan epoch, a time when the life of England, viewed as one great mass, would appear to have been as stately, magnificent, and joyous as the world has ever witnessed. Had they followed their hereditary taste, the New England settlers would have illustrated all events of public importance by bonfires, banquets, pageantries, and processions. Nor would it have been impracticable, in the observance of majestic ceremonies, to combine mirthful recreation with solemnity, and give, as it were, a grotesque and brilliant embroidery to the great robe of state which a nation, at such festivals, puts on. There was some shadow of an attempt of this kind in the mode of celebrating the day on which the political year of the colony commenced. The dim reflection of a remembered splendor, a colorless and manifold diluted repetition of what they had beheld in proud old London—we will not say at a royal coronation, but at a Lord Mayor's show—might be traced in the customs which our forefathers instituted with reference to the annual installation of magistrates. The fathers and founders of the commonwealth—the statesman, the priest, and the soldier—deemed it a duty then to assume the outward state and majesty, which, in accordance with antique style, was looked upon as the proper garb of public or social eminence. All came forth, to move in procession before the people's eye, and thus impart a needed dignity to the simple framework of a government so newly constructed.

Then, too, the people were countenanced, if not encouraged, in relaxing the severe and close application to their various modes of rugged industry, which, at all other times, seemed of the same piece and material with their religion. Here, it is true, were none of the appliances which popular merriment would so readily have found in the England of Elizabeth's time, or that of James—no rude shows of a theatrical kind; no minstrel, with his harp and legendary ballad, nor gleeman, with an ape dancing to his music; no juggler, with his tricks of mimic witchcraft, no Merry Andrew, to stir up the multitude with jests, perhaps hundreds of years old, but still effective, by their appeals to the very broadest sources of mirthful sympathy. All such professors of the several branches of jocularity would have been sternly repressed, not only by the rigid discipline of law, but by the general sentiment which gives law its vitality. Not the less, however, the great, honest face of the people smiled, grimly, perhaps, but widely too. Nor were sports wanting, such as the colonists had witnessed and shared in long ago, at the country fairs and on the village greens of England; and which it was thought well to keep alive on this new soil, for the sake of the courage and manliness that were essential in them. Wrestling matches, in the different fashions of Cornwall and Devonshire, were seen here and there about the market place; in one corner, there was a friendly bout at quarterstaff; and— what attracted most interest of all—on the platform of the pillory, already so noted in our pages, two masters of defence were commencing an exhibition with the buckler and broadsword. But, much to the disappointment of the crowd, this latter business was broken off by the interposition of the town beadle, who had no idea of permitting the majesty of the law to be violated by such an abuse of one of its consecrated places.

It may not be too much to affirm, on the whole (the people being then in the first stages of joyless deportment, and the offspring of sires who had known how to be merry, in their day), that they would compare favorably, in point of holiday keeping, with their descendants, even at so long an interval as ourselves. Their immediate posterity, the generation next to the early emigrants, wore the blackest shade of Puritanism, and so darkened the national visage with it, that all the subsequent years have not sufficed to clear it up. We have yet to learn again the forgotten art of gayety.

The picture of human life in the market place, though its general tint was the sad gray, brown, or black of the English emigrants, was yet enlivened by some diversity of hue. A party of Indians—in their savage finery of curiously embroidered deerskin robes, wampum belts, red and yellow ochre, and feathers, and armed with the bow and arrow and stone-headed spear—stood apart with countenances of inflexible gravity, beyond what even the Puritan aspect could attain. Nor, wild as were these painted barbarians, were they the wildest feature of the scene. This distinction could more justly be claimed by some mariners—a part of the crew of the vessel from the Spanish Main—who had come ashore to see the humors of Election Day. They were rough-looking desperadoes with sun-blackened faces and an immensity of beard; their wide, short trousers were confined about the waist by belts, often clasped with a rough plate of gold, and sustaining always a long knife, and, in some instances, a sword. From beneath their broad-brimmed hats of palm-leaf gleamed eyes which, even in good nature and merriment, had a kind of animal ferocity. They transgressed, without fear or scruple, the rules of behavior that were binding on all others; smoking tobacco under the beadle's very nose, although each whiff would have cost a townsman a shilling; and quaffing, at their pleasure, draughts of wine or aquavitæ from pocket flasks, which they freely tendered to the gaping crowd around them. It remarkably characterized the incomplete morality of the age, rigid as we call it, that a license was allowed the seafaring class, not merely for their freaks on shore, but for far more desperate deeds on their proper

element. The sailor of that day would go near to be
arraigned as a pirate in our own. There could be little
doubt, for instance, that this very ship's crew, though
no unfavorable specimens of the nautical brotherhood,
had been guilty, as we should phrase it, of depredations
of the Spanish commerce such as would have perilled
all their necks in a modern court of justice.

But the sea in those old times heaved, swelled and
foamed, very much at its own will, or subject only to
the tempestuous wind, with hardly any attempts at
regulation by human law. The buccaneer on the wave
might relinquish his calling, and become at once, if he
chose, a man of probity and piety on land; nor even in
the full career of his reckless life was he regarded as a
personage with whom it was disreputable to traffic or
casually associate. Thus, the Puritan elders, in their black
cloaks, starched bands, and steeple-crowned hats, smiled
not unbenignantly at the clamor and rude deportment
of these jolly seafaring men; and it excited neither surprise nor animadversion when so reputable a citizen as
old Roger Chillingworth, the physician, was seen to enter
the market place in close and familiar talk with the
commander of the questionable vessel.

The latter was by far the most showy and gallant
figure, so far as apparel went, anywhere to be seen among
the multitude. He wore a profusion of ribbons on his
garment, and gold lace on his hat, which was also en-
circled by a gold chain and surmounted with a feather.
There was a sword at his side, and a sword cut on his
forehead, which, by the arrangement of his hair, he
seemed anxious rather to display than hide. A landsman
could hardly have worn this garb and shown this face,
and worn and shown them both with such a galliard air,
without undergoing stern question, before a magistrate,
and probably incurring fine or imprisonment, or perhaps
an exhibition in the stocks. As regarded the shipmaster,
however, all was looked upon as pertaining to the character, as to a fish his glistening scales.

After parting from the physician, the commander of
the Bristol ship strolled idly through the market place;
until, happening to approach the spot where Hester
Prynne was standing, he appeared to recognize, and did

not hesitate to address her. As was usually the case wherever Hester stood, a small vacant area—a sort of magic circle—had formed itself about her, into which, though the people were elbowing one another at a little distance, none ventured, or felt disposed to intrude. It was a forcible type of the moral solitude in which the scarlet letter enveloped its fated wearer; partly by her own reserve, and partly by the instinctive, though no longer so unkindly, withdrawal of her fellow-creatures. Now, if never before, it answered a good purpose by enabling Hester and the seaman to speak together without risk of being overheard; and so changed was Hester Prynne's repute before the public, that the matron in town most eminent for rigid morality could not have held such intercourse with less result of scandal than herself.

"So, mistress," said the mariner, "I must bid the steward make ready one more berth than you bargained for! No fear of scurvy or ship-fever, this voyage! What with the ship's surgeon and this other doctor, our only danger will be from drug or pill; more by token, as there is a lot of apothecary's stuff aboard, which I traded for with a Spanish vessel."

"What mean you?" inquired Hester, startled more than she permitted to appear. "Have you another passenger?"

"Why, know you not," cried the shipmaster, "that this physician here—Chillingworth, he calls himself—is minded to try my cabin-fare with you? Ay, ay, you must have known it; for he tells me he is of your party, and a close friend to the gentleman you spoke of—he that is in peril from these sour old Puritan rulers!"

"They know each other well indeed," replied Hester, with a mien of calmness, though in the utmost consternation. "They have long dwelt together."

Nothing further passed between the mariner and Hester Prynne. But, at that instant, she beheld old Roger Chillingworth himself, standing in the remotest corner of the market place and smiling on her; a smile which —across the wide and bustling square, and through all the talk and laughter, and various thoughts, moods, and interests of the crowd—conveyed secret and fearful meaning.

22

THE PROCESSION

BEFORE HESTER PRYNNE COULD CALL together her thoughts and consider what was practicable to be done in this new and startling aspect of affairs, the sound of military music was heard approaching along a contiguous street. It denoted the advance of the procession of magistrates and citizens on its way towards the meeting house, where, in compliance with a custom thus early established, and ever since observed, the Reverend Mr. Dimmesdale was to deliver an Election Sermon.

Soon the head of the procession showed itself, with a slow and stately march, turning a corner, and making its way across the market place. First came the music. It comprised a variety of instruments, perhaps imperfectly adapted to one another and played with no great skill, but yet attaining the great object for which the harmony of drum and clarion addresses itself to the multitude—that of imparting a higher and more heroic air to the scene of life that passes before the eye. Little Pearl at first clapped her hands, but then lost, for an instant, the restless agitation that had kept her in a continual effervescence throughout the morning; she gazed silently, and seemed to be borne upward, like a floating sea bird, on the long heaves and swells of sound. But she was brought back to her former mood by the shimmer of the sunshine on the weapons and bright armor of the military company, which followed after the music and formed the honorary escort of the procession.

This body of soldiery—which still sustains a corporate existence and marches down from past ages with an ancient and honorable fame—was composed of no mercenary materials. Its ranks were filled with gentlemen who felt the stirrings of martial impulse and sought to establish a kind of College of Arms, where, as in an association of Knights Templars, they might learn the science, and, so far as peaceful exercise would teach them, the practices of war. The high estimation then placed upon the military character might be seen in the lofty port of each individual member of the company. Some of them, indeed, by their services in the Low Countries and on other fields of European warfare, had fairly won their title to assume the name and pomp of soldiership. The entire array, moreover, clad in burnished steel, and with plumage nodding over their bright morions, had a brilliancy of effect which no modern display can aspire to equal.

And yet the men of civil eminence, who came immediately behind the military escort, were better worth a thoughtful observer's eye. Even in outward demeanor, they showed a stamp of majesty that made the warrior's haughty stride look vulgar, if not absurd. It was an age when what we call talent had far less consideration than now, but the massive materials which produce stability and dignity of character a great deal more. The people possessed, by hereditary right, the quality of reverence, which, in their descendants, if it survive at all, exists in smaller proportion, and with a vastly diminished force, in the selection and estimate of public men. The change may be for good or ill, and is partly, perhaps, for both. In that old day, the English settler on these rude shores —having left king, nobles, and all degrees of awful rank behind, while still the faculty and necessity of reverence were strong in him—bestowed it on the white hair and venerable brow of age; on long-tried integrity; on solid wisdom and sad-colored experience; on endowments of that grave and weighty order which gives the idea of permanence and comes under the general definition of respectability. These primitive statesmen, therefore— Bradstreet, Endicott, Dudley, Bellingham, and their compeers—who were elevated to power by the early choice of the people, seem to have been not often brilliant, but distinguished by a ponderous sobriety rather than activity of intellect. They had fortitude and self-reliance, and, in time of difficulty or peril, stood up for the welfare of the state like a line of cliffs against a tempestuous tide. The traits of character here indicated were well represented in the square cast of countenance and large physical development of the new colonial magistrates. So far as a demeanor of natural authority was concerned, the mother country need not have been ashamed to see these foremost men of an actual democracy adopted into the House of Peers, or made the Privy Council of the sovereign.

Next in order to the magistrates came the young and eminently distinguished divine, from whose lips the religious discourse of the anniversary was expected. His was the profession, at that era, in which intellectual ability displayed itself far more than in political life; for —leaving a higher motive out of the question—it offered inducements powerful enough, in the almost worshipping respect of the community, to win the most aspiring ambition into its service. Even political power—as in the case of Increase Mather—was within the grasp of a successful priest.

It was the observation of those who beheld him now, that never, since Mr. Dimmesdale first set his foot on the New England shore, had he exhibited such energy as was seen in the gait and air with which he kept his pace in the procession. There was no feebleness of step, as at other times; his frame was not bent; nor did his hand rest ominously upon his heart. Yet, if the clergyman were rightly viewed, his strength seemed not of the body. It might be spiritual, and imparted to him by angelic ministrations. It might be the exhilaration of that potent cordial, which is distilled only in the furnace-glow of earnest and long-continued thought. Or, perchance, his sensitive temperament was invigorated by the loud and piercing music that swelled heavenward and uplifted him on its ascending wave. Nevertheless, so abstracted was his look, it might be questioned whether Mr. Dimmesdale even heard the music. There was his body, moving onward, and with an unaccustomed force.

But where was his mind? Far and deep in its own region, busying itself, with preternatural activity, to marshal a procession of stately thoughts that were soon to issue thence; and so he saw nothing, heard nothing, knew nothing, of what was around him; but the spiritual element took up the feeble frame, and carried it along, unconscious of the burden, and converting it to spirit like itself. Men of uncommon intellect, who have grown morbid, possess this occasional power of mighty effort, into which they throw the life of many days, and then are lifeless for as many more.

Hester Prynne, gazing steadfastly at the clergyman, felt a dreary influence come over her, but wherefore or whence she knew not; unless that he seemed so remote from her own sphere, and utterly beyond her reach. One glance of recognition, she had imagined, must needs pass between them. She thought of the dim forest, with its little dell of solitude, and love, and anguish, and the mossy tree-trunk, where, sitting hand in hand, they had mingled their sad and passionate talk with the melancholy murmur of the brook. How deeply had they known each other then! And was this the man? She hardly knew him now! He, moving proudly past, enveloped, as it were, in the rich music, with the procession of majestic and venerable fathers; he, so unattainable in his worldly position, and still more so in that far vista of his unsympathizing thoughts, through which she now beheld him! Her spirit sank with the idea that all must have been a delusion, and that, vividly as she had dreamed it, there could be no real bond betwixt the clergyman and herself. And thus much of woman was there in Hester, that she could scarcely forgive him—least of all now, when the heavy footstep of their approaching Fate might be heard, nearer, nearer, nearer!—for being able so completely to withdraw himself from their mutual world, while she groped darkly, and stretched forth her cold hands, and found him not.

Pearl either saw and responded to her mother's feelings, or herself felt the remoteness and intangibility that had fallen around the minister. While the procession passed, the child was uneasy, fluttering up and down like a bird on the point of taking flight. When the whole had gone by, she looked up into Hester's face.

"Mother," said she, "was that the same minister that kissed me by the brook?"

"Hold thy peace, dear little Pearl!" whispered her mother. "We must not always talk in the market place of what happens to us in the forest."

"I could not be sure that it was he; so strange he looked," continued the child. "Else I would have run to him, and bid him kiss me now, before all the people; even as he did yonder among the dark old trees. What would the minister have said, Mother? Would he have clapped his hand over his heart, and scowled on me, and bid me begone?"

"What should he say, Pearl," answered Hester, "save that it was no time to kiss, and that kisses are not to be given in the market place? Well for thee, foolish child, that thou didst not speak to him!"

Another shade of the same sentiment in reference to Mr. Dimmesdale was expressed by a person whose eccentricities—or insanity, as we should term it—led her to do what few of the townspeople would have ventured on; to begin a conversation with the wearer of the scarlet letter in public. It was Mistress Hibbins, who, arrayed in great magnificence, with a triple ruff, a broidered stomacher, a gown of rich velvet, and a gold-headed cane, had come forth to see the procession. As this ancient lady had the renown (which subsequently cost her no less a price than her life) of being a principal actor in all the works of necromancy that were continually going forward, the crowd gave way before her, and seemed to fear the touch of her garment, as if it carried the plague among its gorgeous folds. Seen in conjunction with Hester Prynne—kindly as so many now felt towards the latter—the dread inspired by Mistress Hibbins was doubled, and caused a general movement from that part of the market place in which the two women stood.

"Now, what mortal imagination could conceive it!" whispered the old lady confidentially to Hester. "Yonder divine man! That saint on earth, as the people uphold him to be, and as—I must needs say—he really looks!

Who, now, that saw him pass in the procession, would think how little while it is since he went forth out of his study—chewing a Hebrew text of Scripture in his mouth, I warrant—to take an airing in the forest! Aha! we know what that means, Hester Prynne! But, truly, forsooth, I find it hard to believe him the same man. Many a church member saw I, walking behind the music, that has danced in the same measure with me, when Somebody was fiddler, and, it might be, an Indian powwow or a Lapland wizard changing hands with us! That is but a trifle, when a woman knows the world. But this minister! Couldst thou surely tell, Hester, whether he was the same man that encountered thee on the forest path?"

"Madam, I know not of what you speak," answered Hester Prynne, feeling Mistress Hibbins to be of infirm mind; yet strangely startled and awe-stricken by the confidence with which she affirmed a personal connection between so many persons (herself among them) and the Evil One. "It is not for me to talk lightly of a learned and pious minister of the Word, like the Reverend Mr. Dimmesdale!"

"Fie, woman, fie!" cried the old lady, shaking her finger at Hester. "Dost thou think I have been to the forest so many times, and have yet no skill to judge who else has been there? Yea; though no leaf of the wild garlands, which they wore while they danced, be left in their hair! I know thee, Hester; for I behold the token. We may all see it in the sunshine; and it glows like a red flame in the dark. Thou wearest it openly; so there need be no question about that. But this minister! Let me tell thee, in thine ear! When the Black Man sees one of his own servants, signed and sealed, so shy of owning to the bond as is the Reverend Mr. Dimmesdale, he hath a way of ordering matters so that the mark shall be disclosed in open daylight to the eyes of all the world! What is it that the minister seeks to hide, with his hand always over his heart? Ha, Hester Prynne!"

"What is it, good Mistress Hibbins?" eagerly asked little Pearl. "Hast thou seen it?"

"No matter, darling!" responded Mistress Hibbins, making Pearl a profound reverence. "Thou thyself wilt see it, one time or another. They say, child, thou art of the lineage of the Prince of the Air! Wilt thou ride with me, some fine night, to see thy father? Then thou shalt know wherefore the minister keeps his hand over his heart!"

Laughing so shrilly that all the market place could hear her, the weird old gentlewoman took her departure.

By this time the preliminary prayer had been offered in the meeting house, and the accents of the Reverend Mr. Dimmesdale were heard commencing his discourse. An irresistible feeling kept Hester near the spot. As the sacred edifice was too much thronged to admit another auditor, she took up her position close beside the scaffold of the pillory. It was in sufficient proximity to bring the whole sermon to her ears, in the shape of an indistinct, but varied, murmur and flow of the minister's very peculiar voice.

This vocal organ was in itself a rich endowment; insomuch that a listener, comprehending nothing of the language in which the preacher spoke, might still have been swayed to and fro by the mere tone and cadence. Like all other music, it breathed passion and pathos, and emotions high or tender, in a tongue native to the human heart, wherever educated. Muffled as the sound was by its passage through the church walls, Hester Prynne listened with such intentness, and sympathized so intimately, that the sermon had throughout a meaning for her entirely apart from its indistinguishable words. These, perhaps, if more distinctly heard, might have been only a grosser medium and have clogged the spiritual sense. Now she caught the low undertone, as of the wind sinking down to repose itself; then ascended with it, as it rose through progressive gradations of sweetness and power, until its volume seemed to envelop her with an atmosphere of awe and solemn grandeur. And yet, majestic as the voice sometimes became, there was forever in it an essential character of plaintiveness. A loud or low expression of anguish—the whisper, or the shriek, as it might be conceived, of suffering humanity, that touched a sensibility in every bosom! At times this deep strain of pathos was all that could be heard, and scarcely heard, sighing amid a desolate silence. But even when

the minister's voice grew high and commanding—when
it gushed irrepressibly upward—when it assumed its utmost breadth and power, so overfilling the church as to
burst its way through the solid walls and diffuse itself
in the open air—still, if the auditor listened intently, and
for the purpose, he could detect the same cry of pain.
What was it? The complaint of a human heart, sorrow-
laden, perchance guilty, telling its secret, whether of
guilt or sorrow, to the great heart of mankind; beseeching
its sympathy or forgiveness—at every moment—in each
accent—and never in vain! It was this profound and
continual undertone that gave the clergyman his most
appropriate power.

During all this time, Hester stood, statue-like, at the
foot of the scaffold. If the minister's voice had not
kept her there, there would nevertheless have been an
inevitable magnetism in that spot, whence she dated the
first hour of her life of ignominy. There was a sense
within her—too ill-defined to be made a thought, but
weighing heavily on her mind—that her whole orb of
life, both before and after, was connected with this spot,
as with the one point that gave it unity.

Little Pearl, meanwhile, had quitted her mother's side,
and was playing at her own will about the market place.
She made the sombre crowd cheerful by her erratic and
glistening ray, even as a bird of bright plumage illumi-
nates a whole tree of dusky foliage, by darting to and
fro, half seen and half concealed amid the twilight of
the clustering leaves. She had an undulating, but, oftentimes, a sharp and irregular movement. It indicated the
restless vivacity of her spirit, which today was doubly
indefatigable in its tiptoe dance, because it was played
upon and vibrated with her mother's disquietude. Whenever Pearl saw anything to excite her ever-active and
wandering curiosity, she flew thitherward, and, as we
might say, seized upon that man or thing as her own
property, so far as she desired it; but without yielding
the minutest degree of control over her motions in
requital. The Puritans looked on, and, if they smiled,
were none the less inclined to pronounce the child a
demon offspring, from the indescribable charm of beauty
and eccentricity that shone through her little figure, and

sparkled with its activity. She ran and looked the wild Indian in the face; and he grew conscious of a nature wilder than his own. Thence, with native audacity, but still with a reserve as characteristic, she flew into the midst of a group of mariners, the swarthy-cheeked wild men of the ocean, as the Indians were of the land; and they gazed wonderingly and admiringly at Pearl, as if a flake on the sea-foam had taken the shape of a little maid, and were gifted with a soul of the sea-fire that flashes beneath the prow in the nighttime.

One of these seafaring men—the shipmaster, indeed, who had spoken to Hester Prynne—was so smitten with Pearl's aspect, that he attempted to lay hands upon her, with purpose to snatch a kiss. Finding it as impossible to touch her as to catch a hummingbird in the air, he took from his hat the gold chain that was twisted about it, and threw it to the child. Pearl immediately twined it around her neck and waist with such happy skill that, once seen there, it became a part of her, and it was difficult to imagine her without it.

"Thy mother is yonder woman with the scarlet letter," said the seaman. "Wilt thou carry her a message from me?"

"If the message pleases me, I will," answered Pearl.

"Then tell her," rejoined he, "that I spake again with the black-a-visaged hump-shouldered old doctor, and he engages to bring his friend, the gentleman she wots of, aboard with him. So let thy mother take no thought, save for herself and thee. Wilt thou tell her this, thou witch-baby?"

"Mistress Hibbins says my father is the Prince of the Air!" cried Pearl, with a naughty smile. "If thou callest me that ill name, I shall tell him of thee, and he will chase thy ship with a tempest!"

Pursuing a zigzag course across the market place, the child returned to her mother and communicated what the mariner had said. Hester's strong, calm, steadfastly enduring spirit almost sank, at last, on beholding this dark and grim countenance of an inevitable doom, which —at the moment when a passage seemed to open for the minister and herself out of their labyrinth of misery—

showed itself, with an unrelenting smile, right in the midst of their path.

With her mind harassed by the terrible perplexity in which the shipmaster's intelligence involved her, she was also subjected to another trial. There were many people present from the country round about who had often heard of the scarlet letter, and to whom it had been made terrific by a hundred false or exaggerated rumors, but who had never beheld it with their own bodily eyes. These, after exhausting other modes of amusement, now thronged about Hester Prynne with rude and boorish intrusiveness. Unscrupulous as it was, however, it could not bring them nearer than a circuit of several yards. At that distance they accordingly stood, fixed there by the centrifugal force of the repugnance which the mystic symbol inspired. The whole gang of sailors, likewise, observing the press of spectators, and learning the purport of the scarlet letter, came and thrust their sunburnt and desperado-looking faces into the ring. Even the Indians were affected by a sort of cold shadow of the white man's curiosity, and, gliding through the crowd, fastened their snakelike black eyes on Hester's bosom, conceiving, perhaps, that the wearer of this brilliantly embroidered badge must needs be a personage of high dignity among her people. Lastly the inhabitants of the town (their own interest in this worn-out subject languidly reviving itself by sympathy with what they saw others feel) lounged idly to the same quarter, and tormented Hester Prynne, perhaps more than all the rest, with their cool, well-acquainted gaze at her familiar shame. Hester saw and recognized the selfsame faces of that group of matrons who had awaited her forthcoming from the prison door seven years ago; all save one, the youngest and only compassionate among them, whose burial robe she had since made. At the final hour, when she was so soon to fling aside the burning letter, it had strangely become the centre of more remark and excitement, and was thus made to sear her breast more painfully, than at any time since the first day she put it on.

While Hester stood in that magic circle of ignominy where the cunning cruelty of her sentence seemed to have fixed her forever, the admirable preacher was looking down from the sacred pulpit upon an audience whose very inmost spirits had yielded to his control. The sainted minister in the church! The woman of the scarlet letter in the market place! What imagination would have been irreverent enough to surmise that the same scorching stigma was on them both!

███

23

THE REVELATION OF THE SCARLET LETTER

THE ELOQUENT VOICE, on which the souls of the listening audience had been borne aloft as on the swelling waves of the sea, at length came to a pause. There was a momentary silence, profound as what should follow the utterance of oracles. Then ensued a murmur and half-hushed tumult, as if the auditors, released from the high spell that had transported them into the region of another's mind, were returning into themselves, with all their awe and wonder still heavy on them. In a moment more, the crowd began to gush forth from the doors of the church. Now that there was an end, they needed other breath, more fit to support the gross and earthly life into which they relapsed than that atmosphere which the preacher had converted into words of flame and had burdened with the rich fragrance of his thought.

In the open air their rapture broke into speech. The street and the market place absolutely babbled, from side to side, with applauses of the minister. His hearers could not rest until they had told one another of what each knew better than he could tell or hear. According to their united testimony, never had man spoken in so wise, so high, and so holy a spirit, as he that spake this day; nor had inspiration ever breathed through mortal lips more evidently than it did through his. Its influence could be seen, as it were, descending upon him, and possessing him, and continually lifting him out of the written discourse that lay before him, and filling him with ideas that must have been as marvellous to himself as to his audience. His subject, it appeared, had been the relation between the Deity and the communities of mankind, with a special reference to the New England which they were here planting in the wilderness. And as he drew towards the close, a spirit as of prophecy had come upon him, constraining him to its purpose as mightily as the old prophets of Israel were constrained; only with this difference, that, whereas the Jewish seers had denounced judgments and ruin on their country, it was his mission to foretell a high and glorious destiny for the newly gathered people of the Lord. But, through-out it all, and through the whole discourse, there had been a certain deep, sad undertone of pathos, which could not be interpreted otherwise than as the natural regret of one soon to pass away. Yes; their minister whom they so loved—and who so loved them all, that he could not depart heavenward without a sigh—had the fore-boding of untimely death upon him, and would soon leave them in their tears! This idea of his transitory stay on earth gave the last emphasis to the effect which the preacher had produced; it was as if an angel, in his passage to the skies, had shaken his bright wings over the people for an instant—at once a shadow and a splendor—and had shed down a shower of golden truths upon them.

Thus, there had come to the Reverend Mr. Dimmes-dale—as to most men, in their various spheres, though seldom recognized until they see it far behind them—an epoch of life more brilliant and full of triumph than any previous one, or than any which could hereafter be. He stood, at this moment, on the very proudest eminence of superiority to which the gifts of intellect, rich lore, prevailing eloquence, and a reputation of whitest sanctity, could exalt a clergyman in New England's earliest days, when the professional character was of itself a lofty pedestal. Such was the position which the minister occupied, as he bowed his head forward on the cushions of the pulpit, at the close of his Election Sermon. Meanwhile Hester Prynne was standing beside the scaffold of the pillory, with the scarlet letter still burning on her breast!

Now was heard again the clangor of the music, and the measured tramp of the military escort, issuing from the church door. The procession was to be marshalled thence to the town hall, where a solemn banquet would complete the ceremonies of the day.

Once more, therefore, the train of venerable and majestic fathers was seen moving through a broad pathway of the people, who drew back reverently on either side as the Governor and magistrates, the old and wise men, the holy ministers, and all that were eminent and renowned, advanced into the midst of them. When they were fairly in the market place, their presence was greeted by a shout. This—though doubtless it might acquire additional force and volume from the childlike loyalty which the age awarded to its rulers—was felt to be an irrepressible outburst of enthusiasm kindled in the auditors by that high strain of eloquence which was yet reverberating in their ears. Each felt the impulse in himself, and, in the same breath, caught it from his neighbor. Within the church, it had hardly been kept down; beneath the sky, it pealed upward to the zenith. There were human beings enough, and enough of highly wrought and symphonious feeling, to produce that more impressive sound than the organ tones of the blast, or the thunder, or the roar of the sea; even that mighty swell of many voices, blended into one great voice by the universal impulse which makes likewise one vast heart of the many. Never, from the soil of New England, had gone up such a shout! Never, on New England soil, had stood the man so honored by his mortal brethren as the preacher!

How fared it with him then? Were there not the brilliant particles of a halo in the air about his head? So etherealized by spirit as he was, and so apotheosized by worshipping admirers, did his footsteps, in the procession, really tread upon the dust of earth?

As the ranks of military men and civil fathers moved
onward, all eyes were turned towards the point where
the minister was seen to approach among them. The
shout died into a murmur, as one portion of the crowd
after another obtained a glimpse of him. How feeble
and pale he looked, amid all his triumph! The energy—
or say, rather, the inspiration which had held him up,
until he should have delivered the sacred message that
brought its own strength along with it from heaven—
was withdrawn, now that it had so faithfully performed
its office. The glow, which they had just before beheld
burning on his cheek, was extinguished, like a flame
that sinks down hopelessly among the late-decaying
embers. It seemed hardly the face of a man alive, with
such a deathlike hue; it was hardly a man with life in
him, that tottered on his path so nervelessly, yet tottered,
and did not fall!

One of his clerical brethren—it was the venerable
John Wilson—observing the state in which Mr. Dimmesdale was left by the retiring wave of intellect and
sensibility, stepped forward hastily to offer his support.
The minister tremulously, but decidedly, repelled the
old man's arm. He still walked onward, if that movement
could be so described, which rather resembled the
wavering effort of an infant, with its mother's arms in
view, outstretched to tempt him forward. And now,
almost imperceptible as were the latter steps of his
progress, he had come opposite the well-remembered
and weather-darkened scaffold, where, long since, with
all that dreary lapse of time between, Hester Prynne
had encountered the world's ignominious stare. There
stood Hester, holding little Pearl by the hand! And there
was the scarlet letter on her breast! The minister here
made a pause, although the music still played the stately
and rejoicing march to which the procession moved. It
summoned him onward—onward to the festival!—but
here he made a pause.

Bellingham, for the last few moments, had kept an
anxious eye upon him. He now left his own place in
the procession, and advanced to give assistance, judging,
from Mr. Dimmesdale's aspect, that he must otherwise
inevitably fall. But there was something in the latter's

expression that warned back the magistrate, although
a man not readily obeying the vague intimations that
pass from one spirit to another. The crowd, meanwhile,
looked on with awe and wonder. This earthly faintness
was, in their view, only another phase of the minister's
celestial strength; nor would it have seemed a miracle
too high to be wrought for one so holy, had he ascended
before their eyes, waxing dimmer and brighter, and
fading at last into the light of heaven.

He turned towards the scaffold, and stretched forth
his arms.

"Hester," said he, "come hither! Come, my little
Pearl!"

It was a ghastly look with which he regarded them;
but there was something at once tender and strangely
triumphant in it. The child, with the birdlike motion
which was one of her characteristics, flew to him, and
clasped her arms about his knees. Hester Prynne—slowly,
as if impelled by inevitable fate, and against her strongest
will—likewise drew near, but paused before she reached
him. At this instant, old Roger Chillingworth thrust
himself through the crowd—or, perhaps so dark, disturbed and evil, was his look, he rose up out of some
nether region—to snatch back his victim from what he
sought to do! Be that as it might, the old man rushed
forward, and caught the minister by the arm.

"Madman, hold! what is your purpose?" whispered
he. "Wave back that woman! Cast off this child! All
shall be well! Do not blacken your fame and perish in
dishonor! I can yet save you! Would you bring infamy
on your sacred profession?"

"Ha, tempter! Methinks thou art too late!" answered
the minister, encountering his eye, fearfully but firmly.
"Thy power is not what it was! With God's help, I shall
escape thee now!"

He again extended his hand to the woman of the
scarlet letter.

"Hester Prynne," cried he, with a piercing earnestness,
"in the name of Him, so terrible and so merciful, who
gives me grace, at this last moment, to do what—for my
own heavy sin and miserable agony—I withheld myself
from doing seven years ago, come hither now, and twine

thy strength about me! Thy strength, Hester; but let it
be guided by the will which God hath granted me! This
wretched and wronged old man is opposing it with all
his might!—with all his own might, and the fiend's!
Come, Hester, come! Support me up yonder scaffold!"

The crowd was in a tumult. The men of rank and
dignity, who stood more immediately around the clergyman, were so taken by surprise and so perplexed as to
the purport of what they saw—unable to receive the
explanation which most readily presented itself, or to
imagine any other—that they remained silent and inactive
spectators of the judgment which Providence seemed
about to work. They beheld the minister, leaning on
Hester's shoulder and supported by her arm around
him, approach the scaffold and ascend its steps; while
still the little hand of the sin-born child was clasped
in his. Old Roger Chillingworth followed, as one intimately connected with the drama of guilt and sorrow
in which they had all been actors, and well entitled,
therefore, to be present, at its closing scene.

"Hadst thou sought the whole earth over," said he,
looking darkly at the clergyman, "there was no one
place so secret—no high place nor lowly place where
thou couldst have escaped me—save on this very scaffold!"

"Thanks be to Him who hath led me hither!" answered the minister.

Yet he trembled, and turned to Hester with an expression of doubt and anxiety in his eyes, not the less
evidently betrayed that there was a feeble smile upon
his lips.

"Is not this better," murmured he, "than what we
dreamed of in the forest?"

"I know not! I know not!" she hurriedly replied.
"Better? Yea; so we may both die, and little Pearl die
with us!"

"For thee and Pearl, be it as God shall order," said
the minister; "and God is merciful! Let me now do the
will which he hath made plain before my sight. For,
Hester, I am a dying man. So let me make haste to
take my shame upon me!"

Partly supported by Hester Prynne and holding one
hand of little Pearl, the Reverend Mr. Dimmesdale

turned to the dignified and venerable rulers; to the holy ministers, who were his brethren; to the people, whose great heart was thoroughly appalled, yet overflowing with tearful sympathy, as knowing that some deep life-matter—which, if full of sin, was full of anguish and repentance likewise—was now to be laid open to them. The sun, but little past its meridian, shone down upon the clergyman, and gave a distinctness to his figure, as he stood out from all the earth to put in his plea of guilty at the bar of Eternal Justice.

"People of New England!" cried he, with a voice that rose over them, high, solemn, and majestic—yet had always a tremor through it, and sometimes a shriek, struggling up out of a fathomless depth of remorse and woe—"ye, that have loved me!—ye, that have deemed me holy!—behold me here, the one sinner of the world! At last!—at last!—I stand upon the spot where, seven years since, I should have stood; here, with this woman, whose arm, more than the little strength wherewith I have crept hitherward, sustains me, at this dreadful moment, from grovelling down upon my face! Lo, the scarlet letter which Hester wears! Ye have all shuddered at it! Wherever her walk hath been—wherever, so miserably burdened, she may have hoped to find repose—it hath cast a lurid gleam of awe and horrible repugnance round about her. But there stood one in the midst of you, at whose brand of sin and infamy ye have not shuddered!"

It seemed, at this point, as if the minister must leave the remainder of his secret undisclosed. But he fought back the bodily weakness—and, still more, the faintness of heart—that was striving for the mastery with him. He threw off all assistance, and stepped passionately forward a pace before the woman and the child.

"It was on him!" he continued, with a kind of fierceness, so determined was he to speak out the whole. "God's eye beheld it! The angels were forever pointing at it! The Devil knew it well, and fretted it continually with the touch of his burning finger! But he hid it cunningly from men, and walked among you with the mien of a spirit, mournful, because so pure in a sinful world!—and sad, because he missed his heavenly kindred!

Now, at the death-hour, he stands up before you! He bids you look again at Hester's scarlet letter! He tells you that, with all its mysterious horror, it is but the shadow of what he bears on his own breast, and that even this, his own red stigma, is no more than the type of what has seared his inmost heart! Stand any here that question God's judgment on a sinner? Behold! Behold a dreadful witness of it!"

With a convulsive motion, he tore away the ministerial band from before his breast. It was revealed! But it were irreverent to describe that revelation. For an instant, the gaze of the horror-stricken multitude was concentred on the ghastly miracle; while the minister stood, with a flush of triumph in his face, as one who, in the crisis of acutest pain, had won a victory. Then, down he sank upon the scaffold! Hester partly raised him, and supported his head against her bosom. Old Roger Chillingworth knelt down beside him, with a blank, dull countenance, out of which the life seemed to have departed.

"Thou hast escaped me!" he repeated more than once. "Thou hast escaped me!"

"May God forgive thee!" said the minister. "Thou, too, hast deeply sinned!"

He withdrew his dying eyes from the old man, and fixed them on the woman and the child.

"My little Pearl," said he, feebly—and there was a sweet and gentle smile over his face, as of a spirit sinking into deep repose; nay, now that the burden was removed, it seemed almost as if he would be sportive with the child—"dear little Pearl, wilt thou kiss me now? Thou wouldst not, yonder, in the forest! But now thou wilt!"

Pearl kissed his lips. A spell was broken. The great scene of grief, in which the wild infant bore a part, had developed all her sympathies; and as her tears fell upon her father's cheek, they were the pledge that she would grow up amid human joy and sorrow, nor forever do battle with the world, but be a woman in it. Towards her mother, too, Pearl's errand as a messenger of anguish was all fulfilled.

"Hester," said the clergyman, "farewell!"

"Shall we not meet again?" whispered she, bending her face down close to his. "Shall we not spend our immortal life together? Surely, surely, we have ransomed one another, with all this woe! Thou lookest far into eternity, with those bright dying eyes! Then tell me what thou seest?"

"Hush, Hester, hush!" said he, with tremulous solemnity. "The law we broke!—the sin here so awfully revealed!—let these alone be in thy thoughts! I fear! I fear! It may be, that, when we forgot our God—when we violated our reverence each for the other's soul—it was thenceforth vain to hope that we could meet hereafter, in an everlasting and pure reunion. God knows; and he is merciful! He hath proved his mercy, most of all, in my afflictions. By giving me this burning torture to bear upon my breast! By sending yonder dark and terrible old man to keep the torture always at red-heat! By bringing me hither, to die this death of triumphant ignominy before the people! Had either of these agonies been wanting, I had been lost forever! Praised be his name! His will be done! Farewell!"

That final word came forth with the minister's expiring breath. The multitude, silent till then, broke out in a strange, deep voice of awe and wonder, which could not as yet find utterance, save in this murmur that rolled so heavily after the departed spirit.

24

CONCLUSION

A FTER MANY DAYS, when time sufficed for the people to arrange their thoughts in reference to the foregoing scene, there was more than one account of what had been witnessed on the scaffold.

Most of the spectators testified to having seen, on the breast of the unhappy minister, a *scarlet letter*—the very semblance of that worn by Hester Prynne—imprinted in the flesh. As regarded its origin, there were various explanations, all of which must necessarily have been conjectural. Some affirmed that the Reverend Mr. Dimmesdale, on the very day when Hester Prynne first wore her ignominious badge, had begun a course of penance—which he afterwards, in so many futile methods, followed out—by inflicting a hideous torture on himself. Others contended that the stigma had not been produced until a long time subsequent, when old Roger Chillingworth, being a potent necromancer, had caused it to appear through the agency of magic and poisonous drugs. Others, again—and those best able to appreciate the minister's peculiar sensibility and the wonderful operation of his spirit upon the body—whispered their belief that the awful symbol was the effect of the ever active tooth of remorse, gnawing from the inmost heart outwardly, and at last manifesting Heaven's dreadful judgment by the visible presence of the letter. The reader may choose among these theories. We have thrown all the light we could acquire upon the portent, and would gladly, now that it has done its office, erase its deep print out of our own brain, where long meditation has fixed it in very undesirable distinctness.

It is singular, nevertheless, that certain persons, who were spectators of the whole scene and professed never once to have removed their eyes from the Reverend Mr. Dimmesdale, denied that there was any mark whatever on his breast, more than on a newborn infant's. Neither, by their report, had his dying words acknowledged, nor even remotely implied, any, the slightest connection, on his part, with the guilt for which Hester Prynne had so long worn the scarlet letter. According to these highly respectable witnesses, the minister, conscious that he was dying—conscious, also, that the reverence of the multitude placed him already among saints and angels— had desired, by yielding up his breath in the arms of that fallen woman, to express to the world how utterly nugatory is the choicest of man's own righteousness. After exhausting life in his efforts for mankind's spiritual good, he had made the manner of his death a parable, in order to impress on his admirers the mighty and mournful lesson that, in the view of Infinite Purity, we are sinners all alike. It was to teach them that the holiest among us has but attained so far above his fellows as to discern more clearly the Mercy which looks down, and repudiate more utterly the phantom of human merit which would look aspiringly upward. Without disputing a truth so momentous, we must be allowed to consider this version of Mr. Dimmesdale's story as only an instance of that stubborn fidelity with which a man's friends—and especially a clergyman's —will sometimes uphold his character, when proofs, clear as the midday sunshine on the scarlet letter, establish him a false and sin-stained creature of the dust.

The authority which we have chiefly followed—a manuscript of old date, drawn up from the verbal testimony of individuals, some of whom had known Hester Prynne, while others had heard the tale from contemporary witnesses—fully confirms the view taken in the foregoing pages. Among many morals which press upon us from the poor minister's miserable experience, we put only this into a sentence:—"Be true! Be true! Be true! Show freely to the world, if not your worst, yet some trait whereby the worst may be inferred!"

Nothing was more remarkable than the change which took place, almost immediately after Mr. Dimmesdale's death, in the appearance and demeanor of the old man known as Roger Chillingworth. All his strength and energy—all his vital and intellectual force—seemed at once to desert him; insomuch that he positively withered up, shrivelled away, and almost vanished from mortal sight, like an uprooted weed that lies wilting in the sun. This unhappy man had made the very principle of his life to consist in the pursuit and systematic exercise of revenge; and when, by its completest triumph and consummation, that evil principle was left with no further material to support it, when, in short, there was no more Devil's work on earth for him to do, it only remained for the unhumanized mortal to betake himself whither his Master would find him tasks enough, and pay him his wages duly. But, to all these shadowy beings, so long our near acquaintances—as well Roger Chillingworth as his companions—we would fain be merciful. It is a curious subject of observation and inquiry, whether hatred and love be not the same thing at bottom. Each, in its utmost development, supposes a high degree of intimacy and heart-knowledge; each renders one individual dependent for the food of his affections and spiritual life upon another; each leaves the passionate lover, or the no less passionate hater, forlorn and desolate by the withdrawal of his object. Philosophically considered, therefore, the two passions seem essentially the same, except that one happens to be seen in a celestial radiance and the other in a dusky and lurid glow. In the spiritual world, the old physician and the minister—mutual victims as they have been—may, unawares, have found their earthly stock of hatred and antipathy transmuted into golden love.

Leaving this discussion apart, we have a matter of business to communicate to the reader. At old Roger Chillingworth's decease (which took place within the year), and by his last will and testament, of which Governor Bellingham and the Reverend Mr. Wilson were executors, he bequeathed a very considerable amount of property, both here and in England, to little Pearl, the daughter of Hester Prynne.

So Pearl—the elf-child—the demon offspring, as some people, up to that epoch, persisted in considering her —became the richest heiress of her day, in the New World. Not improbably, this circumstance wrought a very material change in the public estimation, and, had the mother and child remained here, little Pearl, at a marriageable period of life, might have mingled her wild blood with the lineage of the devoutest Puritan among them all. But, in no long time after the physician's death, the wearer of the scarlet letter disappeared, and Pearl along with her. For many years, though a vague report would now and then find its way across the sea—like a shapeless piece of driftwood tossed ashore, with the initials of a name upon it—yet no tidings of them unquestionably authentic were received. The story of the scarlet letter grew into a legend. Its spell, however, was still potent, and kept the scaffold awful where the poor minister had died, and likewise the cottage by the seashore, where Hester Prynne had dwelt. Near this latter spot, one afternoon, some children were at play, when they beheld a tall woman, in a gray robe, approach the cottage door. In all those years it had never once been opened; but either she unlocked it, or the decaying wood and iron yielded to her hand, or she glided shadowlike through these impediments—and, at all events, went in.

On the threshold she paused—turned partly round— for, perchance, the idea of entering all alone, and all so changed, the home of so intense a former life, was more dreary and desolate than even she could bear. But her hesitation was only for an instant, though long enough to display a scarlet letter on her breast.

And Hester Prynne had returned, and taken up her long-forsaken shame! But where was little Pearl? If still alive, she must now have been in the flush and bloom of early womanhood. None knew—nor ever learned, with the fulness of perfect certainty—whether the elf-child had gone thus untimely to a maiden grave; or whether her wild, rich nature had been softened and subdued, and made capable of a woman's gentle happiness. But, through the remainder of Hester's life, there were indications that the recluse of the scarlet letter was the object of love and interest with some inhabitant of another land. Letters came, with armorial seals upon them, though of bearing unknown to English heraldry. In the cottage there were articles of comfort and luxury, such as Hester never cared to use, but which only wealth could have purchased, and affection have imagined for her. There were trifles, too, little ornaments, beautiful tokens of a continual remembrance, that must have been wrought by delicate fingers at the impulse of a fond heart. And, once, Hester was seen embroidering a baby garment, with such a lavish richness of golden fancy as would have raised a public tumult, had any infant, thus apparelled, been shown to our sober-hued community.

In fine, the gossips of that day believed—and Mr. Surveyor Pue, who made investigations a century later, believed—and one of his recent successors in office, moreover, faithfully believes—that Pearl was not only alive, but married, and happy, and mindful of her mother; and that she would most joyfully have entertained that sad and lonely mother at her fireside.

But there was a more real life for Hester Prynne here in New England than in that unknown region where Pearl had found a home. Here had been her sin; here, her sorrow; and here was yet to be her penitence. She had returned, therefore, and resumed—of her own free will, for not the sternest magistrate of that iron period would have imposed it—resumed the symbol of which we have related so dark a tale. Never afterwards did it quit her bosom. But, in the lapse of the toilsome, thoughtful, and self-devoted years that made up Hester's life, the scarlet letter ceased to be a stigma which attracted the world's scorn and bitterness, and became a type of something to be sorrowed over, and looked upon with awe, yet with reverence too. And, as Hester Prynne had no selfish ends, nor lived in any measure for her own profit and enjoyment, people brought all their sorrows and perplexities and besought her counsel, as one who had herself gone through a mighty trouble. Women, more especially—in the continually recurring trials of wounded, wasted, wronged, misplaced, or erring and sinful passion—or with the dreary burden of a heart unyielded, because unvalued and unsought—came to Hester's cottage, demanding why they were so wretched, and what the remedy! Hester comforted and counselled them, as best she might. She assured them, too, of her firm belief, that, at some brighter period, when the world should have grown ripe for it, in Heaven's own time, a new truth would be revealed, in order to establish the whole relation between man and woman on a surer ground of mutual happiness. Earlier in life, Hester had vainly imagined that she herself might be the destined prophetess, but had long since recognized the impossibility that any mission of divine and mysterious truth should be confided to a woman stained with sin, bowed down with shame, or even burdened with a lifelong sorrow. The angel and apostle of the coming revelation must be a woman, indeed, but lofty, pure, and beautiful; and wise, moreover, not through dusky grief, but the ethereal medium of joy; and showing how sacred love should make us happy, by the truest test of a life successful to such an end!

So said Hester Prynne, and glanced her sad eyes downward at the scarlet letter. And, after many, many years, a new grave was delved, near an old and sunken one, in that burial ground beside which King's Chapel has since been built. It was near that old and sunken grave, yet with a space between, as if the dust of the two sleepers had no right to mingle. Yet one tombstone served for both. All around, there were monuments carved with armorial bearings; and on this simple slab of slate—as the curious investigator may still discern, and perplex himself with the purport—there appeared the semblance of an engraved escutcheon. It bore a device, a herald's wording of which might serve for a motto and brief description of our now concluded legend; so sombre is it, and relieved only by one ever glowing point of light gloomier than the shadow:

"ON A FIELD, SABLE, THE LETTER A, GULES."

ENDICOTT AND THE RED CROSS

AT NOON OF AN AUTUMNAL DAY, more than two centuries ago, the English colors were displayed by the standard-bearer of the Salem trainband, which had mustered for martial exercise under the orders of John Endicott. It was a period when the religious exiles were accustomed often to buckle on their armor, and practise the handling of their weapons of war. Since the first settlement of New England, its prospects had never been so dismal. The dissensions between Charles the First and his subjects were then, and for several years afterwards, confined to the floor of Parliament. The measures of the King and ministry were rendered more tyrannically violent by an opposition, which had not yet acquired sufficient confidence in its own strength to resist royal injustice with the sword. The bigoted and haughty primate, Laud, Archbishop of Canterbury, controlled the religious affairs of the realm, and was consequently invested with powers which might have wrought the utter ruin of the two Puritan colonies, Plymouth and Massachusetts. There is evidence on record that our forefathers perceived their danger, but were resolved that their infant country should not fall without a struggle, even beneath the giant strength of the King's right arm.

Such was the aspect of the times when the folds of the English banner, with the Red Cross in its field, were flung out over a company of Puritans. Their leader, the famous Endicott, was a man of stern and resolute countenance, the effect of which was heightened by a grizzled beard that swept the upper portion of his breastplate. This piece of armor was so highly polished that the whole surrounding scene had its image in the glittering steel. The central object in the mirrored picture was an edifice of humble architecture with neither steeple nor bell to proclaim it—what nevertheless it was—the house of prayer. A token of the perils of the wilderness was seen in the grim head of a wolf, which had just been slain within the precincts of the town, and according to the regular mode of claiming the bounty, was nailed on the porch of the meeting house. The blood was still plashing on the doorstep. There happened to be visible, at the same noontide hour, so many other characteristics of the times and manners of the Puritans, that we must endeavor to present them in a sketch, though far less vividly than they were reflected in the polished breastplate of John Endicott.

In close vicinity to the sacred edifice appeared that important engine of Puritanic authority, the whipping post—with the soil around it well trodden by the feet of evildoers, who had there been disciplined. At one corner of the meeting house was the pillory, and at the other the stocks; and, by a singular good fortune for our sketch, the head of an Episcopalian and suspected Catholic was grotesquely incased in the former machine; while a fellow criminal, who had boisterously quaffed a health to the King, was confined by the legs in the latter. Side by side, on the meeting house steps, stood a male and a female figure. The man was a tall, lean, haggard personification of fanaticism, bearing on his breast this label—A Wanton Gospeller—which betokened that he had dared to give interpretations of Holy Writ unsanctioned by the infallible judgment of the civil and religious rulers. His aspect showed no lack of zeal to maintain his heterodoxies, even at the stake. The woman wore a cleft stick on her tongue, in appropriate retribution for having wagged that unruly member against the elders of the church; and her countenance and gestures gave much cause to apprehend that, the moment the stick should be removed, a repetition of the offence would demand new ingenuity in chastising it.

The above-mentioned individuals had been sentenced to undergo their various modes of ignominy, for the space of one hour at noonday. But among the crowd were several whose punishment would be lifelong; some, whose ears had been cropped, like those of puppy dogs; others, whose cheeks had been branded with the initials of their misdemeanors; one, with his nostrils slit and seared; and another, with a halter about his neck, which he was forbidden ever to take off, or to conceal beneath his garments. Methinks he must have been grievously tempted to affix the other end of the rope to some convenient beam or bough. There was likewise a young woman, with no mean share of beauty, whose doom it was to wear the letter A on the breast of her gown, in the eyes of all the world and her own children. And even her own children knew what that initial signified. Sporting with her infamy, the lost and desperate creature had embroidered the fatal token in scarlet cloth, with golden thread and the nicest art of needlework; so that the capital A might have been thought to mean Admirable, or anything rather than Adulteress.

Let not the reader argue, from any of these evidences of iniquity, that the times of the Puritans were more vicious than our own, when, as we pass along the very street of this sketch, we discern no badge of infamy on man or woman. It was the policy of our ancestors to search out even the most secret sins, and expose them to shame, without fear or favor, in the broadest light of the noonday sun. Were such the custom now, perchance we might find materials for a no less piquant sketch than the above.

Except the malefactors whom we have described, and the diseased or infirm persons, the whole male population of the town, between sixteen years and sixty, were seen in the ranks of the trainband. A few stately savages, in all the pomp and dignity of the primeval Indian, stood gazing at the spectacle. Their flint-headed arrows were but childish weapons compared with the matchlocks of the Puritans, and would have rattled harmlessly against the steel caps and hammered iron breastplates which enclosed each soldier in an individual fortress. The valiant John Endicott glanced with an eye of pride at his sturdy followers, and prepared to renew the martial toils of the day.

"Come, my stout hearts!" quoth he, drawing his sword. "Let us show these poor heathen that we can handle our weapons like men of might. Well for them, if they put us not to prove it in earnest!"

The iron-breasted company straightened their line, and each man drew the heavy butt of his matchlock close to his left foot, thus awaiting the orders of the captain. But, as Endicott glanced right and left along the front, he discovered a personage at some little distance with whom it behooved him to hold a parley. It was an elderly gentleman, wearing a black cloak and band, and a high-crowned hat, beneath which was a velvet skullcap, the whole being the garb of a Puritan minister. This reverend person bore a staff which seemed to have been recently cut in the forest, and his shoes were bemired as if he had been travelling on foot through the swamps of the wilderness. His aspect was perfectly that of a pilgrim, heightened also by an apostolic dignity. Just as Endicott perceived him he laid aside his staff, and stooped to drink at a bubbling fountain which gushed into the sunshine about a score of yards from the corner of the meeting house. But, ere the good man drank, he turned his face heavenward in thankfulness, and then, holding back his gray beard with one hand, he scooped up his simple draught in the hollow of the other.

"What, ho! good Mr. Williams," shouted Endicott. "You are welcome back again to our town of peace. How does our worthy Governor Winthrop? And what news from Boston?"

"The Governor hath his health, worshipful Sir," answered Roger Williams, now resuming his staff, and drawing near. "And for the news, here is a letter, which, knowing I was to travel hitherward today, his Excellency committed to my charge. Belike it contains tidings of much import, for a ship arrived yesterday from England."

Mr. Williams, the minister of Salem and of course known to all the spectators, had now reached the spot where Endicott was standing under the banner of his company, and put the Governor's epistle into his hand.

The broad seal was impressed with Winthrop's coat of arms. Endicott hastily unclosed the letter and began to read, while, as his eye passed down the page, a wrathful change came over his manly countenance. The blood glowed through it, till it seemed to be kindling with an internal heat; nor was it unnatural to suppose that his breastplate would likewise become red-hot with the angry fire of the bosom which it covered. Arriving at the conclusion, he shook the letter fiercely in his hand, so that it rustled as loud as the flag above his head.

"Black tidings these, Mr. Williams," said he; "blacker never came to New England. Doubtless you know their purport?"

"Yea, truly," replied Roger Williams; "for the Governor consulted, respecting this matter, with my brethren in the ministry at Boston; and my opinion was likewise asked. And his Excellency entreats you by me, that the news be not suddenly noised abroad, lest the people be stirred up unto some outbreak, and thereby give the King and the Archbishop a handle against us."

"The Governor is a wise man—a wise man, and a meek and moderate," said Endicott, setting his teeth grimly. "Nevertheless, I must do according to my own best judgment. There is neither man, woman, nor child in New England but has a concern as dear as life in these tidings; and if John Endicott's voice be loud enough, man, woman, and child shall hear them. Soldiers, wheel into a hollow square! Ho, good people! Here are news for one and all of you."

The soldiers closed in around their captain; and he and Roger Williams stood together under the banner of the Red Cross; while the women and the aged men pressed forward, and the mothers held up their children to look Endicott in the face. A few taps of the drum gave signal for silence and attention.

"Fellow soldiers—fellow exiles," began Endicott, speaking under strong excitement, yet powerfully restraining it, "wherefore did ye leave your native country? Wherefore, I say, have we left the green and fertile fields, the cottages, or, perchance, the old gray halls, where we were born and bred, the churchyards where our forefathers lie buried? Wherefore have we come hither to set up our own tombstones in a wilderness? A howling wilderness it is! The wolf and the bear meet us within halloo of our dwellings. The savage lieth in wait for us in the dismal shadow of the woods. The stubborn roots of the trees break our ploughshares, when we would till the earth. Our children cry for bread, and we must dig in the sands of the seashore to satisfy them. Wherefore, I say again, have we sought this country of a rugged soil and wintry sky? Was it not for the enjoyment of our civil rights? Was it not for liberty to worship God according to our conscience?"

"Call you this liberty of conscience?" interrupted a voice on the steps of the meeting house.

It was the Wanton Gospeller. A sad and quiet smile flitted across the mild visage of Roger Williams. But Endicott, in the excitement of the moment, shook his sword wrathfully at the culprit—an ominous gesture from a man like him.

"What hast thou to do with conscience, thou knave?" cried he. "I said liberty to worship God, not license to profane and ridicule him. Break not in upon my speech, or I will lay thee neck and heels till this time tomorrow! Hearken to me, friends, nor heed that accursed rhapsodist. As I was saying, we have sacrificed all things, and have come to a land whereof the old world hath scarcely heard, that we might make a new world unto ourselves, and painfully seek a path from hence to heaven. But what think ye now? This son of a Scotch tyrant—this grandson of a Papistical and adulterous Scotch woman, whose death proved that a golden crown doth not always save an anointed head from the block—"

"Nay, brother, nay," interposed Mr. Williams; "thy words are not meet for a secret chamber, far less for a public street."

"Hold thy peace, Roger Williams!" answered Endicott, imperiously. "My spirit is wiser than thine for the business now in hand. I tell ye, fellow exiles, that Charles of England, and Laud, our bitterest persecutor, arch-priest of Canterbury, are resolute to pursue us even hither. They are taking counsel, saith this letter, to send over a governor-general, in whose breast shall be deposited all the law and equity of the land. They are minded, also, to establish the idolatrous forms of English Episcopacy; so that, when Laud shall kiss the Pope's toe, as cardinal of Rome, he may deliver New England, bound hand and foot, into the power of his master!"

A deep groan from the auditors—a sound of wrath, as well as fear and sorrow—responded to this intelligence.

"Look ye to it, brethren," resumed Endicott, with increasing energy. "If this king and this arch-prelate have their will, we shall briefly behold a cross on the spire of this tabernacle which we have builded, and a high altar within its walls, with wax tapers burning round it at noonday. We shall hear the sacring bell, and the voices of the Romish priests saying the mass. But think ye, Christian men, that these abominations may be suffered without a sword drawn? without a shot fired? without blood spilt, yea, on the very stairs of the pulpit? No—be ye strong of hand and stout of heart! Here we stand on our own soil, which we have bought with our goods, which we have won with our swords, which we have cleared with our axes, which we have tilled with the sweat of our brows, which we have sanctified with our prayers to the God that brought us hither! Who shall enslave us here? What have we to do with this mitred prelate—with this crowned king? What have we to do with England?"

Endicott gazed round at the excited countenances of the people, now full of his own spirit, and then turned suddenly to the standard-bearer, who stood close behind him.

"Officer, lower your banner!" said he.

The officer obeyed; and, brandishing his sword, Endicott thrust it through the cloth, and with his left hand rent the Red Cross completely out of the banner. He then waved the tattered ensign above his head.

"Sacrilegious wretch!" cried the high-churchman in the pillory, unable longer to restrain himself, "thou hast rejected the symbol of our holy religion!"

"Treason, treason!" roared the royalist in the stocks. "He hath defaced the King's banner!"

"Before God and man, I will avouch the deed," answered Endicott. "Beat a flourish, drummer!—shout, soldiers and people!—in honor of the ensign of New England. Neither Pope nor Tyrant hath part in it now!"

With a cry of triumph, the people gave their sanction to one of the boldest exploits which our history records. And forever honored be the name of Endicott! We look back through the mist of ages, and recognize in the rending of the Red Cross from New England's banner the first omen of that deliverance which our fathers consummated after the bones of the stern Puritan had lain more than a century in the dust.

SELECTED BIBLIOGRAPHY

Works by Nathaniel Hawthorne

Fanshawe: A Tale, 1828 Novel

Twice-Told Tales, 1837; enlarged 1842 Stories

Grandfather's Chair, 1841 History

Mosses from an Old Manse, 1846 Stories

The Scarlet Letter, 1850 Novel (Signet Classic 0451-516524)

The House of Seven Gables, 1851 Novel
(Signet Classic 0451-521714)

The Snow Image, 1851 Stories

A Wonder-Book for Boys and Girls, 1852 Stories

The Blithedale Romance, 1852 Novel

Life of Franklin Pierce, 1852 Biography

Tanglewood Tales, 1853 Stories

The Marble Faun, 1860 Novel (Meridian Classic
0452-009030)

Our Old Home, 1863 Stories and Sketches

The English Notebook, 1941 Journals

The American Notebooks, 1972 Journals

The American Claimant Manuscripts, 1977
Unfinished Romances

The Elixir of Life Manuscripts, 1977 Unfinished Romances

Hawthorne's Los tNotebook: 1835–1841, 1978 Journal

The French and Italian Notebooks, 1979 Journals

Biography and Criticism

Arvin, Newton. *Hawthorne*. Boston: Little, Brown. 1929.

Baym, Nina. *The Shape of Hawthorne's Career*. Ithaca, N.Y.:
Cornell Univ. Press, 1976.

Bell, Millicent. *Hawthorne's View of the Artist*. Albany: State
Univ. of New York Press, 1962.

Brodhead, Richard H. *Hawthorne, Melville and the Novel*.
Chicago: Univ. of Chicago Press, 1976.

Chase, Richard. *The American Novel and Its Tradition*.
Garden City, N.Y.: Doubleday, 1957.

Crews, Frederick C. *The Sins of the Fathers: Hawthorne's
Psychological Themes*. New York: Oxford Univ. Press. 1966.

Crowley, J. Donald, ed. *Nathaniel Hawthorne*. New York:
McGraw-Hill, 1975.

Davidson, Edward Hutchins. *Hawthorne's Last Phase*. New
Haven: Yale Univ. Press, 1949.

Doubleday, Neal Frank. *Hawthorne's Early Tales: A Critical Study*. Durham, N.C.: Duke Univ. Press, 1972.

Fields, James T. *Yesterdays with Authors*. Boston: Osgood, 1872.

Fogle, Richard Harter. *Hawthorne's Fiction: The Light and the Dark*. Rev. ed. Norman: Univ. of Oklahoma Press, 1964.

Hall, Lawrence Sargent. *Hawthorne: Critic of Society*. New Haven: Yale Univ. Press; London: Oxford Univ. Press, 1944.

Hawthorne, Julian. *Nathaniel Hawthorne and His Wife*. 2 vols. Boston: Osgood, 1884.

James, Henry Jr. *Hawthorne*. New York: Harper and Brothers, 1879.

Kaul, A. N., ed. *Hawthorne: A Collection of Critical Essays*. Englewood Cliffs, N.J.: Prentice-Hall, 1966.

Lawrence, D. H. *Studies in Classic American Literature*. New York: Thomas Seltzer, 1923.

Levin, Harry. *The Power of Blackness: Hawthorne, Poe, Melville*. New York: Knopf, 1958.

Male, Roy R. *Hawthorne's Tragic Vision*. Austin: Univ. of Texas Press, 1957.

Martin, Terence, *Nathaniel Hawthorne*. Twayne's United States Authors Series, 75. New York: Twayne, 1965.

Matthiessen, F. O. *American Renaissance*. New York and London: Oxford Univ. Press, 1941.

McPherson, Hugo. *Hawthorne as Myth-Maker: A Study in Imagination*. Toronto: Univ. of Toronto Press, 1969.

Pearce, Roy Harvey, ed. *Hawthorne Centenary Essays*. Columbus: Ohio State Univ. Press, 1964.

Stewart, Randall. *Nathaniel Hawthorne: A Biography*. New Haven: Yale Univ. Press, 1948.

Turner, Arlin. *Nathaniel Hawthorne: A Biography*. New York: Oxford Univ. Press, 1980.

————. *Nathaniel Hawthorne: An Introduction and Interpretation*. American Authors and Critics Series, AC2. New York: Barnes and Noble, 1961.

Van Doren, Mark. *Nathaniel Hawthorne*. New York: Sloane, 1949.

Wagenknecht, Edward Charles. *Nathaniel Hawthorne: Man and Writer*. New York: Oxford Univ. Press, 1961.

Waggoner, Hyatt H. *Hawthorne: A Critical Study*. Rev. ed. Cambridge: Belknap Press of Harvard Univ. Press, 1963.